The List

D1739294

MRC
Chicago, IL

Published by Martha Carr

Chicago, IL

Cover design by	Dave Robbins
Text design by	Brian Fischer
Author Photo by	Nick Bianco

Library of Congress Cataloguing-in-Publication Data

Carr, Martha Randolph, 1959-

The List: First in the Wallis Simpson Series; a novel / Martha Randolph Carr.

Library of Congress Control Number: 2013905444

Printed in the United States of America
ISBN-10: 1620304309
ISBN-13: 9781620304303

The List

A Thriller
First in the Wallis Simpson Series

Martha Carr

Dedicated to Vera Duke and Don Allison, whose guidance in life and literature make so much possible.

To Lori Ames, Brian Hannan, Dave Robbins and Brian Fischer for donating your time and your talents so generously.
Forever grateful for your friendships.

To Deanna Scott, Fitzgerald R. Hannan, Kristen Dean, John Keach, Janna Childs, Carrie Schroeder, Louie Carr, Apple Gunther, Brian Fischer, Emily Fischer, Liz Williams, James Tabor, Daniel Parker, Stacy Bankier, Matt Entin, Karolus Smejda, Kip Helverson, Tina Carr, Susie Oknefski-Hamway, Tracy Nepivoda George, Peggy Thomas, Sheila Love, Raleigh Wilkins, Elizabeth Sawyer, Tracy Thompson, Margaret Lyman, Kimberly Clawson, Paul Davidovitch, Norie Burnet, Christine Steinbeiss, Emily Thrower, Jessica Rooney & Jeff Mauricio, Traci Timmons, Matt Koontz, Nick Bianco, Meegan Scovell and Maurel Samonte for joining me on this journey and making this into group publishing and a wonderful adventure.

And to my son, Louie who reminds me all the time of what really matters and how wonderful life can be in any given moment.

CHAPTER

THE STOUT, ELDERLY EPISCOPAL PRIEST PRESSED THE PALM of his hand hard against his chest, willing the sharp jolt of pain to go away, squeezing his eyes shut for just a moment as he moved as fast as he could along the crowded sidewalk without bringing attention to himself.

There was no time to stop and catch his breath.

His heel caught the edge of a curb and he stumbled, falling against a man who was busy scanning the crowd. The Reverend looked directly at the man and relaxed his face for a moment, trying to look unconcerned.

He quickly took in the expensive clothing and the rigid posture that was out of place at a St. Patrick's Day parade in downtown Savannah. He moved out of the man's reach just in case he had fallen into a trap.

"So sorry, my son," he said as he smiled and turned away before the man could answer. The other eight members of his Order would already be out walking the grid and he could feel the seconds ticking away, faster by the moment.

He caught a glimpse of the minister from the nearby Diocesan office walking through the crowd, shaking the occasional hand as he made his way toward his first appointed drop point in the other direction. Too many clerics headed in one general direction would have caught someone's eye, even in this crowd.

Time was running out. They needed to find the Keeper, or at least the thumb drive that was always with her.

"Thy will be done," he mumbled, trying to calm himself as he hurried, pushing through the throngs of revelers that lined both sides of Liberty Street straining to see the parade.

His knotted hand loosely gripped an old copy of the Book of Common Prayer. He had hurried out of St John's rectory not realizing the small book was still in his hand.

He could see the Six Pence Pub through the crowd that was still gathering along East Liberty for the parade. There was a tight knot of early morning drinkers spilling out of the bar's door, most of them holding mugs of green beer and laughing too loudly for a Saturday morning. Several were wearing large plastic sunglasses with the words Beer Goggles painted around the edges.

Reverend Michael squeezed past a group of girls standing in the doorway who were giggling at the antics of the men at the bottom of the front steps. He pushed through just as the same man from earlier caught him by the elbow at the bar.

"Reverend, do you have a moment?" he asked, gripping the parson's elbow tightly.

A Watcher had identified him.

The cleric straightened out his other arm, letting the small, thin knife slide forward into his palm. He swiftly thrust the tip of the blade into the man's side hard enough to make him recoil but not enough to cause more than a shallow puncture. The Watcher let go as the minister shoved him hard enough to topple into the crowd, green beer sloshing everywhere.

"The drink will kill you one of these days, son," he yelled over his shoulder as he ran through the kitchen and out to the small office in back.

The owner was nowhere to be seen but there wasn't time to find him. The Reverend quietly shut the office door and locked it, shoving a chair under the handle. He grunted and felt another sharp pain in his chest as he pulled the large filing cabinet away from the wall. The cabinet teetered as a drawer suddenly popped open, nicking the cleric in the ribs just beneath old, ropey scars made the same night his hand was crippled. He dropped the small prayer book and took a deep breath, wrapping his arms around the cabinet as he shoved with his hip.

It slid over just enough to reveal a low, wooden door. He pulled out the small flashlight dangling from his keychain and shone the black light on the wooden frame.

The mark of the saltire was there with the right key of excommunication drawn in haste over the left for absolution. The Episcopal symbol was reversed. So Carol was still alive and knew she was in trouble.

Two short diagonal lines next to the two keys meant she was making a run for the Pirates House right by the river. He could feel his heart beating faster as he saw her final mark. The thumb drive was still with her. They were too close to her for her to take a chance by leaving it at any of the checkpoints.

Reverend Michael got down on his hands and knees, feeling the thick scars that wrapped around his waist straining as he quickly crawled through the opening. There was no time to worry if someone would follow behind him. There was only a question of who would get to the river first.

He passed out of the hidden door onto East Perry Lane and started to move faster, leaning forward until he was falling into a run.

He ran through the center of Oglethorpe Square and came out onto East State Street trying to pick up speed.

"Reverend Michael, are you alright?"

It was a parishioner walking with her family in the direction of the parade.

"Last rites," he said, gently patting her on the shoulder, as he kept moving.

The Pirates House was on Broad Street with a passage in the back that led directly onto the edge of the Savannah River.

Reverend Michael pushed inside the restaurant through the throngs of people till he reached the main room and the handwritten pages of Treasure Island that were encased on the wall. He shone the black light on the case and saw the sign of the Ionic cross.

"No," he gasped and felt the blood drain from his face.

There were too many people drinking in the entrance to the passageway. He pushed out the front door again and shoved people aside trying to get to the river's edge.

"Hey, old man, what the hell?" said a young man dressed in green running shorts and a t-shirt, still wearing his number from the Shamrock Shuffle that was ending over on River Street.

Reverend Michael quickly scanned the crowd for the Watcher but there were too many people. He scrambled to the back of the restaurant and found the older entrance to the tunnel blocked by empty boxes. He pushed them over and pried the door open as a splinter dug deep into the skin of his hand.

The narrow opening was barely wide enough and he squeezed through and into the tunnel.

The hard soles of his shoes sank into the soft sand that covered the floor of the tunnel as he raced the last few blocks toward the river. As he grew closer he heard a commotion and a woman suddenly cry out.

He reached the end of the tunnel and looked out at the two men who had her pinned against the sixteen-foot sailboat. She had almost made it. Reverend Michael let the knife drop down again as he started to cross the narrow road behind Magnolia Spa to make a run at them. Perhaps he could distract them long enough for the Keeper to slide into the river. The swift moving current would quickly carry her away and other boats were awaiting her at different points along the river. He was certain this would be the last act of his vow.

"Never again," hissed Carol Schaeffer before there was a crunch and her neck was snapped. Reverend Michael doubled over as he pulled back into the shadows and pressed his body against the interior of the tunnel. He fought the bile rising in his throat as tears came down his cheeks.

"My God," he cried out, "we have failed," he said quietly, tasting the tears on his lips.

"Oh, but failure is really a personal inventory, don't you think?"

"George Clemente," Reverend Michael said, as he pressed his back harder against the wall to keep from falling over. "They let you loose on the world again." He felt his throat tighten as he tried to get out the words.

The Watcher sneered. He was holding the Reverend's old copy of the 1928 Book of Common Prayer.

"How's the hand?" asked the Watcher. He was tapping the Reverend's prayer book gently against his chest.

"None the worse. Management must really be trembling to unleash a jackal like you in their midst."

"More of a promotion, really. World events have changed and the times call for people like me with a unique ability to focus."

"There are more of you," said the priest, trying to cover the feeling of panic creeping up his spine.

"Oh yes, spread across the world."

"Much like the plague."

The Watcher stepped closer and Reverend Michael felt himself involuntarily flinch as the Watcher let out a laugh that resembled a low grumble.

"I prefer to have closure in everything, don't you? No matter how long it takes."

"For once we agree," said Reverend Michael and lunged at the Watcher, grabbing him around the throat, digging his thumbs deep into the Watcher's windpipe. He could feel the delicate muscles begin to shred. The Watcher grabbed his hands and squeezed as hard as he could till the pain became almost unbearable for the minister and he let go, just a little.

The Watcher boxed his ears and pulled away, as he shoved the priest to the ground. Reverend Michael felt his ribs crack as the tip of the Watcher's boot made contact, pushing into his side, over and over again. He curled up in a ball and prayed for God's mercy until he could see his chance.

His arm darted out and caught the Watcher's foot in mid-air pulling him off balance. Reverend Michael kept lifting his foot as Clemente fell backward. His back landed hard against the old Georgia clay bricks, the wind knocked out of him.

Reverend Michael got to his feet as quickly as he could. Easy now, deep breaths. The last thing he needed was to throw up or pass out. The knife slid forward till the handle was securely in his hand. He dropped to his knees next to the Watcher and dug in, but only the tip was able to puncture the skin. The Watcher grabbed his wrist just in time and was quickly regaining his strength.

The Reverend picked up the only other weapon he could find and brought his arm down as hard as he could, willing his twisted hand to hold on to the prayer book as he slammed the spine into the Watcher's head over and over again. He raised the knife again, ready to at least exact revenge.

"What's going on in there? Over here, there's more of them."

A police officer stood at the entrance to the tunnel and was waving frantically for help. It was the only thing that stopped Reverend Michael from finishing what the Watcher had started forty years ago. He slid the book, wet with blood, into his pocket and rose to his feet. Wiping his hand on the inside of his jacket, he staggered out toward the light.

"Mugging," he whispered to the officer as he looked around for a familiar face. He started to sway just as an arm came around his back and pressed painfully against his broken ribs.

"I have him, Officer." It was Reverend Wright's voice. "We'll get him to medical care."

"The ambulance is on its way," the cop protested. "He really doesn't look good."

"I agree, we'll make a point to hurry," said Wright, nodding in the direction of the car.

They walked as quickly as Reverend Michael's injuries would allow over to a black Lincoln Continental with the name of the Georgia Diocese in small gold lettering just under the door handle. Next to the words was a small, discreet depiction of two keys, one silver and one gold laid across each other.

Reverend Wright opened the back door and helped the brother into the back seat, gently sitting him up against the leather.

"We failed," said Reverend Michael to the cleric already sitting in the back seat. He gripped his arm, trembling. "We lost everything."

Reverend John didn't look at him but said to the driver, "Take him to Bethesda Home for Boys. They'll know what to do."

"The list, the list is gone," whispered Reverend Michael, his breathing becoming more labored.

"I was a step too late as well. The list is in their hands for now but that is for another day and different people. We have a vow to fulfill. As soon as you're able, you'll join us."

"Wisconsin."

"Yes, we'll be fine until you can join us. Rest now, it's in God's hands."

"What have we done? If they find out…" Reverend Michael began to weep. "You can't take me to Bethesda. It will only confirm the list."

"There is still hope. Do not forget about the one who lives in Richmond. We've managed to keep that identity a secret, even now. We still have a chance to stop them."

CHAPTER

②

CRAY was flipping through channels during a commercial when the doorbell rang.

He had hesitated and thought about calling out to Lily to get the door before he remembered she wasn't living here anymore. A momentary pang of sadness came to rest in his belly. He wasn't used to being alone and hadn't tried very hard to get past it.

"Okay," he muttered, slowly getting up from the couch, pushing up and out of the sagging middle to go look out the front window. Not too many people came by at night.

He pulled back just enough of the gauzy curtain in the family room to get a glimpse while checking to make sure the long strands of hair were in place on the top of his head. Three men in long coats bundled up against the cold stood on Ray's front step, their gazes fixed on the front door.

A shiver went down Ray's back shaking him hard enough to let go of the curtain. He took a step back trying to decide what to do as the doorbell rang again, this time accompanied by a sharp and rapid knocking.

"It can't be," he whispered.

He walked quickly to the front hall and reached inside the drawer of the small table for the key to the back door, scooping up the small thumb drive in the shape of a racecar with the number 3 on the side. The knocking grew more insistent.

One step away from the door was the loose floorboard. He pried it open just enough to let the long thin USB device roll in and drop between the two layers.

Thank goodness, I was too lazy to fix that, he thought, gently pushing the board back into place until it was level with the rest of the floor.

He looked at the key still in his hand and considered scaling his back fence. The neighbor's dog would quickly give him away.

"Who is it?" he called out, buying a little time to think.

"F.B.I., sir. Are you Ray Billings?"

Ray felt a sense of relief wash over him. It's not them, he thought.

"Yes, just a second."

Ray peered out of the peephole at the fish-eyed view of the men's heads.

"Can you show me some I.D.?" he asked. The short man in front deftly reached inside of his coat and pulled out a thin leather wallet, flipping it open to reveal a gold badge.

Ray let out the breath he'd been holding and unlocked the front door. He stepped aside as the three men pushed past him into his house.

It wasn't until the door shut that the first blow hit him. They hustled him quickly to his office, his feet barely touching the ground, before securing him to a chair.

"Where is it?" asked the little man who had shown him the badge.

"Are you really with the FBI?" Ray asked. It had never occurred to him that the list could spread that far. Another blow came swinging down.

"What did you do with it?" The little man wasn't angry, wasn't yelling or gesturing at all. He asked the question quietly and gave Ray a moment to answer before hitting him with the butt of the gun again. It went on like that for minutes.

How long will this take to be over, he thought. His tongue darted to the corner of his mouth. Blood.

Ray knew his life was coming to an abrupt end. He let his arms sag against the ropes and let out a deep sigh.

An unhappy wife, too many bills, an occasional twinge that made him wonder what might be going wrong just underneath the surface of his skin. It all seemed so pointless now. All that wasted time.

The butt of the gun swung down again, landing neatly against Ray's right ear replacing the sounds of the three men ripping through the room with a round, expansive tone that rang in his head. The folds of his ear momentarily flattened out as his head snapped hard to the left, wrenching his neck.

His arms pulled hard against the ropes wrapped around his wrists holding him fast to the back of the dining room chair. His shoulders ached. There was a pause as the wooden chair teetered for a moment; his right foot taped to the leg that was hanging in the air before gravity pulled it all slowly, back down to rest.

He grunted, sweating hard to right himself back into a normal position, head on straight, chin up, shoulders down.

His eyes opened briefly, the lids barely raised, taking in the orderly trickle of red hitting his favorite shirt. It was soaked in large patterns of sweat and blood. A small white button, its face upturned where his belly hung out over his belt, held a drop of blood that was slowly seeping through the four tiny holes, staining the white threads.

Round, even drops fell onto the neatly pressed pocket from the tip of a long lock of misplaced brown hair. It bothered Ray to know he'd be found with his bald spot exposed.

Panic came over him again, bile filling his throat. He tried to focus instead on all the times he had worn the shirt, putting himself in another room with different people.

He took in another deep breath and let it seep out between his lips, surprising himself. Something inside of him let go and the panic subsided.

It's almost done, he thought.

Knowing he was at the end was making it a little easier. He stopped trying to figure out when things might get a little better. It was all a downward spiral from here.

There's a certain satisfaction in that, thought Ray.

The pain in his head momentarily subsided as Ray took another quick inventory of his body, squeezing his eyes shut so he wouldn't see the end coming. He was sure the moment was upon him and he didn't want to know the precise second there would be no more chances, nothing left to worry about or hope he might get someday.

Ray said nothing, counting the seconds between each blow, trying not to throw up. Minutes finally passed. Poor Stanley, he thought, as he watched the blood continue to trickle down his shirt. But I can't let it happen to the others.

"I'm sorry," he whispered.

One of the other men looked up at the small man before going back to pulling out drawers and shaking books.

"You know he had it with him," said the little man.

"Yeah, then find it. You've had your fun, move on."

Ray let out a small nasally whimper, his mouth quivering as he tasted the blood dripping from his swollen lips. "The Lord is my Shepherd," he whispered, as he raised his head and opened his eyes for a moment just before a pillow exploded, its contents flying as his head slumped.

CHAPTER

③

DISASTERS happen slowly. But by the time everyone's wringing their hands and calling their friends to let them in on the details, it's done. The substance, the moments when the tragedy is agonizing and painful, happen in bits and pieces unseen by all but a few. Alice was figuring that out.

She stood in front of the 1993 green Chevy Celebrity that she'd always kept as neat as a pin, looking at the remains of her windshield. The splintered glass that spread out over the front seat sparkled in the late afternoon light making the vinyl appear fancier than its usual faded grey-blue.

Alice wasn't even surprised at the destruction. She saw it from halfway across the lot and felt relief it was such a quiet message. She could explain this away to the garage.

It occurred to her to look back at the squatty yellow brick building she'd just emerged from to see if anyone else had noticed. She was struggling to appear more than resigned. The parking lot was deserted.

I don't need this, she thought. I can let go and leave everyone to their own devices. If everyone doesn't survive, so what. I didn't start it. I don't have to finish it.

She cupped her hand around her face to look in the back window, not ready to open a door and claim what had happened as her own. A glimpse of her yellowing, pale loose skin caught her eye as she raised her arm, making her feel a little more worn out.

I can leave, she thought, and start over one more time.

She saw a rusted crow bar on the back seat resting on top of square, blue bits of tinted glass. They weren't even worried enough to hide. That was the real message.

Alice needed her cell phone. She fumbled with her oversized faded brown leather purse, and for a moment she felt the excitement she had when she first bought the purse at Macy's department store. She had just arrived in Richmond, Virginia and was looking forward to her new job as supervisor of the finance division in the city's utility department. The purse was to mark the start of a new phase in her life.

This time she was going to build something permanent that was only hers, something no one could touch. No ex-husband to steal away half, which was really everything. Nobody can afford to buy back half of everything they have just to keep it, she thought.

The thought always made her screw up her face a little. She hated that part, that someone she hadn't even laid eyes on in, what, ten years could still make her feel anything.

"This was supposed to be my new life," she hissed, pushing on the tight clasp. It had become more stubborn over time, just like Alice, and made her thumb ache for a moment before it would relent and open wide, revealing all the contents at once.

She took out her dollar store reading glasses and put them on before finding her cell phone.

"Hello? Is Marty there? Marty? This is Alice Watkins, I own the green Chevy? Someone's broken my windshield and I need a new one. Yes, vandalized. No, I'm not going to bother. They'll only tell me they don't usually figure these things out. Could you come and replace it? No, I'm paying cash. Do I get a discount for that?"

Someone would be there soon. No need for Alice to wait by the car. Everyone at the station knew her. She could drop a check off in the morning. Marty gave her the usual senior discount of 10 percent off. Alice hated turning 55 last year and discovering she was sometimes stuck in the senior category.

She picked up her white cotton tote bag with the green handles and a large green tree on each side under the Ukrop's Grocery store logo. They were an institution, founded in 1936 and well-loved by everyone in town even though they'd sold out to Martin's and were even open on Sunday's now. That's why Alice had bought the sturdy sack. It was to let everyone know she was part of the old crowd, putting down roots. Packed inside was a pair of blue Keds with an empty water bottle, a worn paperback mystery someone had lent her, and some files from work she needed to get to tonight. She slid the straps over her left shoulder, balancing the weight with the purse in the other hand, and headed back toward the building and her cubicle.

Maybe everyone has left by now and no one will see me come back inside. Maybe I'll never have to explain.

Alice took small, mincing steps despite being almost six feet tall with extra wide feet. Her feet were crammed into brown leather Clarke's that matched her purse. The only brand she'd ever found that fit.

She got to the back door and punched in her security code slowly. Swollen fingers made it easy to punch two numbers at once.

"Damn," she muttered, as she felt her finger mash down the six and the nine. Everything had become harder to do lately. Alice was permanently on edge. She jiggled the handle hard till it clicked, letting her start over. This time she tried using another finger and pushing with just the tip of her fingernail.

The handle started to turn as she pushed the last number and Alice backed up, waiting for whoever was trying to leave to emerge through the door. She took in small sips of air to steady herself and decided to say she had forgotten something. Keep it simple.

"Alice!" It was Lynn Hedgepeth. She sat in one of the smaller cubicles downstairs from Alice listening to customer complaints all day. She always looked distant and not quite all there. Alice figured that was how Lynn made it through a day.

"Hey, Lynn," said Alice, trying to sound cordial as she pulled the door open a little wider to start to squeeze past Lynn, "forgot something."

"Did you hear?" asked Lynn. Alice thought about acting like she didn't hear her but she wasn't in the door far enough to pull it off.

"Hear what?"

"Ray Billings, he's dead. I heard it was an apparent suicide, whatever that means. Shot to the head just a little while ago. Hasn't even been reported in the news yet. He seemed happy enough to me. Just goes to show. Didn't he work under you? Weren't you two working on some project together?"

Alice let her purse and Ukrop's bag drop to the ground. The bag fell over and a shoe slid out, pulling a file with it. She let herself fall backward and sat down hard, her teeth clicking together. The crying started, grieving really, for what she could see was already gone. Maybe for what she might never have again. Some kind of simple life.

"I quit," she mumbled.

CHAPTER

④

A cold snap had settled over the suburbs of Richmond during the night, making the tops of the trees heavy with frost. The tall pines bent slightly toward the ground, trembling in the cold wind. There was still another hour before sunrise.

Larry Blazney looked up at the trees and shivered as he pulled up the collar of his worn sheepskin coat, hunching his shoulders. His thick gray wavy hair was doing nothing to keep his head warm and the wind was easily cutting through the dark blue flannel pajama bottoms.

"Damn, it's cold," he muttered, giving the leash a shake to make Happy, his old yellow lab, stop sniffing and keep moving. "If you're not gonna' go there, keep movin'," he said, his lips stiff from the cold. "Didn't need a coat yesterday, today I'm freezing my butt out here. Damn Richmond weather. Come on dog! You're trying my patience," he said half-heartedly. He didn't really mean it. Since his kids had grown up and moved out the dog was his pride and joy.

Happy was nosing the ground around the tall English boxwoods that lined the edge of the property in front of the neat gray Colonial. Larry gave a small jerk on the leash to try and make her start walking again.

The large dog stumbled to the side for a moment and went back to the bush, burying her nose at the roots.

"What are you doing?" asked Larry, annoyed. He grabbed Happy by the collar and pulled her head toward him. The dog let out a low growl, her mouth shut firmly around something, as she tried to turn back to what she was doing.

"Oh, you think you've found breakfast, do you? A little road kill du jour?" Larry spread his feet wide and carefully grabbed hold of Happy's jaws, prying them apart till she dropped what was in her mouth. The dog was old but she could put up some resistance to hold on to food.

"That kind of thing'll make you sick, Happy."

A small bone no bigger than the tip of his finger with the faintest bit of flesh still attached rolled out and came to rest at the tip of Larry's shoe.

"What's that?" he said, as he gave the bone a small kick to make it roll over. He held Happy back as he picked up the bone with his gloved hand, turning it around to get a better look.

"What have you found, girl?"

He walked toward the bushes, still bent over at the waist and brushed the dirt away uncovering two more small bones, the same size as the first.

He straightened up, feeling an ache in the small of his back.

"Oof," he muttered, still holding on to the bone from Happy's mouth.

Larry startled as he noticed the man slowly walking toward him from the other end of the street just as a cold breeze suddenly blew straight into his face making his eyes water.

He blinked hard and looked at Happy squatting by the bush getting ready to relieve herself, and gave the leash a hard pull till Happy gave up and started trotting slowly toward the man.

Larry let the small bone drop not noticing where it fell, and started walking again. "Probably some new dumb gardening tip," he mumbled to himself.

"Morning," he said, as he passed the man. The man nodded in return and kept moving. Larry stopped and turned back toward him.

"Your car break down?"

The man turned and looked at Larry, a faint smile on his lips as he squinted in the early morning sun. He didn't answer and started to turn away.

"Your car? Wouldn't it start in the cold?" The man turned back again and faced Larry. Larry took a few steps toward him as Happy trotted to catch up.

"Not too many people exercise in such a nice suit," said Larry, admiring the open charcoal grey cashmere overcoat and polished wing tips. "You trying to walk to a bus line? Need to use a phone?"

Larry liked being helpful. He was raised on a farm just across the river and had never let go of some of the old ways even if he did sell the farm years ago to make way for a mall.

"No, have a cell phone," said the man, patting his jacket.

"Oh, sure," he nodded. "You must be new to the neighborhood. I pride myself on knowing everyone," said Larry, smiling as he offered his hand to shake. The man made no effort to extend his hand.

"Larry Blazney, I live right back there," he said, pointing over his shoulder from where the man had come from. "I'm the one with the purple door. That's how people give directions around here. Go past the purple door and hang a left," he said, letting out a small snort. "Was my wife's idea. Which one's yours?" He looked back toward home, trying to figure out which house nearby had recently sold. As he turned back he caught a glimpse of a leather shoulder holster.

Larry's face gave him away, the surprise obvious in his raised eyebrows even if only for a moment. "Oh," he said, as he quickly tried to get back his easy-going smile.

The man hesitated and looked pained for a moment before he turned away from Larry and gave a small wave in the direction of Pump Road, the main thoroughfare that would be busy in just about an hour with people heading to work, but was deserted so early in the morning.

"Oh, you have a ride," said Larry, looking at the dark blue Ford Explorer as it crept toward them. He felt a chill underneath his coat and a momentary fear passed through him. He turned to walk toward home, pulling on the leash to make Happy walk faster. "Come on girl," he whispered.

Larry's last glimpse of his quiet little neighborhood was of his neighbor Wallis, turning around and around in an upstairs window, looking down at the ground. He tried to cry out to her, make her look outside, but the soft leather glove clamped down over his mouth didn't let any of the sound escape.

A man in the front seat of the Explorer got out, pulling a handkerchief out of his back pocket as he bent down to scoop up two small bones. He wrapped them up tightly, pushing the small collection into his coat as he glanced up at the panicked look in Larry's eyes before his head was pushed down into the car. Larry was straining to see his purple door.

The man slid back into the front seat as he quietly shut the door, scanning the street for any movement.

Happy let out shrill barks as the car turned around and headed back in the direction it had come from. She chased the car all the way to Pump Road but stopped at the edge and sat down to patiently wait. Larry had trained her to never try to cross Pump Road alone. It was too dangerous.

CH APT ER

WALLIS Jones was in her bedroom turning around and around in a tight circle hoping to spot her other shoe quickly. Up, down, up, down, as first a naked foot hit the carpeted floor, and then a mauve, high-heeled shoe bought on sale at Marshall's.

The shoes were a perfect reflection of Wallis, high-end, but a bargain.

She loved competing and looked for ways to win, no matter what she was doing, keeping a mental tally throughout the day of wins and losses. There were always more victories, but sometimes it was because Wallis was willing to make quick, small compromises to get to her real goal, whatever it was. She understood the practicality of making some small deal while holding the truth of her real desire hidden.

People don't often give you what you really want, baby girl, her mother said, especially if it seems like they'll end up with less. Wallis was sure it was some sort of southern woman's creed.

Smile, don't mention any flaws no matter how obvious, and make sure you always walk away with more than the other fellow.

Maybe it wasn't such a surprise then, that Wallis became a lawyer.

A family court lawyer, which gave her more than the usual number of opportunities to parse out small victories. It was only when they were added up months later that the other side saw how much they'd actually given away. Compromise for Wallis was another way to win.

She felt under the edge of the tall dresser with her foot but didn't feel anything.

A dog barked out front, short loud barks that Wallis knew were meant as a warning. She took a quick step to look out her bedroom window, saw nothing but a black SUV pulling away and went back to trying to find her shoe.

Must be another stray, she thought, looking behind the closet door. There had been a problem lately with dogs emerging in the early morning darkness from the nearby park to forage for food.

Please don't let them be in my garbage, thought Wallis.

Wallis was an only child who was named after Wallis Simpson, the peculiar concubine and eventual wife of the abdicated King Edward of England. Wallis' mother, Harriet, was enamored of the small woman's stiff demeanor, severe red lips and perfect boxy suits that never wrinkled. Edward's abdication in favor of his bride was a nice touch. Harriet had heard all of the adulterous stories about Wallis over the years but refused to believe any of it.

"People always try to pull down those better than themselves," she'd say, checking a pin curl at the back of her teased and captured hair. "Sometimes the vociferousness of the crowd is only an indication of how well you're doing."

To show her continuing devotion even after the original Wallis had passed away, Harriet kept collecting any trinket that was somehow connected to the woman and always managed to tuck a tea towel with the exiled couple's faces or a set of coasters with their entwined initials into the box of Christmas presents she gave to Wallis every year. Most of the memorabilia was put away under the large antique four-poster bed Wallis shared with her husband, Norman.

The bed was so high off the ground it had come with wooden steps for either side. It made it easier to stuff things underneath and then hide them with an extra-long bed skirt. Norman liked the height because it kept their dog, Joe, out of the bed. Joe was a middling-sized mutt who looked like he was mostly Bichon Frise, but nobody really knew. Norman and their only child, Ned had picked him out at the pound.

Wallis felt around under the four-poster bed with her stockinged foot, nudging against the lost shoe.

"There it is," she said, accidentally pushing it further away. "Damn."

She knelt down and slid her arm underneath the bed, pulling out the errant shoe with a clump of dust clinging to the heel.

"Not my department," she said, briskly pulling off the dust and stepping into the shoe. Housecleaning of any kind and cooking were Norman's jobs. They'd been married twelve years, all of them happy because it was hard to ever complain about a man who never said much and was willing to vacuum.

Mostly, Norman was a blank pool waiting for others to momentarily reflect something onto him. It unnerved people all the time that he never laughed at anyone's jokes or added a comment to some aside about the outcome of a case.

He had only one 'tell' that had taken Wallis years to pick up on and she had never mentioned it to anyone, including Norman. If he was concerned he'd gently pat-a-pat the growing bald spot at the back of his head, before trying to smooth the remaining dark brown waves of hair. That was it, and even that didn't happen very often.

Norman was a lawyer as well, a corporate lawyer, and was always getting desperate phone calls from more clients than he had time for who needed calm measured advice to get out of a problem they had created, sometimes knowingly. Norman knew all that and would say to Wallis from time to time without a flicker of emotion, "what would I do for a living if there weren't so many people who thought they knew everything?"

"You'd find something, Norman. You're too practical to sit still."

"That's true," he'd answer and return to the brief he was writing.

Together, along with a young attorney, William Bremmer, they formed the law firm of Weiskopf, Jones, and Bremmer. Norman was the Weiskopf and his parents were German Jews who had escaped Nazi Germany when there was still time eventually settling in Richmond along the promenade, Monument Avenue.

Once the Weiskopfs were in America, they decided to think of themselves as American and left their past behind them, heartily celebrating every American holiday. Norman came from a long line of practical people.

His best friend was a popular local Episcopal priest, the Reverend Donald Peakes, who was always called Pastor Donald by most everyone as an affectionate nickname as much as an official title. Norman told Wallis their friendship gave him balance.

The area surrounding the newest statue on Monument Avenue that was also the furthest west, the native-born tennis ace, Arthur Ashe, became the Jewish suburbs of Richmond in the 1920's and '30's. The refugees who would come later, the survivors, would settle further downtown in the older business district, starting over with small businesses on the first floor and a home right above. The two groups rarely mingled even now.

The Weiskopfs settled in, opening a drugstore that eventually became a local chain of four and raised three sons. Norman was the youngest. The oldest, Harry, was a lawyer in Florida helping retirees set up their estates. The middle child, Tom, was an aging hippie in Wisconsin doling out legal advice to indigents from a storefront.

"I didn't know there were real hippies in Wisconsin," said Wallis.

"Tom is their official representative," said Norman, never forming even a small smile.

Wallis was a lapsed Baptist who would boogie if given enough wine as motivation. Neither one of her parents had believed in much of anything but a childhood nanny had insisted on giving the little girl a foundation in her Baptist faith. Occasionally, Wallis still snuck into the back of a service to gather comfort from the familiar but she had never felt the need for anything more than an occasional drop-in and less now that Ned was getting older.

Wallis believed in God, even liked Him and had occasionally prayed for the benefit of someone else, but Wallis saw church as layers of rules between her and any kind of Supreme Being and knew she would fall short on purpose. She was never one to be defined by someone else's rules.

"Ned? Ned?" Wallis yelled, trying to wake her nine-year-old son from a floor away. There was no sound of movement but Wallis knew he could be lying still in his bed wide awake listening to her yell and waiting her out.

"You know, for such a smart kid it amazes me how reluctant you are to go to school," she said, taking each step with determination.

Ned lived on the top floor, which consisted of his room, a bathroom, a small balcony and a crawl space for storage.

Ned was a late-in-life baby who had come along after Wallis had turned thirty-five. Wallis had been in no hurry to get married. Norman changed all of that with his way of accepting whatever came along and his love for Wallis.

She had gotten pregnant easily and was feeling fine till she leaned over to get a glimpse of her file at twenty-eight weeks along and saw the doctor's notation. A geriatric pregnancy of a well-nourished woman.

"They're calling me a fat old broad!" she had told Norman when she got home. He smiled for a moment and kept stir-frying the chicken in his wok.

Wallis never touched anything in the kitchen but the refrigerator door. Norman was particular about his things and moving any of them around, particularly in front of him, would usually evoke a small, quick worrisome head pat.

Ned was born right on time with no complications but quickly developed several. Sitting in the NICU unit of St. Mary's Hospital rocking her eight day old son Wallis wondered if she was at long last in over her head.

He had trouble breathing which made the doctors wonder about asthma, which cleared up on its own, and then there was a mention of a possible kidney problem, but that disappeared as well. A rash that crept from his belly to his chest made them wonder what it meant but it slowly faded and the skin returned to a perfect alabaster that reminded Wallis of Norman.

The doctors had said as an afterthought that there might be a possibility of learning disabilities down the road because of the complications. Wallis made a mental note not to worry about it and took her son home, grateful to be out of the hospital and away from everyone else's decisions about what was best for Ned.

Ned did turn out to be a special child, but in the opposite direction. He was reading in preschool and quickly took to asking complicated questions, particularly when Wallis was driving in heavy traffic. By first grade he was taking apart anything he could pry open, laying out the pieces in an orderly fashion and then putting them back together, sometimes improving the appliance.

By third grade Wallis was even letting him fix the occasional small appliance for a neighbor, giving out her usual warning that he was just a kid and if it still didn't work, or didn't work in a new way, there were to be no complaints or even comments. So far, though Ned's record was perfect.

His room was a study in mindful chaos. K'nex wheels and joints were laid out on the floor next to Star Wars models Ned had built and added onto from generic kits he bought at the local hobby shop he hung out at on West Cary Street.

Next to Ned's bed was an old TV stand he had fixed and added onto with wheels and an extra shelf. The bottom shelf had his collection of baseball cards Norman had passed down to him plus the ones Ned had added, and a large notebook filled with Magic game cards of elaborately drawn figures that were ordered according to their usefulness in a battle. The middle shelf was devoted to science fiction paperbacks, magazines on the latest computer updates and an army of War Hammer 40K figurines that Ned had carefully painted in an army green and blue with an occasional dab of red for a bloody wound. Piled in a corner of the shelf was a large assortment of dice. Ned usually spent Wednesday evenings in friendly games of Magic or War Hammer at the hobby shop, played out on long tables set up by the owner with mostly high school kids and middle-aged men in variations of striped polo shirts and Cargo pants.

The top shelf had the guts of the latest appliance he was working on with a small notebook next to it where Ned kept notes on what he discovered and ideas he had for improvements. Wallis had asked Ned if she could look through the notebook and he had shrugged and said okay in a way that made Wallis think Ned was pretty sure most of it would go right over her head. He was right and Wallis knew that before she even picked it up. She was really looking for a glimpse into the way Ned figured things out and came away with something close to awe.

"You realize the rest of us can't do this sort of thing," she had told him, as she flipped over another page.

"I've noticed," he answered, in the same sort of way Norman might have, making Wallis smile at the similarities in father and son.

Ned even had the same kind of tell as Norman, running his fingers through the back of his thick brown hair when he was puzzling over a problem or on the threshold of a new idea.

The two Weiskopf men also liked to cook together and Ned was the only person allowed to use Norman's pots, under Norman's supervision, which meant while he was in the room. Norman wasn't worried about Ned dropping a pot. They were both too calculated in their moves for that kind of accident. He was more concerned with Ned using one in an experiment just to find out how durable a Teflon coating really was or attempting to slowly melt a Space Marine down so it would look more horrible and disfigured in battle than it already did. Ned had already tried that with the microwave when he was younger sending out a shower of sparks from the small metal figurine. Wallis had heard the 'ssspppft' sound from the living room and came running to find Ned calmly watching the small beast spin inside the dying microwave. Ned later rewired the appliance and calmly explained to Wallis that he had known what he was doing all along. Wallis looked down at her then-seven year old's placid face and wondered if that was possibly true.

"I'd prefer you don't do anything that causes fire or electrical sparks until further notice," she told him.

"Okay," he had shrugged, with an arced eyebrow he reserved for when he thought adults were overreacting.

Wallis gave her watch a glance and took the last two steps to his room in a run and called out.

"Ned?" she yelled, as she turned the corner into his room. He was sitting in front of his computer, dressed in his favorite khaki Cargo pants and 'check your fly' t-shirt with a fishing lure under the suggestive heading. So far, no one at school had objected.

"You could have at least answered me. What are you doing?" asked Wallis.

"Chasing worms," Ned said calmly, his eyes focused on the screen as he made sudden rapid movements with the mouse followed by a click, click and fevered typing. "And if I had answered you, you would have yelled at me to come downstairs awhile ago."

"We have worms?" asked Wallis. Her stomach quickly tightened at the thought of a complicated computer issue that she wouldn't understand.

"Yeah, I put one in there."

"Why?" Wallis stretched the word out to let Ned know she was annoyed.

"So I could hunt it down and kill it." Ned spoke slowly only annoying Wallis more. Wallis took in a deep breath and slowly let it out.

"Mom, why do you worry so much? Do I look worried?" he said, still looking at the glowing screen.

"I have no idea. What does worried look like on you?"

"Very funny."

"You've done this before?"

"Only a hundred times. It's getting boring. I'm waiting for something better to hit my honey pot."

"Honey pot?" asked Wallis, moving directly behind her son.

"Unprotected computer," said Ned, pointing backward without turning his head at an old lap top he had put together from spare parts that had been headed for a landfill. "No firewalls. Eventually some worm or virus hits it and then I can play."

"You know, Ned, I expected you to surpass me, I just didn't think it would be before you were ten."

"It's okay, Mom, I'm on your side."

"And a grateful household thanks you, although I probably wouldn't know the difference for quite some time."

"Or ever."

"Yeah, that's one way to make me feel better, Ned. Socks and shoes?"

"Five more minutes. I can't stop before I purge the wailer."

"I have no way of knowing if you're telling me the truth or not."

"So, you'll have to trust me."

"It's like you're already a teenager and have driven off with the car."

"I could explain what I'm doing in more detail."

"Good maneuver, son. Kill me off with details. No, no, I'll take the high road and trust you because we have the five minutes to spare, but only five minutes."

"So, you're not really trusting me, then."

"It's against the mother rules. I'm only conceding ignorance and hoping you never hack into any secret government web sites."

Ned smiled and let out a small sinister laugh, looking up at his mother's reaction.

"At least when the suits show up at the door, I won't be completely caught off-guard," said Wallis. "Try to give me some warning so my underwear is clean."

"Gross, Mom. Okay, done!" said Ned, lifting his hands high off of the keyboard and standing up to face his mother. "Take off your heels. Stand up straight. Look, I'm already a little taller than you are," he said letting his hand float from the top of his head over to Wallis's. "I'm going to start calling you Yoda, small wise one."

"Thanks, that's very nice, Ned. Already humoring me."

It was true, though. Ned at nine years old was already surpassing Wallis at five feet four inches and seemed to be headed for Norman's nice average height of five foot nine.

"I'm hoping for six feet," said Ned.

"Then you need to hope for some mutant genes."

"Grandma said she had a very tall uncle."

"My mother? Did you ask her what tall meant to her? She's shorter than I am and she likes to make you happy even if she has to ignore what you were really asking and make up a new question in her head. Watch her eyes when she's answering, Ned. If she's looking over your shoulder and won't make eye contact she's selling you a happy-land bill of goods. I had a childhood of them," she said, stepping back into her shoes.

"Bitter, Queen Wallis?"

"Wallis never got to be queen, Ned-lee," said Wallis, giving Ned a friendly tap on the shoulder. "Got you last," she said, smiling. Ned quickly tapped her back.

"You're it," he said. They had been playing this game for years, just the two of them. Norman found it pointless. Wallis couldn't remember how it had started and it never really had an ending. Ned was as competitive as his mother and would wait hours if he had to, to catch Wallis off guard and swipe her in the arm as he ran off, never saying a word. Wallis usually tried to swat him back before he was out of range. Ned loved to quietly tap his mother in public firmly enough so she'd know the game was in progress, even if it really wasn't his turn. He knew she was too conscious of what it would look like if she were to go out of her way to get him back, especially when no one had seen him do anything. Sometimes, to even the score, Wallis would claim she had tapped Ned while he was asleep and Ned would protest it couldn't possibly count.

"Why not?" Wallis would ask, raising an eyebrow, "You were there."

"Not all of me," Ned would answer. He was known to hit extra hard after bouts of logic he didn't feel he was winning.

Wallis tapped Ned on the arm with her left hand, knowing he would quickly counter. She tapped him hard with her right, momentarily winning before Ned grazed her arm and backed up out of the way. She leaned in and caught him on the top of his head, turned and ran out of his room before he could get her back. She went down a few steps before turning back. "Socks and shoes now, Ned," she said, making him stop at the top of the stairs as he seemed to realize she was using their little game to get him downstairs faster.

"I know what you're up to," he said.

"You only think you do," said Wallis, turning to walk down the stairs. "Bring your backpack with you and come on."

"What's for breakfast?"

"Like I'd know."

"Other mothers cook," he called out to her retreating back.

"And that means?"

"I'm going to win, you know," he yelled.

"Let me know when," she said, rounding the corner and walking into the kitchen.

CHAPTER 6

"HE'S NOT GOING TO LIKE THIS."

"When has he ever liked any news? When has he ever liked talking at all?"

"No, this is different. They're getting closer. Do you think they suspect him?"

"No, if they did, he'd be dead," said Mark, putting out his cigarette. "That's why you don't know who he is." He looked down at his iPhone, sliding his thumb over the screen as he quickly sent a short text.

"But it's not good, that guy turning up dead. An outsider and an apparent suicide," muttered Fred. "What makes a murder look like it is apparently a suicide? And that's the third one this year," he squeaked out. "Doesn't anyone notice that the forensics crew in this town is hedging their bets?" Fred fidgeted with the small pin on his lapel, spinning it around and around. The tight circle of 13 stars disappeared into a white blur against the deep blue background. Mark wore a matching pin in the exact same spot on his lapel.

"We're not talking about this any further. What's done is done."

The two men were standing outside of the James Center, one of the taller buildings that passed for a skyscraper in Richmond. Fred was slowly nursing an overpriced cup of gourmet coffee he had gotten from one of the nearby carts.

The low, early morning sun bounced off of the polished brown granite that was harvested in the next county over, just beyond the suburbs of the far West End and well out of the city limits. It put a glare right into the faces of the drivers coming down the steep hill as they headed toward work and made winter commutes particularly slow.

The gleaming tower situated along the lower end of Main Street had a duplicate sitting right next door and locals differentiated between the two buildings by the statues that sat in front of them. This one had an enormous bronze of well-endowed larger than life naked men trying to haul up a sail.

Law offices, restaurants, upscale shops and adjuncts to the nearby Federal Reserve building occupied the tower behind the two men. They were meeting in the middle of the usual breakfast crowd bustle as they did every morning whether there was news to trade or not. It had been Mark's idea. That way they would go unnoticed by casual observers and the Watchers that were always around might miss the few moments that were actually worth listening in on.

Small clusters of people were gathered everywhere in the urban paved park that stretched between the building and the mostly upscale food carts parked along the street.

"Quit playing with that, Fred. Don't draw attention to it," said Mark. It came out like more of an order. Fred's hand fell away from the pin on his lapel.

Neither one of the men stood out easily in downtown Richmond. Both had on the uniform that defined staid upper middle class men in the small southern city. Grey suit with a barely visible light grey or blue pin stripe and a tie that often reflected an alma mater. Fred's graying hair was neatly trimmed, cut just above the collar and ears while Mark had an afro that was just this side of being shaved. Fred wore the Florsheim's and Mark mixed it up a little with Italian loafers. There wasn't much to notice.

"Like they don't know who we are," said Fred, letting out a deep sigh. "They've always known who we are, remember? They picked us out."

Fred nervously looked around and nodded discreetly in the direction of the small group of women sitting on the ledge near the basin by the entrance to the building.

"Secretaries are the worst," he said, "constantly going through the files, asking questions."

"Or they're just doing their job, Fred. You can't let this stuff get to you. Come on, you used to be better at all of this. What happened?"

"They killed some guy who was never on the list, that's what happened."

"Yeah, I know, but they see us as harmless and I'd like to keep it that way," said Mark. "I have a nice quiet life going on and it'd be nice to make it to old age with my streak intact."

"How do you think they even knew about some country boy who's living in the suburbs?" asked Fred. Fred stuffed his hand into his pants pocket where he began to clink together the few coins he had left after stopping at the Gourmet on the Go cart. Mark gave him a withering look but it was just to hide his own growing restlessness. Fred's information about the missing Circle file worried him but he wasn't about to let Fred know that.

"Well, I have to do something with my hands," snapped Fred.

"I have to get back to work anyway," said Mark. "Quarter's almost finished, numbers will be due out soon." Mark was a senior technology architect with the Richmond office of the Federal Reserve.

"Someone's going to have to deal with it," began Fred, but Mark abruptly cut him off.

"Not you," he hissed. "You drop it. There are channels to go through and it'll get taken care of. You did your part. I'll take it from here. You forget all of this and go back to your job."

Fred looked like he was about to say something but finished the last of his coffee instead.

"Talk to you later," he mumbled and he tossed the cup in a nearby trash can as he turned to head toward the building.

"I'll see you later," said Mark, as he walked toward the Gourmet cart, giving a quick glance around to note how many people were still left outside. The numbers were thinning as he reached for his iPhone, quickly tapping the screen and sliding a new picture into view. The swift slides and tapping quickly turned off the small frequency generator that was installed to put out a low level white noise undetectable to human ears.

The family photo of his kids popped into view as he gave a slight tap and dropped the phone back into his coat pocket.

"A large coffee, leave room for cream," he said, pulling out his wallet. The two dollar bills were tucked behind the rest with the corners carefully bent. He always paid with cash wherever he went so that it was less noticeable when he was passing messages.

Carefully chosen bills were always at hand, the serial numbers ending in three digits that specified whether or not it was necessary to meet or if someone had been pegged by the larger forces. Or, even worse, if information was sliding in and out of hands that were never meant to have it. The meanings behind the short series of numbers changed every quarter and varied depending on the region of the country. Even then, only certain cells within the Circle knew their own series and even fewer knew the numbers of other regions. They were all playing games with a large, well-organized force that had more members that were trained from a very early age to be loyal to Management. It was better if information about who was an active part of the Circle was kept to a minimum.

"Let me get it." The man had suddenly appeared by Mark's side and ordered a muffin. Mark glanced up to see if it was a stranger and looked for the familiar lapel pin, but there was nothing there.

"Thank you, but I have it," he said, trying to sound distracted, feeling his heart rate picking up speed. It was unusual to see anyone he didn't recognize hanging around this time of day.

"No, really," insisted the man. "My good deed for the day." He had a distinctive southern accent and looked the part of a Richmond businessman as Mark quickly tried to assess if he'd been made. He kept his hand out, the dollar bills hanging in the air.

"I thought I knew everyone around these parts. You new?" said Stephen, the owner of the Gourmet cart. Stephen was well known to all of the regulars. "It's nice when everyone's trying to throw money at me," not giving the man a chance to answer. "Good sign for business," he said as he deftly took both men's money and made change before anyone could argue.

"Thanks anyway," said Mark, as he quickly took the cup from Stephen.

"Robert, Robert Schaeffer. I just started up the street," he said, pointing toward the large grey Federal Reserve building. "Just moved here from Savannah."

"Mark Whiting, I'm in the same building." Mark was watching Robert's every move, trying to quickly figure out whether or not information was being offered or taken away.

"I know, I saw you head down the hill. I've had to move around a lot," said Robert, "and I've learned if you want to find the good coffee you have to follow the locals," he said raising his cup with the familiar Gourmet logo. "I like your pin," he said, gesturing toward the small circle of stars. Mark flinched just a little and stepped back as the last of the morning stragglers squeezed past him to buy something from the cart. Stephen made a point to leave the two men alone.

"I used to have one," said Robert, "but I lost it in one of those moves."

So it was a warning, thought Mark, to let him know he had his own personal Watcher now. A made man who had decided to rejoin Management. They always made the best Watchers.

Everyone in this game knew who they were playing against. That was never a secret. After all, Management had chosen each of them for the list when they were only twelve years old and had guided them through their education and first jobs, calling on them occasionally to make a certain choice, vote a certain way or join a particular group. It was generally never heavy-handed so that all of it would go unnoticed by the masses of people who, generation after generation, were never chosen to be a part of the network.

Every town, every country had the disenfranchised who were unaware of how the system really worked but railed anyway against how closed-off it all appeared to be.

What was at stake in this game was knowledge and how the rules were being manipulated. That's what the missing file might tell the wrong people.

Knowing he was picked out changed everything for Mark and made him wonder if the file had already found a new home. He thought for a fleeting moment about his three kids but knew that it was pointless to try and get out.

If he was already in harms way there was very little he could do at this point to change whatever it was Management had in mind. The best he could hope for was to get an idea of what they were planning and pass it on later if he got the chance. Maybe the guy would say just a little too much. Suddenly his mouth was dry.

"Are you hoping this is more of a permanent move?" asked Mark.

"For at least a year or two, maybe. It'd be nice to settle down with the boys for some time. I'm a widower and its tough dragging the kids everywhere especially since they're all starting to get a little older and entering middle school."

Mark hesitated for a moment. Robert appeared to be reaching out for shelter. Mentioning the boys' age was a message. Perhaps they had been chosen and were about to start entering the right groups and attend the right schools. This was where it became impossible to turn back.

"Sorry about your wife. That's tough, being a single parent."

"Yeah, and I'm fairly new at the job. Carol, my wife, she's only been gone for about a year. We're all still adjusting and now this move. The boys aren't all that happy with me right now." He looked nervous, quickly licking his lips. Mark noticed his fingernails looked chewed to the quick and he had dark circles under his eyes.

"Maybe we should head up the street," said Mark, suddenly acutely aware of how vulnerable they were talking out in the open. "I need to get back to my desk. Thanks Stephen," he said, waving goodbye. Stephen nodded and started packing up the cart. The morning rush was over.

The two men started slowly walking up the sidewalk toward the Federal Reserve at a pace that passed for quickly in the south but resembled more of a stroll.

"You have any family in the area?" asked Mark.

"No, all of my people are from Georgia, have been for generations. I still have a brother in Macon who works for Mohawk Industries. Two sisters but both of them moved to Florida. I guess most of us felt the need to head out on our own." He dragged out the words, glancing at Mark.

"How many places have you lived?" he asked. It had turned into a game of cat and mouse but Mark wasn't sure who was the prey. If Robert were really a Watcher he was good at drawing out sympathy and knew a lot about the Circle.

It would be easier to treat him as a hostile and exchange pleasantries hoping he'd slip and give away even the smallest bit of information. If he were friendly to the Circle he could still be full of valuable information that with the right pressure could be removed by either side.

The lapel pin wasn't easy to come by and if he was really a member of the Circle but had lost his pin and his contacts were dead, he was floating dangerously free of any support with no way to easily connect back to a cell. The Circle had started out with the idea that only one member of each cell would know who to contact up or down the line of command for the two units above or below. The danger had been exposed though when a generation back an entire group was found out and too many links met tragic ends.

However, the system could leave individual members out in the wind, unsure of what to do next but with families to protect. It was possible Robert had been on his own since his wife died. It was also possible that was why she died. If that were true he was taking a risk chatting with Mark at all.

"So, how did your wife die?" Mark gently asked, giving Robert the chance to tell him more.

"Died in a boating accident. It was ruled an accident," he said, looking worn out as he gave a small shrug. "Ten years of sailing without a problem and she dies on a calm lake right before Christmas. I found her entangled in the sail."

Mark felt his stomach tighten as he held open the door to the building. First this woman, now Ray Billings, maybe others. Something was bothering the Management enough to clean house and risk others putting the pieces together. Mark wondered if the missing file held the answer.

"I'm sorry, that sounds awful," said Mark. "Look, here's my card. Maybe we can talk some more, later." If Robert was a Watcher, handing over his card wouldn't make any difference. If he was a lost member of the Circle then time wasn't on the guy's side. Mark would have to try and figure it out quickly and act.

"Thanks." Robert took the card and reached out to shake Mark's hand. Mark felt the folded dollar bill pressed into his palm and tried not to show any reaction.

"For the coffee," said Robert quietly and he quickly turned and headed toward the elevators.

Mark quickly headed for the stairs and the climb up to his fourth floor office. He often took the stairs trying to constantly create patterns that had been known to come in handy at opportune times.

When he was safely behind his desk he unfolded the bill to put into his wallet, carefully taking note of the three-numbered sequence. 8-4-2. He typed the numbers swiftly into his iPhone and sent a query, surprised at the sudden response. The decoded message back was clear.

He had given them an out of date distress code not used since the end of last year throughout the Georgia region. Bring the missing Circle agent back at once. He was valuable property.

CHAPTER
7

WALLIS heard the sound of a spatula scraping against a pan and knew it was pancakes. There were already plates set up on the island. She sat down on a barstool and took a sip of her only coffee for the day. Cream, no sugar.

"Blueberries?" she said.

"We ran out. I added a little cinnamon and some banana," said Norman, piling three pancakes onto the plate in front of Wallis.

"I can still psyche Ned out, but I don't think it's going to be much longer," said Wallis. "Eventually, he's going to figure out what I'm doing."

"Not as long as you make it part of a competition, he won't. He gets too focused on the wrong goal and can't see what you're up to. Of course, it also means you're playing with our only off-spring's head."

"Wouldn't that be our reason for having him around?"

"I thought it was free nursing care in another thirty years."

"Ned'll figure out a way to get somebody else to do it. It may not be a legal means but I don't see him wiping off drool."

"Me neither," said Norman, "but I figure Ned will either end up living under a bridge or richer than Rockefeller and as a parent I'm very optimistic." Norman said it without a hint of a smile.

"Did you smile more as a child?"

"Yes, but my mother beat those out of me."

"Norman! If your mother knew what you were saying, and anyway, it wouldn't explain Ned," she said, biting into a forkful. "Teachers have sent home notes asking if Ned is happy, you know that. And I know they're thinking I'm covering up something or why wouldn't he smile more?"

"We Weiskopf men keep our strategies very close to the chest."

"More people would realize you were funny if you would smile a little more."

"Too many of the people I'm dealing with are too busy listening to themselves talk and at two hundred dollars an hour I prefer to let them run on and on," said Norman.

Wallis smiled. "Practical, even in your jokes." She speared another bite of pancake.

 Ned walked in and took the stool next to his mother. A pocket on the side of his shorts shifted as a heavy object inside of it slid to one side.

"You have every pocket filled with something, don't you?" said Wallis. "All I want to know is, if any of those things are combined would it become a bomb?"

"I'm not that stupid, Mom. If I was making a bomb I'd do it after hours and hide the components, especially from Dad."

"Owww. I might catch on to what you were doing."

"You haven't yet."

Wallis frowned and peered into her son's green eyes.

"Nope. I've got nothing," she said. "Okay, I'll settle for, don't take any of it out during school unless it's homework. Okay?"

"That was already the plan," said Ned. "I'll take six, Dad," said Ned, reaching for the butter and cutting the stick, carefully guiding half of it onto his plate.

"Ned, some day that bad habit is going to have some very real consequences," said Wallis.

"I already checked. Dad and both of my uncles have very low bad cholesterol and Uncle Harry eats scrapple for a snack."

"There's a chance you got some of my DNA, Ned."

"Meh," he said, shrugging his shoulders. It was his usual signal he was done talking. He stuffed his mouth with two pancakes letting butter drip down his chin. "Oooh, bafana," he mumbled, "good job, Dad."

Ned gave Norman a thumbs-up as Norman kissed his son on the top of his head. Ned swallowed and folded up another pancake sliding it into his mouth while staring blankly at Wallis.

"That's okay. The first date is always easy to get. It's the second one you may find a bit more difficult, young man," said Wallis. "I'm going to go get my things and put them in the car. Be ready by the time I get back."

Ned folded another pancake and pushed it into his mouth.

Wallis grabbed her over-sized briefcase and a small box of files she had been going through for a divorce case that was coming up next week and backed her way out of the laundry room door. She felt her shoe squish as she stepped on the old horse hair mat by the back door.

"Ned," she softly muttered, wondering what was stuck on the bottom of her shoe. She tried to balance the box and look down at her shoe as she kept moving but the box kept getting in the way. She gave up and kept moving.

CHAPTER 8

WALLIS was almost to her car, still scraping the bottom of her shoe along the driveway before she noticed the man pacing next to her car door. He was tall and lanky dressed in faded brown corduroys and a short-sleeve, pale blue dress shirt, badly stained under the arms, grasping a folder tightly in his hand.

Wallis sharply drew in her breath and almost dropped the box. She took a quick read of the man, wondering how far this was going to go. Should she start screaming now and risk looking silly? The man looked like he hadn't slept in awhile.

"Are you Wallis Jones? You're the Black Widow, right?"

"If you're looking for a lawyer, you need to contact me at my office," she said, bristling, making her voice as even as she could manage. "I don't even consider taking clients who show up in my driveway. And for the record, I don't appreciate the nickname." Wallis glanced back at the front door hoping Ned was dragging his feet.

"Ray Billings said to find you…"

Wallis cut him off before he could finish. "I'm not Mr. Billings' attorney, I'm his soon to be ex-wife's and I can't discuss the case.
You need to leave, now." This is a new one, she thought. Intimidate the opposing counsel with your crazy friend.

"Please," he said in a bleating tone, moving quickly toward Wallis and grabbing her by the arms. "We need to talk." A piece of paper slipped out of the folder in his hand and floated to the ground sliding behind the rear tire.

"Mom?" Ned was coming out of the front door, trying to maneuver a school project that had gotten stuck in the doorway. "Should I call Dad?"

Wallis jerked her arms away and hissed quietly at the stranger, "Leave now or I call the police and the judge, in that order. Never show up here again. If Mr. Billings has a problem, tell him to take it up with his lawyer. That's the way the game is played."

"You don't understand…" he said, backing up, a look of fear creeping up on his face. "Don't call anyone, not the police. Don't even call me. Don't say anything to anyone." He glanced over at Ned who had stopped trying to get anything out the door and was nervously keeping an eye on his mother.

"Dad?" Ned called out, watching the man in the driveway.

The man leaned in and whispered, "My name is Stanley, Stanley Woermer. We have to talk." He looked quickly back at Ned again, lingering a little too long for Wallis' comfort, and turned, taking a quick jog up the driveway, turning right at the end and disappearing from view, hidden by the tall bushes that grew at the edge of the driveway. Wallis noticed the expensive running shoes and the easy, loping way he had taken the long hill that led from the house to the street, keeping his posture erect.

"Have to get Laurel to check this one out," she said quietly.

Norman came out of the door wiping his hands on a kitchen towel.

"Everything alright?" he said, looking at the expressions on Ned and Wallis' faces.

"Everything's fine, dear," said Wallis, letting out a long breath. She realized she'd been clutching her keys in her hand. "Just a desperate move by a desperate client. He's gone, come on Ned. Do you need some help?" said Wallis, trying to smile at Ned and let him know it was all okay. She put the box down on her trunk and quickly bent down, picked up the piece of fallen paper and folded it, sliding it into her skirt pocket.

Norman and Ned came out of the door carrying a school project almost as big as Ned made out of Styrofoam and painted gun-metal gray with coiled arms and wooden legs. It had a pair of race cars for feet. Wallis raised her eyebrows, relaxing a little. Being around Ned had a way of making her do that.

"It's an alien. Mrs. Ward asked us to do it."

"It's scientific?"

"I don't know. We had to include motion somehow."

"Hence the cars."

"They're remote control cars. I can make the robot move and there's a giant spring on the inside so it'll bounce some while it goes."

"Very clever. What are you studying in science right now? Energy and motion?"

"Weather patterns."

"Really?" asked Wallis.

"You're way too easy, Mom."

Norman gave a small smile. "I'm going back inside if you people no longer need a man around." Wallis smiled a little, and made a face at him.

"So, where's the fun in it?" she said to Ned.

"I can't always resist."

Wallis carefully put the alien in a seat of his own next to Ned, gently pulling the seat belt around the middle and started driving in the direction of the school. Ned could take the bus but Wallis liked having the few minutes alone with him every morning and it was the one place Ned was most likely to tell her about how he was really doing. It didn't happen often, but Wallis was always hopeful.

"Why don't I have red hair like you?" asked Ned.

"Because you're too young to dye your hair," said Wallis, glancing at Ned's face in her rearview mirror.

"And besides, the box clearly says this is auburn."

Ned smiled and Wallis felt her stomach jump a little at the small unexpected gift so early in the morning. Strange morning, she thought.

As she pulled her older blue Jaguar into the long circular driveway in front of the school she saw children getting off of the bus in the side-by-side matching curved driveways. Some of them were holding similar concoctions as Ned's but everyone else's was no more than a foot tall. Wallis looked back at Ned's project.

"Were there any instructions on size?"

"No, not really."

"What does that mean? She gave hints?"

"She gave suggestions and I decided to do this," he said, gesturing toward the project.

Wallis let out a sigh. "Do you need help carrying it in?"

"No, I've got it. Thanks, Mom," said Ned, leaning forward to get a kiss. "See you later. Love you."

"Love you more," she replied, another of their games.

"Nah ah," he answered, without looking back.

"Yah, hah," she said, and waited for Ned to walk around and get his science project out of the car.

"I love you times infinity," he said, once he had the project out, and quickly tapped her on the shoulder before closing the door. She could barely hear the muffled 'got you last' before he turned and walked away. Good one, she thought, and drove off, headed for work.

She came down Quioccasin Road and turned the corner back on to Pump to head toward the office. The route took her near her house. That's how Wallis spent a lot of her days, crisscrossing the same paths. It made her wonder sometimes what she was accomplishing.

As she neared her corner she saw the neighbor's dog, Happy, sitting quietly with her leash still attached and hanging down beside her. Wallis thought about forgetting what she saw and going on to work but she knew if something happened to the Labrador the guilt would kill her. She pulled up to the corner and leaned across the seat to push open the passenger side door.

"Hi Happy! Hi girl. Come on, come on," she said, in a sing-song voice, waving her arm to try and coax the dog into the car. "It's me, Happy, Ned's mom, Wallis. Come on. Don't make me get out of the car, please. Come on," she said, waving harder.

Happy looked around and started toward the car. Halfway in she tried to change her mind and get back out but by then Wallis had the big Lab firmly by her collar, pulling her the rest of the way in and yanking the door shut.

Wallis tried both doors at the Blazney house but got no response.

"They must not know you're out," she said, looking down at Happy patiently waiting by her side.

She walked Happy around to the back yard and put her in behind the privacy fence, shutting the gate. As she walked back to her car she had the strange feeling of being watched but there were only a couple of cars parked along the street and no one was in sight.

Strange morning, she thought again, rubbing her arms through her coat, trying to shake the cold.

CHAPTER 9

WEISKOPF, Jones and Bremmer was less than five miles from Wallis' house, nestled in a small row of Colonial style white townhouses that fronted the busy corner of Church and Broad Street Roads between a fortune teller and a real estate agent. The far end was a Chinese restaurant. The fortune teller, Madame Bella, was on the end closest to Broad Street Road and had a giant sign in the manicured grass out front displaying a glowing purple hand with neon white lines inside the palm. A smaller multi-colored neon eye was in a first floor window. At Christmas the Madame would decorate all of it with small white twinkling lights. Ned called her sign in front the fickle fingers of fate. Harriet saw the proximity as a scandal in the making and was always trying to get Wallis to call the county and protest.

"Protest what, mother? That it lights up?"

"Well, I don't know what people will think."

On more than one occasion Norman would hand Harriet a twenty after a few minutes of listening to her whine and tell her to go ask the Madame, that she would know. Harriet would look hurt but always kept the money.

Only two yards away was the smaller, white wooden sign of the law firm with the three names painted in understated black script. In an equal distance of two yards each were similar quiet signs for the real estate agent and the Chinese restaurant. Sometimes, when Wallis had to work late at night she would glance out of her office window on the second floor at the purple hand and try to figure out what neon sign they could erect. When she was tired she thought of things like a big giant mallet. That could be taken so many different ways.

Wallis walked into the office from the back door that faced the parking lot and said hello to her paralegal, Laurel, a pretty young woman with two small children. Wallis had handled the divorce and child arrangements for her last year. No one in the office, not William's assistant Patty, an older heavy-set woman twice-divorced, or William, still a bachelor, was happily married except Wallis and Norman.

"Norman in yet?" asked Wallis, "Hi Patty."

Patty looked up over the half-glasses she was wearing and gave a small wave.

"He's on the phone with an irate client," said Patty, rolling her eyes. "Amazing how you two start out together in the morning but still need to ask us to figure out each other's schedule."

"Nice dress," said Wallis, ignoring the comment and looking at the larger-than-life pattern of roses that enveloped Patty. "Maybe it'll make spring get here a little faster. Not too fond of the last days of March. So dreary right to the bitter end. Out like a lamb is a lie."

Patty looked up over her half-moon glasses and raised her eyebrows making the tight gray bun move on the top of her head. "I'll remind you when it's August and a steam bath."

"Positive attitude as usual, Patty."

Patty was a fixture in the office and had originally worked for Wallis and Norman before William had come along. "Just trying to keep your feet on the ground, dearie."

"Thank you, keep up the good effort."

Wallis put the box she had been carrying on the floor near Laurel.

The waiting area was comfortable but sparse. Two small brocade upholstered sofas and two hardback chairs were separated by small wooden mahogany tables and brass lamps with green metal shades. The magazines on the small tables were all at least a few months old and well-worn. Wallis wasn't very fond of the style but didn't care enough to change it. Harriet had done the decorating. Norman's contribution was a small clay pot with a cork in it and an inscription on the front that read 'Bad Clients'.

"I'll get with you in a few minutes, Laurel. Let me get settled first," said Wallis, starting up the stairs. It was Wallis' routine. Check her messages, unload her briefcase, look at her schedule for the day and then find out what had already changed or gone wrong. That was the nature of family law, someone or something was always throwing a curve into the plans.

She took a turn at the top and headed to her office with a nice view of the street and the fickle fingers. Norman's office was on the back and overlooked the parking lot and a few more small shops across the way.

Wallis put her briefcase down on the large oak desk that had been her father, Walter's, when he worked for the fabric mills as a salesman. It was plain and sturdy, which was a good description of her father. He had worked long hours traveling all over the mid-Atlantic region carting samples of corduroy and sateen when there were still enough clothing manufacturers left in the states.

Eventually, trying to make ends meet and keep Harriet moderately happy wore him down and he quietly passed away in his beloved recliner one night while watching the news. His starched collar was loosened and his polished brown leather Florsheim's with the well-worn spots on the soles were neatly lined up next to the chair. His dinner was getting cold on the tray beside him. Wallis had already moved out and was living in D.C. but missed him terribly all the time. He had been easy-going and quick with a joke and unlike Harriet, always saw the best in everything.

"Your mother doesn't just see the glass as half-empty," he had once said, "she wonders who the hell stole the other half. I, on the other hand, wonder if I can interest them in buying just a little bit more."

Wallis knew, though, that Walter was the love of her mother's life and

Harriet never got over the loss. She once noticed her mother gingerly tucking a gold chain into the top of her dress, her beloved Walter's wedding band dangling from the bottom.

Harriet still even wore her matched platinum set with the quarter karat diamond on her finger where it had rested since Walter had placed them there and she had never mentioned taking them off.

Wallis glanced at her schedule, noting the child support hearing that afternoon and the recorder concert at Ned's school. She knew it was going to be tough to make it in time to the school. Maybe Norman could go alone, she thought, already feeling a little guilty.

She headed down the steps pulling the dropped paper out of her pocket as she quickly took the stairs and unfolded it, stopping halfway down. It was a spreadsheet of boys names cross-referenced with schools, churches, clubs, awards. Wallis recognized a few of the names. The boys were the same age as Ned but according to the piece of paper they all went to one of the three private schools thought to be necessary to maintain a social standing in Richmond. The clubs were mostly elite social clubs where only the right family name could gain someone admission. Same with the churches. A regular body could get into one, but they'd never let you feel comfortable enough to stay.

Wallis didn't really socialize with any of the names that were listed but had been the attorney, sometimes several times, for some of them as they remixed their families. In the last column on the paper was a series of short numbers next to each boy's name, sometimes repeated. 845 or 671 or 907, repeated as if at random.

"Wallis?" Laurel was calling to her. "You coming down?"

Wallis refolded the paper and put it back in her pocket, heading down the last few steps and around the corner.

Laurel was walking toward the storage room with the box Wallis had left on the floor.

"Hey, where are you going with that? We couldn't have won yet, could we?"

"Don't you listen to the morning news? We won by default, Ray Billings is dead. Shot himself in the head yesterday. His widow won't be needing a divorce after all."

Wallis self-consciously pushed against the paper in her pocket, startled.

"They're sure it's suicide?"

"I think the phrase the news used was apparent suicide. What's wrong? You have that look."

"You know, for such a small city, there are an awful lot of people who meet a violent end," said Patty, looking up over her glasses.

Wallis looked over at Patty and felt her stomach tighten. She looked back at Laurel and tried to shake the feeling of dread that was growing. "I don't have looks," she said, raising her eyebrows. "Keep the box out for awhile, Laurel, just in case."

"You do have looks and you're not spilling. Okay, okay, enough said, need to know basis."

"And could you call Jim at the Road Runners Club and ask him if a Stanley Woermer is a member?" said Wallis.

"Sure, do I give him a reason why I'm asking?"

Wallis hesitated, "Tell him I'm looking for a running partner and someone recommended Woermer. Could you ask Norman to find me when he gets off the phone?"

Wallis stood at the fax machine tucked into the small closet across from Laurel's desk trying to remember which way to feed the paper into the machine. Norman was in charge of buying office equipment and he was forever finding a guy who had rebuilt a copier or a shredder from old parts and then sold it for way under cost. Sometimes that meant none of the arrows meant much of anything.

Norman wasn't cheap by nature, but it bothered him that they kept coming out with new features every few months. Mixing up old parts to make something new was Norman's little act of anarchy against the system.

Wallis slid the paper around feeling herself growing more frustrated.

"Laurel? I can't remember, does the paper go face down or face up? We should really put a sign on this thing," she said, sounding more agitated than she had meant.

Laurel squeezed in behind Wallis, ducking under the fuse box on the back wall to get around her.

"Face down, just like the arrow says. I didn't put a sign here because this one is correct," she said, emphasizing the last word.

"Problem?" asked Wallace, trying to force the tension out of her voice.

"It's not like I don't know who 'we' is, meaning me, and it's not like I don't see something that needs doing and take care of it, all the time."

"I'm sorry, bad morning. You're absolutely right," said Wallis, slipping her hand into her pocket again, feeling the edge of the paper with her finger.

"It's not like you to snap. We've had clients worried about the safety of their children and you were still as calm and cool. I can't imagine how bad it would have to get before you'd tense up." Laurel eyed Wallis, scrutinizing her for clues.

"Did you reach Jim yet?" said Wallis.

"Second time today you've used Jim as a diversion. Okay, but I'm going to figure this one out. I always do. You could save both of us a lot of trouble and trust me now, but either way, I'm putting the pieces together."

"And Jim?"

"Yes, I got him. The message is in your pile as per your usual routine, if I'm not being too insubordinate, that is."

Wallis managed a small smile, rubbing her forehead, feeling the beginning of a headache.

"Thank Goodness for you, Laurel, or I might actually run the risk of ever being too big for my britches."

"It's on my resume, as you recall. And Jim said Mr. Woermer's a little out of your league, a seven minute runner, but he has a list of more appropriate names. I think he meant slower."

"Did he say anything else?"

"He mentioned he used to train with Stanley when he was still running marathons, and he said Stanley still shows up for the Saturday morning runs over at Runner Bill's on the South Side. Is that where you know him from?"

"I'm due in court." Wallis jabbed send on the fax machine and started to slide past Laurel out of the closet. Laurel put her hand on Wallis' arm and stopped her, dropping her voice to a whisper.

"Are you in some kind of trouble? You do know you can trust me, right? Because I'd really be insulted if I found out you even had to wonder about that."

"I do know that," she said quietly, "thank you."

"Excuse me." A young woman with a serious expression under short blonde hair against pale skin, wearing charcoal grey trousers and a white shirt with embroidered vines across the front stood at the door to the closet. "I'm here to see Mr. Weiskopf?"

"Sure," said Patty from behind her, "let me ring him for you. What's your name, honey?"

"Annie Brody," she said turning slowly toward Patty. "I have an appointment. Sara Kaye recommended him." She sputtered out toward the end of the sentence, the words trailing off.

Annie Brody stood at the corner of Patty's desk listening to her page Norman and glancing nervously back at Wallis and Laurel, never showing any expression except the small hints of worry in her eyes. The color of her skin and hair made her blue eyes stand out on her face, the one spot of color that came naturally to her.

"Hi Annie," said Wallis. She recognized her from her occasional visits to church. Annie gave a small half-wave but didn't move from the spot.

"You want to take a seat?" said Patty.

"Sure, sure," she said, looking around like she'd just noticed there were seats in the room. "Over there," she said, pointing to the chair nearest the stairs and looking back to Laurel and Patty.

"Sure, honey. Take any chair you like. We won't mind," said Patty, her usual tone of voice making it sound like more of a judgment. The woman gingerly sat on the edge of the seat.

Laurel turned her back and made a face at Wallis.

"Norman, Annie Brody is here to see you," said Patty into the phone. "Sure, okay. He said to go on up, these stairs here, and it's the office to the right. Good luck honey," said Patty, hanging up the phone and pushing her glasses back up her nose.

"It's become like a code word around here, Sara Kaye sent me," said Patty, once Annie Brody was safely out of range. "I feel like I'm part of some women's network for Baptist-owned businesses," she muttered.

"They like Norman, they find him to be absent of judgment," said Wallis. Patty and Laurel both let out a laugh.

"Amen," said Patty.

"Hello, ladies." A nun who worked at the local Episcopal Church located just across the river, St. Stephen's darted in the back door, dropping a brown padded envelope on Patty's desk.

"Hi Sister," said Patty. "I'll see Norman gets this. Is it a rush?"

"No, the Reverend said it was just a little routine church business," said the nun as she headed back out toward the parking lot.

"Tell the Pastor hello for me," yelled Laurel.

"Will do," said the Sister as she held the door for an extra moment before letting it swing shut.

"Baptists and Episcopalians," said Patty. "Surely, this will help me get into heaven. I didn't even know there was such a thing as Episcopalian nuns before I started working here."

"Norman's ecumenical," said Laurel.

"And best friends with the minister," said Wallis.

"Your mother called, by the way," said Laurel turning back, "said she found the same brocade pattern on sale at Fabric Barn that your namesake used in one of her houses. She wanted to know if you wanted a few yards. You think that's really possible they'd have it at Fabric Barn?"

"Harriet doesn't joke about anything to do with the Duchess. If she says it's the same, it is. Tell her I'll take a few yards. If I say no, she'll be hurt, talk about it for months under her breath and give it all to me anyway."

Laurel was smiling as she picked up the phone, "I'll let her know. By the way, I can't believe I forgot. Madame from next door has requested an appointment with you. She said it was urgent. I had to put her off till Friday and she was not happy. I think I may have gotten the evil eye."

"Any clue to why?" asked Wallis.

"No, only that it's not legal so you can't charge her for the time."

CHAPTER

WALLIS drove over to the Henrico County Juvenile courthouse off of Parham Road trying to picture the men who ran in the Runner Bill's group. She usually made it over there at least once a month but ran in the back of the pack, far behind the small cluster of men who always turned it into a friendly four mile race. Wallis couldn't remember Stanley. He must have always been at the lead getting back in his car to go home by the time Wallis would have made it back to the shop for bagels and juice.

She wasn't surprised to find out that Stanley was someone she had probably caught a glimpse of before. That was typical of a small town like Richmond where lives intersected all the time at odd places, often depending on what part of town someone lived in.

Where do you live, was one of the first questions people asked each other, and depending on the answer either lost interest or started comparing notes. Each part of town gave away little bits of information. Church Hill or the Fan meant there was a greater chance of no children, might still have a nightlife and less likely to want to conform to anything.

The North Side was a bridge with a mixture of everything and good for antiques at the yard sales.

The West End and South Side were suburbs with purpose, filled with people determined to get ahead and help their children get a firm footing. Often those yard sales had shiny new things still in their boxes, already unwanted.

Wallis found a parking space along the small road that fronted the courthouse parking lot in front of the long, cream colored low-slung building that sat down in the dip of the hillside. She slid her cell phone into the glove compartment, locked the car, and headed for the cement steps on the far right side and entered through the glass doors. She skipped the metal detectors, walking to the side and waving at the deputy sheriff who was patting down a middle-aged man wearing numerous small chains as accessories to his pressed jeans and t-shirt.

"Hello, Ms. Jones. Nice to see you again," said the portly deputy sheriff in a tight grey-blue uniform. "Okay, you can go," he said to the man, handing him the plastic cup to scoop out his keys and change.

"Hello, Oscar, thanks. I was here yesterday," said Wallis.

"And, as usual, it perked up my day."

"You're a charmer, Oscar. That's why I look forward to our chats. Are you doing alright?" asked Wallis, gesturing toward the white bandage across Oscar's cheek.

"T'weren't nothing. I hear tell that's your client down the hall. Quite an outfit, and that's saying something."

Wallis turned back and took a look at Oscar to see if he was trying to rattle her.

"What do you mean?"

"Perhaps you should go look for yourself. Hope it's not a custody case, or maybe I should say, hope you got paid in advance," he said to her retreating back as she took measured steps down the long hallway packed with lawyers and clients waiting to be summoned into any of the four courtrooms.

As Wallis passed the first courtroom the door opened and a tall thin deputy stepped out, glancing down at the name written on a card.

"Lassiter case," he boomed, "anyone in the Lassiter case." A small group of people stirred on a nearby bench and made their way toward the door.

Everyone always walks in looking like they've already lost, thought Wallis.

"Hey Jeffrey," she said, to the short, older man in a dark suit that was too long in the arms and too tight around the neck. "This your case?" Wallis knew she had a little extra time and she wanted to put off seeing exactly what kind of disaster was awaiting her at the far end of the hall.

"Yep, tell Norman hello for me," he said, placing an arm around an older woman who was attempting to hold a fidgeting baby while watching a toddler who was trying to crawl underneath the crowded bench.

"You'll need to wait out here," he told her, "Children aren't allowed in the court room."

"But it's about them," she said, sounding frustrated.

"You're absolutely right, but it's in their best interest to not have to participate in any of it," he said firmly, keeping his hand on her shoulder. Wallis had to give the same speech at least once a week.

"They ought to know now what their mother's like, save 'em a lot of heartache later. Told William the same thing. He didn't listen neither," the woman said, curling her lip.

"Please take a seat somewhere. This shouldn't take more than a half hour," said the bailiff, ignoring the woman's comments.

The woman tsked and moved the squirming baby from one great hip to the other, pulling her flowered shift in the same direction. The baby's toe got caught in one of the large front pockets but she didn't make a move toward any of the benches.

"Suit yourself," said Jeffrey calmly and pulled his hand away, turning to go in the court room. The woman didn't budge but didn't follow him.

Jeffrey shrugged at Wallis, licking away the sweat on his upper lip. The bailiff gave the lawyer a sympathetic look before glancing down at the name of the case on the index card in his hand.

"Everyone in your party here?" he asked, not looking up from the card.

"Yeah, we're all here," said Jeffrey, the beading on his forehead picking up.

"Okay, let's get this show on the road."

"See you around, Wallis. Hey, heard about your client's unfortunate fortune. Husband turns up dead. Only thing that could have made it better is if it had been an accident. Then maybe there'd be some insurance."

Jeffrey said it without a hint of sarcasm or amusement. He was doing what he'd been trained to do, hunting for the angles and settling for what was.

The door swung shut and Wallis turned to see the glare on the face of the unhappy mother-in-law left minding the children. Wallis still managed a tight smile and walked briskly away. As she neared the end of the hall she could sense the unease. Everyone seemed to be facing away from the last bench as if the hall ended right where they stood and didn't go on for a few more yards.

Tucked behind them, sitting uncomfortably on a bench by herself was the client, June Reynolds, wearing a sleeveless silk top too small for an ample bosom, most of which was squeezed together and blossoming out of the top of her shirt. June was nervously tugging at a short tan skirt trying to pull it down another inch over a large thigh but not succeeding. Her feet were shoved into high heeled clear plastic sandals. She looked like a stripper dressed up for a date. Wallis immediately began practicing in her head the speech she would give the judge to explain her errant client.

"Hi, Ms. Jones," June squeaked out, giving another tug to the skirt. "I got here early, like you asked."

Tug, tug.

"These were the best clothes I could find."

Tug.

"I hope they're alright."

Wallis looked at what June thought would pass for appropriate courtroom attire and suppressed the urge to sigh.

June fidgeted, looking overwhelmed and frightened as her hands still nervously worked the sides of her skirt. Wallis gave her a confident, unyielding gaze, trying to gauge whether or not it would make things worse to suggest June try to sit still.

"Everything will be fine," she said, her usual response when the truth was out of place.

A bailiff stepped out into the hall, ready to yell out a name. Wallis took two quick strides toward him.

"How's it look for us?" asked Wallis.

"Hi, Ms. Jones, all of your parties here?"

Wallis stepped back and glanced for a moment, spotting the other counsel, Richard Bach, and nodded at the bailiff. Richard gave his usual smile showing a perfect row of overly-white teeth.

"We're all here."

"I'll let the judge know, thank you. Sherman case? Everyone in the Sherman case?" he yelled. Two small groups of people, a man and woman separated by lawyers, rose up from different benches and cautiously approached the door, looking wary about walking so close to each other. Wallis felt grateful for Norman all over again.

June was still patiently waiting on the long narrow pine bench that resembled a church pew, folding and unfolding her hands in her lap.

"Will it be soon?" she said, in the same, high pitched small voice.

"Maybe another half hour or so. They're not too far behind today." Wallis pulled out a file and sat down next to June.

Richard approached nearby and gave Wallis a small wave, smiling broadly, a bright white glow between his lips, as he took an obvious but quick glance at June's get-up.

"I'll be right back," she said, not looking at June.

"We'd like to discuss a settlement," said Richard, talking through the smile.

"What are you offering?"

"An increase to five hundred a month, more than fair considering my client's financial status as a small business owner."

"No deal. We believe the financial records will show your client's..."

"We're not going to share those..."

"We already have them," said Wallis, her face taking on the calm, stony expression she used when she sensed the game was in motion. She had subpoenaed the man's records from the bank over a month ago, bypassing him altogether.

Richard looked momentarily taken aback, the smile slipping off of his face.

"How...? I mean, what exactly are you saying?" he sputtered.

"I'm saying, we already know how well your client is doing, we also have his list of monthly bills that you provided and based on the state's calculations, your client should be paying nine hundred and fifty dollars a month, beginning from when the request was filed." Her face never changed expression. The smile slipped back on Richard's face, the sides pulled a little tighter.

"We'll need some sort of assurance your client is actually spending the money on the child."

"She is. That's all the assurance you're getting. If you want to go in and fight about it, we can, but we'll also be asking for a percentage of all household and medical bills over a hundred dollars and an extra thousand every six months for any extracurricular activities, if you want to break it down and argue the individual points."

Wallis knew Richard was only trying to save face now. He knew the game was over and there was nothing to be gained by going before the judge, especially not Judge Pearson. He went strictly by the state guidelines and was bound to notice how far back the father had been making substantially more money than he'd been letting onto.

"Let me ask my client," said Richard, the smile growing more tense.

"We'll need the back monies owed, today," said Wallis, in a calm even tone.

Wallis could have sworn he muttered, Black Widow, quietly as he turned and she felt the skin on her neck prickle. That's going to cost you, Richard, she thought.

She hated the nickname. The old boy network of lawyers with old family names that did most of their business at the Country Club of Virginia, a beautiful expanse of land that stretched out along River Road where the old money lived, or the Commonwealth Club, a boys only private dining club where the men liked to swim in the nude, had given her the name. They didn't like losing, especially to a woman and even less to a name that didn't have past presidents or generals attached to it. Wallis had been born outside of the network that was always at work in the small city, easily helping the favored to get the advantage. That only meant Wallis took particular pleasure when she was able to get in their way.

Wallis turned and made a point of walking loudly back to June, letting her heels click hard on the parquet floor. She kept her back to Richard and his client and stood in front of June so they couldn't get a clear view.

"Just another minute, June, okay?"

June nodded vigorously. "Is it going okay?"

"Yes, it'll be fine. Just another minute."

June nodded again. Wallis walked back toward Richard who was still chatting with the husband. The husband was shaking his head no, but Richard was making chops through the air with his hand, telling his client something over and over again, wearing him down. The husband looked over at June and sneered, said something to Richard and turned away.

"He'll take the deal," said Richard. "Will a check be okay for the back money?"

"Yes, but my client is also going to want seventy percent of all medical bills over a hundred dollars paid by your client, as well."

Richard's face grew dark. He looked like he was holding his breath for a moment.

"Let me know," said Wallis, still calm, and turned to walk back and sit down by June.

The bailiff emerged from the courtroom, the woman from the previous case sailing past him, walking hurriedly back down the hall with her lawyer keeping pace behind her. The man came out more slowly, peppering his lawyer with questions. Hard to tell who won that one, thought Wallis.

"You're up," said the bailiff.

"We may have a settlement. Do you have just a minute?"

"Just a minute, because that's all you've got," said the bailiff, taking a glance back at Richard, watching the two men's heads bobbing first in one direction, then another.

"Are you two ready?" called the bailiff.

Wallis stood by the bailiff, waiting for the answer. Either way would have been fine with her. She knew the ability to be happy with whatever came at her was a key part of why she usually won, and she at least took skin with her when she lost.

Richard rose slowly, still nodding at his client, who reluctantly nodded back to him, and came over to the court room door.

"We have a deal," he said to Wallis, "but he wants thirty days from when he receives the bill to pay the funds."

"That should be fine," said Wallis. "We have a settlement," she said to the bailiff. "I'll present the parameters to the judge, draw up the agreement and send it over to your office." She didn't look for a nod. "You have the check?"

"He's writing it now." I'm going to tell her to go cash it now, thought Wallis.

"Wallis? Wallis?"

Wallis turned to see Lilly Billings coming down the hall, her orange hair visible like a moving dot in the crowd, clutching her purse tightly under her arm. She was wearing her usual odd version of a suit. A sensible dark wool skirt with a matching vest over a brightly colored silk blouse with billowy sleeves and sensible shoes. Ray Billings' new widow in all her splendor.

"Lilly, what are you doing here?" said Wallis, taking a step away from the small crowd and dropping her voice. "Shouldn't you be taking care of the arrangements?"

"Ray's family is doing all of that. It's their right now, anyway. Ray and I weren't really speaking there in the end, and I think they hold me a little responsible." She glanced down and blinked her eyes hard a few times.

"You're not, you know," whispered Wallis, her voice softening.

"I know, but it wasn't suicide, Wallis. Ray and I may have been fighting but he wasn't depressed over it, just a little mad I wasn't more supportive."

"Supportive?"

"He was up to something at work, you know, at the utility department. He said he was trying to do the right thing. All I know is he had a lot of late nights and strange meetings. I thought it might be women for awhile, that seemed like the saner reason, so I followed him. Did I ever tell you that? But he was meeting with his supervisor, Alice Watkins, in a diner, and there's no way Ray was attracted to that old tired thing."

"What were they doing?"

"Talking, and not casually. They were leaning over the table, practically in their coffee, arguing about something. Ray had a file he was trying to give her and something else that I couldn't really make out, but she wouldn't take it. He looked disappointed, hurt even, and got up to go. That's when I left. When he got home I told him I saw him and he went through the roof," she said, her arms flying up over her head. "Still wouldn't tell me what was up, only that he was raised right and somebody had to do it."

"Do what, Lilly? I don't understand."

"That's the problem, neither do I. I only got a peek at that file. Saw it just for a moment before Ray caught me and took the file someplace."

"What did you see?"

"Names, all men's names, on a grid with different headings like where they went to school. And little rows of numbers. That's all I saw. Ray works for the utilities department. Why would he need that? You think Ray was doing something bad? That wouldn't be like Ray, I swear," she whispered, tearing up. She blotted her eyes with a neatly folded tissue she had pulled out of a sleeve, careful not to smudge her elaborate eye makeup.

"Why didn't you tell me all of this before?" said Wallis, trying to keep her breathing even. Lilly didn't answer, still blotting at her face.

Wallis felt the same lurch in her stomach she'd felt earlier and wanted to find Norman immediately. Take off at a dead run, if necessary. I should have told him this morning, she thought. Not men's names, boy's. Boys I know. What have I done?

"I'll tell you, Wallis," she said, clutching at Wallis' arm with a perfectly manicured hand, "he was scared, worse than I've ever seen. When I really figured out he didn't trust me enough to tell me anything, I knew it was over. Thirty years and all gone."

"If he was so upset and keeping secrets, how do you know it wasn't suicide after all?" asked Wallis, hoping Lilly didn't have a good answer.

"Because of something he said," she said, lifting her chin like it was already obvious. "He said if something happened to him, I was to tell you. No matter what it looked like I was to tell you. That you'd know what to do. I thought he was just getting crazier and crazier when he said that, but now this. What'd he mean by that?"

"I have no idea," said Wallis, the last of her calm of a few minutes ago finally seeping away.

"You know, Ray may not have liked you, but it was only out of respect for your nickname that his lawyer was always saying. Black Widow. He didn't like knowing he was going to lose."

"That was it? That's all he said?"

"No, one other thing. But that sounds as crazy as the rest. He said this whole thing was bigger than he could even tell and if it wasn't for the list, he wouldn't have gone anywhere near it." She shrugged, as if to say maybe it was all a little crazy after all.

"Ray was a good husband for twenty nine of those years," said Lilly, "that ought to account for something. I owe him this much, I figure. Not sure what to tell you to do with it all, but Ray was determined. This was no suicide."

Her eyes welled up again and she let the tears slide down her cheeks making lines through the powdered exterior.

"Did Ray ever mention Stanley Woermer?" asked Wallis, knowing she was slipping into something unasked for and unwelcomed.

Lilly looked momentarily startled.

"You know Stanley? That was Ray's best friend. Why'd you bring him up?" She took a step back from Wallis.

"He paid me a visit. Said something about Ray." Wallis wished she had let Stanley talk, given him a few more minutes.

"You think Stanley knows? I asked him, he said Ray never mentioned anything, was just mad about the whole divorce. You think Stanley lied to me?" Lilly looked confused and more worried than when she had first found Wallis.

"Asked him when?"

"Before I came looking for you." Lilly grew pale behind all of the makeup and leaned in and hissed, "What's going on Wallis. You in on this?"

Wallis looked at Lilly, not sure what to say.

"Ms. Jones? Could we finish up here? I have other places to be."

It was Richard making a point of checking his watch every few seconds like time was racing away from him. Wallis was grateful for his condescension for once.

"I have to go, Lilly. I don't know. I'm not sure what I can do. It's not really my area. I'm a family court attorney. I don't know," she mumbled, as she backed away. Lilly looked like she wanted to say something, but fear had spread across her face when Richard had approached. She quickly turned and hurried down the hallway toward the exit without ever looking back. Wallis watched her go, taking a glance over her shoulder but only saw Richard and the usual clusters of people nervously waiting their turns.

"Everything alright?" asked Richard, the same even smile of perfect teeth.

"Yes, everything's fine," she said, wondering if there was more to the question than she realized.

The bailiff had come back, a little more impatient this time.

"Are the parties ready? If you're not, the judge says to come on in and argue it there. Enough in the hall."

"No, no, we're ready," said Wallis, glancing once more toward the exit. What was all that, she thought. She felt for the paper inside of her pocket. It was still there. She knew better than to tell anyone before she had more information.

Have to find Norman, she thought, looking at her watch. Ned's recorder concert. Maybe Norman will be there. She felt a little desperate, so out of character, as she followed everyone into the courtroom. Norman will make sense of all of this, she thought as the door shut behind her.

CH APT ER

AN hour later Wallis was driving as fast as she could, taking the long, narrow back road to Ned's school, trying to get there before the concert was really under way. She pulled onto the grass in front of Ned's school, lining up with the other cars that had turned the side lawn into an impromptu parking lot.

She got out and ran as fast as her high heels would let her for the door closest to the auditorium, hoping they hadn't started yet. She looked around quickly for signs of Norman's old Jeep but didn't see it and wondered if he had managed to get there at all. Have to put it out of my mind for now, she thought. Concentrate on Ned.

She ran across the foyer, becoming aware of how loud her heels sounded on the green tile floor and stopped short in front of the large double doors. The assembly had started and she could hear Mr. Beasley's muffled voice through the doors talking about what a great year they were having and how proud we all are of our teachers and children.

Wallis pulled on the large curved black handles of the heavy wooden door, opened it far enough to slide inside and stood at the back with a few other late-comers.

A few heads turned to look and she gave a small wave and smiled. Sorry, she mouthed to a disapproving father, rolling her eyes as he turned away. She noticed Ned's class sitting in the first few rows on the right side and tried to pick out Ned, but in the low lighting it was too hard to spot his perpetually tousled head in a small sea of them.

"Hey Wallis, nice to see you again," whispered a tall, blonde woman. Wallis quickly squeezed up next to her, getting out of the way of the door as it slid open again and another anxious parent entered still breathing hard from the run across the grass. The man turned around and sneered again. Wallis felt better.

"Hi, Sharon, how much did I miss?"

"You missed the business meeting. Perfect timing. We all dutifully raised our hands to pass amendments one and two."

"What are they?"

"I have no idea," she said, smiling and shrugging her shoulders, "but I voted yes. It seemed to be what Mr. Beasley wanted."

Wallis liked Mr. Beasley, the school principal. He looked more like an insurance salesman in his suits and hair-sprayed helmet hair. The kids begrudgingly liked him, even though he made them toe the line, because he was fair and was willing to make the occasional fool of himself by dressing up in an ape costume for the talent show or a clown costume when enough books had been read by the students. The parents gave him respect for running a good school on what was always a tight budget.

"How's Paul?" Paul was her son, a new addition this year to Ned's class and had become one of Ned's best friends.

"Doing fine. Can't wait till school's over for the year, but he feels that way the day after Labor day."

"And David? Did you two work it out?" David was the ex-husband who was always floating on the edge of Sharon and Paul's life, not really participating, not really gone. He owned a software company, Whittaker Technology, which catered to manufacturing companies, large and small. Sharon was a receptionist at Phillip Morris headquarters and was barely making ends meet.

"Sort of. I was finally able to prove he cashed the insurance check from the dentist after, what, two years of haggling, so he coughed that up."

Wallis knew she was making Sharon uncomfortable. The shy woman never liked talking about David or money and particularly the two subjects combined. But it always annoyed Wallis to notice Sharon's old car pull up in front of the house, large patches of white primer where Sharon had tried to cover up peeling paint. Ned never had to watch for them if Sharon was driving the boys to get a Slurpee or drop them off at the soccer field. The car made so much noise he could hear it from his room and knew when to come running. Wallis always let Ned go with a faint feeling of apprehension, wondering if the car would make it down the road.

The last time Paul had spent the night he had bragged through most of dinner about his dad's new Jeep with the custom package, leather seats, special rims. It took all of Wallis' resolve to look happy about it and say, "How nice" to Paul's open, smiling face.

"He wants to be proud of his dad, too," Norman gently said later. "It can't be easy on the little fellow. I know, I know, you'd like to cream the guy, but you can't save them all, Wallis."

Mr. Beasley left the stage and took a seat in the front row. Sharon pointed toward two seats along the side and they sat down just as the curtain opened and Ned and Paul's teacher, Mrs. Ward stepped out. She was wearing her usual uniform of a sensible dress that started at her collar bone and traveled in a straight line only hinting at the idea of bumps, bulges or curves, before stopping at her ankles, hanging right above sensible leather shoes with a thick rubber sole. Her hair was kept in a salt and pepper style that was a tower of teased hair and pin curls and was probably the same style she had proudly worn when she had been in high school.

Wallis opened her mouth to say something else and boost Sharon's confidence when the same father in the last row leaned forward and loudly hushed them. Wallis did her best blank, uninterested lawyer look and fixed her gaze on the stage instead. The show was starting and she'd probably said enough already anyway. Besides, the day had really rattled her.

The children got up and dutifully marched toward the stage, a few of the children trying to look at the seats to spot their parents. Wallis finally saw Ned and he was vainly scanning the seats with a worried look on his face. Wallis half-rose out of her seat to let him see her and his face broke into a grin as he walked onto the stage and took his place on the second row of the platform.

"Welcome parents," said Mrs. Ward, a friendly-enough teacher who the children both loved and feared, "to the annual recorder concert." She paused and Wallis could hear the familiar slurp, click over the speakers as Mrs. Ward briefly bit down on dentures before breathing deeply and starting again. "The children have all been working very diligently and are very excited to show you the benefits of all that hard work. We are going to present a medley of songs beginning with America the Beautiful and we ask that you hold all applause till the end."

That was a tough request at any event involving children and parents, especially if there was any kind of performance. Parents seemed to always be on the edge of their seats waiting for any opening to clap wildly and let the children know they were just thrilled to be there.

The concert was the perfect length. Long enough that the parents were becoming aware of just how hard and scratchy the seats were, and not so short that they didn't feel their little offspring hadn't had a chance to really shine. All of the songs were easily recognizable no matter what random notes occasionally appeared and all of the students looked pleased with their individual performances. Even little Connie Babcock who was known to burst into spontaneous tears over a perceived slight no one else could fathom looked happy.

Wallis had managed to get out of the auditorium ahead of the crowd and stood near the door into the cafeteria where the cookies and soda were set up, waiting for Ned to appear.

"Hey," he said breathlessly, shoving the recorder at her as he dashed by, heading straight for the cookies.

"Hey, yourself," said Wallis, still standing back a little, waiting for Ned to return from the mass of kids who were trying to grab a handful before all of the good ones, anything with chocolate, were gone.

"Where's Dad?" asked Ned, balancing the cookies against his chest as he chewed on a mouthful. "You see any soda?" He looked around the room, his attention already gone.

"Being your parent is good self-esteem training," said Wallis.

Ned turned back, amused. "Okay, I'll give you a second, but only because it's easier to pay up now, than later."

"I'll take it. I'm also hoping this early training is giving me a thick enough skin when you go away to college to not try and move in next to you."

Ned arched his eyebrows and stuffed another cookie into his mouth.

"Dad would never let you," he said, spraying out cookie crumbs.

"You're awfully confident your Dad won't be a problem when it comes to letting go. You might be surprised."

"I don't think that. I just know he'd miss you."

Wallis smiled. "Good save, child of mine. Go get your soda. I'll be over here. Did you see where Paul's mom has gotten to?" she said, straightening a lock of dark hair on his forehead.

Ned ducked away from her hand and pointed toward the far wall. "She's leaning over there," he said.

Wallis looked in the direction Ned was pointing and saw Sharon glumly leaning against a wall not talking to anyone but trying to look happy about it.

"Fifteen minutes Ned, and then we're out of here," she said, tapping him hard on the shoulder so he'd know the game was back on and he was last. Wallis stepped back into the crowd of people, smiling hard as she watched Ned grow mildly frustrated trying to decide whether or not to go for the soda or follow her. He popped another cookie in his mouth and turned for the tables.

"Hey, Sharon," said Wallis, taking up a space next to her and leaning back against the wall. "Did you get a cookie?"

"No, it looked a little dangerous and once the chocolate ones are gone there are only those bland round cookies. You two staying much longer?"

"Not too much. Been a long day, time to go home, find Norman, watch him make dinner."

Sharon let out a short laugh. "You're so lucky. Norman have a brother?"

"Yes, two, and they both appear to be very helpful, but they're no Norman."

"Even Norman-lite would be a good idea."

"Can Paul come over and have dinner with us?" Ned and Paul had run up breathless and sweaty. A smudge of chocolate had appeared in the center of Ned's shirt.

"You'll still eat dinner?"

Ned drew his mouth up into a small look of frustration.

"Of course, don't I always?" he said hurriedly. "Can he?" he said, looking first at Wallis and then at Sharon. Must be so hard to have to get so many people's approval before you can do anything, thought Wallis.

"It's okay with me, if…" she gestured toward Sharon.

"Sure," she said reluctantly. "I'll come by around eight to get him?"

Wallis knew Sharon didn't like eating alone and was hinting at being included, and normally Wallis would have suggested it before Sharon even had a chance to wonder, but she needed to get Norman alone for awhile before dinner. Sharon was going to have to buck up her own chin tonight.

"Norman can drop him off and they can work on any homework together after dinner, right?" she said, giving Ned a look.

"Sure, sure, yeah, yeah," said Ned, bobbing his head.

"Then you have a deal," said Wallis.

"Great," whispered Paul and the two boys were off, dodging in and out of the crowd, weaving their way back over to the table.

"I suppose I should have said something about no more cookies before I completely lost Paul," said Sharon.

"Oh well, sometimes you have to eat dessert first."

"Hey, Wallis. Hi, Sharon! Saw the article about David in the Times Dispatch this morning. Man, I hope you're getting a piece of that!" said Rhonda Bridgeforth, the class mom. Every time Rhonda smiled her eyes grew larger until Wallis could clearly see white all the way around the brown irises. Made her look a little crazy. Wallis wondered if someday over a class project Rhonda might finally snap.

Sharon looked up nervously, glanced at Wallis, and mumbled, "Well, can't be sure if it's true. David's been known to polish the apple a little."

"What article?" said Wallis. She didn't always get a chance to read the paper.

"Oh, you should have seen it. Nice big write-up in the business section how Whittaker Technologies just got the big Cardinal Group account for all of their software. Boy, that must be worth millions!" Rhonda looked breathless just thinking about all of that money.

Wallis' face dropped into her best lawyer face with a stony expression of resolve. "I won't charge you, Sharon. Just let me represent you," she said, trying to keep the annoyance out of her voice.

"Wow, when a lawyer wants to take a case without the money then you know it's time," said Rhonda. Wallis ignored the dig, she was used to them.

"Okay, then," said Sharon, not looking directly at either one of them. "Maybe you have a point."

"Oh! Glad I could help," said Rhonda, smiling, her eyes growing wild.

Just getting Sharon that far did make Wallis feel like there'd been some kind of victory.

Wallis piled the two boys into the car, stuffing their backpacks into the trunk amongst her files. She waited till a few of the cars closer to the curved driveway had a chance to pull out before she backed up and made a semi-circle in the grass, slowly going over the curb with each tire, back onto the pavement.

She'd felt pretty calm through the concert and short reception but now that she had a chance to think and knew she could finally find Norman the sense of urgency was returning and her stomach was tightening up all over again.

The boys chattered the whole way home occasionally wrestling in the back seat with their seat belts firmly in place, but still managing to get an occasional head-lock on each other.

"Five, four, three..." said Wallis, firmly, glancing at them in the rear view mirror. Ned knew that if she ever got to one privileges would start getting stripped away with ever-increasing speed. The two boys giggled and sat still for a moment.

Ned turned toward his window and let out a long breath, fogging up a small patch of glass. He took his fist and made the imprint of a baby foot, using his pinky to add the toes. Paul giggled and turned toward his window, fogging it up and drawing a scary face. Wallis knew it was only a matter of time before somehow this descended into bathroom humor. It always did.

Ned was the first to get there. No surprise, thought Wallis as she saw the word, poop, materialize on Ned's window. The boys let out shrieks of laughter before Ned wiped it away with his sleeve, the boys glancing at Wallis in the rear view mirror with looks of shared conspiracy.

Wallis let it go. A little tasteless humor was usually in order when you're a nine year old boy and fogging up the windows wasn't trying to cut off each other's air supply. They were almost home anyway.

She made herself get out of the car at a normal pace and reminded the boys to come get their backpacks out of the trunk. They each grabbed one and raced for the door, disappearing inside and Wallis guessed, straight up to Ned's room and the computer.

She left her briefcase and purse just inside the door and called out for Norman.

"Norman? Norman?"

She knew he was home, the front door had been unlocked and the Jeep was blocking the entire bottom half of the driveway near the house, as usual.

"Hey," said Norman, coming out of the kitchen. "What's up? You forget where the kitchen is?"

Wallis suddenly didn't know what to say. She could hear the explanation in her head and realized she didn't really know anything. Her anxieties were based on rumor or guesses and her own gut instinct.

"Wallis? What is it? Did something happen? Is it Harriet?"

"No, no," said Wallis, quickly. Boy, what does my face look like, she thought, trying to take a deeper breath.

"Well, what? Is it…"

"No, no one's dead, well, no one we really know anyway. I'm not sure what's happened, but I need your help," she said, pulling out the paper and holding it out for Norman.

"What's this?"

"That man in the driveway this morning, he dropped it. He was a friend of Ray Billings…"

"The guy who died? I heard it on the news. Do you know him?"

"I was representing Lilly Billings. They were getting a divorce. She tracked me down in the Henrico courthouse. She said it couldn't have been a suicide."

"No one ever wants to believe it's a suicide. What's this?" said Norman, reading the page of names. "Hey we know some of these kids. What is this?" he asked again, his hand rising toward his head. Wallis watched as he gently tap, tapped the back of his head.

"I don't really know. Stanley Woermer, the man in the driveway was Ray Billings' best friend. He dropped it. It's a list of some sort but I have no idea what it means or if it means anything. But Ray Billings thought I would, he told both his best friend and his wife to find me if anything happened to him, anything at all."

"Why you?"

"I have no idea."

"Considering you've dealt with your share of child abusers, why are you so scared over what seems circumstantial at best?"

"Good question. Call it a gut feeling. I can usually spot the liars and I'm having a hard time finding one, as much as I'd like to. The people who knew this man best don't believe he took his own life."

"You're not usually a good one for conspiracies. If it's really good old-fashioned murder, then the crime portion is over. If it's suicide maybe the crime involving these kids is over," said Norman, waving the list.

"I don't know which one is better. What should I do?"

"Are you sure this is anything to really be worried about? I don't know. Call the police? Call these parents?" Norman's hand started to look for the back of his head again.

Wallis wasn't used to Norman being at such a loss for ideas.

"No, no, not yet. I don't know where the lines cross here. That man, Stanley, he was so afraid and he said not to call anyone, not the police, not even him. And I can't imagine the conversation with any one of these parents. What would I be suggesting? No, first I need to find Stanley Woermer and ask him what this means," she said, taking the paper out of Norman's hand. "Find out why me."

"Do you think this is the kind of conversations most happily married couples have?"

Wallis smiled at Norman, leaning in to his body, placing her arms around his waist and resting her head on his shoulder. "Love you," she said.

"I'm well aware of that," he said, kissing her shoulder.

Wallis didn't sleep well that night. She kept snapping awake with a peculiar feeling that what was going on in her reality was only some continuation of a nightmare she'd had while asleep and the two sides were now bleeding into each other. She waited for her heart to finally move to a slower rhythm but then the small panic that began in her driveway crept back.

"Why me," she whispered in the darkness. "And how do I find Stanley Woermer." It was a prayer of sorts.

The next morning she got up feeling like she had an unjustified hangover. The early morning light hurt her eyes as she dragged herself out to get the morning paper.

"Aaggh, not again," she muttered, when she spotted the familiar yellow plastic bag at the top of the driveway. "Is it so hard to toss it a little ways toward the house?"

As she got to the top of the driveway she could see the familiar purple door just down the next street. Several cars were parked outside and the driveway was full.

Wonder what that's about, thought Wallis.

She bent down to pick up the paper hoping no other neighbor was about to come outside to get in their car and spot her in her pajamas, her hair still wild from tossing and turning. She'd still have to wave and yell a friendly hello and she wasn't in the mood. She picked up the paper and felt something stiff inside of the bag.

Another ad, she thought. They'd become popular, sometimes even the plastic bag was decorated with information about a sale at the local hardware store. I suppose the paper has to figure out some way to make money with the few readers it has left, she thought.

She slid the piece of cardboard out of the bag and saw it was half of a dry cleaners insert. Written on one side was a message, 'meet me at Book People on Granite Avenue at 10:30 this morning in the European Travel section. Tell people you're going there and come up with a good reason. Don't attract any attention. I'll tell you what I know. Please come.'

It was signed, S. Woermer and the 'please' was underlined twice. The whole thing looked like it had been written in a hurry.

Well, at least that answers one big question, thought Wallis, her stomach tightening up, warning her of something unseen.

I seem to have found Stanley Woermer.

CHAPTER

WALLIS found the bookstore easily. Granite Avenue was only four blocks long and as she neared the corner of Patterson Avenue she saw a large wooden sandwich-board sign propped up in front of a small two-story cottage that looked worn down around all of the edges. The sign was hand-painted in over-sized letters with the words, 'Book People' and an outline of an open book.

She pulled into the small gravel parking lot and looked around. There were only two other cars in the parking lot. An old blue Chevy wagon and a boxy yellow Volvo that had seen better days. She pulled up next to the Volvo and parked as close as she could to the tall faded wooden privacy fence that bordered the back. Stepping out of the car she dodged the variety of potholes in need of gravel.

The short cement walkway up to the front porch was lined by over-grown grass bending in to cover the path. At the edge of the walk was another old Chevy station wagon with the tail end backed up so it faced the sidewalk. The back gate was flipped up and cardboard boxes of used books were piled inside with the price scrawled on the outside of each box.

The boxes had the name of an old moving company, Ownby's, now defunct, on the side with the words, 'Moving Families Since 1924'.

Wallis remembered Stanley's admonishment in his note to come with a purpose and she stopped to look in the boxes, ducking her head under the open tail-gate. She didn't really read much anymore unless it was a legal brief or a deposition but had loved to read novels before law school. Maybe there's an old treasure in here, she thought.

The boxes were mostly filled with old school books from the 30's and 40's and had the names of children now retired or passed away written in the front with the name of their teacher and their grade. The handwriting was loopy and large and done with deliberate care. She peered into another box before turning for the wooden steps and heading into the store.

The bell over the door gave out a small tinkle as she entered. Don't see that too often anymore, she thought. A small woman with short, curly salt and pepper hair was bent over a large wooden desk at the far end of the small room. An old brown cash register was perched on the top of the desk next to her. On her other side was tall piles of new children's picture books.

The entire room was crammed with books. Small mismatched wooden dining tables were scattered in the space, covered in different colored table cloths and topped with stacks of books. Built-in book cases lined every wall that didn't have a window and more books were propped up in the windows. Wallis had never seen anything like it. Ned would love this, she thought.

"Can I help you?" said the woman, lifting her head to look up over half-glasses slid halfway down her nose. "Were you looking for something in particular?" she said, in heavily accented English. Wallis guessed she was probably European by birth.

"Do you have a travel section?" Wallis asked.

"What kind? To where?"

"Europe?"

"Sure, sure. Follow me," said the woman quickly, pulling off her glasses and letting them dangle from a long black cord around her neck. She gestured to Wallis with her arm to follow her down a small, narrow hallway lined with bookcases that began behind the large desk. Wallis hadn't even noticed the passageway before.

"My name is Esther," she said, rolling her r's. "I own the place with my husband, Herman. If you need a book, ask me, I'll know where it is. If we don't have it, even if it's out of date, I'll find it. That's our specialty." Her voice rose and fell, ending on a high note.

Esther looked back at Wallis as they turned a sharp corner and headed down another narrow hallway that wound past small offshoots of rooms filled with books. She scanned Wallis up and down, making Wallis uncomfortable, while still walking through the odd angles of the halls, not bumping into anything. Occasionally her hand darted out and touched a book as if checking to make sure she was still navigating correctly, her steps never slowing.

"Have you ever been to Europe?" asked Esther, her head turning away from Wallis to face front, not waiting for an answer. Wallis wasn't sure if she should answer. Esther turned back to her with raised eyebrows.

"No, no, I haven't. Would like to, though."

"Any place in particular?"

"No?" Wallis wasn't a very good liar without a mapped-out strategy. It was something Norman was always pointing out that made her a very unique lawyer.

"Transylvania is beautiful. I know, I know," she said waving her hand in the air, "I've heard all the jokes. Maybe that's why it's still beautiful. No one takes the place very seriously. The castles and the town are still very much like when I was a girl. No modern ugly apartment buildings, no tall cell phone towers." Her face turned into a sneer as she glanced over her shoulder at Wallis. They turned at last into a small room on the far side of the house. Stanley Woermer was already there looking at a fat paperback book about the sights of Paris. He was dressed in dark blue nylon shorts with a blue and yellow windbreaker zipped up to his chin. Wallis tried not to look at him.

"Start with this," said Ruth, pulling a tall, thin hard-back book off of a shelf and handing it to Wallis. "Hello, Stanley. I didn't see you come in.

Finding everything?"

Stanley started, the book in his hands momentarily shaking. "Yes, Ruth, I'm fine. I know my way around."

"You okay Stanley? You're not normally the nervous type." said Ruth, all of the r's rolling. She didn't wait for an answer and was turning the corner before her sentence was finished.

Stanley glanced up at Wallis, quickly looking back down at the book cradled open in his hands. "Thanks for coming. Wasn't sure you would."

Wallis reached into her pocket and pulled out the list of names she'd been keeping close since she found it.

"You left this behind in my driveway."

"Oh, thank Goodness," said Stanley in a breathy whisper, reaching out for the paper, momentary relief crossing his face. "I couldn't find it. I was worried someone might have taken it."

Wallis moved the paper just out of his reach. Stanley pulled his hand back, looking hurt.

"First we talk," said Wallis. "I know some of these boys on this list, know their families. Why does a list of names of nine and ten year old boys have you so frightened?"

"Because people are willing to kill to get that list." Stanley looked ready to cry. "Ray died trying to figure out what it all meant. He was my best friend since childhood." Stanley's lip quivered, the last words coming out in starts and stops. "You know Richmond, not too many of us leave. Moving to Hanover is moving away for these parts."

"Are you saying he didn't know? What made him even care?" Wallis felt a wave of anger go through her.

"I had almost the same reaction." Stanley gave a half-smile, his face relaxing for a moment into deep lines. "Does everything have to be our business? That's what I said to Ray. We had good lives going for us. Families, jobs, church, running. It was a nice list." A long sigh escaped Stanley. "It pissed me off, Ray messing with all of that." Stanley brushed the tears off of his face with the back of his hand. "Sorry 'bout that. Not usually much of a crier. Haven't slept much in awhile." He let out a small snort.

"What made him care, Stanley?" Wallis leaned in, whispering to Stanley, her hand firmly on his arm. Stanley looked down at her hand and sighed again.

"Makes me wonder if this is the way it gets played out all the time. Each new person that gets pulled in. First you're surprised and a little scared, then mad as hell, then frustrated. I'll let you know now, it's a cycle. This is pretty much it, except each stage gets a little more intense." He pulled his arm away from her grip. "Okay, okay, I know I'm rambling. So what. Blast! You know, I didn't want to know any of this either!" He threw the book into an old red velvet wingback chair set up in the corner for customers to pause, get absorbed in an expensive travel book.

Stanley started pacing in the small space, his hands laced together, pressing down on the top of his head.

"Ray came to me with these lists. This pile of papers that had charts of all of these boys. Some of the boys were from good families, a lot of them we knew, and said there was a problem. One of the boys on the list, Jimmy McDonough, his mother was complaining to anyone who would listen that her son was getting the short shrift."

"Jimmy McDonough? I know that name," said Wallis.

"Yeah, you would. He's the kid that took a neighbor's car for a drunken joy ride through the front doors of Midlothian High school. Remember? Right at the beginning of the year. Left it parked right inside the door. His parents paid the damages and got him community service. You'd think the woman would be grateful and be quiet, but Kristen was so mad."

"At what?"

"She said she was promised Jimmy would be taken care of. He'd get into a decent college, get a good job, have a career and now it was all gone. Jimmy's last stunt had sealed it."

"Promised by whom? You're still not telling me anything, Stanley. Do you not know anything?"

"You don't read the paper all the time, do you?" He shrugged. "Yeah,

I figured. That's the way it is. Gossip on one side of the James River doesn't really travel to the other. Got to watch the news, read the paper."

"I'm going to go," said Wallis, looking at her watch. "When you get your thoughts together call me at the office," she said sternly. "I don't have this much time to throw away."

"There aren't any more McDonoughs." Stanley blurted it out. "All dead, killed in a freak accident crushed between two large semis. Happened just after St. Patrick's Day."

"Are you trying to be funny, Stanley? Because it's not really working for you," said Wallis, spitting out the words.

"The driver of the second semi said he had reached down to change the stations on the radio and didn't realize the semi in front was slowing down. The paper said you couldn't even tell there was a minivan in there somewhere until they pulled the two trucks apart. Nothing left, no survivors. No more McDonoughs."

"And that's part of a plan? That's an awfully elaborate plan for the suburbs. You're making no sense." Wallis did remember the news story on the television and remembered switching the television off when they started talking about the family. Too much misery that had nothing to do with her.

"Just before that so called accident Kristen cornered Ray, told him what she knew. They worked together at the utilities department, down in the city. Better pay there and great benefits. I gotta sit down."

Stanley sunk into the old chair that still clung to some of its lost elegance and picked up the book on Paris, letting it rest in his lap. He pulled a starched white handkerchief out of his back pocket and wiped his face and neck. For a moment it made Wallis think of her dad, of Walter, trying to unwind after a week on the road selling brocade and seersucker further south. Seersucker had always been big further south.

"Stanley," she said more softly, "I can see that you're upset and because of Ray it's understandable but you have five minutes to pull some of this together or I'm out of here and we don't speak again, on any topic, ever." Wallis saw the small shake in her hands.

"She claimed she'd been recruited," he said, waving his hands around, raising his voice for a moment, before taking a deep breath. "She said she was invited into this group but Ray called it recruited. Kristen had gone to a tea in her neighborhood that was supposed to be a kind of welcoming party for a new neighbor, Faye something. This was all years ago when Jimmy was still in elementary school, but he was having problems even then. Not drinking, not yet, but he wasn't exactly doing well in school. Kristen had to miss a lot of work to meet with the school or specialists trying to do something about Jimmy. She was a little desperate. She went to this tea and they all started talking about their kids and of course, Kristen started complaining about Jimmy, saying she wasn't sure what she was going to do. Someone told her about a therapist who was supposed to work wonders and gave her a name and number. You know how parents are always a little desperate when it comes to their kids."

"I've seen it a few times in my profession," said Wallis.

"Yeah, right," said Stanley, snorting again. "Black widow, I forgot. Sorry, no offense." Stanley shifted uneasily in the chair, the sharp lines of his arms and legs moving around, trying to find a comfortable position.

"Keep going, Stanley."

"Kristen said the therapist offered her a plan. A kind of civil service plan. The way she explained it was the therapist had given Jimmy a lot of tests and interviewed the entire family and said Jimmy had a lot of untapped potential. Boy, don't you know Kristen bit at that one." Stanley's voice came out in a whine. "She said there was an opportunity for Jimmy, a long-term opportunity, but it was a little unusual. Kristen claimed it was a secret society, you know, like the Masons, to help young men and women from good families who weren't getting what they needed. But they had a few conditions."

"Like what?" said Wallis, feeling her stomach sour.

"Like keeping it secret, for starters. And sticking with the plan they laid out, no veering, no grilling. They apparently never actually said making a public nuisance of yourself was grounds for dismissal, and maybe it wouldn't have been if Jimmy hadn't managed to make the newspapers."

"Who exactly are they?"

"I'm not sure I know that."

"How can you be sure your friend didn't kill himself? How can you be sure this isn't all paranoia on his part? How can you be sure he didn't draw up this list?"

"For one thing, Ray was afraid of guns. He had been all his life. His uncle used to take the two of us out hunting when we were small boys. He said it was to toughen us up. But all it did to Ray was turn him against guns of any kind, forever. That's unusual for most men who grew up around here. Not everybody would realize that unless they really knew Ray, like me." Tears ran down in slow streaks across Stanley's cheeks, pooling in the corners of his mouth. "And I was with Ray when he first looked at the list."

Wallis felt it, knew it was the tipping point over onto the other side. The moment she knew what he was saying was true and even if she walked away and refused to do anything about any of it, she'd carry the weight of the secrets.

"Do you know who killed Ray Billings?" Wallis' body shuddered. I don't really want to know, she thought. Then I'll have to do something about it. I can still stop and walk away.

"No, not really. But I know they're there. They leave nasty little messages everywhere to let me know."

"Know what?"

"That I could end up like Ray." Stanley was shaking. He put one hand over the other against his belly, pushing hard enough to make the knuckles white. "I sound crazy, don't I?"

"A little." Wallis watched Stanley slowly creeping toward a breakdown, struggling to hold it off for as long as possible. Wallis had seen this before. Mothers or fathers on the stand who knew the person they had pledged their life to, created a household, children, an entire life with, had turned out to be a monster. The betrayal was laid bare, but too late, the children were harmed. Desperation would come over their faces as they realized strangers would decide the fate of their children. They were helpless and were realizing that what came next depended on who told the most convincing story to the judge, a stranger, and not whether it was the truth or a lie.

Clients were forever asking Wallis for reassurance, insisting the judge had to at least follow the rules.

"Not really," Wallis would reply casually. Better they get used to being treated this way. All that awaited them was indifference. Wallis had seen too many cases with too many people dripping with venom and emotion. Often the clerks looked sleepy. "He can do what he wants to do. In family court the laws end up being guidelines," she would say.

A controlled look of horror was a common response, thought Wallis, and appropriate. Better they understand and let go of any ideas of fair play. He who played the game well always won.

Maybe it was the same here, thought Wallis.

"What are you really afraid of Stanley?"

"Not knowing anything. Who they are, what they're really doing and when they might decide I'm too much trouble." He grasped his hands tightly to his chest, letting the book slide out of his lap to the ground.

She knew if she pushed him there was a good chance he was going over. She took a deep breath and made herself relax. Courtroom mode.

"What kind of messages are they leaving?"

"They broke Alice's windshield. Left the crowbar behind. I think someone's been in my house, gone through all of my things." His voice trailed off.

"Stanley? Stanley, look up. Look at me. You seem to want help, but you're making it harder for me. Who's Alice? Why did someone break her windshield? How do you know it wasn't just stupid kids? How do you know all of this is connected to anything?" Wallis was talking too fast, trying to argue a different outcome.

"Alice works in the Utility Department too, or at least she did."

Wallis remembered Lilly's description of Ray's meeting with the woman.

"She left me some crazy message last night," said Stanley, "saying she was leaving town and starting over and not to call her. Man, she practically screamed that part. She worked in the accounting department and was helping Ray with the paper trail. You know, follow the money."

"They found a trail? Connect some of these dots, Stanley."

"I'm doing the best I can here. Look, my main purpose is to honor what Ray told me to do. After I've done that, I'm out of it. I've had enough," he said, waving his arms like an umpire signaling the runner was out. He was quietly crying. "I have things to live for and bottom line, I don't give a damn what's going on around me. Not anymore. Perfectly happy to go back to being ignorant."

"So, why not do that now?"

Stanley looked up at Wallis. "Because Ray mattered that much to me," he whispered. "Because he deserved better than this and because as much as I'd like to ditch all of this and go back to what's left of my life, I get the uneasy feeling the sons of bitches aren't going to let me."

Stanley pulled out a file that had been hidden under the chair and held it out to Wallis.

"How did you get this in the first place?" she asked.

"It was off of a thumb drive Kristen gave to Ray. She stole it from her Watcher. At first we thought it was just music downloaded off the net. That's what it looked like. But Ray was good with computers, it was his thing. He knew how to find the files, said people did it all the time. Hid files in with the audio tracks."

"Do you have the drive?"

Stanley pulled out the little race car thumb drive with the small '3' on the side. He looked relieved to let go of the burden.

She looked at Stanley. "Were these lists the only files you found?"

"As far as I know. I wasn't too eager to learn everything."

Wallis took the file reluctantly and flipped it open. Inside were more of the same flow charts broken down into categories with groups of ten boys per column. Each group was separated by two years in age with a short series of numbers under each name in different three number combinations. Other pages had a list for each boy of accomplishments and goals still to be met. It was a careful, orderly mapped out plan to ensure success in life.

"Everybody should have one of these, Stanley," said Wallis, turning over pages. "This isn't a plot. This is an old boy network. Clubby, snobby maybe, but not diabolical. Of course they knocked Jimmy McDonough out of this club. His career path was to become an even better alcoholic."

"Yeah, well there's a pretty nasty catch," said Stanley, his head sinking toward his chest. "There's no out clause. Once you're in, you're in for life. That's what Kristen had been screaming about. That's why she had been desperate and gone to Ray. The dumb bitch was so desperate about Jimmy she talked herself into believing it would all be alright, until it wasn't."

"No out clause."

"Well, unless you consider death a way out. That's it, that's what I'm saying. You can't sign up for the program one year and then decide you've had enough the next. Once in, you're in forever. No alternative career plans, no dropping out and becoming some lame artist or joining the Peace Corps. They tell you what you'll be, where you'll live and occasionally, what you'll do for them. It's a very orderly system, alright."

"They were planning to kill Jimmy McDonough?"

"They were planning to give him very limited career options. To contain him and keep him from becoming a problem. Sales in some dead-end company had been mentioned as an option. Jimmy wouldn't have amounted to more than middle class, but maybe that was higher than he would have made it on his own, anyway. Death was the other alternative, and the one that won out. You see, until the very end, Kristen still believed in her young Jimmy and was unwilling to let them suddenly limit what he might become. She wasn't having any of their ideas and kept pleading with the Watchers to come up with some other way. She told Ray that Jimmy was young and could sober up, but the Watcher had said they'd been doing this for a long time and knew the outcome. There was no place to go for an appeal."

"Who is it that cares so much what happens to a bunch of boys? The Watchers? What's a Watcher?" The more Wallis learned the less she felt she knew and the more she knew she would have to find out.

"That's what I don't know. I told you, I tried not to ask too many questions. I don't know, maybe I should have. Ray said he'd found something out and we had plans to meet the next morning when he turned up dead. They must have found out. I tried going through his things but there was nothing left but the thumb drive. Somebody had beaten me to it. I wouldn't have that if he hadn't told me where to look, just… just in case. I'm surprised they didn't find it."

"So why me?"

"That was one of the last things he told me on the phone. To find you if something happened. You and only you because as much as he was sorry you were Lilly's lawyer he admired what you could do, but that was only part of it. Ray said you knew someone they were trying to recruit. He'd found the name on a list and saw you with her. He thought you might have a chance to find out what was going on. That and you're from here too. You have the right kind of roots. People might trust you enough to talk." Stanley was talking faster, getting lost in the knots of what had happened to him.

"Who do I know that's mixed up in this?"

"Sharon Whittaker, that's the name he gave me. They want her son. They want Paul."

Wallis caught the look of surprise across her face a little too late. Stanley saw it and Wallis could see the look of fear grow in his eyes. He stood up as a shudder went through him, ending with a shake of his bony knees.

"I have to go."

"Not yet. Where do I go from here? Do you have Alice's phone number? Who else knows?"

"Give me a pen. I'll give you her new cell number. She gave it to me with the promise that I don't give it to anyone, but I'm making an exception. She'll just have to get over it. I can't take any of it anymore." Stanley hurriedly wrote the number on the back of the file and handed the pen back to Wallis. "She's taken off for Williamsburg this morning. She didn't even bother to have her mail forwarded. I'm supposed to pick it up for her and send it along. Tell her I'm sorry."

"You said one of the things Ray said, what else did he say?"

"Just that most of these names had no home of their own and they weren't all from Richmond. I don't know what that means. Ray was going to tell me when we got together."

Stanley turned to leave as Wallis grabbed his arm.

"Who else, Stanley? Who else knows anything?"

"I don't know. Don't you get it? I wasn't supposed to be involved at all. Ray only told me because I was his best friend and he became so afraid. I don't understand any of this computer stuff. I don't understand the money or any of it." He leaned in close to Wallis and whispered in a hiss, "I just want to be left alone. I've done what Ray asked and now I'm out of it. You do with it what you want."

Stanley pulled his arm away, wiping away tears, and headed down the narrow hall between the bookcases. As he was about to turn the corner Wallis could see him startle and take a step back before quickly turning the corner.

Wallis gathered up her purse, the file and the disc and hurried after him to try and see what scared him but only caught a glimpse of a man's polished, well-worn heel quickly turning the far corner. He must have been waiting around the next stack of books and left right behind Stanley. By the time Wallis got to the front only Ruth was left standing behind the old desk.

"Did two men just leave the store?" asked Wallis in a rush, stopping at the desk.

Ruth raised an eyebrow and looked Wallis up and down.

"No, only one. Stanley, the man you were talking to. Was he alright? He looked flush and was sweating like he'd gone for a run." Her voice was doing the same sing-song, the r's rolling along. "Stanley's usually so easy-going."

Wallis stopped moving and tried to listen for any other sounds besides Esther's voice. Where had the other man gone to?

"Why, did you see someone else?" asked Esther.

Wallis turned away from Esther trying to get her to stop talking and listened for any kind of movement.

"I've been out front for the entire morning going over inventory. We still do it by hand, don't trust computers. They're always breaking down."

"Excuse me," said Wallis and she retraced her steps back into the bowels of the small house, not stopping at the travel section but following the zig-zag labyrinth all the way to the back till she came to a small kitchen still decorated in 1950's linoleum, glass-fronted cabinets and squatty white appliances. The back door at the other side of the small room was shut tight.

"Is there a problem?" said Esther, coming up behind Wallis. "Was someone supposed to be meeting you?"

"Where does that door lead?" said Wallis, ignoring Esther's questions.

"To the back yard. We don't really use it except to take out the trash. It's very inconvenient and besides, I have a hard time getting Herman to mow the front. You should see the back. It's chigger heaven."

Wallis looked out the small panes in the door at the overgrown backyard. The grass was neglected to the point of blooming its own tiny white flowers. Someone had made a path through the grass, trampling it down in a direct line to the gate in the tall privacy fence that ringed the yard.

"Hhmmph," said Esther, standing next to Wallis, looking out the window. "So he did take the trash out. He should have said so instead of letting me go on like that."

"What do you mean?"

"Herman's so absent-minded. If I don't keep telling him, nothing gets done. Trash is his job, I won't do it. Maybe if he mowed, but…" she said, shrugging her shoulders.

"How can you tell from here? Where's the trash cans?"

"Right by the gate, see? The grass is bent down, that's my little way of knowing without having to ask Herman. Makes him think I trust him, maybe just a little, but I don't. The grass in that yard, good stuff if only someone would mow it. It pops right back up the next day after he's walked across it. Just like a great green carpet," said Esther, her voice rising and dipping. "Must have carried the bag for once," she said. "See?

A small path. Usually he drags it. Herman's not big on doing chores. If he doesn't want to do something he has little ways of making you suffer for the favor."

Wallis placed her hands on the door, leaning in to get a better look through the dirty glass at the trampled grass. It was a narrow path of someone's footsteps. She took a small step away from the door, her hand sliding down the door, briefly rubbing against something sticky.

She kept her hand at her side, casually rolling the tips of her fingers together, making a small gummy ball out of the residue, as she glanced back at the door. She could just make out the faint square outline of residue that started at the edge of the door and stopped right before the old twist lock. The lock had been taped. She looked away before Esther could notice.

"You know, any other store owner would have asked a lot more questions by now," said Esther. "You zipping through here like somebody stole something from you. But I don't do anything the way I'm supposed to and it's served me well so far. Learned that rule living under the Soviets. I go by what my gut tells me," she said, patting her belly. "I'm going to trust that you'd tell me what's bothering you if I needed to know."

Wallis stood quietly, considering for a moment telling the older woman what she knew, eager for someone to tell her it was all an unfortunate set of coincidences and conspiracies only happen in the movies. But she remembered what Stanley had said. What it was like for each new person that gets dragged into the story.

"Well," said Esther, "the offer remains open." She put an arm around Wallis, leading her back toward the winding halls made of books. "Take good care of Stanley. He's a good egg. Yes, I know you came to meet him. I told you, I have a lot of practice watching and waiting. It's a good survival tip," she said, winking. "You're questioning everything, that's a good idea too. I'll help you out with this little observation. Stanley is by nature a cynic, believes in very little. If something has scared him this badly, he has good, concrete reasons."

They came to a turn in the hall near an old bathroom with small black and white tiles inlaid in the floor; small sections missing here and there exposing the concrete underneath.

"That's odd," said Esther, "he didn't empty this one. Tsk, that Herman," she said, before another idea seemed to grow inside of her. She looked up at Wallis with a stony expression, the lines deepening on her face. "Remember what I said, I trust you to tell me if there's something I should know."

Wallis kept her silence, too unsure to know what to do. Never say anything, never ask anything if you don't already know the outcome. The first rule of being a good courtroom lawyer.

"Wait," said Esther, tapping Wallis on the shoulder as she tried to leave. "At some point, you may be looking for a friendly ear. Don't underestimate an old woman. I don't make that offer to just anyone, but this is Richmond. We're all somehow connected and once you can see which way a web spins, you know what you need to know. I've known Stanley since he was a boy coming in here for comic books. I knew Ray too," she said, a look of momentary anger. "Don't underestimate an old woman," she said, tapping a pin Wallis hadn't noticed at first. It was a small, tight circle of 13 stars set against a deep blue background.

CHAPTER 13

BY the time Wallis got to her car Stanley was gone and there was no sign of anyone else. She slid into the front seat of the Jaguar, shoving the file under the seat and dropping the race car into her purse. It made her uncomfortable to have any of it out in plain view. She made herself sit and take a few deep breaths, calm down, think rationally.

She turned the key, the car easily jumping into a quiet hum and fit the car phone's ear piece into place. She dialed the number from the back of the file and put the car into reverse, rolling backwards as she listened to the long rings.

"Hello?"

"Hello, Alice?"

"Yes? Who's this? Nancy?"

"No, my name is Wallis Jones. Stanley gave me…"

"I know who you are, the Black Widow. Stanley shouldn't have done that," she said, her voice pitching into a whine. "I don't want to be bothered."

"I don't want to get you involved again," she said quickly, trying to avoid losing Alice before she'd had a chance to find out anything. "I was wondering if we could meet. Maybe I could ask you about what happened. It might help me fill in a few holes."

"No. I'm starting over. I don't want to be bothered."

"I need your help."

"Then you're out of luck. You should do what I should have done sooner. Let it go and be glad you can."

"I don't know if I believe there's a conspiracy at all, Alice. Maybe it's more old fashioned than that. Sad, but old fashioned." She put the car in drive and pulled out of the parking lot back onto Granite Avenue.

"If that helps you sleep, go with that. More of a reason to let go."

"But until I know, I need to make sure that a friend of mine hasn't gotten mixed up in something she can't handle."

"Sharon Whittaker, I know. Ray told me. Why is she your responsibility, or do you make a habit of rescuing people?"

"How about if we leave my motives alone and you and I get together for lunch?" she said, turning onto Libby Avenue.

"I told you, no. Not a chance."

"Give me something, Alice, and I'll leave you alone. Give me a thread."

"Okay, okay. I suppose you earned your nickname…"

"Not really," said Wallis, a little tersely.

"Don't be so sure," said Alice, "even if you don't like it. It's more a compliment, the way I see it. Anytime you can get those good old boys to fear and respect you, it means you're something powerful. They're too arrogant to be afraid of much."

Wallis pulled up to the light at the corner of Libby and Monument Avenue and looked over at the fountains in front of St. Mary's Hospital. "So, tell me, Alice. Where do I go from here? What was Ray going to tell Stanley Woermer?"

"Stanley talks too much. Ray should have never told him anything. I don't know everything Ray knew. Or at least not what he found out right before he died. He must have figured out the next layer."

"The next layer of what?"

"Oh no, you don't. That's something you'll figure out on your own. The list of children you don't know, start there, that's your thread. Look underneath and pay attention. You'll see it. And follow the money trails, all of them."

"What do you mean, all of them?"

"Quit interrupting. I'm not going to give you any details. Just don't assume anything and remember that the little guys often mimic the big ones but they do a much sloppier job of it. And, so you don't waste your time, I'm going to change this number. Should have never given it to Stanley."

Alice hung up abruptly leaving Wallis to wonder what she was supposed to be looking under. What money trails? Wallis turned right onto Monument Avenue, down toward the city proper on her way to the Richmond juvenile courts. The tree-lined avenue was one of the oldest roads in the city, stretches of it further down still paved in old cobblestones, occasionally protected from being paved over by old southern white women willing to lie down in the road. Older homes, small cottages dating from after the Second World War dotted the sides of the western end of the street, postage sized lawns in front and large green expanses in back.

As Wallis entered into the Fan district closer to the city the homes changed and became grander, older, dating back to the turn of the nineteenth century when most of Richmond was rebuilt. The homes were built in closer together, almost to the edge of the wide sidewalks, many of them with sweeping porches that stopped at the edge of narrow alleys built to accommodate coal deliveries into basements.

Large statues took up space in the center of the road the closer she got to the downtown starting with Arthur Ashe, a hometown favorite with everyone until the idea of putting his likeness on Monument Avenue at the head of the line in front of Lee and Jackson.

Richmond was a place where people had their heads permanently swiveling in two directions, the past and the present, and they were willing to argue about disagreements long settled that came to nothing. Wallis knew that to get along in Richmond was to give in to the understanding that hurt feelings were passed down like an inheritance. Walter had understood that.

"First, you know the white southerners lost the war," said her father, smiling wryly. "And losers never forget, never stop rewriting. What you have in this town is a very old editing job that has only begun to wear thin, thank Goodness. But I find, once a morsel of respect is given, they're willing to move on to other subjects. Not until, mind you."

It was something to remember either way, Wallis had decided. Pay a morsel of respect to hurt feelings, no matter their source, before getting to the matter at hand.

Wallis turned on the phone and said, "Office," waiting as the phone dialed the number. Laurel picked up on the second ring.

"Weiskopf, Jones and Bremmer."

"Laurel, I'm on my way to court. Any messages I need to know about now?"

"Norman's been looking for you. He wanted to know how your meeting went this morning. What meeting? You didn't have anything scheduled. New case?"

"No, not really. Personal matter, thanks for digging."

"Not subtle enough, huh?"

"Laurel, I think you could make me smile while sitting in the middle of an open field during a hurricane," said Wallis, letting out a long sigh.

"That an old southern saying? You sound tired."

"Where's Norman now?"

"He's comforting a tax scofflaw, telling him there is life beyond poverty."

"Would you tell him I'm on my way to court downtown and I'll catch up with him after Bunko? I'll check in when I can."

"You know, it's actually something I like about you, this abruptness."

"You're not actually the typical paralegal type either, Laurel."

"Which is my cue to exit. I'll make sure and tell Norman, he looked worried. And I'll be home tonight if you'd like to fill me in as well. Madame stopped by again. Apparently Friday is too far away. She looked very unhappy."

"Everyone always thinks their problem can't wait. Goodbye, Laurel, and for the record, I'm grateful you're not standard issue."

"Right back at you, Boss."

The day passed uneventfully for juvenile court in downtown Richmond. Some crying, some angry words, some compromise, no threats of violence. The hours in court had returned a sense of calm to Wallis to be back in her element after the meeting with Stanley.

Wallis walked out onto Marshall Street in the early evening, slowly walking down the wide stone steps in front of the over-sized red brick building with stately white pillars. She felt worn out down to the bone, glad to feel so exhausted. It made it harder to really worry about what might be happening to the pieces of her life. Everyone had used words like calm, hard to rattle, and cynical to describe Stanley Woermer, the opposite of what Wallis had seen in the bookstore and she knew the same words could be a pretty apt description of her.

The Jag was parked in an open lot two blocks away and as she slowly made her way down the wide sidewalk she had to pass by the small dramas giving out their last gasps along the short marble wall that ran the length of the sidewalk in front of the court house. The building took up the entire city block, ending before the smaller, old John Marshall house the city fathers had decided not to disturb but had built around instead.

Families were heard exclaiming their innocence to each other on the sidewalks outside. A mother was yelling out her virtues, two young men there for support nodding their heads in agreement while keeping a short distance between themselves and the wildly pacing woman. Further down, a woman cautiously put her arm around her friend saying with as much conviction as she could dredge up that things could only get better from here. A father marched down the sidewalk, angry he couldn't keep the woman who had been his wife from getting any more of his money.

"If I'd 'a known I had to pay the dentist's bill, I wouldn't have bought him those shoes," the man shouted before he slammed shut his car door, glaring at no one in particular. A couple of people looked up with bemused silence and went back to their conversation. A woman, quietly and quickly walked to her car in the other direction down the block, suppressing a smile as best she could. She had won a small battle. It was something to build on.

Everyone is always right in family court, thought Wallis, getting back to her car well after six, even if they think they won or lost.

These kinds of days always wore her out. She had gone before Judge Henderson with a custody case that had to be settled before the couple could get a divorce. It was the fifth continuation, mostly by opposing counsel on behalf of the husband. The judge's patience had grown thin. When it became apparent the other lawyer was going to attempt to drag things out even further, the judge coolly informed everyone that the case was going no further than today, no matter what.

"By the time you two leave my court, you will no longer be married and your children will have an answer to where they'll be living and when," he said, leaning forward as he pulled the billowing black sleeves out of the way. Clearly visible at the collar of his robes was a small pin with a tight circle of stars.

Judge Henderson didn't look at either party as he spoke. He never looked at anyone, never lifted his head. His mottled face wore a perpetual scowl of indifference as he glanced around at his lap or nearby papers. His pale brown skin was as thin as onion paper and gave away his real moods, changing from pale tan when he was bored to a rosier brown when he was listening and deep purple when he had had enough. Both lawyers knew better than to challenge him, no matter the mood.

"There will be two scheduled bathroom breaks, no meal breaks, and no leaving the court room for any other reason until all matters before me are settled. Counselors, do we all understand?"

Wallis could hear the husband sputtering in the ear of his lawyer, something about his rights and noticed the lawyer batting away at his client, trying to get the annoying fly to sit down, be quiet. Both men were wearing the more common flag pins. Everyone in this town is patriotic and has to wear some measure of it on their sleeve, thought Wallis.

The wife sitting at her elbow looked up toward Wallis, but Wallis never looked her way. No need for an explanation, this was the way it was going to be. Wallis stole a glance at Jane Ely, the court reporter to see if she had flinched when she had learned of her connected fate. She was still staring straight ahead, dutifully taking down every word. She was one of the best in town and was always Wallis' first choice.

"Yes, your honor," said both attorneys in unison.

"Was there something your client wanted to say, Mr. Hicks?" asked the judge.

"No, your honor. Thank you, your honor."

Even though she was hungry walking into court and it would be worse by the time she left, Wallis was glad to hear the ruling. It was a good sign.

She was right. It had taken eight hours with only the two promised fifteen minute breaks and a couple of outbursts from the now ex-husband, but Wallis' client had walked out with custody of the children and her name back. The property had been split up months ago during a screaming match in their driveway.

Mr. Hicks' client had child support and visitation set up for him, against his protests and had stormed out ahead of everybody. Wallis knew Judge Henderson didn't veer from the tables set up for these kinds of decisions, even though he could have, but she was used to the complaints about being taken. Sometimes it was her client, sometimes it wasn't. She had a feeling both of these parties would be back, time and again, to let the courts iron out what they had never learned how to discuss.

"Where do I go from here?" the woman had asked Wallis, suddenly looking lost. So much of her life had been taken up with first a bad marriage and then a bad divorce.

"That's for you to figure out, which I know you can. Start with the children and work from there," said Wallis. "Call me if you have any problems," she said, turning to leave. Wallis knew not to hold anyone's hand for long after the decisions came down no matter how much she might like the client. People who gave into seeing themselves as victims never got around to a thank you anyway.

"Hello Wallis."

It was Richard Bach, walking toward the courthouse.

"Richard, late night?"

"No, left a file behind," he said, smiling evenly, his bright-white teeth never giving away too much. Wallis noticed he was wearing a small American flag pin with a white background, trimmed in gold.

"Nice pin, Richard."

"Thank you," he said, smiling harder. "I wear it with pride. Have a good night," he said, as he stepped around Wallis.

"Richard?"

Richard Bach stopped and turned back to Wallis. "Do you know Lilly Billings? Ray's wife, that man who killed himself?"

"No, sorry. I have to run before they close up for the night. Good night."

Wallis noticed the small shake in Richard's shoulders when she said Lilly's name.

She got into her car and felt for the file underneath the seat. It had been stupid to leave it in the car, she thought, but she wasn't sure what to do with it. The thumb drive was still in her pocket. She started the engine and called home.

"Hey," she said, relaxing at the sound of Norman's voice. "I'm just leaving court. Yeah, it was Judge Henderson. Two pee breaks, that was it. Is that you laughing? Yeah, I guess we won. How's Ned? She loved his robot? Give him a kiss for me. I saw Stanley. He was only a little informative. Yeah, it was strange, I don't know. We can talk about it when I get home. I think someone was following Stanley. No, no, I'm okay. I love you too. It's Bunko night and I'm late already. I'll see you after the girls. Wait up, okay?"

Norman hung up the phone, wondering if he should have told his wife about Mr. Blazney. He went back to the front door to speak to the young detective.

"Sorry, Arnold, just my wife checking in. I'm sorry I can't help you. Where did they find his body?"

"In Deep Run Park near the playground in the middle of one of the soccer fields. Looks like he was hit by an SUV that didn't stick around. Any idea why he'd be that far from home still in pajamas?"

"No," said Norman, rubbing the back of his head. "Unless he was walking Happy, his yellow Lab. Is she okay?"

"Yeah, we found her in their back yard safe and sound, her leash still on her."

"You think some kids were joyriding and accidentally hit poor old Larry and left him there to die?"

"I might, except for a couple of things."

"What's that?"

"The human bone found in the cuff of Mr. Blazney's pajamas and the human remains found in Happy's stomach."

CHAPTER

IT was Angie Estaver's turn to host the monthly Bunko game. Her house was in the same neighborhood as Wallis, set at the opposite edge of the subdivision. It sat on the corner of Star Lane Way in a cul de sac, backed up by a thick stand of trees that blocked a lot of the noise coming from nearby Ridgefield Drive. Most of the yard stretched out on the left side of the yellow paneled Colonial hemmed in by a split rail fence. A portable basketball hoop was parked in the street near their driveway.

A cluster of mini-vans, SUV's and smaller sedans were already parked near the Estaver house. Wallis was the last to arrive. She parked in front of the small L-shaped rancher next door and made her way up the brick path, pushing the car key's button over her shoulder to lock the Jag as she hurried along in the dark.

She was so intent on her path she didn't see the man coming out of the shadows until he was almost in her path. She sucked her breath in hard, stopping and bracing herself. The man hesitated and took a step back, his face still too deeply in the shadows for Wallis to be able to get a good look.

"Wallis Jones," he said in a calm, confident voice, with the slightest trace of an accent. "We need to talk."

"Take another step back," she said, trying to sound menacing. "What is it you want?"

"Things are a little more complicated than you know. I can help, I think. We need to talk."

"Dammit," said Wallis, feeling her heart pound and the anger rise, tightening her throat. "What's with the bushes? I have an office, a phone," she hissed, not wanting to attract attention from anyone already inside. "I'm going to go out on a limb here and assume you're not here for a divorce. So, maybe you're another friend of Ray's or is this some new kind of fun?"

Wallis was clenching and unclenching the keys in her hand, feeling the edges press against her skin

"You're being watched, carefully watched by some very capable people. A little caution is called for these days."

"This is ridiculous," said Wallis. "We're standing in the west end of Richmond playing cloak and dagger. What the hell is going on here?"

"More than you know. I'm sorry you've been dragged into this, but now that you are, I can use your help."

"How did you find me? Are you following me?"

"More like keeping my eye on you. But there are others keeping tabs on you. May I see your shoes?" he asked, holding out his hand.

"My shoes? No, why would I do that?"

"Because I've been watching them track you and it's been too easy. Did you step in anything right around your house?"

Wallis shuddered, remembering the door mat right by her kitchen door and shifted her feet but didn't move to take off her shoes.

"Why should I trust you? You haven't told me anything and now you're saying I'm a target." Wallis' voice sounded high and thin. "I need this to stop," she whispered.

"Allow me to introduce myself," he said, his tone an attempt at being calm and reassuring. "My name is Helmut and you have stumbled into a very old fight that is bigger than you have yet to grasp."

"I've been told. Whose side of the fight are you on?"

"I like to think the side of the righteous but I'll let you judge after you hear everything. Wallis," said Helmut, taking a step closer, "we need to talk. It's imperative you know more than you do now. Ignorance will only get you hurt."

"By whom?"

"By people who learned a long time ago how to mete out just enough power to others to never really have to let go. It would mean nothing for me to start giving you names. You need the entire story and that will take a little time. The shoes?"

"I did," said Wallis, not moving.

"You did?"

"I stepped in something, I mean something was in my door mat. What was it?"

"I suspect it was a resin that can be easily tracked and is almost impossible to wash off. I hope those aren't a favorite pair." Helmut smiled softly but his voice was determined. "Give them to me."

"No. I'm not walking in there in my bare feet until you tell me something. How much danger am I in? Is my family in danger?"

"Not yet. But all of us, myself included, are inconsequential to this game. The only thing keeping you safe right now is no one knows just how much you've been told and they have decided you're worth the risk. What exactly do you know?"

"I know about the list."

"Ah, but which list. Their BIGOT list or the Circle's? You're a good player, Miss Jones. The list holds so many secrets, possessing it imparts nothing. They know you have the thumb drive. So do we. The shoe," he said suddenly, shaking his hand, "We don't have much time. I must insist."

"Why is it a bigot's list?"

"No," said Helmut, his voice still calm. "BIGOT. It's an old spy acronym for a list of players in any operation. It dates back to WWII when Allied orders for officers in Gibraltar were stamped TO GIB before the invasion of North Africa. Please, I'm wasting precious time. It was at a moment of our greatest disaster. The Circle was almost destroyed."

"The circle?"

Suddenly, the sharp staccato barking of a small dog started up from the other side of the door. Wallis startled and dropped her keys, not taking her eyes off of Helmut.

Ralph, Angie's long-haired Chihuahua, started barking on the other side of the door, letting everyone know Wallis was there. No one ever got the chance to ring the doorbell before Ralph sensed their presence and started barking.

"Leave the shoes behind. Let them know you're on to the game. Make them work harder. It will keep you safer," he said.

"Who?" said Wallis, but Helmut turned and started walking away briskly, fading deeper into the darkness of a well-populated suburbia that didn't appreciate the look of street lights.

"Wait," Wallis called out as loud as she dared. Helmut never slowed down. Wallis suddenly felt the cold March night on the back of her neck. Her clothes were damp from sweat.

Wallis watched him fade into the darkness before she walked up the front steps and cautiously opened the door, trying not to let Ralph escape into the night. She nudged him back with her foot as she eased inside. As Ralph aged and his hair turned greyer, he had begun to resemble a moving mop head, zipping from room to room, up and down the stairs. Sharp barks emanated from one end of the mop as the other end twitched from side to side.

Hector, Angie's husband answered the door.

"Hey, Wallis, come on in," said Hector, in his usual booming delivery. He scooped up Ralph and tucked him under one arm as he held the screen door open for Wallis.

Hector's nature was shy, particularly around women and he always kept his sentences short and to the point before disappearing to another room in the house or wrestling with some of his young sons.

"You okay?" asked Hector, taking a closer look at Wallis. Wallis opened her mouth to say something but couldn't come up with anything reasonable to explain away the fear that must show on her face. She shrugged and started to take off her coat.

"Let me take that," said Hector. Wallis mumbled a thank you, as she let go of a deep shudder and eased past him and a frantically yipping Ralph.

A little army of children anchored on the ends by teenagers were lined up at the long narrow kitchen table, eating away and talking loudly over each other about school or the high school football team or video games. Wallis recognized most of them. The older ones were the small cluster of babysitters used by everyone in the neighborhood.

"Hector, are you going to play Tetris with us tonight?" asked a small boy on the far side of the table. Wallis felt herself relax a little as she watched Hector blend back in with the kids, bragging about how he was planning to win every game.

I'm safe here, she thought, knowing it was irrational and shaking slightly from the new idea that there could be familiar places where she could be in danger.

She gave a small wave to the women at the two card tables set up in the family room, the necessities for Bunko night laid out before them. Four women to a table with three dice at each table and two small bowls of treats to munch on as each woman waited her turn to roll the dice or a new game to start. One bowl was always devoted to chocolate, the other to something salty.

Around the corner in the dining room were two more tables set up the same way with a small hand bell resting on the table closest to the kitchen door. A seat was still vacant at that table.

"Come on, Wallis," said Julia, an over-sized blonde in matching orange knit pants and top, "we saved you a seat at the head table. Have a sit-down so we can get going. My lucky hand is feeling itchy tonight." She let out a seasoned cackle that ended in a wet cough.

"Those patches aren't working for you, are they Julia," said Bridget, a tall, lanky brunette with an outdated shag wearing the same kind of outfit, but blue, as she patted Julia hard on the back. Wallis recognized the Wal-Mart fashions from her grocery shopping last week. The ensembles were part of a large display of matching coordinates set up underneath an aging celebrity's likeness.

"Not wearing one right now. Forgot last night and lit up while I had one on. Nearly passed out from the rush." Everyone let out a laugh.

Most of the women were close to Wallis' age and a few, like Bridget were older. All of them were talkers. Wallis liked coming to Bunko and listening to the women make bawdy jokes about their husbands or playfully moan about their weight or their bad habits. None of them ever gave Wallis a hard time about contributing so little and no one used the time to get too serious about anything. It was a nice little slice of middle-class suburbia without the accompanying angst Wallis usually swam through every day.

Wallis took her seat and quickly wrote her name on the index card at her place.

"Thanks," she said, handing the stubby yellow pencil back to Angie. "What's traveling tonight?"

"Threes. I'll keep score this round," said Angie, pulling the small yellow pad closer to her. Similar negotiations were quickly decided at the other tables.

Angie raised the bell and said, "Ready?" giving the bell an easy shake. "You go first, Wallis. You look like you had the longest day."

Wallis let a smile creep up her face and picked up the dice. Her first roll resulted in two ones and a five.

"Snake eyes," said Maureen sitting opposite her. "Good job, partner. Roll a few more like that." Each player took their turn rolling the dice three times, the desired 'ones' getting marked down as notches on the yellow pad at each table.

"Bunko!" yelled out an excited Silvia at the next table over, raising her arms over her head. All three dice had turned up ones, giving her and her temporary partner five extra points.

The turns traveled around the tables over and over as the women chatted and ate, sometimes forgetting to count the dice, laughing as they tried to remember.

"Twenty one," said Maureen, as Angie rang the bell calling an end to that round. "Better luck next time," she said to Angie and Paulette as they rose to move to the next table over.

"I'll switch," said Wallis, getting up and sitting down at Maureen's right elbow.

Ginger sat down across from Wallis becoming her new partner for the next round. Yvette slid into the chair across from Maureen. "We all ready?" said Maureen, not bothering to look before she rang the bell and everyone started rolling for two's.

"I'll go," said Maureen, grabbing at the dice.

"You really want the prize tonight, don't you Maureen?" said Ginger. Maureen stuck her tongue out and hissed, "Yes," as two two's turned up. Yvette unwrapped a miniature Hershey bar and slid it into her mouth.

"How's it going with Lance?" asked Maureen. Lance was Yvette's six year old son.

"I can't complain," said Yvette, "but I'm not sure what to do. His teacher says he's way too far ahead of everyone else in the class and wants to jump him to second grade. But it's already March. He'd be starting in the middle of everything and wouldn't know a soul."

"Did she just mention it?" said Wallis.

"No, and good point," said Yvette, laughing. "She mentioned it last December before the new semester started, but I suppose I don't want to do it so I dragged my feet. I'm going to keep up my passive resistance till summer, I think. Sure, he's making her come up with lesson plans just for him, but he's small for his age and she should do the heavy lifting here, not Lance."

"How's Fred doing?" asked Yvette, turning to Maureen.

"Worried about the economy, which is a good thing. He seems to need something to worry about and when he can't figure out what it might be he starts to look at me," said Maureen, letting out a snort of laughter.

"What does your husband say about Lance?" asked Maureen.

"He's so busy at work. He asked me what I was doing and when I said I wasn't all that interested, he stopped asking. I'm all for waiting to see how this plays out."

"Sounds reasonable to me," said Wallis.

"Yeah, just say no," said Ginger. "How's Ned getting along? He's running ahead of his teachers, isn't he?"

"Yes, but the teachers don't seem to be aware of it, which is how Ned likes it. Ned's better at playing his own game and does just enough to get the A's but not so much they'll notice he's not getting challenged."

"That's okay with you?" asked Maureen. "Oh, Bunko, Ginger, good for us." Maureen made five notches on the notepad.

"Sure, it's fine. Ned's naturally curious and he's not going to stop himself from learning and if he feels he needs to be under the radar then so be it. He'll find his way."

Wallis thought of Paul and some unseen force's interest in him and she let go of a shudder.

"You cold?" asked Ginger. "You want to use my sweater?" she said, reaching around to peel the fuchsia cardigan off of the back of her chair.

"No, no, I'm fine. Just thinking about some of the cases I see." Getting a little better at lying quickly, thought Wallis.

"Yeah, that must be hard not to take home," said Maureen. "I don't think I could do it. I'd be yelling at people all the time to straighten up and fly right." The women chuckled.

"Twenty one!" said Ginger. Maureen vigorously rang the bell.

"Okay, who's my next partner?" said Maureen, pushing herself up and moving over to the next table.

"Maybe you'll win for having the least tonight, Maureen," said Yvette.

"A prize is a prize," said Maureen, pulling a chair out a little further at a nearby table.

"Did you hear about Blazney?" said Maureen to her new table partners.

Wallis looked up, trying to catch what she was saying but couldn't hear her over the general chatter.

Dot, a newcomer to the neighborhood who looked far younger than her forty years sat down across from Wallis. "Two holes, good going Wallis," she said, glancing at the file card by Wallis' place.

Ginger took the chair Maureen had left as Julia settled into the empty folding chair.

"Hello again," said Wallis.

"Glad to be back," said Julia.

"Are we on three's?" asked Dot, looking around.

"Yes!" yelled Angie who was around the corner.

"Are we ready?" asked Ginger, raising the bell. "Yes," several voices yelled out in unison and the bell rang, signaling the start of another round.

The sound of dice hitting the table mingled with the delighted sounds of hitting the right number and the good-natured moans of scoreless tosses.

"Oooooh, traveling," said Dot, surprised at her own luck of tossing a straight line of three's. Angie hopped up from her seat, pulling off the bracelet made of strung together dice and handed it to Dot.

"Congratulations," she said, smiling, as she turned to go back to her seat.

"Traveling!" shouted Bridget sitting two tables over. She looked around eagerly for where the bracelet had gotten to. Angie turned back to Dot who was slowly sliding the bracelet back off, trying not to look disappointed.

"It didn't even have time to cool off," said Angie, smiling at Dot before handing the bracelet over to Bridget and retaking her seat.

"Did I tell you?" said Julia, "Roger's been offered a scholarship to Sutler, right out of the blue!" Roger was Julia's tall, curly haired twelve year old son. Wallis liked him. He was easy to get along with and would talk to her about what was going on in his life. Wallis always felt privileged to get a peek inside of any middle school life.

"Really? Somebody just called you up and asked if Roger wanted to go there?" asked Ginger. "Wow, you must be living right."

"Well, it wasn't exactly out of the blue," said Julia, talking a little too fast. Wallis felt a sense of dread coming over her, sensing what Julia was about to lay out before her.

"Sam and I have been talking to this group for a few years," she said.

"Group?" asked Dot.

"Yeah, like the Masons, except they're called The Stewards. They do good works for children. They've been around for hundreds of years. Anyway, they took an interest in Sam and have been helping us get him ahead."

"How did you meet them in the first place?" asked Dot. Wallis watched each of the women, keeping her silence, making herself take measured breaths. She didn't say a word, too worried that in her attempts to disguise her growing dread her voice would come out too controlled, too calculating.

"Tina introduced me to one of their Watchers at a tea she had. Roger must have been around nine. I've mentioned it before, when he got into cotillion at the Women's Club? Remember?"

"Oh yeah, I thought Pamela helped you get in."

"She did. She wrote a letter."

"Watcher?" interrupted Ginger, "That sounds a little creepy. Why are they called Watchers?"

"Who knows," said Julia. "You know how those old societies are, they like their drama. All I know is they've made our lives a little easier and helped Roger. All I need to know."

"They haven't asked you to join?"

"Nope. Apparently they have rules about joining if they're helping your child. If you're really interested Tina's having another tea in a few weeks. She said I could invite y'all. You want to come, Wallis? Ned would be about the right age. They like to get them young," she said, smiling.

Julia reached into her purse on the floor by her feet and pulled out several invitations, offering them to the women at the table. Dot grabbed at one of the stiff cream-colored engraved cards.

"They only accept a handful, mostly boys, big surprise, but I figure even if you only end up with a little help, it couldn't hurt, right? You want one, Wallis? You're awfully quiet. Looking for the loopholes?" She held a card out to Wallis.

Wallis slowly took the card and smiled back at Julia. She was working hard to press the anger back down inside of her. The effort was taking its toll and she could feel some of it seeping out of the sides.

"And they want nothing in return?" she said, a little louder than she had intended. The sound of dice hitting plastic tablecloths stopped for a moment as the collection of women looked toward Wallis. "They don't have expectations about what your child might become?"

"No...No," mumbled Julia. "It's just guidance." Her voice had taken on a slight whine, so unlike her. "It's hard to give your children everything you want to these days."

"Or even everything we had," said Yvette from another table. A grumbled murmur of approval rolled around the room. Wallis breathed in slowly, held her breath for a moment and let it back out.

"Fred wants nothing to do with it," said Maureen. "He was put through that whole rigmarole as a child and he said it stops with him. Well, that and we have no children," she said with a laugh.

"Sorry," said Wallis, trying to give Julia's hand a reassuring pat. Her head was pounding. "Long day and I guess I'm still partly in lawyer mode. I'm sure you checked it out."

Her last words were more of a warning that she was hoping Julia would remember.

"My grandfather was a Shriner," said Ginger, picking up the dice. "Always had to wear the little fez in pictures. So proud of it. I don't understand any of it, but if it's helping kids get ahead it can't be all bad. Oh, twenty one!" She rang the bell.

Wallis won the random drawing that night, taking home a large purple candle. She walked to her car slowly looking around for anyone lurking by the bushes but the street seemed empty. She felt badly about how the night had turned out. The conversation had never managed to reach the same level of good-natured fun after her comments.

CHAPTER 15

THE crowd was gathering early. The parking lot of Baldwin's Funeral Home was quickly filling up with well-kept late model European sedans all parked carefully within the white lines.

Anyone driving home down Parham Road from the office or the local Martin's grocery store that night would have thought someone important must have died. The reverence of the gathering said it was a prominent business owner who was well respected by everyone who worked for him or at least someone who was still feared, even in death.

But no one was there to honor the dead. The funeral home was being used as the perfect cover for an impromptu large meeting. The leaders of Management knew no one ever looked too closely as they sped by out of respect for the grieving.

The sky was cooperating with the mood and was gray and overcast as the sun slowly set over the wealthy suburb. There was a wet chill in the air that made everyone want to draw the collar of their coat closer and walk a little quicker toward their destination.

Somber men and women were quietly walking toward the building. The loudest noise was the rhythmic shuffle of their heels along the blacktop. Everyone was dressed in conservative southern business attire topped with dark overcoats.

A few of the men greeted each other with a nod or mouthed hello but no one spoke.

The dark grey or blue suits were standard issue for the chosen so that they would always blend into any group. Hair was always above the collar for men and a shoulder length bob for the women. Each town had their own version of what was acceptable and everyone followed the specifications. Outsiders noticed the herd mentality and pegged it to wanting to fit in and not rock the boat. Members everywhere had been taught from an early age that odd or poor grooming could be a distraction to the work at hand and make someone too memorable. The point wasn't to stand out and be remembered, it was to get the job done and go back to the easier routines of life. Standards made everything easier.

After all, rule number one was that the principles of the organization mattered more than any handful of personalities and individual expression was to be sacrificed for the common good.

As the men and women entered the building they quickly handed their coats over to the two men who greeted them with a short set of instructions and handed back a ticket stub to retrieve their belongings later. It was only then that the small lapel pin became visible across the sea of bodies, dotting the left side of every jacket. A small round pin of an American flag against a white enamel background trimmed in gold leaf. It was the passport into the cavernous room and made each member recognizable anywhere in the world as a fellow traveler. Every country had their own version of the pin with their own national flag. Only one small company run by Management made the pins. It was a necessary precaution in order to control who received the gold-enameled marker.

Regular meetings were held at the beginning of every quarter in different funeral homes around town. Members were called together to keep everyone on track with the same message. But this one was quickly put on the calendar and held more importance than usual to the local leaders. Things were starting to appear too lax in the Richmond delegation and a few recent and unfortunate incidents had made plans vulnerable to being detected. That could not be tolerated.

Richard Bach stood just outside the doors that lead to the small stage in the sanctuary. He was glancing in to take note of who had already arrived and settled into the first rows of seats as he straightened the cufflinks on his shirt with the familiar symbol of small flags. Their abundance on his lapel and at his wrists denoted to anyone that Richard was a vice president in a local group. Someone who could make things happen without having to always check with anyone else.

The American public knew the covert society called Management vaguely as the Stewards. It had its roots in the formation of the United States back in the late 1700's when democracy was an idea that looked like it might actually take root. Older monarchies realized that the era of reigning over their flocks as they had ordained was coming to an end and to survive they would have to adapt. Louis XVI resisted the idea and tried to plot against the early organizers.

Loyal staff members were quickly dispatched to Paris where they infiltrated the new movement and encouraged bloodshed rather than negotiations. Once the stubborn king and queen were beheaded the Management set to work romancing the new leaders and feeding their egos with the idea of a controlled democracy where their power would be ensured.

The old system of raising children with the right blood lines according to a strict regimen of the right schools, the right clothes and the right connections was opened up to include families with more moderate genes and purses. Slowly over time, these children became the new middle class that was easily manipulated into doing upper management's bidding in exchange for a fairly comfortable life with an identifiable track. Politicians were put in place, corporations were carefully managed and army generals were groomed all over the world.

Emerging countries were thoroughly researched by diplomats whose mission was to scout out the easiest way to start a new outpost without being heavy handed and detected.

The British took it too far though and insisted on standing out in front of everything they touched, boasting that the sun never set on their empire. Something had to be done and by the early 1900's the British arm of the Management was cowed into place.

As a concession to mollify the occasional protests from local chapters a certain amount of leeway became permissible so that local groups felt more autonomous as long as they didn't stray from the main goal.

After all, even insiders don't like to find out they are being oppressed. But those who had witnessed the lengths Management was willing to go to, however, never forgot.

However, the upper echelons were willing to go to great lengths to keep certain boundaries intact. They had found out over time just where the lines were that when crossed tended to lead to uprisings and the violent end to entire Management chapters.

Things sometimes became messy and had to be quietly rebuilt, which takes time. India's new world order had taken generations to become effective and Pakistan and Vietnam were proving to be slow and difficult works in progress.

The purpose of an artificial democracy was simple, really. A certain amount of replacements were going to be needed in every generation to insure management level positions at every level were filled with their own recruits. The projections along with an updated list of intentions were sent to local groups so that they could identify the right children. Intentions differed with the times but held the implicit idea to keep the power base right where it was as efficiently as possible with the smallest amount of risk. In exchange everyone received a modicum of the good life with very little change.

In order to protect the core, the locals only met the Management officers directly above them. No one really knew who was running things at the top but speculation and gossip always swirled around the wealthy and the famous.

If things were going well, neither side heard from each other beyond the regular missives and everyone was relatively happy.

But lately people he had never met but he was smart enough to fear had heard of Richard and his management style and they weren't very happy. An associate had been dispatched to help Richard lead the meeting and bring everyone back into line. She was due to arrive at any minute.

"Richard Bach?"

Richard startled only slightly and turned to see his senior vice president, Robin Spingler striding toward him. Normally, Richard had no time for women. He saw them more as accessories than fully realized human beings but Robin's large frame and cold demeanor made it easier for him to make an exception.

Robin was wearing a skirt and jacket similar in style to most of the women in the meeting but on her tall frame it appeared to be more of a costume.

"Robin, so glad you could make it."

"Don't be glib, Richard. It doesn't look good on you, and we all know how much illusions matter to you. Are your people here?"

"Yes, everyone is assembled and breathlessly awaiting your words."

Robin stopped abruptly at the door and turned back to Richard, leaning in close to his face.

"Everyone is expendable, dear boy," she whispered coldly. "Me, you, every person in that room. You don't have some invisible aura protecting you. People are dying all around you and its getting noticed. Your work is even inspiring the opposition to take note and we don't like that. Don't become such a pain in my ass that I find it easier to make you the last incident in this unfortunate turn of events. At the very least I'd find it necessary to remind you much like the last time you decided to start making decisions on your own." She slapped her hands together for emphasis.

Richard's smile froze into place and he found it difficult to take a deep breath. He felt the sting of the bamboo whip Robin had once wielded with precision against his back raising large, red welts. It had taken a week before he could sit back against a chair.

"There are still loose ends to take care of but your lack of skills has made it difficult to easily maneuver. We should have had that file back by now, and it's not. I promise you this," she said, pointing a short, red nail very close to his face, "if we missed a chance to break into the Circle because of you, I will take care of you personally, again." She spat the last word out as a sneer.

Robin stepped back and smiled broadly before lumbering through the door and out onto the stage. Richard followed meekly behind her and folded himself into one of the chairs on the stage. He had a smile firmly in place but made a point of not making eye contact with anyone.

Three attempts and he still hadn't been able to get the file. A Watcher had the file for a moment but before anyone could open it, the McDonough woman had stolen it. That had been the last straw for Richard.

At this point he wasn't even sure where it was anymore. It had to be quickly travelling back up the ranks of the Circle by now, if it even existed anymore. Follow Stanley Woermer, Richard thought, wiping away the uncharacteristic sweat that was forming on his brow. He'll lead me to it.

CHAPTER 16

"**YOU** didn't mind when I told you about all of this three years ago, Wallis." It was Julia, slowly walking up behind her in the darkness, moving the straps of her large green Jelly bag further up her shoulder. Bunko was over and everyone was quickly heading home, back to familiar routines.

"What are you talking about?"

"Remember? That time we met at your office and we went for lunch at Appleby's? I told you about the tea party and what they had offered and you said it sounded nice. Like the old boy network was finally growing up and inviting newcomers. You even congratulated me."

Wallis had a flicker of a memory about the lunch.

"I know. You weren't really listening, which is okay," said Julia, stopping right in front of Wallis. There were tears in her eyes making Wallis regret her words even more. "My life isn't all that interesting. But I don't see why you'd suddenly think there was something wrong now just because Roger gets such a nice opportunity. I mean, I know how you feel about the old Richmond crowd, but..."

"It's not that," said Wallis, quietly.

"Look, Sam and I will be lucky if we can pay for Roger's college, and Roger's a good kid. He deserves to get a chance at whatever he wants to be."

"That's kind of my point."

"And, if taking a little help gets that for him then we'll swallow our pride and do it."

Wallis suddenly saw what Julia was getting at and grabbed her hand, squeezing tight. "No, no, Julia. I didn't mean... Of course I'm happy for any great things that come your way. Roger's a great kid and you're doing a great job. You know I wouldn't judge..."

"Well, I wouldn't have thought so," she whimpered.

"No, I wouldn't," she said firmly. "But how do you know you're getting something for nothing? How do you know for sure?"

"We haven't had to sign anything," said Julia, "and they gave us a document that says as long as Roger maintains a C average they'll pay the tuition through high school. We had a lawyer check it out. We're not liable for anything." A tear slid down Julia's cheek.

Wallis hugged Julia close, whispering, "Then why are you so upset?"

"We're good parents," said Julia, still in Wallis' embrace.

Wallis pulled back and looked at Julia's face.

"I know that. Never doubted it, even for a moment. I am sorry about my tone back there. Chalk it up to my annual outburst. Look, I'll come to the tea and make nice. Okay?"

Julia smiled, a tear getting caught in her lips. "Okay, but without the lawyerly interrogation. It's a tea, deal?"

"Yeah, deal."

Wallis knew Julia wasn't telling her everything but didn't know how far in Julia had already gotten herself, or Roger, and couldn't risk telling Julia anything just yet.

What more is there to know, she thought.

Wallis drove off, turning out of the neighborhood and heading up

Ridgefield Drive toward Pump Road. She turned right and drove to the new mall where Pump Road changed names and drove around the almost empty parking lot, curving around to the back near the super-sized Dick's Sporting Goods store that faced a thinning woods. Richmond had a hard time not developing every square inch of land. Those trees won't last long either, thought Wallace.

She slowed the car down enough to slip her shoes off and pulled neatly between two parked cars, checking her rear view mirror. No one in sight. She dropped the shoes gently out of the window as small phosphorescent flakes glittered on the bottom of the right shoe. She pulled her feet up off of the floor of the car and carefully rolled up the floor mat, depositing it next to the shoes. The engine churned as she pushed the gas pedal down with her bare foot and headed back toward Pump Road.

Norman was sitting up in bed reading when she got home. He had his half-glasses on and the covers pulled up to his chest, exposing the faded white t-shirt he loved to wear to bed.

"Hello," he said, putting down the paperback.

"I made a complete ass of myself tonight," said Wallis, dropping her purse. The folder was sticking out of her open purse. She gently shut the door behind her, placing the prized candle on the tall-boy and peeled off her blouse and skirt, letting them drop to the floor. "Where's Ned?"

"He fell asleep reading about black holes and what might lie on the other side of them. I tucked him in. What'd you do?" he asked with his usual placid expression firmly in place. "And may I say I have always appreciated your sense of lingerie, dear. Thank you for never giving in to parachute pants."

"I had a mild outburst during Bunko. Questioned someone's motives a little too loudly." Wallis glanced down at the matching pale green lace bra and panties and let out a sigh. She climbed the two steps and got on the bed, resting on her knees.

Norman raised an eyebrow and sat up a little straighter. "That's not like you. Someone try to take your candle?"

Wallis glanced back at the candle and smiled. "There was a whole candle theme. It'll come in handy on some stormy night," she said. "No, I won that fair and square. But Julia Croft mentioned Roger's getting a free ride to Sutler next year and she used some of the same language as Stanley. I'm afraid I snapped at her just a little."

"That's enough to make you an ass? Take longer looks at some of our clients, my love. That doesn't even qualify as an outburst. More of a brief rude comment."

"You should have seen Julia's reaction, then. She was crying on my shoulder."

"That's something," said Norman, "but nothing to do with you. Come here," he said, holding out his hand across the bed. "This Woermer's paranoia is spreading to you. Julia could have so many other things going on that are completely unrelated. Take you, for example. Did you snap at her because you were mad at her?"

Wallis let out another sigh and shook her head. "No, but I was good and mad. You're right though, Stanley Woermer did get to me." She moved closer to Norman. "And I think someone followed him. I can't be sure, but I caught a glimpse of someone in the bookstore and he seemed to leave in a hurry by the back door. Apparently that door was only used to occasionally take out the trash. The lock looked like it might have been taped open, like someone knew we were meeting."

"What did Stanley say? Did he notice?"

"He had already left, but something or someone startled him on the way out. He said Ray Billings had found some system of promoting certain boys that had a nasty out clause."

"Ah, a conspiracy."

"Yeah. Why are those always so hard for any of us to get on board with?" she said, resting back on her heels.

"Because humans by nature are all blabbermouths to some degree. We expect to know about it."

"Yes, well, that raises another good point. Julia reminded me that she'd asked me about this whole thing three years ago and I had barely blinked. Congratulated her on cracking the system around here. Wouldn't a really good conspiracy be like a good lie?" she asked, reaching out to pull back the covers next to Norman. "Make it as innocuous as possible? Put it out there in front of everyone?"

"Well, what would be the master plan of this particular conspiracy?"

"I don't know," said Wallis, stretching out next to Norman. "But for the second time in a day someone was waiting for me in bushes."

"Stanley again?" said Norman, sitting up and taking off his glasses. "Come back to finish his story?"

"No, and I'm not sure Stanley knew much more anyway. This one called himself Helmut. He was big into the conspiracies. Hinted at bigger things. Ran off though when Ralph started barking."

"Were you scared?"

"Not any more than I already was. He seemed to want to help. Of course isn't that what they teach in serial killer school? Kill them first with kindness?"

"Apparently this Helmut flunked," said Norman. "What now? There seems to be something going on."

"Right, but what," said Wallis. "Helmut wanted my shoes and said people were using them to follow me."

"Your shoes? Where are they?"

"I dumped them," said Wallis. "Which means either I dumped credible evidence or got spooked enough to get rid of a good pair of shoes."

"Was there something on your shoes?"

"Yes, it came from the back door mat. Why would you ask that?" asked Wallis.

"I didn't think they'd be interested in just the shoes. Maybe I'll take a look at the mat tomorrow, just to be sure," he said, his face calm.

"I already dumped the car mat."

"Good thinking," said Norman, smiling just a little.

"I got invited to a tea," said Wallis. "Apparently that's how they cast out their net for possible recruits. Sorry, ladies only."

"I have never regretted your gender," he said, sliding a finger under the silk strap on her shoulder and tracing the outline of the curve of her breast.

"You're making it difficult to care about telling you what I know," she said as he rolled toward her, putting a leg between hers and reaching around, unhooking the bra.

"Will it still be going on an hour from now?" he asked, tossing the bra in the direction of the floor behind Wallis as he pulled her up against his chest.

"An hour? You're very ambitious," she said.

Later, Norman finally got up and turned off the light, crawling back into the bed, reaching out for her body in the darkness.

"Come here, love of my life," he whispered, pulling her close again, spooning behind her, their feet entangled. Wallis reached down for the sheets that had been forgotten at the bottom of the bed, pulling them up over their bodies, settling back in against Norman, letting herself fall off to sleep in his arms.

"I love you, Norman," she whispered as she drifted off to sleep.

The alarm startled her awake at six o'clock. Norman was still asleep, curled up behind her. She gently rubbed his shoulder and leaned over to kiss his forehead.

"Norman, wake up. Morning," she said, "and thank you."

He smiled without opening his eyes and reached out his hands, searching for her. He brushed a hand against her belly as she turned and pulled away, feeling for the step with her foot.

"No time for that now, husband of mine. It's another work day, although the shower's kind of roomy." Norman smiled and opened his eyes. He sat up and stretched his arms over his head.

"I love being married to you," he said, in the middle of a yawn. She smiled as she looked at the slight paunch he had started to develop lately.

"Any chance you and I can grab coffee together this morning, outside of our usual haunts?" asked Wallis.

Norman stopped stretching and looked at Wallis. "Still worried?"

"Yeah," she said. "But maybe if I can explain it all to you, you can tell me why I shouldn't be. Maybe Shoney's? Not too many people there after nine."

"Okay," he said, swinging his legs out of bed, "then it's a date. I'll warm up the shower." He ambled toward the bathroom, absently scratching his back, the hair on his head pushed forward, exposing the growing bald spot. Wallis felt a sudden rush of love for him and was grateful that at least everyone in her small nest was safe.

Ned bounded out of the car at school that morning, spotting a cluster of his friends and quickly forgetting even a goodbye for Wallis. She watched him hurrying over to his friends, grateful it was so easy for him to set out without her but feeling a momentary tug. She watched him telling them all something in a rush of words, remembering when he used to talk to her that way, as he gestured with his hands. She smiled as the car behind her honked and she waved in their direction, reluctantly pulling away from the curb.

Norman was already at the Shoney's settled in a table near the back. None of the nearby tables were filled.

"I requested this particular spot," he said after the waitress deposited the menus and left to get their coffee. "Although it doesn't seem upscale enough to hear a good conspiracy."

"I know you're smiling on the inside," said Wallis, sliding over on the padded red leather bench.

"My game plan is to not worry until I officially see reason to worry. So far, I'm good."

"Okay, well you let me know before we leave if we've moved up to an amber alert."

"Those things don't mean anything, anyway," said Norman, "except who's up or down in the polls."

Wallis pulled out the manila folder and opened it between them, showing Norman the charts of boys in different age groups.

"Where did these come from?" asked Norman.

"Off a thumb drive that the late Kristen McDonough stole from her Watcher. The drive has music on it, but Stanley said that somehow Ray Billings figured out there was something else there and came up with all of this."

"Who was Kristen McDonough?"

"She was supposedly a mother in the program. Remember that freak accident a while back where the two semis crushed the minivan? So much for the McDonoughs," said Wallis, pushing her palms together.

"Ooooooh," said Norman, wincing. "That has to be a coincidence."

"Not according to Stanley."

"What are those numbers under each name?" he asked, pointing to the short series of numbers.

"I don't know, but they don't appear to be random. I have no idea. I was just starting to get answers out of Stanley when he got spooked and took off. But it was Kristen McDonough who got everyone so stirred up. Apparently her son, a recruit, had become a public drunk and embarrassment to the system and she didn't like what was going on. Made a lot of complaints, started talking to her coworker, Ray."

"And suddenly no more McDonoughs."

"Right. And then Ray tells everyone he can get a hold of that he's found out some key part of the puzzle and to make sure everyone lets me know what's up if something happens to him…"

"And he apparently commits suicide."

"Right again and suddenly there are too many coincidences. And Paul Whittaker is a potential recruit in what appears to be a life time commitment that your parents make for you. But for what reason or really to who, I don't know."

"Okay, I can't say I'm panicked, but maybe a wee bit worried," said Norman, hesitating as the coffee was placed before them.

"We'll just do the breakfast bar," said Wallis, as she waited for the waitress to turn and leave.

"You're hungry again?" said Norman. "Not that I care."

"No, it just came out. Didn't want to sound cheap."

"That's not like you. You normally don't care what anyone thinks."

"You're right. I'm a little off center at the moment."

"Apparent suicides can do that. Got anything else, any ideas?"

"I was thinking of asking Ned to look at the drive for me, but I didn't know if that was really, really stupid."

"Ned's probably the smartest computer guy we know and very reluctant to ever share information with adults. He's perfect for the job," said Norman. "Maybe you'll find out more at that tea. Are you going to try and quiz Sharon?"

"Not sure. I thought I might talk to Lilly Billings first and get a look at everything on that disc and then decide."

"You have an assignment for me?" asked Norman.

"Just the usual support," she said, sliding the papers back into the folder and putting it back into her purse.

"Yours without asking," he said, sliding out of his seat, checking his watch.

"I have to get to court. How about if I pay for the coffee?"

"A gentleman as always. I have to run too. Catch up on some things at the office. Walk me to my car?"

Norman held out his arm and Wallis took it as they walked through the restaurant making their way to the cash register.

"You're not staying?" the waitress asked Norman as they neared the front.

"No, onto other things," he said, "good coffee, though."

Wallis smiled and stepped aside as a middle aged man in a business suit tried to get by her.

"S'cuse me," he muttered, as he slid between Norman and Wallis, heading back toward a booth in the small atrium off to the side.

Wallis shrugged and said to Norman, "This must be the hot spot for meetings."

"I forgot to leave a tip," Norman said, "I'll be right back." He walked quickly in the direction of where they had been sitting and turned, disappearing around the corner.

A small woman in a blue business suit who had been sitting in the other row of booths got up, draping her coat over her arm and quickly approached Wallis.

"No good can come of what you're doing," she hissed at Wallis. "You're only an incidental."

"What?" Wallis was caught off-guard and quickly looked around for Norman. "What are you talking about?"

"No good can come of it. It's a much larger web than even the Black Widow is used to, let it go," she said and turned for the door, quickly walking out to the parking lot.

Wallis leaned against the counter, trying to make herself calm down, suddenly feeling clammy.

Norman came strolling back up but picked up his pace when he saw Wallis.

"You okay? What happened?"

"A woman, she told me to let it go. Said, no good can come of it."

Norman looked all around. "What woman?"

"She headed for the parking lot," said Wallis, running outside quickly followed by Norman. "She's gone. She must have really been moving."

"Did she threaten you?" said Norman, putting his arm around Wallis.

"Not exactly, but it felt like a threat."

"What did she look like?"

"Our age, shorter than me, brown hair. Pretty non-descript Richmond white woman," she said, frustrated. "This must have been how Ray Billings felt trying to explain all of this to Lilly." Wallis looked down at her purse still swinging off of her arm. "The file! The file is gone! Do you see it?"

"No, I'll check inside. You okay out here?"

"Yes, go, go. I'll be okay."

Norman took the few steps back to the Shoney's in a run, his silk tie fluttering up over his shoulder, leaving Wallis by herself in the parking lot.

Wallis looked around at the parked cars trying to see if anyone was huddled down inside one of them. She took a few steps out further into the lot, trying to shake the feeling of being watched.

"Not there," said Norman, running up next to her, a little out of breath.

"I put it in my purse, I know I did. I couldn't have lost it in the past five minutes."

"Maybe we should call the police," said Norman.

"What are we reporting? Stolen paperwork? Rude strangers?" Wallis was getting angry, something she rarely did. She knew she had no control over what was happening, no way to get control.

"Try to take a deep breath, Wallis. You still have the drive?"

"Yes, I think so, it's here," she said, pulling the small race car out of her purse. "But that damn file."

"There must be something," said Norman, rubbing the back of his head, looking out toward West Broad Street.

"I know one damn thing I'm going to start with," said Wallis. "I'm going to stop playing by their rules and make up some of my own."

"What does that mean?"

Wallis' cell phone started ringing. She dug it out of her purse and looked at the caller I.D. It was Stanley Woermer. Before she could answer the ringing stopped.

"It was Stanley," she said to Norman, calling the number back. "No one's answering. He made a point of saying he was never going to call me. Something must be wrong."

"Do you know where he lives?"

"No, but I think I can come up with the address," said Wallis.

"Call Alan, let him check it out first," said Norman. Alan Vitek was a former Navy Seal with his own investigative firm and was a regular consultant for the more complicated cases at Weiskopf, Jones and Bremmer.

"Okay, okay."

"You want me to follow you to the office?"

"Have we ever done that before?" asked Wallis. "No, no, I'll be okay. They were just trying to scare me."

"I'm afraid it's working," said Norman.

Wallis looked at Norman and realized he was still breathing hard. "You're really worried, aren't you? That can't be good if a Weiskopf is sweating. They're very good, Norman, whoever they are. If I didn't have you, I'm not sure I'd be able to find anyone else who would believe any of this. It's like someone is trying to chip away at me."

Norman walked Wallis to her car and hugged her tight, waiting by the car as she drove off, turning back out onto Broad Street. She gave him a wave and watched him get smaller in the rear view mirror. It wasn't until she got back to the office and went to take her brief case out of the back seat that she saw it. Carefully scratched into the paint on the other side of the car was a small spider inside of a tight circle of stars with a line cut diagonally through the middle.

CHAPTER

TOM Weiskopf sat outside of the local coffee shop in downtown New Berlin, nestled in Waukesha County, Wisconsin taking quickly glances down at his iPhone waiting for the transmission that came every day at this time. Top of the hour every afternoon at four o'clock central time.

New Berlin was former farm country that had reluctantly become a suburb back in the 1970's to accommodate a white flight while still managing to hold on to some of its old rural identity.

Everyone knew who you were, what you did and what you had done to someone else. That kind of broad-based knowledge made it harder to hold a grudge and easier to forgive most transgressions. It also meant that after enough years had passed and Tom had ingratiated himself into the community he could ask for help, no questions asked, and there would be plenty of people at the ready.

There were very few lapel pins in this territory from either side of the dangerous game.

Here, everyone was still related to everyone else unlike the New South where a steady stream of outsiders had made it easier all across the Bible Belt for Management to move in and start scouting out new recruits at the elementary school and warm up to parents at local civic groups.

Tom saw the potential in New Berlin when he first arrived back in 1987. He drove up West Main Street in a beaten up blue Ford E-150 van and saw the subtle glances from everyone in town. He knew they'd pass the word quickly that a suspicious looking character had arrived. That made it a perfect staging area. The next few years were spent joining the biggest local church, Church of the Redeemer, swinging a hammer on the annual volunteer repair crew for elderly folks around town and hanging out at the spring fish fries until he was accepted as one of their own.

He knew he was on the inside the afternoon someone arrived in town and the local gossip quickly reached him at the coffee shop.

It was a perfect system.

Tom looked at the clock hanging in the store window across the street as the local Presbyterian Church tower pealed off four loud bongs from a prerecorded CD. His iPhone quickly converted the series of three-numbered transmissions it was receiving into a short message.

'The Citizens of each State...'

He felt his throat tighten as the prelude spilled onto the small screen.

What's gone wrong, he thought, as he tried to make himself take a deep breath and relax back into the chair.

The phone was a fully functioning computer that had been adapted to do double duty as a hand-held radio receiver with an XOR operation to make moments like this less conspicuous. Tom was receiving a sudden burst transmission from a numbers stations far away, which was used to get a message out quickly to everyone in cells spread out across the country. Different times of day were assigned to different operational cell levels.

Anyone could pick up the signals but unless they also had the right thumb drive with the OTP, the electronic one-time-pad with the decoded encryptions to the random pairings, it meant nothing. No level of cells possessed another level's OTP.

The system could not be broken unless one of the drives fell into Management's hands and they were able to discover the hidden algorithms underneath the music tracts or word documents that were carefully laid over the sets of numbers or letters. If a drive were found by anyone other than a member of the Circle or Management they'd overlook its real importance.

Transmissions usually began with the opening lines from one of the twenty-seven Amendments to the Constitution, which was meant as a signal that the message was either nonsensical or mundane, depending on the chosen amendment. Reams of them were sent out each week as cover and to crowd the airwaves, making detection of just where the transmitters were more difficult. Only a handful of the transmissions were of any value and most were updates on possible activity by people of interest, nothing more.

Tom had gotten used to seeing the words fly by and had seen most of the amendments so often he had almost memorized the text over the years.

But this time was going to be different. The broadcast began with the opening lines to Article IV, Section 2 of the Constitution.

'... shall be entitled to all Privileges and Immunities of Citizens in the several States. A Person charged in any State with Treason, Felony, or other Crime, who shall flee from Justice, and be found in another State, shall on Demand of the executive Authority of the State from which he fled, be delivered up, to be removed to the State having Jurisdiction of the Crime.'

It was an opening Tom had never seen on his phone before and had hoped to never see. The carefully laid out plans that had been meticulously cultivated for the past sixty years by the Circle were in danger of being exposed. Management had detected a thumb drive and may already be in possession of the encryptions. If they had identified a handler and their family in a high enough cell it was possible that torture had exposed other key players. The inner American Circle may already be in danger.

No new faces had recently arrived in town but Tom instantly began to wonder if he was being watched. The short message took less than a minute to download and unscramble before being immediately dumped after sprawling across the screen. He couldn't afford to take his eyes off of the phone for very long to check his surroundings.

'Richmond, Virginia. SOS009 Leave immediately.'

"Hey, Tom, why so serious?"

Tom jerked the phone, his thumb instinctively jamming down on the off button as the screen faded to black. He looked up into the fading sun at the face of his elderly neighbor, Wilbur Vernon, dressed in faded overalls and a Deere hat tilted down toward his nose. His lined face and curved shoulders gave away that he'd spent too many seasons hunched over a crop, willing it out of the ground.

"Hey Wilbur, just looking at the news crawl. Probably shouldn't do it, just pulls me into a mess that doesn't really have anything to do with me."

"Know what you mean. My TV gets a hundred channels, makes me feel like I ought to watch a few of 'em. Suddenly I'm worried about Chinese wheat crops till I remember I don't grow wheat no more and I never sold to foreigners no how. Fancy phone you got there. I remember when they couldn't even get moved around in the house," said Wilbur, who was already walking away.

Tom slowly let out a breath as he called out, "Point taken, Wilbur. Maybe it's time for a rest." He was already laying the groundwork for leaving town without raising any suspicions.

Wilbur raised his hand in a salute but kept walking.

SOS009 was a direct communiqué to Tom to head back to his old hometown. It stood for Survivors of the Original Solution with Tom's designation as a member of the top cell, number nine out of the twenty. They had earned their way into the inner circle by surviving the slaughter of the original plan. The original strategy had been put into motion across Europe in 1918 after the First World War. Its origins were with German Jews who had faithfully served the Kaiser only to watch him sell out to the ever-growing menace which had nicknamed itself the

Management.

Many of them had seen what happened in the pogroms of Russia and were determined to see a different outcome this time. Jewish residents of Berlin banded together and spread the word through the synagogues. They would create their own network and call it the Circle or Kreise.

Norman's grandfather, Tom, held some of the first meetings in his parlor. But Management had found out about the plan and came up with a solution to their problem. It began across Germany in November of 1938 with Kristallnacht and by the time it was over in 1945 most of the original members had died in camps or as part of the underground.

The SOS, as they came to be called, escaped with their lives, erasing enough of their heritage to go undetected as the remnants of the first great design to overthrow the Management. Only twenty members remained and one of them was Tom' son and namesake. He took his young wife and left immediately for America with the help of some unusual allies.

By 1942 a new plan started to evolve and right underneath the noses of everyone who had conspired to murder the Circle. The twenty young men and women who had survived the Holocaust were smuggled to America through an underground created by a chain of sympathetic Episcopalian nuns and priests. Together the twenty vowed to build again and learn from their mistakes.

Management was learning from its past mistakes as well. They had learned to coat their threats with promises of power and money and began working with smaller governments in other countries, creating bands of insurgents when they ran into too much opposition. A vast system eventually grew over the past decades until it was difficult for anyone but the few at the top to know just how far Management's reach extended. Most members of either side assumed it was everywhere.

That was when the Circle looked for a new entity to cultivate that was disregarded by Management and seen by them as useless and beyond saving.

Management's greatest weakness had always been their inability to see that those with nothing to lose could still believe in something better.

The Circle knew that and laid the groundwork to foster and care for the misbegotten as they built a new counter of force that could spread across the globe.

The plan quietly grew as they waited patiently for two generations to grow older and relinquish their power. Management grew as well, infecting every government across the globe until they believed the fight was all but over. As far as they knew, the Circle had been contained and was seen as an ineffective nuisance.

Tom was to go and see his handler, the number two member of The Circle.

Things must be bad, he thought, to risk putting anyone from the top twenty within shouting distance of each other. He turned his phone back on and hit the speed dial.

"Wallis? It's your favorite brother in law, Tom. I'm coming for a visit. Need to relax a little, away from the busy streets of New Berlin. You got room for one more?"

Wallis hung up the phone, wondering what that was about. Tom rarely left Wisconsin as far as she knew. She went in search of Norman to tell him the string of strange occurrences hadn't ended just yet.

"It's not even a holiday," she mumbled, trying to recall if Yom Kippur was imminent.

"Does your brother, Tom celebrate Jewish holidays?" asked Wallis. Norman was sitting at the kitchen table poring over the local paper. The sections were spread out as if he were sampling from each one, simultaneously.

"What? Not that I recall. That was a good one. Normally, your questions have a lot more to do with something relevant."

Wallis smiled and raised an eyebrow. "They still do. I'm far too practical to start asking for random bits of information. If that's what I wanted I'd read the local paper too."

Norman didn't look up but Wallis thought she detected the faint beginnings of a smirk.

"Okay, I'll bite. Why the interest in Tom's eternal soul or what's left of it?" said Norman.

"He called and said he's coming for a visit. I was trying to figure out the why."

Norman looked up from the paper.

"Now, that is interesting. You didn't ask Tom why he was gracing us with a visit?"

"I don't like to ask questions when I don't already know the answer," said Wallis, laughing. "That and he hung up too quickly. The whole, Tom leaving Wisconsin thing caught me off guard. Plus, I didn't want him to think we weren't delighted at the thought of seeing him."

"Which we are," said Norman, as he went back to scanning the business page for a small classified ad buried in the announcements. Underneath a grainy photo of a local print shop was the phone number that ended in the sequence, 680. Norman slowly sat back and let out a long breath. All hell is breaking loose, he thought. Not again.

CHAPTER 18

MARK Whiting was never a stupid man. He knew from his early days in training with the Circle that the Richmond Federal Reserve was the key to the entire U.S. banking system. It controlled all of the information technology for the entire banking system. Mark was aware of that when he arrived on the Reserve's doorstep in 1993 at the dawn of the internet age.

The Circle had given him the assignment to take his prodigious talents as a software specialist and offer them to Management.

Management knew who he was, of course. He had originally been one of their children and was seen as a boy genius who was being groomed for bigger things. That was all before he grew disenchanted and crossed the aisle. Mark was smart enough to know that he couldn't leave the game altogether but perhaps he could find a different team.

However, massive organizations that are old and entrenched have massive egos. That led Management to believe they still understood him and could therefore use him, all the while keeping watch over him as he toiled away in one of their offices using all of their bugged equipment.

Every keystroke he made was recorded and analyzed by their spyware for the thousands of potential security problems.

Over the years he had moved up in ranks and was now the Senior Technology Architect responsible for maintaining the software that directed the Fedwire Securities Service's business strategy and personally managed the processing infrastructure.

He was a small but very important cog in the pipeline of data that was translated to all of the central banks and beyond.

It was perfect for his unique retirement plan that wasn't sanctioned by either side.

Mark had grown tired of the cat and mouse game a long time ago. Let the two giants conspire for power, he thought. He had decided years ago to find a way to bow out without death being a necessary element.

He had watched what happened to other Circle families who had tried to maintain their family's security and their integrity. Their children were slowly drawn into the family business and became part of the war. More than once he had questioned what the difference was between the Management's recruitment and this insidious pull by the Circle. Neither side seemed to have much of any choice about their lives. Things would be different for his small sons and little girl. It was enough that his wife had left him a long time ago without looking back. She had wanted to be free of all of the responsibility and had left it all to Mark. That was fine with him. He loved being a father but he wanted to make sure his family got a real chance at a normal life.

However, successfully pulling away would require a large influx of cash that could go unnoticed and not get traced back to him or cause too many questions. That was the hard part.

It required staying very close to the heartbeat of Management's central technology operations and choosing his targets very carefully. But it was imperative to his plan that the Circle not catch on either till it was too late.

Timed correctly, they were more likely to just cut him loose if they could already see that it didn't threaten any of their own plans.

The last year had been a bloody one for Management and they were becoming more aggressive. Several of their puppet dictators were murdered although Mark wasn't sure which side was doing the shooting. However, he realized he was growing older and more wary and it was time. He decided to put his plan into action.

Besides, unrest always made the large giant restless for reform by force, if necessary. Wars usually followed and new, stricter regulations would be put into place. He had to act now so that his small change in the infrastructure would become usual, routine by the time new eyes would be scanning the records.

He planted into the software accounting code a small error that only randomly occurred, shaving off less than a penny from accounts that were trading money. Any bank on the watch list from the old Soviet Socialist Union, the Middle East or South America was left out of the plot. Once the money from any of those countries rose over $5,000 someone might have noticed and thought it was part of a money laundering plot. But funds coming to or from almost any other country were left out of the scrutiny and the small and steady drain would go by unnoticed amongst the billions of trades.

Trades were set up by Mark to only be done with foreign currencies, which were also subject to the fluctuating exchange rates, further masking detection. Monies from the process were then diverted through multiple foreign accounts before winding up in a series of accounts known only to Mark.

If he was successful, by the time he was done he would be able to retreat with a few million dollars. Not enough to warrant the Circle chasing him down but enough to keep his family safe on a Montana ranch near the Canadian border. He was starting to see how it all might even come together by the fall. The money was already stockpiled for the most part but he was making sure he'd found the right piece of property. There would only be one chance to get it right. Everything was lining up perfectly.

"Please, I hope so," he whispered, not sure who he was praying to but hoping God was listening anyway.

It was easy to get around Management's detection system. It turned out that they had been right about him all along. He was naturally gifted when it came to the cyber world and he used the inherent weaknesses of technology to his advantage. His growing portfolio spread out over several banks continued to go unnoticed by everyone.

Mark stood in his quiet kitchen and watched the daily message come up on his iPhone. The sun was just cresting the suburban rooftops visible from his kitchen window. Everyone in his household was still asleep.

His day always started early with a wakeup call from a distant numbers station. This morning's transmission began with Article I, Section 4.

'The Times, Places and Manner of holding Elections for Senators and Representatives, shall be prescribed in each State by the Legislature thereof.'

It was a warning from an unseen Circle cell. Security had been breached and the Management was aware of an opportunity. The message was brief.

'Protect Robert, begin Kirchenfenster operation', was the entire message. So the upper cells knew the two men had made contact. But why was Robert so important?

"Hello, Robert? This is Mark. You still need a ride to the boys' soccer game?"

They had run into each other two more times since the initial gathering around the coffee cart just one week ago. Once in the hallways of the Federal Reserve and once back down on the plaza. Robert had let loose just enough information to give Mark something to work with if he ever needed an excuse to meet. That was basic training.

"Great, pick you up in an hour."

Mark set to work on the other half of the message, the Kirchenfenster operation or Stained Glass Operation. Certain top members of the Circle had German roots that went very deep. It was an old plan meant to create mistrust and misinformation and was much more effective than outright aggression. Those who keep secrets and lie as a matter of habit tend to worry too much about who else is lying and when they detect a flaw, they start to question everything and make mistakes. It was a far more effective method to bring down an enemy than bombs or guns.

Mark had no way of knowing how many others were responding to the same message. No one was ever told who received the same OTP or whose iPhones weren't just phones. It wasn't the first time he'd been asked to create confusion but there was an added urgency. He picked up the land line and dialed.

"Hello Fred? How are you? Hope I didn't wake you. Just wanted to check on you. Everything okay?"

Mark was using Fred as bait. He knew Fred was a weak link and calling him at an irregular time would only make him worry more, become more conspicuous. A land line made it easier for eavesdroppers to suddenly be following him making the rest a lot simpler. It wasn't fair to Fred but some people are only pawns, thought Mark. Fred had never accepted that death was a possibility and it made him more of a target, not less. Mark was well aware, though that he was just a more arrogant but equally as helpless player, at least for now.

"Okay, well, see you on Monday. Let's get coffee."

He hung up before Fred had a chance to vent. That would make him more likely to talk to his wife, make a mistake and continue to be overheard. But Fred didn't know anything of value. All he could do was speculate about what was going wrong within the Circle and inadvertently plants seeds of mistrust in anyone who was listening.

Step one was done. Step two was a quick search on Google for information about Cardinal Group, the largest credit card company in America laying people off in early 2001. He found the article he was searching for and called it up, clicking on 'recommend', just as he had been directed. It was a small column that predicted a decline in the stock without giving too many details that pointed out it was from nearly ten years ago. Management would soon wonder who was targeting one of their giant cash cows and start to look for answers, misdirecting them away from Circle operations.

The third step required a little funding but that would have to wait for Monday. He gathered up the kids and headed out to pick up Robert and his boys.

"Hello," he called out. The boys came running happily toward the minivan, piling into the back. Robert got in front, reminding his kids to buckle up and quiet down a little.

"Inside voices, boys," he said. "Thanks for the ride, greatly appreciated."

"No problem, we were headed there anyway," said Mark. "Diana has the day off today. I think she's headed to the mall with some friends. You know which fields your boys are playing on today?"

They were headed to a vast open field of ten acres along Pouncey Tract Road that had been developed into a soccer complex dotted by different soccer fields with the occasional refreshment stand. Both men knew better than to try and start a conversation in front of their children. It could place the boys' lives in danger under normal circumstances and after the warnings Mark was getting he was taking every precaution.

"I think our fields abut each other," said Robert. "We can stand in the middle and cheer for both."

Once the boys were settled along the various sidelines the fathers took up camp between the two fields where they had a clear view of both matches. Mark took out his phone and scrolled through the screens, quickly turning on the low level white noise.

"How are things these days?" he asked as his son waved to him from the center of the field. Mark smiled and waved back at him.

"Not good. I suppose you've wondered about my wife's death."

"It's crossed my mind."

"Carol was not only an expert at sailing, she was also a strong swimmer. My wife was murdered."

"What did the autopsy show?"

"That she had drowned." Robert looked down at his shoes. Mark let a little time pass, watching his oldest in the soccer game as the two younger ones ran up and down the sidelines.

"Do you know anything more than that?" asked Mark.

"There was no toxicology report, no blood tests done. Her lungs were filled with water and they stopped at that. But, there were also no signs of a struggle. There was nothing to indicate that she fought like hell to stay alive."

"Why would they have wanted your wife dead?"

"I'm hoping that I don't really know the answer to that. If it's what I suspect we are all in a lot more danger and it's only a matter of time before I turn up as an accident as well. My wife was an orphan of sorts. She grew up on an orphanage, anyway. Did you know that most of the children who have ever grown up on an American orphanage were only social orphans? They had a close, living relative but not one who could take care of them or maybe wanted them. That was Carol's story. Her mother died and her father couldn't take care of Carol or her two younger sisters. They all ended up at an orphanage."

Robert's son scored a goal and was doing a small dance that resembled a chicken. Robert smiled and yelled, "Good job, son!" Mark waited patiently for him to go on with his story.

"Her father dropped all contact when Carol was nine and went on with his life but refused to sign away his rights as a parent. That made Carol and her siblings' part of this vast, lost generation that had no family to speak of but couldn't be adopted. That's when she was taken into the Schmetterling Project," said Robert, looking up at Mark.

"What are you talking about?" asked Mark, a little too loudly. "That idea was dropped," he hissed, "a long time ago."

"No, it was put into action but all references to it were dismissed and then destroyed, or so we thought. One Holocaust was enough."

Mark remembered the idea from when he first came into the Circle. Even then it was already just a legend of something that was bandied about but eventually discarded as too risky.

"Then how do you know about it?"

"Carol's maiden name was Baumann. Her father was one of the original twenty."

Mark glanced back at Robert. "That explains a little bit about why the Circle wants to protect you."

"So you got an order? I'm not surprised. I know a lot about the grand scheme to collect as many children as possible worldwide. The Circle looked for children who were either tangled in social services or left to fend for themselves and helped them eventually get placed at orphanages. These would become the new recruits to infiltrate every aspect of governments, Fortune 500 Corporations, large non-profit organizations. It was devised as a vast web identifiable only by where someone started out in life."

"But why wouldn't the Circle want to keep you quiet?"

"Because they don't know if I left a record and because in some cells murder is still seen as a sin."

"Lucky for both of us."

It was a vague reference to the continued influence of both the Anglican and Jewish hierarchy.

The Schmetterling Project was supposed to beat Management at its own scheme but it had also become a lesson in humility.

The Circle had been looking for inroads since its inception and understood the Management's distaste for anyone they couldn't use. It was what the original members from the European Jewish community had harnessed to their advantage, that is, until they were detected.

But by then their foothold was so strong the Circle was sure they would be able to persevere. The mistake had cost them well over six million lives, most of them completely unaware of the cause. Management had wanted to be thorough.

"No, it's not right" whispered Mark. "It's not possible. Orphanages in this country were closed back in the 1980's."

"You haven't been paying enough attention. Most closed or morphed into rehabilitation centers, you're right, but the rest were given the new name of residential education facility. They started billing themselves as more of a boarding school for the underprivileged. A new name and an old mission that only the head of each home was aware of. They were told to aggressively stay away from the media and even each other. Drop below any kind of radar. Most stopped taking public money for that reason."

Mark felt his stomach sour. As cynical as he was, he didn't want to believe that the Circle was willing to use children just because there were no parents around keeping track. Apparently he had been wrong. It made the mathematician in him start to recalculate all of the other risks.

"Why did you keep paying attention?" he asked.

"Even though Carol's father burned out from all of the stress, Carol was still a part of that dynasty, which I believe is what put her in the line of fire. That means my children have the same bull's-eye on them. You see, I don't think she was murdered just because of her involvement with the Circle. I think someone figured out her background."

"I'm not sure which one is worse," said Mark, "both'll get you killed."

"And if I'm right, and they have figured it out, there may be other methods for Management to figure out who was raised within the ideals of the Circle."

"The records at the children's homes," mumbled Mark, feeling a chill come over him.

A sudden hush came over the field where Robert's sons were playing and adults rushed to the sidelines. A parent had collapsed and was lying on the ground as concerned faces all turned toward the growing crowd. The news rolled out over the ten acres quickly as game after game paused and parents called after curious children who were trying to get closer.

"Grab your son, now!" said Mark as he quickly switched off his phone. He didn't look back as he marched quickly toward his own two boys never taking his eyes off of them. As he got to Jake he grabbed his hand firmly and kept staring straight ahead at Peter. It would only take a moment, he thought. Once Peter's hand was safely wrapped inside his father's, Mark turned and scanned the growing crowd in the opposite field.

It has to be a set up, he thought. Robert and his sons were nowhere to be seen. Mark dialed the number quickly but it went immediately to voicemail. The phone was turned off. He searched the fields for over an hour on foot never letting go of his boys' hands. He finally had to give up and quietly put the boys in the van, slowly driving up and down the narrow road that wound through the acreage hoping for a sign.

There was nothing.

As he pulled out of the complex he saw Richard Bach standing by the entrance pretending to shoot him with a gun, a wide grin across his face. It was all he could do to keep from trembling in front of his boys.

CHAPTER 19

NORMAN stood in the parking lot watching Wallis' car pull out into traffic and saw the scratches in the Jag at the last moment. He thought about calling her on the cell phone, but he knew she'd see it soon enough.

He had come close to telling her over coffee about their neighbor's demise but saw how rattled she already was and decided to wait until tonight. After seeing the symbol etched into her car he was glad he kept silent. This would only unnerve her further and make her wonder about the significance of the timing. Norman wasn't ready to tell her.

He checked the trunk and saw that the mat from the back door wrapped in heavy plastic was still there.

"Donald?" he said into his cell phone.

"Yeah, you busy? Something's come up. We need to talk. No, the usual place. Let's avoid the office."

Norman and Pastor Donald had set up alternate meeting places long ago that were out in the open where they could go mostly unnoticed.

It would have been difficult in Richmond to find someplace where they wouldn't run into someone who recognized them and if it looked clandestine word would have travelled fast. Better to find a haunt close to home that looked like a break from work. The parking lot of Panera's was a good choice.

"You had to wear the collar?"

"It's company policy," said the priest, "kind of like being a Rockette."

"Episcopalian humor, no doubt," said Norman.

"Which is why we get along so well, Mr. Weiskopf. We both have these highly developed frameworks for what's funny that involve the longer view of anything."

"I assume you're referring to eternity."

The Reverend took a sip of his coffee, letting the conversation drop for a moment.

"My brother, Tom is coming for a sudden visit," said Norman.

"Is that so?"

"I'm assuming you already knew about it."

"Did you call me here to check my social calendar?"

"The force is disturbed," said Norman.

"Star Wars reference in the middle of all this. I like it."

"Both sides seem to be a little testy right now." Norman glanced up at his friend, squinting. "My wife has gotten drawn into it."

"Ah, at last we're getting to the point."

"A neighbor of mine, an innocent old man was killed this week while walking his dog in our sleepy little subdivision."

"Larry Blazney, yes, I heard. Very unfortunate."

"That sums it up in an understated sort of way. It appears they picked him up in front of my house. Did you hear that as well?"

The old priest didn't react and kept sipping his coffee. Norman gave the back of his head a quick, nervous pat.

"Who were they really after, Don?"

"Not who, so much as what. They believe Wallis has something of interest, so do we."

"Why is that?"

"Ray Billings and his apparent suicide. I got the chance to see the corpse before he was abruptly cremated. For a suicide he really took the hard way out of here. His wife, Lilly is a good Episcopalian, you know. The official cause of death put us in quite a pickle, even the Episcopalians balk at taking your own life. We decided to focus more on the apparent side of things and give him the burial he really deserved. You know, Ray told quite a few people to get in touch with Wallis if anything happened to him. Do you know why that is?"

Norman let out a deep sigh. "No, and I'm really beginning to take a dislike to this Ray Billings. His good buddy, Stanley Woermer showed up on our doorstep looking for Wallis. What is it everyone is looking for?" asked Norman.

He was a good lawyer, never asking a question he didn't already know the answer to. They wanted the thumb drive.

But Norman was part of the original line descended from the zwanzig and had been taught well. Trust no one completely, ever.

"Never hate the dead, Norman, bad karma," said the Pastor. "What, a priest can't make a religion joke? You look a little tired, Norman. This has been a long week and it's only the first of many. A war has started or at least come out in the open and like it or not, Wallis has been enlisted. She just doesn't know it yet, or does she?"

The Reverend looked up from his cup.

"No, she doesn't really know. I was hoping to never tell her."

"Yes, your father told me about your reluctance. I have always thought it was foolish. Knowledge is power."

"It's also a manipulation."

"Very true and there is no avoiding that paradigm but better to be aware you are being manipulated than to walk into a trap, completely blind.

Get some rest, you're going to need it, particularly when Tom comes to town."

A white paneled van drove slowly past them taking the corner and turning out onto West Broad Street.

"Things are never going to be the same around here, I fear," said Pastor Donald as he watched the van gather speed. "The usual checks and balances are quickly falling away. People are starting to become desperate and old ties may soon come loose."

"You think that van was a warning, don't you?"

"It was at the very least a small courtesy. I had better go. We have been standing here long enough to exchange simple pleasantries." The Reverend turned to get back into the black Lincoln Continental that had the name, St. Stephen's in small gold scroll under the driver side handle.

Norman leaned back against his car and waited for the Minister to start the engine. Pastor Donald put down his window and leaned out a little. "Oh, by the way, just so you know, some young zwanzig went missing earlier today with their father. The mother is sadly already dead in another apparent suicide and after she had struggled so much as a child. She had been left a kind of orphan, you see." The Pastor gave Norman a long look as he pulled away.

Norman waited until the Minister had pulled away in traffic till he placed a call to Alan Vitek. He was beginning to feel like things were slipping out of his control.

"Alan, I have a job for you. I need you to go and check on a man named, Stanley Woermer. Just see what kind of condition he's in and get back to me. No, I don't have an exact address but he's an original Richmonder and with a name like that. Yes, call me as soon as you know."

Alan took the information and hung up without another question. He had been trained to ask as few questions as possible. Questions tended to muddy up the situation anyway.

Norman had been right. Stanley Woermer's address was easy to find. Native Richmonders never tried to hide. It didn't matter if they were millionaires or thieves. It would have been bad manners.

Stanley lived over on Roseneath Road in an older suburb of Richmond not too far from the Fan district.

Alan parked a block away and slowly strolled toward the address. Parked out front was Wallis' Jag with the spider and the circle of stars with the line scratched on the side. He considered calling Norman back to give him a heads up but decided to find out more information first.

He approached the open door quietly and as he neared he could hear someone rooting around inside.

"Wallis?" He said it without concern, hoping she would be the one to emerge as his fingers lightly touched the gun strapped just under his jacket.

"Alan?" Wallis came out into the light with a look of surprise on her face. "Did Norman call you? He told me to let it go, but something is wrong. Stanley's not here." Her voice was strained, so unlike her.

"Why does that mean something's wrong?"

"Good point. I'm not sure I know the answer to that one," said Wallis, looking quickly around at the small mess she had made. Tucked under a small pile of newspapers she saw the travel book Stanley had carried out of the bookstore.

"Can you look for Stanley?" she asked Alan. "Till you find him?"

"Yes," he said, slowly. He had never seen Wallis so out of balance. "Absolutely. I'll make it a priority."

"Good, good." Wallis stepped around the piles on the floor as Alan came further into the room. "Until you find him," she said, "and then call me. Me," she said with emphasis, tapping her chest.

Wallis drove off toward Patterson Avenue playing a hunch. Esther was sitting behind the front desk in the bookstore carefully writing down all of the week's sales in an old bound composition notebook. She looked up as the bell jingled above the door and saw the look of concern on Wallis' face.

"It's Stanley, isn't it?"

"How did you know?" asked Wallis, hesitating for just a moment. She reached out to steady herself, placing a hand on top of a tall pile of children's books that were stacked on a table just inside the door. There were books piled on the two tables in the front room and on the floor nearby.

"Why else would you seek me out?" she said. "Is he alright?"

"I have no idea," said Wallis. "This is going to sound selfish but I came because I didn't know where else to go and I feel like the ground is slipping out from under me a little."

"Self preservation must come first, dear," said Esther, "otherwise the other side already has the advantage. You do know there are two sides here, no?"

"I have no idea what you're talking about, Esther. Only that there are a few strange things going on and I have pitifully little information."

"I told them that was a mistake, keeping you out of the loop like that. No one listened."

"Who? Who wouldn't listen?"

Esther came from around the counter and locked the front door, turning the closed sign around and dimming the lights.

"Come with me inside this maze of books. There is a little genius to my style of housekeeping. No one will see or hear us in there, I am sure of it. I have taken precautions," she said with a wink.

Esther gently took Wallis' hand and led her back into the stacks till they were sitting in a little cove of books.

"Sit," said Esther, gesturing toward a small velvet loveseat. She stood in front of Wallis and began to pace the small space. "This is an old story. It's not generally worth telling because no one would ever believe it. It's brilliant really and so easy to dismiss."

"We're still talking about Stanley, aren't we?" Wallis was taking long deep breaths willing herself to calm down.

"Indirectly, yes. Normally, I would tell someone that Stanley got mixed up with the wrong characters and hint at some criminal element. People can understand that and they feel better. All is right with the world. But you, my dear, are in a unique situation and I like you, I always have. Yes, I've known who you are for quite some time. It's a small town and you are a big fish," she said, shrugging her shoulders. "Besides, it has always amazed me how you can be in the middle of such a big plot and know absolutely nothing. It's breathtaking really and I don't mind admitting just a little envy. I was actually hoping Norman was right this time."

Wallis sat up at the mention of her husband. "Norman? You know about Norman. What does he have to do with any of this?"

"Now, now, no need for anger although it's touching. Norman sits at the center of this too, but very reluctantly. You see, he is a second generation zwanzig, descended from one of the twenty survivors, but with a twist. I know all of this means nothing to you, my dear and sweet Norman hoped to keep it that way. But things have changed and not for the better."

Esther settled into the seat next to Wallis and took both of her hands.

"Money corrupts nothing but power infects like a virus and can only be contained, never completely destroyed. For centuries that power was centralized in monarchies that ruled all of the civilized world and there was some order to everything. At least the greed and manipulation was out in the open. But times changed and the old orders were coming apart. Those in power weren't going to let something like a revolution or a few beheadings separate them from the lifestyle they believed they deserved."

"Really?" said Wallis, annoyed. "You're really going to go back 200 years for this fairytale? Norman is caught up in a 200 year old power struggle?"

"See why it's so brilliant? But really, why wouldn't there be shenanigans going on behind all off the pomp and circumstance? And make no mistake my dear, you are just as caught as Norman."

"Why, because I'm a Republican?" said Wallis sarcastically.

Esther smiled. "No, my dear. Those parties, Democrat, Republican really are just games for the average citizen to play to distract them from realizing that so much has already been decided. Always remember that the most effective schemes are meant to inspire suspicion and cause a distraction. The election ads certainly fit that bill," said Esther. "Violence is always the move of someone who is truly panicked. Besides, the real manipulations go across all lines, including the artificial borders set up by governments and have more to do with the bloodlines that can't be chosen. That's what has caught you in its web and I'm afraid, Ned as well."

Wallis felt a shiver go down her back at the mention of her son. "What are you saying?"

"Ned is Norman's son as well, which makes him a zwanzig, a twenty and the other side is beginning to wonder about Norman's heritage. You see, Tom, Norman's grandfather, wanted to give his family a clean slate and made a point of destroying all records of where the family started. No one outside of the immediate family knew how close they came to being annihilated in Nazi Germany and no Weiskopf has ever mentioned it. The new back story was that they emigrated earlier. You believe your in-laws came to America long before the murderous rampage across Europe but that's a lie. But I'm getting ahead of myself and you will not understand if I don't fill in some missing pieces.

"Norman would never lie to me."

"Norman has been lying for so long I'm not sure he realizes anymore that it's not the truth. You see, back when this country was beginning to form there were two groups vying for power. One side believed in the old system of keeping all of the power for a few favored bloodlines and raising the subordinates that would be needed from a few trusted families. It was all they had ever known and of course they thought that was best. But a new spirit was gripping this country and there was a revolutionary idea that even a commoner should have the right to decide his own fate. It sounds commonplace now but really, it takes quite a bit of faith to believe that so many people will vote for the greater good, ever.

"It was a spectacular beginning, really, but it didn't last past the first few administrations. The other side, which came to be known colloquially as the Management learned how to ingratiate itself into power through the grassroots. They used an old method and tweaked it just a little. Soon all of those good intentions were slipping away, not only here but all across the world. Remember the old saying, the sun never sets on the British Empire? Technology only helped Management to grow. But there were still those who believed in a purer form of democracy and they were determined to be free. They have tried again and again but for an entire century all of them failed miserably. It is never good to come at a giant from the front. They step on you like an annoying bug. A new idea formed to infiltrate the seats of government and the financial world with a second set of eyes and ears and they became the Circle."

Esther pulled back one side of the cardigan she was wearing to reveal the small lapel pin with the circle of stars.

"That's scratched into the side of my car," said Wallis, feeling her heart beating faster. "There's a line scratched through the middle."

"Yes, a warning, I'm not surprised. Does Norman know?"

"He was with me when it happened. Someone stole a file I had in my purse."

Esther grasped Wallis' hands tighter. "They got the file? What was in it, what exactly? Did they get anything else?" she hissed, spitting out the words in a rapid fire.

"No, no," Wallis stammered, "It was a BIGOT list, that's all, I think, as far as I know."

"Who told you that word, BIGOT?"

"Some strange man with an accent tried to warn me last night. He said I was being followed, tracked somehow. He said his name was Helmut."

"I don't know him, best to be cautious. They are getting careless. My word, how much do they know?" said Esther. "Enough of an old woman's story. Here is what you really need to know. The first real effort against Management was at the beginning of the last century. The Circle chose a small European country, Armenia that interested no one. They had learned that it was better to go undetected as much as possible. But the Management learned of the effort to undermine them and sent in Turks from the great Ottoman Empire. It took only two years to kill one and a half million men, women and children and wipe Armenia off of the map forever." Esther stopped for a moment as she let out a deep sigh. Her entire body tensed as she looked down at her lap. "It was meant as a warning but the Circle didn't listen and tried again. The second attempt ended in a greater Holocaust. Ever since it seems the tug of war between the two sides, well…" She hesitated as if she were trying to figure something out. "Maybe all we accomplished was to play out our part in creating a wasteland across the twentieth century."

"What are you saying? That Hitler was part of this, what, Management?" said Wallis, almost at a shout.

"He was a clever and twisted part of a vast empire but in the end not welcomed even there. I'll grant you that there were those within his own organization that regretted ever helping him get elected. It has been the only time so far that Management has ended up warring with itself. It was heartening to see that even Management had its limits but a ruthless opportunity was seized at the same time to wipe out a problem. Millions of people died, many of them had nothing to do with the Circle but they paid as well. Management couldn't be sure and they weren't taking any chances. However, not all of the Circle perished."

"The twenty."

"Yes, the zwanzig. Twenty young men and women who managed to escape to this country and start anew. By that time they had new allies as well. The Armenian atrocity had enlightened others to the greater good as well, like that uprising in India and Gandhi. But in the end he paid for his efforts as well, didn't he? But there were those who joined together and formed a larger Circle. Management was aware of the possibility of a new threat and as distasteful as they found anyone from that horrible Nazi regime they helped many of them escape as well. Right next door to us in fact, in South America. It was a policy of keep your enemies closer and in this case, I suppose, both elements were suspect."

"The list in that file. The list someone stole from me today, this Management stole, it was a list of boys' names, some of them boys I know. What was it? And there were numbers after each name," said Wallis.

"Some of them are Management's newest recruits. If that's all they got from you they must be very disappointed tonight. The numbers are nothing, not to ponder at all," said Esther, patting her hand.

"Why is Ned in danger?"

"I like that about you, your focus. It will serve you well. Legacies and their ways die very hard and Management has always seen the blood line of the zwanzig as particularly dangerous. It's as if they believe there is something more powerful about what can be passed through DNA. We have worked hard to protect the lines and keep them a secret as much as possible but something has happened and I'm afraid we aren't sure exactly what. Some of their number has been thinned."

"That's a disgusting word for murder," said Wallis.

"Yes, it is. But if you are to at least stay alive in this game then you must see things from the same angle as your opponent. And they would see the zwanzig and all of their families as a poisoned herd with only one solution. Do not ever lull yourself into thinking that reasoning will be possible. If they have figured out that Norman is a zwanzig then you and Ned are in grave danger, which is why I don't believe they know that small fact just yet." Esther sat back, suddenly looking very tired. "Ray Billings did you no favors."

"Did he know?"

"I don't believe he did. He singled you out quite innocently for a completely different reason. He saw you as an honest lawyer," said Esther, with the beginning of a smile, "and a local girl. You see, it proves my point. Webs are very easy to weave and very difficult to break apart."

"How do you know so much?" said Wallis.

"Ah, at last, the question just as you have finally figured out the answer, correct? I am a zwanzig as well. The only one of my family to make it to America. I am not exactly Romanian as everyone believes. I am German, through and through."

Wallis heard the slight change in Esther's accent.

"Tom, your dear brother in law, is coming to see me. A war has begun and we would like to prevent another slaughter. You, my dear may be key to that."

"Me? How is that possible?"

"You not only hold information dear to the Circle but you are also a precious commodity to Management. It's brilliant really. It's why Norman was allowed to leave the cell he was in and settle down with you in the suburbs. Enough, though, eyes are watching and I'm sure they've seen your car outside by now. You must go home. Talk to Norman and he will tell you the rest."

"I have Bunko tonight," said Wallis, almost to herself. "I have to go."

CHAPTER 20

25 steps from the small basement office at the bottom of the B-ring and a left turn to the wide stairs straight up near the entrance of the Pentagon. Heel, toe, heel, toe. Turn right and walk a hundred steps down the hallway, through the security turnstiles and out the glass double doors to the South parking lot. One minute flat, he thought, looking down at his watch, and he was standing by his car.

Fred Bowers counted each step, every time, willing himself to remember which role he was playing today.

Every year he thought it might get easier but after twenty years he realized he was at a baseline. Counting the steps, finding a pattern made the transition between the two worlds bearable. He was a mole within his own country, even within his own organization.

At the dawn of the internet the Circle became a little more like Management and grew wary of its own members. To quell the uneasy feeling the zwanzig created deeper cells within the structure that were hidden from everyone else.

Fred was tagged as the perfect recruit to be of service to the upper echelon within the Circle and overnight he was split into two distinct lives. One was spent as a forensic accountant located in the James Center in downtown Richmond, Virginia and the other was as an Assistant Director in the Department of Defense as a part of the Senior Executive Service corps with an office inside of the Pentagon.

The dual roles were like having an affair with a passionate, out of control woman and going home to her controlling, murderous sister. The two sides are related and both need you but there are boundaries. Beyond them he was very expendable.

The first role required him to be the good family man and capable lawyer who was always the follower attracting attention for the nervous fear that seemed to cling to him. In this persona he was the low-level member of the Circle who was never entrusted with anything of importance. Neither side saw him as much of a threat, only a pawn.

The other role was closer to the truth. He was serving in a top cell stripped of anything but the duties at hand. It was a role that measured every thought, every action and every word out of his mouth and always with a glance at the bigger picture.

He saw himself as a necessary part of the game at hand but he was also keenly aware that parts can always be replaced.

He had accepted that death was a likely part of the mission a long time ago when he was sworn in to serve the highest elements in government that belonged to the Circle. Over the years the strata fluctuated, sometimes within a few heartbeats of the oval office. Once again, though one of their own was elected president and it was Fred's job to keep him informed.

Misinformation could advance an enemy plot far more than the threat of any missile and without the right kind of advisor at his side it would be very difficult for any president to know what to do.

Most of the struggle between the two giants was played out in the open. American members infiltrated both political parties, sat in both Houses and were sprinkled at the top of every major corporation. The lobbyists, however, were by far the most interesting group.

Their express purpose was to represent the will and intention of whoever was paying their tab but with a hard slant toward their team, Management or the Circle. They were the enforcers dressed up in very expensive suits who spent their days reminding legislators what happened to anyone who betrayed their cause. Management had the advantage in those moments and bared their teeth more openly. The Circle lobbyists always had to spin the story into what lives would be lost at the hands of the Management. But every Circle Senator or Congressman knew there were limits even within their own group.

Fred's life in the Washington area consisted of a small triangle that sometimes went from a small high rise apartment in Alexandria along Seminary Road to the Pentagon in Arlington to the White House along Pennsylvania Avenue and that was it. He had direct orders to never walk down the long halls in the Old Executive Office Building or the Capital or anywhere else he might be recognized. He never went out at night when he was in D.C. and the apartment where he stayed was kept clean and stocked full of food by an unseen member. He was never detected and slid easily in and out of town along the interstate.

While it was true that technology had made it possible for either side to locate and follow anyone, they first had to be aware they wanted to and Fred was not on Management's list. It was an impossible task to keep track of everyone and Fred's Richmond persona had made it clear that he wasn't valuable to the Circle and therefore to the other side. They never noticed his occasional weekend trips.

His wife, Maureen, was a Circle operative as well, put in place to give him cover. It was an arranged marriage of sorts but over the eighteen years they had been together they had grown to respect each other and were close friends. In all those years, however, they had never discussed the Circle or their real purpose, never slipping even when their heads lay inches from each other.

There was no mention to anyone when Fred slid out of town. On those weekends when Fred was gone, Maureen made a point of being seen puttering around the garden and stayed close to home. She joined only the groups that she was directed to in the encoded messages such as the neighborhood Bunko game or the large Episcopalian church, St. Tom located just down Pouncey Tract Road that was full of young families who were eager to get ahead.

She had been trained well and knew her purpose out in public was to establish common routines and tell stories about Fred in order to reinforce the outline that had been so carefully created right in front of everyone.

Both of them were filling out shadows of a suburban life and in that sense Maureen had the worst of it. There was never a break from the role she had been directed to play out until further notice. Fred sometimes looked at her and wondered if she minded or had she slipped somewhere in all of these years into the role so completely that she didn't know anything else anymore. The thought never lasted long though; it would have been a distraction.

Four hundred and thirty two steps, a short turn and then back, three hundred and eight steps, turn again all the while still heading straight. Two hundred and two more steps to get from the East Portico of the White House to the small elevator hidden behind the folding partition that was the official separation between the East and West wings. Each time a small distraction was timed to take place among the Secret Service who helped to turn away the few faces that may have wondered who he was and why he had access to the First Family's elevator right next to the old winding stairs that were used by past presidents such as Lincoln or Coolidge. Both lead up to the private quarters.

The family quarters was one of the only secure places left where only the team that held the presidential office knew exactly what was happening at any given moment.

To ensure discretion, whenever an administration changed sides every cook, every valet, every maid was let go and an entire new team was put into place. Even with that, extra precautions were taken whenever Bowers walked the halls.

Sixteen steps from the elevator to the front sitting room.

"Mr. President."

"Mr. Bowers, so good to see you, again." President Ronald Haynes was resting back against the cream colored couch. His famous head of thick, snow white hair stood out against the square linen cushion.

"At your service, sir." It was always the same greeting.

"Please, take a seat."

Bowers sat down on the edge of the Queen Anne wing chair and recited the information from memory. None of the short missives, the Special Compartmentalized Intelligence that Fred brought to the President were ever put down on paper.

"Operation Kirchenfenster has begun," said Fred.

"Ah, they do love their German names, even now, don't they?" said the President with a thin smile. "The Stained Glass Operation is again in play. We will work to confuse and deceive rather than come at them directly. But there's a difference this time, isn't there?"

"Yes, sir. We are at war." Bowers said it calmly and evenly, his voice never wavering.

"Yes, so it's official, then. A quiet war, though. Most of the people who walk the streets will never know. They may feel the repercussions but they'll never know what caused it all. It's very interesting, really. Any head of government, anywhere in the world really only gets to declare something is a war after those above him give him the go-ahead." Fred sat motionless waiting for a direct question.

"We look so powerful to the general public. Does it have an official name, this war?"

"No, sir, not at this time."

"It was bound to happen," said the President, with a sigh. "I knew that when they came to me and asked me to run for office. I saw the timing and what was coming. There was so much at stake. I'm surprised I made it into office. I was never sure that Management wouldn't find out or at least wonder. Good Lord, all you had to do was look at who was starting to fill our ranks, really look, and you could see the pattern."

"Yes, sir."

"So, we put the counter measures into play. Are the operatives on their way?"

"We were awaiting your approval," said Fred.

"You mean this office still has some actual power?" The President stopped to absently straighten out his blue silk tie. "Let it be so," he said, giving a nod. "Give them the authority to negotiate whatever they need to. We start with the MPLA in Angola, then Congo, Gabon, Cameroon and Niger."

"Yes, sir," said Fred, waiting for the president to wind down.

"It's a win-win, you know. I wanted to do this last year when I noticed China cozying up to the Sudan. They call it a mutual agreement and then use their land to grow crops but not one blade of wheat would stay in Africa. We may yet get to distribute the food across the continent where it belongs and gain a bargaining chip with China in the deal," said the President.

"If we don't then more than a few Africans are going to starve just a hundred yards from crops that will be shipped back to China but we'll still have our diversion," said Fred.

"An interesting dilemma, which is worse? This deception had better be worth it."

"Sir, if the wrong people found out what the Circle has been creating all of these years and right under their noses then a lot of innocent young lives will quickly pay the price."

"Mr. Bowers, the lives that may be lost in Africa are innocent as well."

"Yes sir, but exposure of the list would be enough to tip the balance of power too far into Management's hands. Millions more would die. And sir, I don't think we're going to come out of this war without some calculated loss."

The President looked up at Fred. "We are at war, aren't we, Fred? Sometimes I forget your military background. Alright, then, well, if we can distract the other powers that be enough to think we actually wanted the land rights I will live to be an old man, Mr. Bowers, God willing. If not, my reelection and my life will once again be in the hands of conniving mortals. No offense," he said, with a short laugh.

"No, sir."

"What is our next move?"

"We send over the agricultural engineers with the Special Forces Unit to start laying the groundwork, sir."

"And if there is resistance?" said the President.

"We are ready to negotiate in good faith, sir, but we will aggressively remove enough obstacles to make our intentions appear genuine."

"Have we pulled at Management's purse strings as well?"

"Yes sir, we are pushing down the value of the Cardinal Group as we speak and shorting the stock. Our deception won't last long but will let Management know that we are moving forward and can hurt them."

"Of course," said the President, slowly getting up and walking to the window. "Is that all, Mr. Bowers?" he said, looking out the window at the lawn in front of the north portico and the familiar front porch.

"No, sir, there is one more directive. One of the zwanzig, the special one, he may have been detected." The President jerked around to look at Bowers.

"You aren't sure? How is that possible with all of this technology?"

"Both sides are being very cautious, sir, very quiet, and there's a special circumstance."

"And that is?"

"A Circle OTP has gone missing. A drive that belonged to an upper level cell originating from the Mid-Atlantic. We believe it was taken from her dead body right after she was drowned."

"Mr. Bowers, this is turning into a very bad day. Do we have a remote idea of where it is now?" said the President in an angry hiss.

"Yes, sir. It slipped out of Management's hands. The special zwanzig, we believe his mother has it, sir."

"Well, I suppose the Management's theory of DNA will be proven at last. If they are right, his mother will give in to some deep, inner need for power and all is lost. If the Circle is right, then we still have a chance to finally bring some democracy back into the world after an absence of more than a hundred years. This contest of wills, it will be very interesting, Mr. Bowers. I suppose both sides are waiting to see what happens next."

"Not exactly, sir. Tom has been called home. We are going to see if we can tip the balance in our favor."

"And Management will likely respond."

"They appear to have already tried, sir. There are several dead in Richmond."

CHAPTER 21

YVETTE Campbell quickly pushed the cart up and down the aisles at the grocery store trying to get everything on the list without thinking too much about what still needed to get done.

"Saturday is just not long enough," she shouted over her shoulder to her husband, Bob as she ran out of the door. There was a Bunko game later and she was determined to get enough of her chores done so that she could relax tonight. Maybe even drink a glass of wine.

"Ah, boxed wine," she said, smiling, as she reached into the glass cooler and pulled out a box of white chardonnay and a box of rose. There was a general agreement among the group to never bring anything in a deep red color that could leave a more obvious stain. Everyone at Bunko was firmly in the middle class and knew that each possession could not be easily restored. A stain would have to be endured until there was room in the budget for a replacement.

"Coffee, coffee," mumbled Yvette, looking up at the markers at the top of each aisle. Two aisles down. She started to push the heavy cart.

There were three kinds of grocery stores in town: high end, discount and bulk and Yvette shopped at all three, never completely memorizing the layout of any of them.

She found the coffee at the far end of the aisle and pulled the cart as far over to the side as she could manage, trying to stay out of the way of other shoppers as she stared at the different brands of coffee. She was doing a social calculation in her head, trying to figure out just how expensive the coffee needed to be for her friends at Bunko divided by how much she had to spend this month. Her hand reached out for the Folgers. It was on sale and was fancy enough for the girls.

"Score," said Yvette. "Now, maybe I can get a little somethin'-somethin' for myself."

She grabbed a small paper bag from the shelf and measured out half a bag of coffee beans from one of the more expensive gourmet bins. The one marked chocolate raspberry. The aroma wafted into the air as she breathed in deeply and her shoulders relaxed. She poured the contents into the grinder on the left with a hand-made sign taped on the front that said, 'Flavored Coffee only'. The beans rattled down into the bottom as she turned the dial on the front till it pointed at the word, drip and she hit the on button.

"Click, click, click"

The dark coffee beans made contact with the sharp, rotating metal teeth in the grinder, picking up small chards from all of the people who had ground coffee that day. Mixed in were also the smallest bits of residue left by a shopper just as the store had opened that morning. A few small drops of polonium 210, popular among some of the deadlier arms of the Management had been placed inside of the grinder. It was all it would take to end the life of everyone who had a cup of the fancier coffee choices.

Later that night the grinder would be flushed out with hot water as it was every night and along with it the evidence would wash away as well. The teenage boys who were charged with cleaning the store would be wearing rubber gloves and inadvertently saving their own lives. Just a small, diluted drop on the skin was enough to stop a heartbeat.

But until then, sixteen random shoppers would stop to fill the little bags with different varieties of coffee before heading home. It would take time for all of them to get around to using the coffee, spreading out not only the locations of the deaths but the times as well and make it just a little bit harder for a pattern to emerge and the local police to figure out exactly what had happened.

The method had been carefully chosen. The oil in the beans stopped the poison from becoming airborne, which could have lead to a death too close to the actual murder weapon. It wouldn't be until someone brewed the beans that the hot water would wash through the grinds and pick up the traces of the radioactive poison, depositing it into the pot and then a cup.

Yvette rolled the top of the bag down, clamping the sides shut and placed the coffee on top of the tall pile in her cart.

I'm going to save that for later, she thought. She looked up and saw a familiar face.

"Hey, Ginger, you shopping for tonight too?"

"Oh, hey Yvette, no, I already have my dish. I forgot to get something for the kids. See you there? Oooh, the expensive stuff, nice."

"Sshhhh, it's my little secret. I hide it in the back of the cupboard."

The two women laughed as Ginger patted Yvette on the arm of her quilted red parka.

"I know what you mean. If I go first Ralph is going to find a treasure trove of chocolate all over that house."

Yvette held up the little bag of coffee. "Yeah, their inheritance." The two women broke into laughter all over again.

"I better run. I left Ralph with the kids and last time he let them eat pizza in the family room."

"I'll see you later, then," said Yvette, as she leaned into the cart. She let out a small, "oof" as she got the cart rolling again. "Have to get back to the Y," she mumbled, as she absently felt her waistline.

At home Yvette carried in all of the groceries, placing her small treat behind the bag of sugar in the cupboard next to the sink. She thought about making just one cup before getting ready for Bunko but wasn't sure there was enough time.

"I'm gonna' take the kids to McDonald's, okay?" Bob was standing in the narrow doorway of the kitchen in his stocking feet holding his work boots in one hand.

Yvette raised her eyes in mock surprise. "What sparked this generous mood?"

"Don't know, been having a good day. Thought I'd spread it around a little. Kids get to eat a Happy Meal, you get a little time to yourself before you head out. Everybody wins."

"You are a good husband," said Yvette, kissing her husband.

"I know that," said Bob. "Kids?" he called out, "come on, hit the road. We're gonna' head for the golden arches."

Yvette listened to their squeals as they raced around the house. It was a rare treat made all the more special by getting to ride along. Usually Yvette or Bob would run out quickly and bring it all back home. Three kids could cause a lot of mayhem and spilled soda in a minivan.

It's a good life, thought Yvette as she turned on the TV to the local news and opened the cabinet by the sink. Just one little cup.

"Two deaths seemingly unrelated but both without a known cause were reported today in the West End of Richmond," said the familiar anchorman on channel 12. Yvette always watched the same news stations. She felt like she knew the entire team and would even wave when she saw one of them around town. Richmond really is a small town, she thought.

"One man was a resident of the Penbrooke subdivision and the other was a woman who was living in the Fairview condominiums. Both were thought to be healthy but in the span of a moment dropped dead in front of their families. Police are not saying whether or not they believe foul play is involved but characterize the deaths as suspicious. A police official noted that it was an unusual circumstance. Autopsies are to be performed."

"Hmph," muttered Yvette. "Probably nothing." Nothing much ever happened in Richmond, thought Yvette. Everybody knows that.

She hummed a little tune as she poured the water into the old coffee maker and measured out an even spoonful. She could hardly wait to taste it.

Later, her family would find her slumped over in the chair, her head on the table with a small purple bruise the size of a half dollar, right in the center of her forehead. The news would be over by then.

Bob had quickly called 911 as he pushed the children into the family room while yelling his wife's name as loud as he could, over and over again in the vain hope that he could still demand she rouse.

The neighbors came running over as soon as they saw the ambulance and police cars gather out front.

"What happened?" said Bob, to anyone in a uniform. Surely, someone could tell him how he could turn his back for just a moment and the neat little lines around his life got the chance to fade away.

Bunko was cancelled that night and all of the girls came over to help Bob with looking after the kids. Someone pulled out a notebook and a makeshift schedule was started with the different women volunteering for bringing over meals, cleaning or babysitting. By then the coffee that had been sitting in the cup next to Yvette's body had grown cold and was poured down the sink. The pot had been left on in all of the commotion and was burned on the bottom. A helping hand shoved it into the dishwasher.

The small brown bag of ground coffee was finally shut and placed into the nearest cabinet as the counters were quickly wiped down. It would be weeks before anyone went looking for it again. Bob never drank coffee. He said it always gave him a sour stomach.

CHAPTER 22

WALLIS stopped by the office on her way home. Laurel had
called several times and said that Madame Bella was insistent that she
see Wallis. She had forgotten about the appointment and tried to beg off
but Laurel told her Madame Bella had climbed the stairs and was sitting
in her office. She was refusing to leave until she saw Wallis.

"I'm going to have to miss Bunko and I forgot to tell Ginger," she said to
Laurel as she came in the door. "No time to call her now."

"She's got the turban and robe and everything," said Laurel.

"Did she say what it's about?" said Wallis as she handed Laurel her coat.

"No, and I tried, like a good assistant will do. She seems prepared to
camp out if necessary. Very determined. Maybe she knew you were
destined to come back here," said Laurel, smiling.

Wallis rolled her eyes as she quickly took the stairs.

"Madame Bella," she said, as the large woman turned in the chair to
look at Wallis.

"This couldn't wait," said Madame Bella, in a firm voice. She was a familiar figure in this part of town. It was hard to miss a large Irish-looking woman who loved to wear Gypsy clothing as costume even while pushing a cart through the local Lowe's store.

She was planted in one of the small side chairs facing Wallis' desk, overflowing the sides in a purple robe with a continuous celestial pattern cinched in by degrees with a pale blue sash. On her head was a matching purple turban with a large yellow amulet pinned in the center. Her hands were tucked into the opposite sleeves as if she were trying to stay warm.

Wallis had caught glimpses of Madame Bella in similar getups over the years and had stopped paying attention to the details a long time ago.

"That's what I heard," said Wallis as she sat down behind her desk. "What can I do for you? I didn't even know you were married."

"This is not about me," said the psychic in a distinctive southern twang found only in the western reaches of Virginia. "I've come to warn you."

Wallis tensed, "Are you here to make a threat?"

"That's good. You've always said exactly what's on your mind. But you've never really been tested like this before. I was a little worried you might turn cautious. No, no, we're not enemies. I'm here to warn you about others." Wallis suddenly noticed that Madame had pulled her left hand out of a sleeve and she was gripping an iPhone. Her thumb was deftly sliding across the face of it as she kept up a steady stream of conversation and glancing back and forth between Wallis and the phone.

"A storm has been brewing for some time now," said Madame, leaning toward the desk until her ample chest rested on the top. "I was told to come and see you, to let you know."

"Told by whom?" said Wallis.

"Not important and too distracting," said Madame, with a dramatic wave of her right hand. Wallis suddenly could see that the hand was heavily bandaged over where there should have been a ring finger and pinkie.

"What happened?" started Wallis. Madame Bella didn't even look at her hand.

"Again, not important. A loss to the other side but as you can see, I escaped with my life so a minor fray. I am here to make sure you stay more intact."

Wallis felt her stomach turn as she noticed the blood stain on the bandage covering the small stump.

"They got nothing for their troubles but two useless, arthritic fingers and a ring. I liked the ring, though," she said, with a wry smile. "It was a nice citrine. I'm very sorry about your Mr. Blazney. That was a mistake."

"Mr. Blazney? What about him?" said Wallis, wondering what her friendly, elderly neighbor could have to do with a complicated intrigue.

"I'm sorry, I thought someone would have told you by now. He was killed just yesterday. How did no one tell you?"

Wallis felt the outline of her cell phone in her pocket and thought about calling Norman but something made her hesitate.

"That poor old man was out walking at the wrong place and time, which happened to be right in front of your house. I was on my way to see you earlier that night and I'm afraid I was seen as well. Tortured in the back of a van near some park, very efficient." She waved the bandaged hand again as if it gave some explanation.

"Nasty, brutal people. They thought the threat of a couple of fingers would reveal something. It did. It revealed that I always keep a spare knife strapped just under the boobs. No one ever likes to search an old, fat broad too closely, you see. Stabbed that one right in the eye," she said, demonstrating the gesture with a twist. Wallis winced and found herself trying to sit up straighter.

"The other oaf was so surprised that he hesitated just long enough for me to get a good swipe at him. Fat old man. He survived but it'll leave a nice mark just across his face." Madame Bella spat out the last words. Wallis had sat there quietly listening, trying to breathe calmly.

"Do you know Esther?" asked Wallis. It was a calculated risk using Esther's name like that but Wallis wasn't sure what else to do. She was desperately trying to figure out how many sides were in this plot and how many of them wanted her dead.

"Ah yes, good egg, that one. And good question, my dear. Most would answer that she sells books but I will tell you that she is a bit more complicated than that," said Madame, giving Wallis a wink. "I'm afraid this is my last night in this good town if I care to go on living, so I need to deliver my humble message and push on. I'd tell you that normally I'm not so pushy but that's not true," she said with a chuckle. Madame Bella raised an eyebrow and pointed her remaining fingers at Wallis.

"You have something that has travelled through a lot of hands, lately. Poor Ray Billings and that Stanley fellow."

"What's happened to Stanley?" said Wallis, in a hush.

"I'm not sure, but you need to stop looking for him and pay very close attention to what I'm telling you now. You are going to feel betrayed, my dear, by all of those you love most but let it go immediately. Too much is at risk for you to waste time sorting through what should have happened and you'd probably be wrong anyway. Just remember that if you start to blame one you will have to blame all. That is going to have a lot more meaning for you over time. Trust those who you have believed to be trustworthy regardless of what you will soon know about them. See the snakes for what they have always been and continue to listen to them without giving anything away."

"Madame Bella, this sounds like a prediction."

"No, no, dear. You know, in all these years you never came to see me read the cards for anyone. My predictions to the lonely and afraid had more to do with a stern lecture about less whining and more acceptance of what had already happened to them dressed up with some tea and tarot cards. What comes next for you will be hard to bear, I can promise you that. But you must take it all in quickly and think clearly if we are to make it through this time."

"This time. You mean, this time after the last slaughter."

"Ah, so Esther has filled in some of the blanks. Good, good, God is good. Yes, yes, I believe in a divine presence and I pray to Him all the time for deliverance but I never try to put any boundaries around what it's going to look like. Today, apparently it looks like you. Just remember, child, everything was done by those around you in good conscience. Keep those you love close but trust no one with the information until you are sure."

"When will that be?" She knew Madame Bella was talking about the thumb drive but she wasn't ready to admit to anything. Just for a moment she saw them holding down the old woman and sawing off a finger and she wondered if she wouldn't have started spilling everything she knew all the way back to nursery school. She was pretty sure she wouldn't have had the nerve to be angling for her moment of revenge.

"You'll know when the time is right," said Madame Bella. "I'm afraid that as so often happens in times of great shifts it is impossible to know anything more beyond what the next step ought to be. Your next step is to go home and open your heart and your mind to the truth that has been with you all along. No, no," said Madame Bella, raising her injured hand, "the rest should be from someone closer. To tell you now would be cruel."

"Cruel as compared to what?"

"Very true, but you're going to have to trust an old woman on this one. I've done what was asked of me. Besides I have very little time left to slip away and as old and useless as they may be, I'm rather fond of the rest of my parts."

"Can I help you?" said Wallis, rising out of her chair.

"My dear, I was right about you," said Madame Bella getting slowly out of the chair. "There is one thing," she said, as she removed the turban to reveal a tight bun of grey hair.

"Madame?"

"Just one second," said Madame Bella in her nasally twang. "Damn it, can't get these buttons anymore on account of," she waved her hand.

"How can you be so calm?" Wallis suddenly felt very tired as a shudder rolled through her body.

Madame looked up for a moment and held Wallis' gaze. "You're usually a pretty cool customer."

"That may not be true anymore," said Wallis. "Here, let me help you."

Madame Bella had slipped her arms out of the purple robe and revealed a blue buttoned shirt and long peasant skirt underneath.

"Please, let me," said Wallis. "I'm assuming you're going to try and slip out of the back? That may not work. You know as well as I do that one side opens on to a busy street and the other onto a wide parking lot. It's impossible to get out without being spotted."

Wallis undid each button as a smooth, black cotton front emerged underneath the loose top. She helped Madame Bella the rest of the way out of the shirt to reveal starched white sleeves underneath the top of a black cotton smock.

"Do you mind?" said Madame Bella, gesturing at the side of the skirt. Wallis gave her a look but did as she was told.

"I'm beginning to get the picture," said Wallis, "but surely a conspiracy as big as this one isn't quite this stupid."

"You're thinking one large woman in costume going in and only one large woman in a different costume going out has to add up to something. Me too, and it was me that you were calling stupid, my sweet."

As the peasant skirt fell to the ground the rest of a nun's habit was revealed. Madame Bella reached down toward a large black patent leather pocketbook. She snapped the small brass clap at the top as the sides sprang apart.

"It's never been about trying to completely fool anyone, it can't be. We work to plant just enough confusion and it's more powerful cousin, suspicion to buy a little time. The rest is left up to God."

"Are you saying that because you're trying to get into character?"

Madame smiled as she dug around inside the purse.

"It looks like a small suitcase," said Wallis, peering over the corner of her desk as she tried to get a better look inside.

Madame chortled as she pulled out a starched white wimple and black veil and proceeded to drape her head. She leaned over and dug around in her purse for a moment, coming up with a few bobby pins. She opened her hand to Wallis without a word.

"Madame Bella?" said Wallis, as she pinned the wimple and veil to Madame's head.

"Mother Elizabeth," said Madame Bella. "Although I have to tell you, Madame Bella has been one of my favorites."

"Is that your real name, Elizabeth?"

Madame Bella stopped and gave Wallis a tight embrace, whispering into her ear.

"Don't let it matter who I really am, honey. This little piece will be a lot easier if you can do that for me." The newly anointed Mother Elizabeth stepped back from Wallis.

"We never got to know each other, weren't supposed to, you know," said the large nun. "It was easier that way to watch you without drawing attention for the wrong reasons. These getups only attract attention when mixed in with regular folks. But otherwise, human nature makes most people look away. Much easier to hide in plain sight."

"I've heard that about conspiracies, too," said Wallis.

"You're a firecracker, you are. Now, no more questions. If you could carry these downstairs for me," she said, nudging the fallen robes with her toe. "That would be a big help. Someone is waiting for those and it's past time for me to depart."

"This isn't going to work," said Wallis.

"You'd think so, wouldn't you?" said the newly disguised, Mother Elizabeth. "But we made plans, you'll see. I've always liked this role, you know. My pushy self will seem to have purpose. I'm going to make a great Mother Superior again," she said, as she waddled toward the stairs.

"I can remember a time just a few days ago when something like this would have made me think about calling the police. But, now I have to wonder who'd show up and who I'd really be betraying," said Wallis as she followed the large woman down the stairs.

"Very good, Black Widow. I know you don't like that name but its okay."

As they came around the corner into the small reception area there stood a small band of women dressed as nuns. Sitting in a chair was a larger woman in a plain skirt and top.

"I take it these are for you?" said Wallis, offering the woman the former psychic's colorful costume. The former Madame Bella winked at Wallis as she pushed the other nuns toward the back door.

"Wait a minute," said Wallis. "I know you." She looked more carefully at one of the younger nuns and realized it was Annie Brody, one of Norman's clients. "And you're Sara," she said, looking under the wipple of one of the other nuns. "How long has this been in the works?"

"There are always contingency plans," said Annie, with a shy smile. "The trick is to not be seen making them. Fortunately, Norman's done a lot of work for a variety of churches, including ours," she said, pointing a finger at Wallis and back at herself. "Everyone needs a good lawyer from time to time."

"Pastor Adler," said Wallis, thinking of the kindly minister who always stood in the pulpit at Pilgrim Baptist Church. "He's a part of this?"

"Don't be fooled by the good pastor's demeanor. His faith has made him a formidable warrior. Read Psalm 18, you're going to need your faith for what's coming, as well. 'For by thee I have run through a troop; and by my God have I leaped over a wall.'"

"I'm kind of a lapsed Baptist," said Wallis.

"I have been in this particular battle for awhile now," said Mother Elizabeth. "And, it has been my experience that without a faith in He who sacrificed everything for us first, the journey becomes too long and the opposition starts to appear sweeter. But a cautionary word, my dear, they are a poison that at best scars and at their worst, drags down an entire family tree. We're off, girls. You," said Mother Elizabeth, pointing at her replacement, "wait at least a good half hour and then you head out as well." She kissed the woman on the top of her turban. "May it all go well."

Wallis realized what she meant. "What will you tell them," she said to the woman, "if someone is over there waiting for you? Why were you here?" Her voice rose slightly with fear in her voice.

"If that happens, then my time is done," said the woman. "But there are others waiting to help me tonight. It's alright, ma'am. It's what I was trained to do."

"Combat training is now part of the Episcopal Church?" asked Wallis.

"A firecracker, that's what you are," said Mother Elizabeth.

CHAPTER 2 3

"**HOW MUCH DID YOU ALREADY KNOW?**" asked Wallis, after everyone else had finally left the office. The new Madame Bella had asked her to quickly close the door and not watch her walk away. Wallis had pressed her ear to the door but heard nothing.

"Not enough," said Laurel. "That was all way above my pay grade. That was a damn circus."

"It was, wasn't it," said Wallis, as she tried to piece how everything fit together. "You know, Laurel, I've always thought there were a few things about myself and this town that I could count on to be consistent. I'm not a sucker and this is a small town."

"I know what you mean and yes, you may be wrong on both counts. No offense."

"None taken. I keep thinking this is all so ridiculous and yet it keeps growing. I'm not sure whether or not to laugh or throw up," said Wallis.

"Both, but one at a time. Look, maybe it's time we did compare notes. You need an ally and I'm standing right here. We have known each other for too many years to not be joining forces."

"Why is it I need an ally more than you do?"

"Excellent point."

"For the record, we already are a team unless you have news that I don't know about."

"No, no, no surprises here. What was that about your neighbor?"

"Mr. Blazney? God," said Wallis, as she sat down hard and momentarily covered her face with her hands. "My sweet old neighbor. I found his dog and took her home," she said, looking up at Laurel. "Must have been the same morning."

"Why is everyone swirling around you, anyway? You're interesting but not on that big of a scale."

"That's a good question. Madame Bella," said Wallis, waving at the back door where the small group of nuns had quietly shuffled out, "said someone closer to me would clue me in on that one. I'm thinking she means Norman."

"Oooh, that can't be good. Norman wouldn't keep information about you from you, would he?"

"Before today I would have sworn that was a no. But now, I'm not so sure. That's how much has happened today."

"That's big. Maybe you're not so smart to just trust me. Lame joke," said Laurel, holding up her hands in protest. "Look, whatever it is Norman Weiskopf has a good reason. Come on, Wallis, think about it. We're talking about Norman. Granted he can keep a secret better than a dead man but he loves and respects you. I'd bet money on it and we all know how I do not like to gamble with my money."

"I know you're trying to get me to take a deep breath and I appreciate it."

"First thing to do in a crisis is take a step back. Otherwise you're a pawn and not a player."

Wallis smiled at Laurel, grateful she had been smart enough to hire her in the first place. Suddenly, the handle to the back door began to rattle and someone began to simultaneously pound on the door. Wallis startled and stood up, not sure whether or not to go to the door or run out of the front.

"Who is it?" she shouted, trying to sound as if she wasn't afraid.

"Do you think that was a good idea?" whispered Laurel.

"Open the door, Wallis. It's David Whittaker. Open this door," he shouted.

Wallis looked at Laurel and stepped closer to the door.

"It's late at night David," she said, as calmly as she could muster. "And I'm not opening this door. It's ex parte anyway, which I'm getting the impression you already know. You have a problem with Sharon or myself, tell your own lawyer. Go home, David."

The door shook as if it had been given a hard kick at the bottom. Wallis wondered if the door would hold. Laurel ran out of the room and returned quickly with two golf clubs.

"William's not going to like that we borrowed his clubs," said Wallis.

"William will have to get over it," said Laurel, holding the club over her head. "All of that misspent youth at a Seminary will come in handy for him."

"He exorcised all of that when he became a lawyer," said Wallis.

"Wallis Jones, you have far more to worry about than a pathetic court case against me. Don't think they haven't figured it out, you stupid bitch. You know where Ned is right now, anyway?"

Wallis ripped the door open and raised the five iron. David Whittaker started to push his way into the office as Laurel swung down catching him in the gut and bringing him to his knees. He reeked of good whiskey.

"No, Laurel," said Wallis, as she put out an arm to stop Laurel from hitting him across the back with the iron.

"You stupid ass," she whispered close to his ear. David was on all fours, still trying to catch his breath and making small retching noises. "Are you so arrogant that you think every woman will run in fear at the sight of you? It's good advice in general but if you ever threaten anyone I care about again I'll be the one swinging for your head." It was the first time Wallis had ever threatened anyone outside of a court of law.

"She means it too," said Laurel, still holding the driver over her shoulder, ready to swing.

"Get out," said Wallis, shoving him over with her high heel. David pulled himself up to a standing position, resting against the wall, breathing hard.

"Do what you want to me. It won't stop anything. I've been waiting for this moment, Black Widow." He straightened up, pushing his hair back into place. "I'm even doing you a favor warning you. Pedigree won't always trump everything."

"What disgusting thing are you trying to say?" said Wallis.

"You don't know, do you?" he sneered. "That's rich," he said, wobbling from foot to foot and slurring his words. "You think it's me. I'm some kind of snob but it's really you!" he said, pointing at Wallis. "Doesn't matter that you never knew, you still used the way everybody was willing to give you a free pass. But no more, that all ends tonight." David lunged forward as Laurel swung again, making contact with his leg and the corner of the wall. He stepped back rubbing his thigh and looked as if he was about to make another attempt as Wallis and Laurel both raised their weapons.

"Huh, you're not worth it," he said, raising up his hands in defeat and sneering. "You're not worth it." He backed out of the door and stumbled down the stairs, making his way across the wide parking lot toward the darkened strip mall. Wallis stood on the small back porch trying to peer through the darkness that was broken up by only one tall street lamp.

"See anything?" asked Laurel.

"No, but we're sitting ducks here. Time to go."

"Nothing is the same, is it?"

Wallis took another look around at the darkness. "Apparently, everything is the same but we've finally been let in on it. Can you grab my purse? I'll keep watch and then we're both getting out of here."

"Yeah, but where are we going?"

"To our respective homes, I guess. You okay with that?"

"No one seems to be after me," said Laurel.

Wallis didn't remember that her coat was still sitting in her office till she was standing by her car. She shivered in the cold and looked up at the dark window of Norman's office on the second floor.

"Get it later," said Laurel. "Do you mind if I advance a little theory before we part ways tonight?"

"Go right ahead. You're usually more on the money than anyone else, anyway."

"You're assuming its Norman. No one's actually said that it's him, right? Well, excluding Ned, there is one more person to consider. What about Harriet? Isn't she a more likely suspect?"

"I have no idea anymore," said Wallis, as she placed a hand on the hood of the Jag to steady herself and bent over at the waist, taking deep breaths and trying not to throw up what was left of the salad from lunch. The scratch in the door was right by her head.

CHAPTER 24

OSCAR Newman loved his job, loved the way people took a step back when they saw him coming in his deputy uniform. It was the only thing in his life that made sense to him.

He walked briskly up to an older brick building in the bowels of Shockoe Bottom, located down near the James River and in the shadow of the few high rises in downtown Richmond. He entered one of the old defunct tobacco warehouses with a faded logo for Pall Mall's painted across the three-storied building.

Oscar was determined and angry as he pulled open the side door and stepped into a large warehouse filled with men, black and white, rich and poor trading slips of paper and quietly reeling off short series of numbers to each other. It was the central count house for the city's numbers organization.

"Six, eight, nine. Give me six, eight nine." "How 'bout triple three's."

The response from a small group standing at the front was always, "Quarter, quarter."

All of the men who were taking the bets were wearing the same style of suit, trading numbers out of the same kind of leather briefcase, filled with more slips of paper and a ledger. They still preferred the old fashioned method to computers, which left too obvious of a trail to follow.

At one side of the room was a chalk board with recent dates and three numbers written next to each date. It was an old form of lottery that worked the same as a daily lottery, only cost less to play and was never legal.

Everyone stopped mumbling and turned to look at the deputy sheriff. "Get out here!" yelled Oscar, his hand moving down toward his gun. A few men slowly rose as if to run or at least get out of the way. Most look annoyed.

"Where the hell is Davey?" said Oscar, his hand resting on the holster. A very large black man, tall as he was wide and sweating profusely, slid a pile of papers into his hands and quietly ducked behind a table. Oscar spotted the movement and barreled toward Davey, his hand clenching the holster. A path was cleared for him as Davey tried to right himself back to standing, a few wisps of paper falling to the floor.

"Come on, Davey! Didn't I tell you these numbers were crap?" said Oscar, his hand sliding off of the gun and into his pocket as he pulled out a wad of small papers and threw them in Davey's face.

"Those were your combinatings," mumbled Davey. "You picked your own combinatings."

Oscar unsnapped his holster, pulled out his revolver and pointed it briefly at Davey as a murmur went around the room. Davey shrank back, letting go of most of the papers and shut his eyes. Oscar hesitated, rolled his eyes, and seemed to resign himself to something as he took aim at the blackboard behind Davey, shooting out the top line.

The sound echoed for a moment in the cavernous building.

"Yeah, like I'd shoot you here," said Oscar, sounding annoyed as he helped Davey to his feet. "Put this on seven, eight, nine," he said, pulling out a dollar bill. He removed a thick brown envelope from the inside of his jacket and put it in front of Davey. "Here's everybody else's. Captain says you owed him a free one."

Across the room two black men in tidy pinstriped suits were going over a ledger. "Somebody's got to do something about that crazy jerk. He's bound to hit Davey one of these days."

"You'd think so, with a target like that, and Oscar being an ace shot. Hasn't he told you yet?" Both men snickered.

"Where's Parrish?" asked one of the men, looking around.

"He's out doing his own thing, you know that. He'll get the job done, always does. One of our best runners. Keeps it all up here," said the other man, tapping his forehead. "Never even writes down a combinating or a nickname. Never had a complaint. Genius for the details, and brings in more money than anybody else in this room. Can't do enough for a man like that."

Across town a well-dressed, tall elegant man with close-cropped hair, Rodney Parrish, was getting ready to head back to work. He gently pushed open the screen door of a well-kept modest blue and tan bungalow on a tree-lined street in an older neighborhood.

Parrish stepped out, quietly and deliberately pulling the door shut behind him while straightening his suit jacket and checking his expensive silk tie, tapping lightly on the white lapel pin of an American flag trimmed in gold. His breathing was even and calm and he wore a faint smile as he walked down the short sidewalk lined with brightly colored plastic daisies turning in the slight breeze.

The briefcase that was hanging loosely from his right hand gave only a small swing, keeping a perfect rhythm with his stride as he took each step down the walk before turning toward the east, heading for the Boulevard and away from the older suburbs. His three-piece pin striped suit, his idea of a uniform, was spotless.

Down the sidewalk from where Parrish had just been visiting, past the row of neat identical bungalows was the little cottage where Lilly Billings had moved to shortly after separating from her husband. The door looked undisturbed and everything was exactly as it should be until a little further into the living room where Lilly still sat with her feet crossed at the ankles, her hands neatly folded in her lap and her back to the door. The only thing out of place was the left side of her head, bashed in past her ear, and a look of surprise on the part of her face that was still intact.

But there was no blood, no mess at all, and no sign of any kind of struggle. Nothing was out of place. Only the best pieces of jewelry were missing, Parrish's payment, but that was all. No blood spatter was left to complicate things, no sign of how the killer got in. No clues at all.

Parrish had a demanding standard for himself and he always liked to keep his customers happy.

Just as he reached North Boulevard where he'd be able to blend into the small bit of foot traffic in the city, he pulled out his cell phone and typed in a short message. 'Job done, no reward.'

Lilly didn't know anything about a thumb drive or the list. She had made that clear, swearing on her life.

Parrish got into the dark blue Ford Explorer that he always kept neat as a pin and drove off to deliver the winnings from the morning bets. It never looked good to miss a deadline.

CHAPTER  ②⑤

STANLEY darted down the alley that stretched for miles behind the row houses between Grove and Hanover Avenue in the Fan District. He was going for a short five mile run to calm his nerves and try to build some kind of routine even if he was in hiding.

Stanley loved running through the Fan and glancing at the architecture as he moved quickly down the wide sidewalks. Everything had been rebuilt sometime after Sherman's ignominious march through the South but with depleted fortunes. It explained the haphazard way the buildings jutted in and out of the cobblestoned alley.

Lately, he'd been sticking to the alleys everywhere he went in an effort to try and go by unseen. The narrow passageways behind the houses worked as a good cover to try and evade the people who kept tailing Stanley everywhere he went.

He thought he noticed the same car popping up every few blocks for the past mile but everyone in Richmond drove an SUV. It was hard to tell.

He'd given up on going back to his small cottage with the Williamsburg blue trim that was tucked in between all of the other cottages.

Instead he'd been begging different friends to let him stay on their couches for a couple of nights. But it always happened that he'd become worried and suddenly move on again. Lacey and Dan, fellow runners who lived over on Park Avenue, had tried to convince him to stay a few more nights till he was feeling a little calmer but Stanley became convinced that he'd already put them in enough danger.

For a moment he wondered if they were in on it and the thought made him feel depressed. That was just a few days ago. He tried calling Wallis Jones but had thought better of it and hung up after only a couple of rings.

He was working his way through his group of running friends, staying with each one for only a couple of nights. There were only a few names left to call but Dan had let it slip that everyone was getting together and making up a Stanley calendar as some kind of way to see him through what they saw as a mid-life breakdown.

But Stanley knew the truth. He was running out of options.

Richmond was a small town and everyone ran in their own small circle of friends. It wasn't going to take very long before word got around about his predicament. Nausea was rising in his throat again.

His mind was never settled, constantly going over his options or reviewing his every move, looking for the mistakes. Stanley was used to being methodical and fixing whatever hitches came up but he couldn't see the edges of this problem. It was going to swamp him.

What if Lacey or Dan told someone he was so jittery? They could easily do that, he thought. They wouldn't think twice about saying something during a run or over sushi at the new mall out by the Powhite Highway.

The word will spread and the wrong person will hear that I can't hold it together. There's no way to contain this, he thought.

He came to the end of the alley at Stuart Circle that was ringed on three corners by large churches and an old hospital that was now condominiums on the other. He stopped for a moment, carefully looked both ways and ran until he had crossed the wide circle of cobblestones and was in the center of the wide boulevard, in front of Stonewall Jackson's statue. Stanley had been looking forward to this part of the run for a week.

He had patted the marble horse for good luck once a week for years. He still needed the little piece of familiarity, the ability to still choose something, in order to grasp a little sanity and keep it.

He got to the over-sized statue and stood there on the narrow pavement that ringed the statue, making himself calm down enough to have one clear chain of thoughts.

He felt his breathing slow down for just a moment and he took in his first deep breath in days.

"Just a couple more miles to go," he said, trying to smile and count up his blessings. It was an old trick of his that he used whenever he had to shake off a bad mood. "I'm sorry, Ray," he said, "but I did what you asked and now I'm going on from here." Stanley patted the statue, looked both ways and started to step off the pavement and dart across the road, back to the relative safety of the alleyways.

His foot touched down on the cobblestone just as he caught the glimpse of the black SUV he was sure had been behind him at the top of Monument Avenue and Glenside Drive. It was heading into the circle at a high rate of speed.

"They're here," he mumbled, his knees trembling for a moment. Stanley quickly assessed his options and knew he had no choice but to go for it. If he stayed he'd be trapped in the open with a road to cross on all sides. They'd be able to pick him off easily.

He bolted onto the road running as fast as he could and reached the sidewalk just as the car came screeching up behind him. He could hear the click, whoosh of car doors being thrown open on all sides as he willed himself to pay attention to the pattern of his feet. "One, two, one, two, one, two," he said, over and over again. He knew that there was a good chance they wouldn't open fire in such a well to do neighborhood. Too many witnesses who actually thought the police were there to protect them.

These guys wanted to capture him and drag him somewhere else.

"The advantage is now mine," he said quietly.

Men in suits carrying heavy weapons were hired for their ability to muscle the enemy, not chase down trained runners on unfamiliar streets.

But Stanley knew these streets well, first as a boy when he lived across the James River and he would come to visit cousins and then as a runner always looking for a new route to stave off boredom.

He heard the men shouting to each other and could tell by their footfalls they weren't seasoned runners. They were running flatfooted, making it easier to track them without having to turn and look. He found his rhythm and started taking small side alleys that he knew lead to only one narrow exit slightly hidden, which would take them an extra moment to figure out. He quickly crossed over to another short jog between two brownstones, running down the narrow strip of alley that had been created to supply coal in the winters. He kept ducking in and out, weaving his way down the blocks toward the downtown district where there would be more foot traffic. His breathing was coming easily as he listened to their frustrated shouts.

Just another block and he would be near the Governor's mansion built to look like the White House where the Capitol Police would be hanging out and nearby office workers would be taking a break on the rolling lawn.

Surely a few grown men in suits running down alleys would grab their attention, he thought, knowing a lone runner would go by unnoticed.

He quickly reached the end of the alley behind what had become older offices used mostly by the state government. He had already run seven miles flat out from the statue but knew that he could keep going for awhile without even getting winded.

He hesitated, listening for the sound of hard soled shoes running on pavement and heard nothing, wondering if they were now tracking him by car.

"This way," a man hissed. Stanley peeked out from the alley and saw a man in an older, white Jetta pulled up at an angle at the curb. He was making small, determined waves. "Hurry," he said, quickly looking around as he kept up the hand waving.

"Why should I trust you?" Stanley hissed back.

"This town," said the man, in heavily accented English, "First the Jones woman has to ask questions and now you. How about because men are after you who don't want information as much as they want to clean up their mess? And, you, my friend, don't have any other options."

Stanley knew he was right. He even knew a moment like this was coming since the day Ray died, less than a week ago. He couldn't even comprehend what everyone was after much less why it was worth killing someone like Ray. He ran toward the open door and slid in the front seat saying a small prayer that it wasn't a mistake. The man started driving toward Main Street as he put out his hand.

"Helmut Khroll," he said. "We've got to get you to a safer spot and then maybe explain a few things."

"Thank God," said Stanley.

"Well, close," said Helmut Khroll, "just a journalist," he said, smiling as he gunned the engine and headed back uptown toward the suburbs.

CH APT ER

WALLIS tried to calm down enough to take the drive down Huguenot Road toward the other side of the James River at the posted speed limit of 45 mph. She knew the four lane winding road was a common speed trap and she wasn't in any kind of shape to take her chances with the local police tonight. There was no one else on the road. Richmond had a habit of closing down after dinnertime.

Normally, Wallis had a faith in the entire legal system that dictated she'd be okay in the end despite the flaws. A speeding ticket was merely an expensive nuisance. But nothing was the same anymore. She wasn't even sure of Norman. That last thought was making it difficult for her to focus on anything else.

Just as the front wheels of the Jaguar touched the Huguenot Bridge a car suddenly appeared in Wallis' rear view mirror. The old silver Volvo sedan seemed to come out of nowhere.

It must have come up from the Pony Pasture, thought Wallis, taking a deep breath and glancing back and forth between the Volvo and the bridge. There was a hidden entrance just to the side of the bridge that wound down to wide open fields that ran along the James River.

She tried to see who was driving the car but there was only the occasional street lamp lining the bridge and that was making it impossible.

She took a quick glance over the far side of the bridge and in the moonlight she was able to see the rushing water below as it pulsed past a small line of large boulders in the center of the river. Just as she glanced back toward the road the Jaguar shook violently, thrusting her head forward before slamming it back against the headrest.

The back end of the car began to fishtail on the narrow bridge as the airbag exploded in Wallis' face, a fine white powder blowing into the air and stinging her eyes. Wallis struggled to keep her eyes open through her tears and the pain as the car behind her attempted to ram her again, catching the right corner of the trunk and pushing the Jaguar against the side of the old green metal railing. There was a sound of metal scraping on metal and the bridge squealing from the pressure. Small sparks leaped along the edge of the passenger side window.

Wallis pulled the steering wheel hard to the left and stood on the brakes, momentarily lifting herself up off of the seat, the deflated air bag resting in her lap. The car responded by sliding sideways and pushing even harder against the old railing.

At the last moment as a four foot section of railing began to pull away from the large iron bolts that held it in place, bowing out toward the water in a 'V', the car started to correct hard to the left. Wallis started spinning the wheel as fast as she could toward the right, giving the car what she hoped was just enough gas to keep it moving. The car stalled out as the engine fell silent and Wallis watched everything moving swiftly past her window in a vacuum of sound. She tried to wrench her head around to the left as her neck spasmed and she instinctively pulled her chin down, squeezing her eyes shut for a moment. As she opened her eyes everything seemed to be happening in slow motion. Her body was hanging inside of the seat belt, her torso leaning over the gear shift in between the seats. The view of the hill just in front of her that lead to Cary Street and the route home pulled out of view and was replaced by the white caps on the water as she tried to turn back to see what was coming next. Her fingernails dug into the arm rest against the driver's side door as she pulled herself over, ignoring the sharp pains in her neck that travelled down into the small of her back. Just as she became sure she was going over the car teetered back and slammed onto the road. The other car finally came into view as the Jaguar came to rest.

The Volvo had come to a stop when Wallis started trying to correct the spin-out and there was now a sizeable distance between the two cars. Wallis was certain she knew what was coming next and could feel the bile rising in her throat. The Jaguar was caught near the far side of the bridge, its nose pointing at an angle toward the water.

"Don't look at the car, don't look at the car," she mumbled, willing herself to quickly turn around and make each move count. She wrapped both hands around the keys still dangling from the ignition and gently turned the key.

"Please work, please work," she pleaded, noticing her bottom lip was growing fatter. The engine caught and turned over with a slight sputter. "Not a guarantee but I'll take it." She turned the wheel back and pressed down on the accelerator as she saw the Volvo quickly growing closer in the rear view mirror. The Jaguar wasn't picking up speed fast enough. She braced herself for an impact and wondered what it would be like to be floating briefly through the air with a ton of steel surrounding her body.

Wallis thought about closing her eyes and taking her hands off the wheel just as the headlights from behind started to fill the entire interior of the car with light.

"I love you Norman," she yelled, as loud as she could, as the car continued to get brighter, and she raised a hand up in the center of the car where the driver behind her could clearly see, thrusting her middle finger into the air.

Suddenly, the Volvo swerved around her, the sound of the engine being gunned as Wallis looked to her right, surprised to still be on the road. Sitting behind the wheel was the bailiff, Oscar, with his belly firmly wedged behind the wheel. He was grinning at Wallis, brown tobacco stained teeth forming a large opening. There was a long thin slash down the right side of his face. Wallis thought about what Madame Bella said about a fat old man and what she'd been able to do to him.

She looked back at Oscar in disbelief wondering why he hated her so much. He was around her car in a moment, squealing across the bridge and running the red light just on the other side. That was when Wallis noticed the car coming from the other direction, wildly honking its horn for her to get out of the way. She quickly pulled into the right lane as the minivan passed and a nervous-looking woman was still honking madly, peering out of her open window but she never came close to stopping.

"Please don't call the police," she yelled, even though the minivan was already disappearing over the bridge. Wallis pressed the accelerator gently and started out slowly, creeping off the bridge, listening to the new sounds the car was making as something under the car scraped the road. She looked over the railing for a moment at the train tracks below as she got to the other side and rolled past the empty parking lots of upscale strip malls.

Her entire body tensed as she tried to look into the darkest corners, wondering if Oscar was waiting to take another shot at murder. The dark parking lots on either side gave way to the deep woods as Wallis continued up the hill by the rolling lawns of the golf course at the Country Club of Virginia.

The car was struggling the entire way, barely pushing fifty even though Wallis' foot was now jammed down on the gas. "I know you're here somewhere," whispered Wallis. She emptied out her purse on the passenger seat and fumbled for her cell phone to call Norman. She dropped the small race car in her lap as she quickly dialed with her thumb while trying to scan both sides of the road.

There was a red light at the intersection of Cary and River Roads that formed a narrow T right in front of the old stately Tuckahoe Apartment buildings that were always reserved for old money. No one was waiting at the light as Wallis tore through, barely missing the cars starting to turn left from the other direction. Just as she sped through the Volvo appeared out of the Tuckahoe's small circular parking lot and pulled in neatly behind her as the irate honking continued behind them. The phone dropped out of her hand, still ringing as both hands went back on the steering wheel.

Wallis got to the second intersection at Three Chopt Road and took the corner as fast as she could, the tires squealing against the pavement, the bailiff not far behind her.

Three Chopt Road was an old two lane road that wound past the front of the country club with old stately homes lining the other side. Cars were streaming past just a door handle away as Wallis took another hill. It was only a matter of time before she would find herself on another stretch of road alone with Oscar.

Just as she got to the corner of Grove Avenue Wallis abruptly turned right hoping there would be people sitting out at the popular restaurants that lined the upper part of the street. Sitting on the corner to her immediate left was St. Stephen's Church, an old Episcopal church attended by all of the old first families of Virginia made of white granite from a local quarry back when the entire area was full of mines and the larger Episcopal churches, like St. Stephen's catered to the owners while the smaller ones were filled to the rafters with the miners. Right next door sat St. Bridget's, a large Catholic cathedral made out of yellow stone pulled from another local quarry.

Wallis scanned the street and quickly saw that all of the store fronts were dark. The only light was coming from the wrought iron street lights along both sides. She crossed over into the left lane and took the curb, bouncing along the sidewalk and rolling down the grass toward the wide open parking lot of St. Stephen's situated behind the church. The bottom of her car bounced along the grass before making a large whomp against the blacktop of the parking lot as Wallis sped for the other side, zipping across the painted white lines. Something fell from the bottom of her car clanging against the pavement as she kept driving.

The Volvo stayed right behind her as she quickly pulled around the left side of the Episcopal Church and aimed straight for the rectory that sat between St. Stephen's and the looming cathedral.

At the entrance to the rectory Wallis threw the car into park and leapt out, scooping up the thumb drive from her lap as she ran for the stone steps. She beat on the side door of St. Stephen's as hard as she could as the Volvo slowed down. Oscar made a quick circle in the parking lot, coming to rest in front of the Jaguar, blocking it from going anywhere. He turned off his lights just as the large wooden door began to open and an older minister appeared with a worried expression on his face.

"Pastor Donald," said Wallis, as she threw up on his feet.

"Wallis?" said Reverend Donald. "Are you alright?" He reached out to gently pull Wallis in by the elbow as she winced. "What's happened?"

Wallis turned to look at Oscar and wrapped her fingers tighter around the small race car in her hand.

"Who is that?" said the Reverend, as he looked past Wallis and saw the remains of her car. "Did he do that?" he asked, almost shouting. Wallis nodded and gingerly wrapped her left arm against her bruised ribs. She was starting to realize how close she had come to dying on the bridge. Reverend Donald stepped out onto the steps and pushed Wallis inside of the church as he grabbed the metal bat he always kept by the door.

"God helps those who come prepared," he said to Wallis, giving her a wink as he started down the steps toward the darkened Volvo. "Call Norman," he yelled, without turning around to see if Wallis was following the order.

Wallis looked at her car and realized the phone was still sitting on the floor where it had dropped. She took the stone steps two at a time, running across the open space as she watched the Reverend walk swiftly toward the Volvo, the bat raised, ready to swing. She got to the passenger side and pulled on the crumpled door but the frame was too badly bent. The door wouldn't open. She stepped out into the street just as Oscar gunned the engine and the Reverend swung the bat connecting with the windshield as the glass shattered into small pieces raining back on Oscar's face. The car swerved, barely missing Wallis yet again as it passed and turned into the darkness.

Wallis quickly opened her door and felt underneath the seat banging her hand against the springs. She ignored the stinging as her knuckles scraped against an unseen sharp point and felt the edge of her phone, pulling it toward her.

She quickly stood up and ran for the security of the church steps, not looking back to see what was happening behind her till she was once again near the open wooden door. Reverend Donald was running to catch up with her, the bat still resting against his shoulder.

"You okay?" he asked, as he dropped the bat on the front step, breathing hard. He gently wrapped his arms around Wallis, her arms tucked against her chest, the thumb drive still in her hand.

"I'm not sure," she said, as she looked past him and out into the darkness. "I have to call Norman," she said, suddenly pulling back. "They want me dead and Ned, what if," she said, dialing the phone.

Norman answered on the first ring. "Wallis? I've been trying to call you back. What was all of that noise? Are you alright? Where are you?"

"I'm with Pastor Donald over at St. Stephen's. There's been an accident. Is Ned with you? What is a zwanzig, Norman and why do so many people suddenly want me dead?"

"I'm coming to get you. Ned's with your mother. Nothing will happen to him there. Wait right there. Don't leave the Reverend's side."

CHAPTER 27

    PASTOR Donald led Wallis quickly through the newer wing that was noteworthy for the tall lead paned windows placed to let in the maximum amount of light. But the same architectural detail offered no sanctuary to those who were trying to elude anyone who might want them dead.

They kept traveling into the depths of the over-sized rectory passing through a heavy, locked steel door and into the older part of the building that was well over a hundred years old, which for Richmond was often marked as the beginning of time.

They moved swiftly into a long hall with high ceilings and large imposing paintings of former rectors lining both sides. The passageway was windowless and the only light came from the occasional small table lamp giving off an ethereal glow that in more normal circumstances the few parishioners who ever traveled this hall always found to be comforting.

Donald pulled out a phone and was quickly typing as he continued to pull Wallis along the corridor. Wallis tried to stop for a moment to get her bearings.

Their rapid pace down the hallway had been throwing off small shadows that kept startling Wallis and making her snap her head around to make sure they weren't being followed. Each time she did the sharp pain reminded her of how much she had been thrown around in her car on the bridge.

She reached out to squeeze Pastor Donald's hand to steady herself as she tried to slow him down.

She had known Oscar for years and just like that he had tried to kill her. Richmond was a city that prided itself on all the small relationships that weave together any small town. Long time residents liked to think that they could turn to their neighbors and even if they didn't always get along they could get a helping hand. Wallis had believed that too.

But there was an entirely different side to things that had become visible to her and pushed and shoved at the boundaries making all of the rules Wallis had grown up with and depended on obsolete. It was making her nauseous all over again to realize how little control was even going to be possible.

The Minister slid the phone back into his pocket and grasped her hand, stepping behind her and firmly nudging Wallis along as they took a short maze of stairs, hallways and doors. He wasn't going to let her rest for even a moment.

"Not yet," he said, softly. "One good thing about not being able to build until we can prove we already needed more space is we end up with so many nooks and crannies," he said in a hushed voice as they continued to hurry down a hallway that curved slightly toward the end. "God bless steering committees."

The hallway ended at another steel door that lead to a small, hidden circular driveway tucked in between all of the large stone buildings just large enough for one car at a time. The Lincoln Continental was parked just by the door in the only pool of light coming from the tall imposing street lamp. Wallis could see her reflection in the thick, dark windows. Her hair was disheveled and she was holding her arm like it was a broken wing.

"Come on," said the older priest as he stepped quickly down the short flight of stairs, pulling Wallis behind him.

"What about Norman? He's rushing over here."

"No, I've let him know where to find us," said the Pastor, tapping his pocket as he slid behind the wheel.

"You think this is safe?" asked Wallis, as she climbed carefully into the front seat, favoring her left shoulder.

"Were you planning on moving in?" said the Pastor, smiling. "It's best not to sit too long in any one place right now. That way they can't rally the troops."

"Troops?" said, Wallis.

"Figure of speech," he said as he drove through the narrow archway and over the mossy bricks till they were on the side street, heading toward town.

"Where are we headed? It's not that I don't trust you but, really, how much experience have you had with intrigue?" said Wallis, glancing in the side mirror repeatedly as she held the seat belt away from her body.

"I'm an Episcopal priest, my dear. Our entire sect was started out of politics, sex and intrigue and not much else has changed in the intervening years. Are you in pain?" he asked.

"I'm okay."

"You are a bad liar, Wallis."

"I've been told that a number of times."

"It's very charming but perhaps not very useful. I know, odd advice from someone in my profession. We're almost there," he said as they turned onto the busy thoroughfare of West Broad Street and the endless seam of upscale shops anchored by a grocery store or a Target. Some of them had already closed for the night as their employees headed home to feed their families. Nothing respectable stayed open in Richmond late into the night except for the Wal-Mart or the movie theaters. Wallis noticed his knuckles were white where he was gripping the steering wheel.

Pastor Donald turned into the parking lot of a strip mall that was fronted by a Chipotle and a For Eyes with a large multiplex movie theater in the back.

"Where are we going?" she asked.

"Just another moment," said the priest.

She thought of all the times she had taken Ned to the movies there or gone out on date night with Norman and been able to rest her head on his shoulder.

Grief suddenly hit her in the middle of her chest making it hard to catch her breath. Everything she held dear felt like it was in jeopardy and the pool of people willing to help her seemed pitifully small.

He took a right through the over-sized parking lot that was in the back and off to the side and turned down a small, narrow side street that was rarely ever used. The tall grass on either side of the cracked pavement looked like it was going to take over shortly and erase the road altogether.

They quickly came to the end of the street and abruptly turned, driving between large stone pillars onto a campus with manicured rolling lawns and clipped hedges. Wallis had never noticed there was anything back here in all of her years driving up and down West Broad Street or parking at the nearby theater. It was like a secret garden hidden in plain sight.

"What is this place?" she asked as they pulled up to a small beige rancher. Here and there along the curving road Wallis could see other identical houses tucked behind trees.

"In the old days we would have called this place a home for foundlings," said Pastor Donald. "Now, they have the moniker of residential education facilities."

"You mean orphanage?" said Wallis, drawing in her breath. "Wait a minute, I know this place. Norman has been sending them donations for years."

"Yes, good cause, nice cover. Your husband is a great multitasker. He's also their legal counsel."

"Why are we here?"

"More will be revealed. Come on, we need to get inside. No one has ever bothered us here but there may be a little more effort put forth tonight." He quickly got out of the car and came around to Wallis' side.

"How is it I have never noticed something this big?" she said, as Pastor Donald held open the door.

"Yes, I hear that a lot and thank The Almighty. We don't notice what we're not interested in or don't see as useful. Troubled or unwanted groups of older children are often overlooked. Some might see that as an insult but I have always seen it as a blessing."

Pastor Donald knocked once before opening the front door of the closest cottage. Wallis entered the small foyer as several boys of varying heights popped up off of a couch and came to greet her.

"Hello, I'm Daniel. Nice to meet you. Can I take your coat?" a boy said in rapid succession. He looked to be about thirteen, tall and lanky with a shock of blonde hair. Wallis started to peel off her coat as a smaller boy stepped forward to help. "Hello, I'm Arthur. Very nice to meet you. May I help?" He kept steady eye contact with her as he helped her get her arm out of the sleeve. Wallis glanced at Pastor Donald.

"Nice job, gentlemen. Points will be noted all around. Let her pass now," he said. The boys stepped back as Daniel gestured with a sweep of his arm toward the main room. Wallis felt an ache inside and wanted to go find Ned.

She stepped into the main room and counted five more boys helping in the kitchen. A man was patiently showing them how to layer lasagna in a large baking dish.

"Stanley Woermer," said Wallis, feeling relieved to see him alive. Still it felt for a moment like the wind had been knocked out of her again. It was startling to see how the pieces broke apart and kept coming together behind the scenes.

"Yes, he's going to be our guest for awhile," said a young woman. "Hi, I'm Lucy. This is my husband, Joe," she said, gesturing toward the large man still sitting on the sofa playing a video game. "Joe's just a giant kid, himself," said Lucy smiling. "We're the house parents for this home. I take it you already know Stanley? He's been great. The boys just love him."

Stanley turned and gave Wallis a small smile as he turned back to the task at hand. "You don't want to put too much in any of the layers or it all starts to ooze together."

Wallis went up behind him and squeezed Stanley's arm to make sure it was really him. "Stanley Woermer, how did you get here?" she asked. "I thought you were, I mean, I was worried you were," Wallis glanced at the boys who were waiting for her to finish her thought, "not doing well."

Stanley glanced back at her but kept working with the boys.

"That would be my doing." Helmut Khroll interrupted as he came in the back door, locking it behind him. "On both counts."

"You," said Wallis. "You helped Stanley?" Wallis willed herself to slow down and take note of her surroundings. Everything has a reason, a motivation behind it, she thought, including all of this. That was basic courtroom training. If I can hang onto that I can keep my bearings.

"Yes, I was driving by at an opportune moment. We never got the opportunity to exchange last names when we first met. My name is Helmut Khroll," he said.

"We can do proper introductions in just a little bit," said Pastor Donald.

Stanley placed a reassuring hand on the boy next to him. "Pete, pay attention," said Stanley, gently. "This is one of my nana's secrets to killer lasagna. You put a little extra fresh oregano just under the top layer of noodles. Then it's a little harder to tell we were using sauce from a jar."

"I have a few questions," said Wallis. "I need to speak with Stanley."

Stanley turned and looked at Wallis. "It'll be okay," he said, gently. "I had no idea, you have to believe me." He was almost whispering, speaking to her as if his words could wound her. "I would have left you alone."

"What is it you know?" asked Wallis.

"We should take that tour," said Pastor Donald, interrupting. "Come on, we can come back in a little while for dinner."

"I have to get home to Ned at some point and soon," said Wallis. "It's already getting late. I can't stay for dinner."

"Someone named Laurel is there with him," said Helmut.

"How did you find Laurel?" asked Wallis.

"I didn't, Norman asked her. It's okay," said Pastor Donald.

"Is Ned your son?" Arthur had sidled up next to her and was holding large sheets of paper at his side. He was about Ned's size and coloring and almost tall enough to look Wallis directly in the eye.

"What?" Wallis looked at him. He seemed so earnest.

"Can we look at my room first? I can lead the way."

"Arthur, that's a great idea," said Pastor Donald. "Why don't you give a quick tour and we'll pick up where you leave off."

"Right this way," said Arthur, giving a little bow. They went down a short hallway that reminded Wallis of the rancher from her childhood. There was a laundry room tucked into the wall, followed by two bedrooms on either side with nondescript framed pictures of different large animals that decorated the walls along the corridor.

"This is my room," said Arthur. "I share it with Pete. Come on in," he said. The walls nearest the door were covered with drawings of men in various stages of combat. "This is my side of the room. My dad was a Marine in Afghanistan but he died over there last year. These are some pictures I'm doing for my mom. She took it pretty hard," he said as he held up the pictures so that Wallis could get a better look.

"These are very nice. You're very good at perspective," said Wallis, "That's not easy."

"Thanks," said Arthur. "That side of the room is Pete's. He's kind of messy," he said, sounding annoyed, as he picked up a tie from the floor and tossed it onto Pete's bed. "Makes me mad because it's a chore and he doesn't do it. I can't wait to leave here," he said, looking around at his room. All of his words tumbled out of him as if he'd been saving them up for awhile.

"It's not so different anywhere else, Arthur. My son, Ned would love to change things, too but he's a kid. He has rules."

"Really?" Arthur looked surprised. He looked like he was going to say something but thought better of it. "I have a stepdad but the cops took him away. He od'ed on heroin and some guys left him in a dumpster. I saw the EMT's stab him in the heart with a needle. I don't know where he is now. Hey, you know, I can tell you all the right doses for any pilz you can name. Try me," he said, in his run-on style. All of the words were bunched up together.

"That's amazing, Arthur. I'm not sure I could get past aspirin."

"I know the right amount for bricks, chill pills, Christmas trees, Jif. Those two are the same. Blues, that's one of my mom's favorites along with vikes. Name one, go ahead, I can do it."

"Tell me more about your dad," said Wallis, changing the subject. She knew she was in tricky parenting territory.

Arthur hesitated and let out a deep sigh. "He died in combat. Some roadside bomb blew his Humvee apart. They said it was an IED. There was even footage, I saw it."

"You saw it?" said Wallis, startled.

"Yeah, the Al-Qaeda filmed it and showed it on YouTube till they took it down."

"Arthur, that was wrong," said Wallis softly, lightly touching the boy's shoulder. "You should never have seen that."

Arthur shrugged. "It's a war."

"Wallis, you ready for the tour of the rest of the joint?" Pastor Donald stood just outside the doorway. "Thank you, Arthur. Are those new pictures? I'd love to see them sometime soon."

"These are for my mom. She's gonna' be here this weekend. I'll show you the next ones." Wallis looked at him standing there alone in his room, still gently holding the present he had made for his mother as she left the room.

"How is it possible to leave someone so young behind and almost forgotten?" she asked. She had seen it hundreds of times a year as an attorney and come to accept that was the way some people were wired but it didn't mean she ever understood their motivations.

"It's not always a choice, Wallis," said the Reverend. "Come on, there's more to see and it's growing late."

Wallis and the Reverend passed back through the living room as all of the boys jumped to their feet again to shake her hand goodbye. She looked over their heads at Stanley who was still in the kitchen as he quickly turned and mouthed good luck.

Helmut was waiting outside smoking a cigarette.

"I've asked you more than once not to do that here," said Pastor Donald.

Helmut dropped the cigarette and ground it out with his heel. "Sorry, long day. Calms my nerves."

"That was interesting," said Wallis. "Did you know that Arthur is a human PDR?"

"Yes, I believe we've all gotten the run down. Arthur, I'm afraid, sees it as a useful skill in order to keep loved ones alive and occasionally to shock other adults," said Pastor Donald. "I picture him someday using it as a pickup line."

"And it will still be a winner," said Helmut, smiling.

"Who are you?" asked Wallis, as they started walking across the campus under a dark, overcast sky. No stars were visible and Wallis had to carefully watch her step.

"In the old days I would have been called a journalist but these days I keep getting mistaken for a blogger." Pastor Donald shot him a look. "I'm sorry. I suppose right now jokes are not very funny," said Helmut. "I'm an investigative journalist who doesn't know when to just say no. I stumbled into this story a few years ago by accident and now it's become an addiction."

"Who do you write for, a German paper?"

"Good ear, but no, I'm on my own. I don't know who'd be willing to take this story. Maybe it's a book someday."

In the past it had been necessary to have Management or Circle operatives inside major newspapers as editors or reporters to make sure that information could be slanted in a certain direction to get the public to easily play follow the leader. If they saw something printed in their newspaper they always took it as gospel and never asked questions. The hard part was always finding talented journalists willing to believe in a large power structure. It wasn't normally in their DNA.

However, in the past ten years both sides had figured out that big money can make anyone rethink their position, even journalists, and they'd found ways to sanitize the payoffs so that busy investigators could still feel good about themselves as they looked for the proof to support the theory they'd been handed by their cell leader.

There were still people who were oblivious to the giant organizations surrounding everything else and did their best to do a good job but the operatives around them worked quietly to portray them as cynical or outliers, just in case they ever caught a glimpse.

These days it was even easier with all of the bloggers and online pundits who never bothered to check facts. All that was needed was a whiff of suspicion from a halfway decent source. They were openly courting corporate cash and didn't even try to look objective or as if they'd ever originated a thought of their own. It was a golden era of information, particularly for Management.

That's why Helmut Khroll was such a thorn in their side.

"Then why pursue it?" she asked.

"You know, that's a good question but journalists have never been good at making sure they get paid when there's a good story involved. Long story for another time."

"Let's take a short tour of the new chapel," said the Reverend, "and we can answer a few of your questions." He held the door open to the small building near the center of the campus.

"That's not the same as offering up information I might not think to ask about, is it?" asked Wallis.

"No, it isn't," said Pastor Donald, "but it's going to have to do."

CHAPTER 28

⌒**ROBERT** sat in front of his laptop quickly scanning the ads on Craig's List. He had made sure the computer's MAC address was already spoofed and he added further layers to any search that was being conducted to rout him out by using a proxy system to hide that he was still in the area.

Computers were regularly pinged by their host providers whenever they were connected to the internet, sending back signals that tracked someone's every move. If someone logged on at home, the host knew they were there and if they went over to Starbucks and logged back on, they could tell how long the user was sipping a latte and updating their Facebook status.

However, it was possible to spoof both an IP and a MAC address, which would still allow a third party to know someone was on the net, just not who was typing the keys. But if there was a long enough trail of an unidentified user it could pop up and alert anyone who was trying to ferret out a lost Circle member. However, doubling up with a proxy made it nearly impossible to know where the unidentified computer sat, masking that someone was actually trying to hide.

None of it though was going to stop the Management from scouring Richmond for what was left of Robert's family. He knew an alert had been sent out and they would keep up the search.

He was squatting with his sons in a newly renovated apartment on Lady Street in the Randolph neighborhood just on the edge of Oregon Hill, which was an old blue collar neighborhood. Both areas were being absorbed by the nearby urban college.

Virginia Commonwealth University had been slowly taking over the area for years pushing out some of the black residents of Randolph and tearing down old boarded up houses for new places to put up the growing student population. Other developers had followed behind them and were back-filling with renovated houses and three flats on the side streets in an attempt to take part in the gentrification. No one would notice with any interest for at least the first few days a man coming and going out of an apartment building. They'd assume it was finally being rented out. Robert's two boys would have to stay hidden till they were ready to move again.

They hadn't said much since the rush from the soccer field.

Robert pulled up the jobs wanted ads and looked for the internships under each category searching for the key phrases. He had to memorize hundreds of new short phrases each year that were taken from the Constitution. They came in the iPhone transmissions and were never to be written down or spoken out loud. Each phrase could be easily reworded to sound more natural and then placed in an ad to help a Circle operative come in from the cold. Somewhere in there would be the regular posting for the new safe house address in the Richmond area. The postings changed daily and the addresses were moved almost as frequently.

He would have to hope that the address wasn't too far across town. He had left his car in the soccer complex's parking lot and the Richmond area wasn't built for walkers. The city and its' suburbs lacked any real public transportation, long stretches of sidewalks or even many taxis. A man with two kids on a bus would be easy to spot.

There, under Human Resources he saw a senior internship stating that there was no pay but 'all receipts from purchases made at appointments would be reimbursed.' The beginning words of Article VI. Robert felt himself relax just a little. It was still possible salvation from this murderous hell was near at hand.

He took down the number and carefully shut down the computer making sure that all the software masking his time online was the last thing to switch off.

His two boys were asleep on the floor curled up in the sleeping bags they had hastily grabbed that afternoon.

He had seen the man slowly fall on the sidelines at the soccer field and the crowd start to gather with everyone's attention turned toward him. Robert knew to immediately look for the telltale signs that it was all a diversion.

Everyone was looking in one direction except for a man or woman here and there who were carefully scanning the crowd. He knew at once they were probably looking for him and even more importantly, his two children. It was too risky to wait around and see if he was wrong. He had to act fast and move out of the Watchers' lines of sight if they were going to have a chance to keep on living.

Mark had yelled to him to get his children as he turned to look directly at his own children. There was no time for Robert to tell him he wasn't circling back and would have to reconnect somehow at a later time.

He grabbed the older twin, Trey hard near the elbow and kept walking till he reached Will and grabbed on, making a sharp turn and weaving his way through the edge of the crowd. He wanted to blend in as much as possible and make his way toward the closest exit as a piece of a small stream of people rather than one man pulling along two boys in soccer uniforms.

They had walked up the rolling hill to the main road where Robert had seen another parent, a woman from the same team trying to make a hasty exit ahead of the crowds. He explained to her that his car wasn't working and he needed a ride home. They didn't live too far from the fields. He knew that his nerves would be written off as frustration over a stalled engine.

It was a calculated move to head home first. There was a chance that

Management was already at the house and waiting for him but he had to take the risk and gather what he could before they hit the road.

The other mother quickly offered to take them all home, asking her own son to get in the back and move all of the books and sports gear out of the way. Small town Southern manners could still be counted on in a pinch.

"Don't get any of that mud on my seats, boys," she had cheerfully sung out, trying to ease the mood for Robert. Trey and Will sat quietly in the back trying not to make eye contact with anyone. Robert had followed protocol as the boys got older and started teaching them about some of the other lessons in life that were a unique necessity for them.

He just hadn't expected to be putting the lessons into action so early or without Carol.

Robert had met Carol in college and at the time was blessedly unaware of any real conspiracies beyond some small controversy over the grading curve in advanced calculus and an old history lesson on Watergate. Carol had introduced him slowly to the idea of larger groups grabbing power with a much more organized and global system that was handed down through family lines by taking him to a few small, open Circle meetings.

That was his first introduction to following protocol.

At first he thought they were one more campus group trying to push an agenda of good will or spirituality or some other vague plan designed to believe in the goodness of everyone. But over time he began to understand they didn't have a specific agenda as much as one clear idea.

"We are part of a circle," Carol had called it, "that is trying to keep the ability to choose in the hands of as many people as possible. We're not trying to tell them what to choose."

"You mean like the democracy we're already a part of?" he had said, with more than a little sarcasm.

"Yes and no," she answered. "It's an ideal that a lot of people believe in but even the existence of the idea is under a constant threat."

Her whole being came alive, Robert had thought, when she talked about being a part of something that gave so much to so many people all over the world.

"People who disagree with each other," she said, "or have no education or they have a list of degrees or piles of money or are struggling to pay the mortgage. They all deserve a chance to believe in being fiscally conservative or welfare for the masses or stem cell research or whatever else it is and argue and compromise and argue again. We all have the right to try and fail and try again. No one should be able to take that away from us. Otherwise, it's all just fate and God gets left out of any of it and then no one is safe."

"Does God really need to be in any of this?" he asked, testing out being a college student and his newfound sense of independence from everything.

"No, but it's all a little too much to stomach without the idea that something bigger is involved."

Robert was worried more about how this was going to affect his chances of getting Carol into bed than he was interested in any big theories on God, conspiracies or democracy. It all seemed like a lot of posturing by some over-educated college students.

"How did you get involved with any of this?" he asked, and was surprised when she cut him off and said all of that would have to be explained later.

It took time but eventually he began to see all of the little connections that created a kind of road map of each member of either side as they went from childhood to college to career. He used the little pins of stars or flags that were everywhere as a starting point to meet someone and under the guise of getting to know them he began to form a pattern out of their lives. He had even tried to buy a flag pin at a local jewelry store without telling Carol just to see what would happen and was surprised when two guys he barely knew from a fraternity started trying to recruit him. They said they had heard about his interest in getting ahead and were interested in helping him out. Some of the people he had been getting to know from the young Management team had already earmarked him as a potential asset. He had tried to ignore the slur they used about Carol being Jewish.

Carol had been so angry with him that she stopped speaking to him for a week.

"Do you not understand that it isn't a game? There's no out, do you get that?" she yelled. He saw her face turning red just before she slammed the door and left him standing there by himself. He was sure they were over till she showed up at his dorm late one night, weeks later and said she was sorry for all of it. She had made an enormous mistake involving someone else and she had no right to do it.

He had missed her so much by then he'd have signed on to anything to have her back. It took some convincing that he was in for the long haul but eventually she had given in and agreed to marry him at last.

He had looked back at that beginning more than once and wondered if he even cared about the Circle at all in those days.

Carol had explained that there was a little more to staying with her than just a ring and a walk down an aisle. It was rare for outsiders to be brought in as spouses but exceptions were made, particularly for anyone from the original twenty. They put him through a few years of training and helped shape the rest of his college courses and then his career. He had asked Carol more than once how this was so different from what the other side did and finally she had sat him down and said, "One side constantly grows this enormous army invisible to even those working or playing next to them so they can control the message and in some twisted way keep themselves safe from ever having to think or act. They don't want to risk losing a life that has fewer questions and nicer stuff and they see it all as an estimation of numbers. Only so many will end up with this easier life and the others who don't were unfortunate and on the wrong side of the statistic. The other side, the Circle, is trying to grow an army just as large and just as invisible so they can preserve the right to let everyone else live a life full of possibilities and choices and interruptions and failures and unexpected surprises. We give in to the idea that some will get more than others and I can't tell you exactly who that will be or what they will look like but it's possible that we'll all be okay. Now, you choose which one you want to see survive. Frankly, God only exists in the places where we aren't trying to control all of the questions."

He had loved her so much in that moment.

Now she was dead. Robert had stopped talking to God after they found Carol. He still hoped some kind of God was there but it was too painful to try and rely on anything that had a part in her drowning.

He turned and looked at his sons curled up, peacefully sleeping. Tears were mixing with the snot from his nose.

He wiped his face on his sleeve, trying to hold back the waves of grief that would come over him at inopportune times and threaten to stop him dead in his tracks. Carol is gone, he thought to himself, and there's nothing I can do about that right now. I have to protect my boys.

That's what matters most, despite what Carol had made him promise, almost on a daily basis, every year they were married.

Somewhere out there in the small Southern city was Carol's thumb drive with the names of her sons on it. He had to get it back before the wrong people had confirmation of just what was happening and who was involved.

"All of those people I grew up with at that orphanage, my home, would be in danger. Their entire families would be at risk. Don't let that happen," she'd insist. "Protect them like they were your family because to me, they are my brothers and sisters and I owe them all my life." Her words kept echoing back to him in the cold, empty apartment.

CHAPTER 29

WALLIS sat back in the pew, letting her bottom slide over the polished northern red oak until the curve of her back fit itself effortlessly against the gentle camber that someone had slowly carved out a long time ago. Helmut and the Reverend were sitting in the pew just in front of her. Wallis looked up at the large, circular Rose window in the front of the church wall, situated just behind the two men. The window held long glass petals of color each displaying a child performing a different virtue. They were all formed around the most inner circle of a stain glass modern depiction of a mother and her beloved child. Wallis wondered how painful the entire scene of parental devotion might be for the throngs of children who sat here gazing up at the window every year.

"Do you think it's possible to really know how to miss what you never had?" asked Wallis. Helmut turned to look back at the window.

Wallis rested her elbows on her knees and put her face in her hands. Never in her life had she felt so defeated without someone to turn to and ask what it all meant.

"Wallis," said Pastor Donald, "we need to talk a little before Norman inevitably comes busting in here. There are a few things you need to know."

Wallis lifted her head. "You mean, like what's that list all about?" She looked at Helmut while pressing down gently on the side of her pants to see if it was still there. The thumb drive was safely in her pocket.

"The BIGOT list," said Helmut, nodding his head. "That's a good place to start."

"You're not going to like a lot of what I'm about to tell you," started Pastor Donald, "but I want you to know that I was the one who told Norman many years ago to say nothing to you."

"Norman is responsible for what Norman decides to do," said Wallis, letting her voice slide into her best attorney tone. "He's not your puppet."

"That is very true and a great observation. Norman is no one's puppet and he made that clear when he turned away from his family heritage as a young man and then sealed it by choosing you as his mate. You, of all the people in the entire world. There wasn't a more controversial choice. I wasn't surprised by Norman's desire for a more normal existence but I was a little reluctant to go along with what appeared to be such a reckless coupling. You have your own way of doing things and when paired with your family tree that makes you an unknown component."

"What are you talking about? Do you have that much of a problem with women who work?" asked Wallis, trying to move so her shoulder wouldn't ache so much.

"No," said Pastor Donald, smiling a little, "and either way I don't have any kind of a problem with you. But to choose to live his life in such close proximity to those who would wish him dead if they only knew his lineage was a little surprising. So contrarian, which I suppose is the definition of Norman Weiskopf's personality."

"What do you mean, Norman's lineage? And who do we associate with that would want Norman dead?" Wallis asked the question slowly, aware that the answer was going to sting and take away just a little more of someone she loved. She just wasn't sure who it would be or how much would remain when they were finally done.

"Norman is a hero," said Helmut. "It's much harder to stay and just live your life among the enemy."

"What?" asked Wallis.

"Wallis," said the Reverend gently, "There are people who are seen as royalty because they took power on a battlefield in some long ago time and then squashed a crown down on their heads. They keep their crowns by any means necessary and justify the mayhem they cause by painting the world as a bleak place that is in dire need of control by human beings. There are others, though who are made into royalty by those around them because they did their best to spread the power around to the masses and resisted ever seeing themselves as special," he said.

"It's as if mere mortals have to find a more divine reason to follow anyone rather than just sound reasoning," said Helmut.

"You are all talking in riddles. What are you trying to say?"

"Wallis, my dear, your family is a part of the original members who tried to take the power and put the crown on their own heads. No, no, it's alright. Don't pull away. You have to hear me out," said Pastor Donald.

"You are all crazy," she hissed.

"No, we're not. Your father, Walter was part of a long, unending line that began hundreds of years ago and is now affectionately referred to as the Management."

"Liar!" yelled Wallis, trying to stand. The pain from her shoulder made it too difficult. "Liar! How dare you say things about a man you never met. My father was never a murderer. He would have never harmed anyone. No, no," she cried, "and to think I almost believed all of this gibberish." She slid out of his reach. It was a comfort, just for a moment, to think that she had fallen prey to a false plot made up by crazy people. Crazy people usually came in small numbers and could be avoided or put away.

"No, I'm not lying and I'm not saying your father was an active participant," said Pastor Donald.

"But he was," said Helmut.

"Not helping right now," said the Pastor.

"Not going to help to lie to her so that she can just find it out later. Besides, I have a feeling she'd try and find out on her own and all of that prying will only put her in more danger. We need to keep her alive. We've already seen how shy Management is to approach anyone in her family, well, until today. It's an asset we can use."

Pastor Donald took a good look at Wallis. "Good point, I would think. Wallis, you can't make all of this mess just about you. There's too much at risk. You're being enormously selfish. Normally, I'd come at all of this from a gentler angle but I just don't have time. Look, you are part of what Management sees as a dynasty and the way those people value DNA makes you some kind of human Holy Grail for them. They had high aspirations for what you might some day do in the organization."

"But Harriet put a monkey wrench in the whole thing," said Helmut.

"My mother, my mother knows?"

"Of course she knows," said Helmut. "Walter had to get permission to marry her. She was deemed acceptable and compliant. Boy, were they wrong."

"What do you mean?" asked Wallis.

"Your mother surprised everyone when she refused to let you be brought up with any knowledge of Management. She put her foot down when you were just a baby and said she'd take you out herself before she'd let that happen. She knew it was powerful leverage because at least in Management's eyes there weren't a lot of direct descendants left from the original founders. You were a precious commodity to them and they badly wanted control over your upbringing but Harriet got in between them and you."

"There were rumors that she actually tried to end her life and take you with her once when you were das kind, a small child," said Helmut.

"How did you know about that?" Wallis stopped herself. She had never talked about the incident when she was only four years old and her mother had made a half-hearted attempt to drown them both by driving the car into a retention pond. She only remembered it as snapshots frozen in her mind, no matter what she did to forget. Her mother left for a long rest that summer and her grandmother took her place for awhile. After that, no one ever mentioned it again. Norman didn't even know about that summer. She had learned to gauge her feelings after that and watch others to detect their true intentions.

"Wallis," Pastor Donald interrupted, as he gave a withering glance at Helmut, "can you imagine what it must have taken to convince some very determined and powerful people not to just take you away? Say what you want about all the rest of it but your mother stayed out of a love for you."

"You may as well know, there were members who encouraged your father to find a way to help your mother onto her heavenly rewards," said Helmut.

"When? I don't believe you. It's not true."

Pastor Donald rolled his eyes. "Have you noticed how often you've managed to startle her in the last five minutes, Mr. Khroll? Perhaps we could let the more gruesome details out a little later?"

"No, I want to know. I have a right to know," said Wallis.

"It's one of those things that once you hear part of it you have to get the rest," said Helmut, shrugging his shoulders. "Walter genuinely loved your mother, loved you too. But he was weak and didn't know how to stand up to anyone. I think he was relieved that your mother took such a bold move and yet everyone lived to tell about it later."

"Did you know him?" asked Wallis.

"No," said Helmut, "I'd be what's considered persona non grata but I've interviewed quite a few people who did know your vati. Walter was trapped under a mountain of expectations that were attached to him by an umbilical cord. Poor sap never stood a chance. But Harriet, now that was the one with the balls. Imagine how far she had to take things to let them know she was capable of killing her beloved child."

"Lovely," said Pastor Donald. "Can I have the story back, now? I have to impart just a little more."

Wallis leaned to her right trying to take some pressure off of her shoulder. "It looks like it might be dislocated," said Helmut. Wallis ignored him. It was a lot to take in to think of Harriet as gutsy for a worthy cause and especially to protect her only child. "It's not possible," whispered Wallis. "Where's your proof?"

"That's all to come," said Pastor Donald. "There is something more important right now that I need to get you to understand. You are not the only heir apparent. Norman is a direct descendant from the other side. He and his brothers are part of the handful of survivors from an enormous tragedy."

"Even though everyone in the Circle swears they don't believe in that sort of thing there's still a certain amount of reverence given to anyone involved in the emigration from Europe. I must confess, I wonder about that a little myself," said Helmut.

"But pay attention to what really matters, Wallis. We are all adults and while an early death for any of us would be tragic we at least got to try out a few things while we were here. That list you keep mentioning, that's what is of vital importance. Those children, your child, they deserve a chance at life as well."

"My child, what about Ned?"

"He is the only one of his kind in this world. A child born out of two dynasties who are trying to tear each other apart. A child who is one of the last descendants of the original founders of both sides. To be able to claim him as a member would boost the morale of one side and crush the other. It would give Management the spiel they need to recruit and grow to a size we may not be able to stop." Pastor Donald let out a tired sigh.

"However, Ned has more power to crush or rekindle the Circle's efforts than they as yet realize. Until now, Management only knew about half of his inheritance, your half. Part of what's on that thumb drive you protect is the other half of that secret," said Pastor Donald.

"And just a little bit more," said Helmut.

"We can address that later. Just remember, Wallis, Norman followed his heart and then he had to play catch up his entire marriage and be careful to always keep his head in order to keep both of you safe from detection. He had to sit there at all of those family functions right under Walter and even Harriet's noses knowing they'd have turned him in if they'd known who he really was in this world. It would not have mattered that he was their son in law or the father of their grandchild. That would have been asking too much, even of Harriet. But Norman chose to play the game because of how much he loves you."

"Wallis! Are you alright?" Norman came rushing in the back of the church looking frantic.

CHAPTER 30

IT was the first time Wallis could ever remember hesitating in front of Norman. He was the one person she had always told everything to, unfiltered, without even trying to edit what was okay, what needed to wait or what needed to stay hidden. He saw the look on her face and stopped halfway down the aisle as if he were afraid to find out that something fundamental to who they were as a family had changed.

Helmut started to say something but Pastor Donald put his hand firmly on Helmut's arm and shook his head, no.

Wallis was trying to weigh the evidence in her mind just like she'd seen a jury do hundreds of times but it wasn't working. The worth of their family couldn't be added up and determined by their mistakes or their virtues.

"I'm sorry," said Norman. He was still standing a distance from her. Wallis had never seen him look so vulnerable. "I knew from the first time that I met you, you'd be better off if I just stayed away. Loving you has been the most selfish thing I've ever done."

She knew he was pleading his case. "Don't," she said. He let out a gasp and his face quickly grew ashen.

"How could you not tell me about Ned?" she said, letting out a sob as her entire body shuddered in a rolling wave.

"I made a choice from the beginning. I couldn't go back and forth just because circumstances changed," he said, his arms outstretched like he was hoping she'd fill them.

"You, you made a choice!" she screamed. "You did! Where was I in any of this? I had a right to know, at least from you. I know about all of it. They told me what I come from," she said, gasping.

"And then what? Watch you try to reconcile every good memory you have of Walter. And what about Harriet?" He was saying everything in a calm and even voice that must have taken him years to develop, thought Wallis. But his eyes gave him away. There was a panic in his eyes that told her how hard he was trying to say all of the things he had spent years acting as if he didn't even know.

"Even if you could do it, why would I want to be the reason you had to always keep your guard up around your mother?" he said. "You know, I know that hell. Watching every word, every gesture. No one gave me a choice, ever. I had to listen to long lectures about the common good as if my entire lifetime was an offering to a cause. The best I could hope for was to try and balance between the two worlds."

"What two worlds? The Circle and Management? They are two sides of one big, plotting world." Wallis was finding it far more difficult to mute how she was feeling. Her one good arm was making pinwheels in the air and her face was splotchy with streaks of dirt and a bruise that was already turning purple. "When did you start to think that I wasn't a part of this team?" she yelled, waving her arm between the two of them.

She saw his shoulders sag and she felt herself give in just a little but then she remembered Ned and the anger welled up inside of her again, making her stomach churn.

"I have never held anything back from you. Never!" she said, jabbing the air with her finger. "We have a son, together, Norman. Even if you didn't think I could bear it as well as you could, I had a right to know, to work this out with you. Please tell me, how often did I skate right alongside something that could have harmed Ned and didn't even know it?"

"I wasn't," he said, halting, "I wasn't trying to make all of the decisions. I was trying to give you what I wished for so often back when I still let myself even think about it," he said. He looked worn out, like he had done his best and failed.

"What was that? What did you wish for that you've apparently never told me?"

"To not know there was so much that was decided all of the time. To be able to believe that it was possible for something random to happen that was good and unexpected." His voice had grown flat and he was no longer looking directly at Wallis. "I had to choose you, to be with you. I had to believe there was something I could do in this lifetime that was without reason and just because I believed in it. If that wasn't possible, well, I wasn't going to hurt you the same way."

Wallis lowered her arm.

"You were trying to believe," Wallis said, quietly. She stopped for a moment and took a deep breath, letting it out slowly. She willed herself to take each step in front of her till the gap was closed and leaned into his body. "Don't tell me why you had to love me. You don't have to explain," she said, her arm gently cradled between their bodies.

Wallis' shoulder jiggled slightly as Norman cried, holding onto her tightly, burying his face in the crook of her neck and her tangled hair, his hands holding on to her wounded shoulders. It was hard for her to endure the pain.

"I'm sorry if I ever let you down, Norman," she whispered. "And I'm sorry if I made you carry all of this by yourself. Maybe, maybe you were right," she said, feeling exhausted.

Norman lifted his head and took a deep breath, clearing his throat. He gave himself a good shake trying to regain his composure.

"I knew a Weiskopf wasn't going to be able to be that vulnerable for very long," she said gently, trying to remind him of what she had thought were more normal times. He made an attempt at a smile and took her face in his hands. She slowly took his hands and held them close to her chest.

"I only have the one good arm," she said, smiling. "Norman, I'm not sure I would have even believed you before tonight. I'd like to think I would have tried but as we both know, I have a very practical mind, and to ask me to believe that Harriet was going against protocol to defend me. That's still the hardest part." They both laughed until Wallis felt the pinch in her shoulder again and let out a soft moan. Norman gently lifted her arm, cradling the elbow to take pressure off of the shoulder.

"You see, this is how we do things, Weiskopf," Wallis said, quietly. "We carry the crap together." She took a sudden step back, remembering the leer on Oscar's face as he tried to push her car off the bridge. "I have no idea what lengths they'll go to, this Management." She pushed her hand against her stomach as she thought of what it all meant. "Oscar wanted me dead and he was only taking someone else's orders. Apparently, I've become expendable. Does that mean Ned is too?"

"Oscar did this to you?" asked Norman.

"The first thing we have to do as a team is figure out how to protect Ned. I'd prefer not to use Harriet's plot of a willingness to kill as a strategy this time."

"She was probably thinking off the cuff. It made me respect her and give her some points and that made being around her all of these years, possible. I've been thinking about how to keep Ned away from all of this from the moment you said you were pregnant. I'm not sure how to do that beyond a day-to-day plan."

"I might be able to help with that a little," said Helmut, who was still sitting in the pew next to Pastor Donald. He stood and stretched out his arm across the pews, waiting for Norman to walk toward him and shake his hand. "I don't believe we've met. I'm Helmut Khroll."

"Yes, I've heard your name before," said Norman. "You're the journalist who keeps turning out stories about what Management's been doing overseas. I'm surprised you're still in one piece."

"Thank Goodness for the internet and a little training on how to move around unnoticed," said Helmut.

"You knew about him?" asked Wallis.

"I've noticed his postings. If you follow all of the pundits you see the patterns and can tell who's playing on what side. Helmut Khroll is the only one who seems to take issue with everyone," said Norman. "He's what you'd call a pain in everyone's side."

"We used to call that news," said Helmut.

"I liked your piece on the new farms China is creating in Africa," said Norman. "I haven't read about that anywhere else."

"Yeah, that was a good one. Getting out of the country was a little tricky. I have a nice scar to show for my efforts," said Helmut, pulling the collar of his shirt to expose a ropey scar along the top of his right shoulder. "I was never sure if the border guard knew who I was or was pissed off that my cheap watch was a little too meager as a bribe."

"It's like you think you can get the ignorant masses to do something if you keep exposing the insides of the machinery," said Norman.

"At the very least I can make it more difficult for them to starve out the villages on their own land or maybe control all of the power in America," said Helmut.

"Yes, you've always aimed low," said Pastor Donald.

"You two already knew each other?" asked Norman, looking at Pastor Donald and Helmut.

"Oh yes, I've sought refuge more than once from the good minister and his ilk. It amazes me how little is getting written about what these new leased farms in Africa will do to the local people. It's horrible enough to be starving and there is nothing growing and you know you're doing the best you can, given the circumstances, for your family. But it's genocide on an entirely different level to grow food in front of someone, on their land and then refuse to share. Not only is there no outcry, there's not even a murmur. Why is the Circle being so quiet?" asked Helmut.

"As worthy as the topic is, can I interject so we can move things along?" said the Reverend. "My old friend, I saw what Oscar tried to do to your bride and he struck me as the sort who only acts upon orders from above. However, that doesn't mean the orders came from the appropriate sources. There have been quite a few slip-ups lately."

"You think someone is trying to clean up their mess," said Norman.

"Yes, and it's someone who isn't high ranking enough to realize who Wallis really is or what a bigger mess they just made. We may be able to use that to our advantage."

"But first things first, we need to fix that shoulder," said Helmut, as he grabbed hold of Wallis' arm and shoulder. "Brace yourself, this may hurt a little." Helmut jerked the shoulder back into place before anyone could stop him.

Wallis let out a scream and started to black out, falling back into Norman's arms.

"That ought to do it," said Helmut. "Try your arm. What? I've had to do that a few times in the field."

Wallis moved her arm around and her shoulder was still sore but moved a lot more easily. As the pain calmed down she knew what had to come next.

"I'm going home to see my son," she said.

"I understand," said Pastor Donald, "but we'll need to revisit what to do next."

On the drive home Norman kept patting Wallis' leg like he was trying to reassure both of them that they were still intact, body and soul.

"Can I tell you something I've never said out loud?" asked Norman.

"There's more?" Wallis blurted out. She immediately regretted it. She was usually so good at not passing along her opinion of anything, relieving everyone of the burden of competition. She tried to smile at Norman to cover her slip. "I'm sorry," she said, "I know it's complicated and I don't understand. Go ahead, tell me and I'll listen."

"I believe in God," said Norman.

"There were a few dozen things I was thinking you might say, Norman Weiskopf and that wasn't one of them," said Wallis.

"It's what's kept me sane. This battle that's been going on for over two hundred years and takes so many innocent lives into it to keep it all moving, it has no end."

"It sounds crazy to think there could even be a conspiracy that vast that goes undetected by the masses," said Wallis.

"That's why they do battle right out in the open most of the time. People accept that there's going to be conflict and everyone at the top is generally part of one side or the other." Wallis watched as Norman kept checking the rear view mirror to see if there were any cars that seemed to be following them. She wanted to ask him about it but she knew her only intention was to get Norman to say something that would reassure her and she knew there wasn't anything. She didn't want to make him point that out to her.

"It's a family feud that can go on in some form forever and probably will. But, there was this moment when I met you." Norman stopped talking and stared straight ahead at the traffic along Three Chopt Road.

"Norman, why was that enough to make you believe in something bigger that cared at all?"

He hesitated, his jaw working from side to side. "Imagine falling for this girl whose family started the machinery that twisted my life and killed my grandfather and his entire family, including every cousin, every man, woman and child they could get their hands on. When I stand in the same room with Harriet I wonder if somewhere inside of her she's glad they all died."

"What a horrible thought," whispered Wallis.

"I knew that Harriet had done something to protect you. I had heard the rumors. Besides, we all had to wonder why you weren't a part of Management, given your blood line."

"It must have really tweaked my mother's nerves when I married someone of the Jewish persuasion," said Wallis.

"Actually, I'm not sure that matters as much as you think it does. There is a lot of animosity that's built up quietly between most religions and Management and they've all done battle with the organization at some point. Some more quietly than others," he said. "It's the Episcopalian Church that's like a flea on their neck right now."

"Pastor Donald," said Wallis.

"He's just one figure. The Episcopal Church has a few things going for it that have made it easier for them to claim small victories. They're organized like a corporation with an elected presiding bishop at the top so there's a centralized system but they don't have the visibility of the Catholic Church so they can maneuver more easily without the notice. No one cares nearly as much if you're Episcopalian than if you're Jewish or Catholic or even Baptist and the Episcopalians sent out just as many missionaries around the world to establish bases."

"You're kidding me? There were political motives?"

"Of course, I would have thought that was obvious," said Norman as he passed Larry Blazney's house.

Wallis looked at the black wreath on the purple front door. "Was Larry part of it?" asked Wallis.

Norman shook his head. "No, he wasn't and if he'd gotten nosy around any other house than ours they probably wouldn't have cared. I don't know."

"Why did they kill Ray Billings? Was it really over this thumb drive?"

"Thankfully, you still have it. There has to be something on there that scares them so much they lost some of their control over one of their main Mid-Atlantic offices. Have you looked at the drive?"

"No, there hasn't been time. I'm not even sure I'd know what to look for without Ned's help and I haven't been able to bring myself to cross that line."

"We may have to. Ned is the only human being I know that is capable of keeping secrets from anyone, including us and Management won't harm," said Norman, as he turned off the engine at the bottom of their driveway.

"You know, we'd be doing to him the very same thing that was done to you. We'd be dragging him into an awareness that you've hated all of these years," said Wallis.

"I know but what if they took Ned from us and I never warned him or told him about the other half of his heritage. What would have been the wrong move then?"

The back door opened and Ned ran out to the car with Laurel close behind him. Joe barked and leaped out the back door running past Laurel to nip at Ned's heels.

"Mom, Mom! Are you alright? Laurel told me about your accident!" he yelled through the glass on her side. Wallis slowly opened the door and got out of the car wrapping her good arm around her son as he hugged her tight. "I was so scared," he said, as he began to cry.

"He was fine right up until the moment he saw your face," said Laurel. "Are you okay?"

"My shoulder has seen better days but it'll be alright. I could use a hot bath and a drink. You think you might stay overnight?" asked Wallis.

"I thought you'd never ask," said Laurel.

CHAPTER

WALLIS made a makeshift sling out of a Chanel scarf that had the large, gold interlocking C emblem against a red background. Her mother had given it to her in one of the familiar Christmas boxes a few years ago.

"Is this homage to Harriet or another defiant gesture?" asked Norman.

"I can't decide. You know, it was a lot easier to know how I felt about her when I could make her one-dimensional. Finding out she's full of spit and vinegar is really throwing me off," said Wallis. Wallis was propped up on her side of the bed with her arm resting on top of a pillow.

Ned lifted his head from where it was once again buried against his mother's good shoulder.

"What?" said Ned.

"Nothing," said Wallis. "I was complimenting your grandmother."

"You must be okay if you're making jokes," said Ned. "Where's Laurel?"

Wallis smiled and kissed her son's forehead. "She's gone to bed, you wore her out. It's about time you were asleep too, young man."

"I could help, you know. I heard what you were saying about a thumb drive," said Ned. Wallis glanced over at Norman who shook his head, no.

"I know you could help and I appreciate it. But, at least for now, your dad and I are going to try to muddle through."

"But," said Ned, "you'll get stuck just trying to open the file."

"I'll probably get stuck trying to put the right end into the drive. I'll make you a promise," said Wallis, not looking at Norman, "if we get stuck, I'll ask for your help. Okay? Go brush your teeth."

Wallis insisted on climbing the stairs to Ned's room and sitting by his bed till he fell asleep. Joe was curled up on his bed and raised his head when Wallis sat down.

"Good boy," she said, gently patting the dog's head. "You watch over him, okay?"

She gently rubbed Ned's back in the semi-darkness and said a small prayer for her son, trying to remember the last time she had actually asked God for anything. Ned started gently snoring and Wallis shifted her weight slowly to get up without disturbing him. She leaned back down to move a strand of wet hair off of his forehead and take one last, long look at her son's face before she left the room.

"What are you doing?" asked Norman, who had appeared in the doorway.

"Praying," said Wallis.

"Do you mind if I ask what your wish list is?"

"Not to make Ned pay for any stupid mistakes that are made by the grownups." Wallis straightened up and winced as her shoulder jiggled. "That and a new shoulder."

"We need to get that looked at," said Norman.

"You ever actually pray?" asked Wallis. As she walked toward Norman he held his arms open wide like he had in the chapel. She could remember him doing this for her at least once a day every year they'd been married.

He gently enfolded her in his arms and said, "I don't know. The good Reverend tries to encourage me to at least talk to God but he may be just trying to fill a quota."

"Jokes in the middle of people trying to kill us," whispered Wallis. "Nice."

"I believe it's one of the perks of marriage," said Norman.

"Tell me true, Norman. Do you believe God is there?"

Norman let out a deep sigh and Wallis felt his shoulders give way just a little. "I have no idea," he said, "but I'm a little worried I'm about to find out."

Wallis let out a small laugh. "What would Pastor Donald say?" she asked.

"It's about time. Then he'd tell me the same thing he's been telling me for years. Pray for His will to be done and then I can let it go. That's what's stopped me for this long."

"What?" asked Wallis, turning in his embrace so that her back was against his chest and she could see the outline of her son, sleeping peacefully in his bed.

"I'm a little concerned about what God's will might be for me. Things haven't always worked out so well for Weiskopfs. I just can't believe it could be that simple."

"Norman, what if we do need Ned's help?"

"No," said Norman, in a loud whisper. "I've been thinking about what you said. No, we do our best not to drag a nine year old boy into this. Let him live in peace a little longer."

"He's in the middle of it already, Norman. I don't think it's going to be about if, but how much and when." Wallis thought she heard Norman swallowing down something and she turned back around to face him. "Hey, none of this is your doing or your fault."

"You didn't feel that way a few hours ago," said Norman.

"I know and I'm sorry about that," she said, resting her head on his shoulder. "I made a mistake, Norman. I built this whole idea up in my head that you were somehow superhuman and would never have a good reason to keep anything from me."

"Can't I have both?" asked Norman.

Wallis breathed in deeply. "Sure, I can try that too."

"Too? What's the other new idea?"

"That God might actually care about my prayer." Wallis felt dragged down by the worry.

"We need to get a look at what's on that thumb drive," said Norman.

"Use my computer," said Ned, as his head popped up from his bed.

"How long have you been awake, young man?" asked Wallis, startled.

"Just now," said Ned, sitting up and rubbing his eyes. "Come on, Mom. Besides, if they encrypted it by hiding the real data underneath something else, you won't be able to find it. That's what I'd do if I was trying to hide something."

"Where did you learn something like that in the first place, Ned?" asked Norman.

"I'm a little afraid of that answer," said Wallis.

Ned rolled his eyes as he kicked off the covers and crawled out of his bed. He was wearing his favorite pajamas that had the phrase Defense Advanced Research Projects Agency printed in binary code all over. Wallis had found them online and when they showed up even Ned was impressed that she got the inside joke. She looked at her young son in his pajamas and thought about how vulnerable he looked.

"You people worry too much," he said. "Kids talk at school. We're not stupid you know and some of the guys at the job showed me some cool spy gear."

"When did we become, you guys?" asked Norman. "And what job? Have I been working that much lately?"

"He's talking about Computer City. I've been letting him hang out with the Mobile Geeks on the occasional Friday," said Wallis.

"When I get my homework done early, it's our deal," said Ned, as he turned on his computer and got himself situated in front of the screen. "I fix computers," said Ned, "and sometimes during our break the guys will show me the newest stuff."

"Guys?" asked Norman. "More guys?"

"Really, Norman, this is the least of our worries right now," whispered Wallis. "Focus. He's talking about some twenty-something guys who repair computers for a living. Ned usually ends up showing them a thing or two and I think we're about to have him do the same thing for us."

"It's called steganography. Hiding stuff should be easy."

"Stega what? I'm already lost," said Wallis.

"Very funny, Mom," said Norman.

Ned smiled softly at Wallis. "I told you he had a high opinion of you," whispered Norman.

"In coding all of the code is actually invisible. An image or an audio file is just a code that some software knows how to interpret into an image or song. You know, there's always data included in those files, metadata where you can put information like the artist's name, album, song title, bitrate, beats per minute. All that kind of stuff."

"All what kind of stuff?"

"The stuff I just listed, Mom, pay attention. You can attach whatever you want in the metadata. It'll be invisible until something knows how to read it."

"What's the something?" asked Norman

"Like an MP3 on a computer. You'd also need audio playing software. All those softwares know how to read that stuff."

"I get about every third word of what you're saying but I think I'm hanging in there," said Wallis.

Ned let out a snort and laughed. Joe barked and ran in a small, tight circle, which made Ned laugh harder. Wallis was grateful that he didn't understand how much danger surrounded all of them. If Esther or Helmut were to be believed a lot of it circled right around her son.

"When somebody plays the song they wouldn't know anything had been added or changed and it would be impossible for them to know what's in the metadata."

"Is it possible to hide a message from someone who's looking for it?

"Sure, that's easy. You create additional tags that the software isn't looking for and the information would just sit there until something asks for it."

"What's a tag?" asked Norman.

"Just a line of information. The stuff someone's trying to hide."

"What if we don't have the software?" asked Wallis.

"We download it, don't worry, Mom. I've got this. Hold on." Ned went to his backpack and pulled out an orange thumb drive. "Barry gave me some software when we were talking about it. I was hoping I'd get the chance to try it out but I wasn't sure how to find some really good metadata. Who knew it'd be my mom," he said laughing.

Wallis felt her stomach tighten.

"Ned, hold on just a second. I need to ask your dad something. Norman?" she said, signaling him to follow her to the hallway. "Look, I'm having second thoughts about this. You were right. He's just a little boy. He doesn't understand at all, which is how I'd like to keep it. If he even remotely started to catch on I don't think he'd ever sleep again."

"Someone tried to kill you tonight, Wallis," said Norman, keeping his voice low. "We don't know if they're planning to try again or who they'll target next."

The color drained from Wallis' face. "Do you think they'd go after Ned?"

"I have no idea but I'm hoping that drive tells us something. We need to get ahead of them just a little. We aren't exactly handy with a gun. All we have going for us is information but we have to be able to get at it."

"Should we be trying to hide?" asked Wallis.

"Hide where? Of all the people in the world you and Ned are the most recognizable people to Management. Please, let's just keep going and keep it light and hope that the information is just lists or so detailed that Ned doesn't connect the dots. It's all we have and we don't have a lot of time. You haven't seen the news today, have you?"

"No, why?" asked Wallis. She could feel her stomach churning again. Her entire body ached and all she really wanted to do was get in a hot tub and stay there for awhile.

"Look, I don't know how to tell you this one. Apparently, you haven't been answering your phone either."

"No, I was being chased down by crazy people," said Wallis, her voice straining. "What, what is it?"

"Julia tracked me down. Yvette Campbell died today. They think she may have had a heart attack."

"Oh no," whispered Wallis. She was finding it hard to catch her breath. "No, no." She bent over and put her hands on her knees, willing herself to stay upright. "Do you think it was something else? I missed Bunko night and didn't have a chance to tell anyone. Why would anyone want to kill Yvette? Good Lord, how much is there that we don't know?"

"Breathe, Wallis. Take in a breath and hold it. We can't afford to panic, even a little. I'm sorry for all of this," said Norman.

"You can't possibly hold yourself responsible for who my parents turned out to be."

"Look, we aren't going to find out much more about anything else tonight other than what might be on that thumb drive. We are going to do our best to always protect Ned even if we have to lay down our lives to do it. Right now, that means getting our son's help because he's smarter than the two of us combined," said Norman.

"You think there's an end to this nightmare that doesn't involve any harm coming to our family?" asked Wallis.

"Yes, yes I do and I'm going to make sure of it," said Norman. "Tom should be here by tomorrow and together I think we can come up with something."

"We're relying on Tom? Is there more to him than I knew about the first go round?" asked Wallis.

"You're in for at least one pleasant surprise," said Norman. "But he's got a stop he has to make before we meet up with him."

"You guys ever coming back?" Ned called out.

Norman walked back into the room with Wallis right behind him. She did her best to shake off the feeling of dread and put any image of Yvette laughing and enjoying herself at their last Bunko game out of her mind.

"Okay," said Ned, "squirming in his seat till he was comfortable. "You have the drive?"

Norman nodded at Wallis and she reached into her pocket. She'd been keeping the drive close by ever since she got out of the damaged Jag. "Here, Ned. How will you know if we've gotten all of the information that's hidden?"

"We might not but there are a few things I can do that should answer that question. We look under all of the images first. Every image you take has metadata imbedded in it," said Ned as he pushed the drive into the port.

"They do? Every image there is?" asked Wallis. She watched Ned typing and clicking.

"Yeah, by the camera. Date taken, kind of lens, the camera setting, that kind of stuff. There's metadata hidden in all kinds of electronic things we use. The guys at the store claim that the government is constantly tracking us," said Ned.

Norman cleared his throat.

"What are the limits to what someone could track?" asked Norman.

"Metadata could include where you were, when and if someone has a lot of that data on one person it forms a picture of who they are that's better than breaking into any actual files," said Ned.

"Did the geeks, the guys at the store say if there was any way to counter it?" said Norman.

"It's possible but it's not easy and everyone gets tracked these days. You draw more attention if you suddenly fall off the grid," said Ned. "There's even a new program that can be attached to anything with a GPS without the user knowing about it that can track when you're in the aisle of a store, what kind of store and not only what aisle but where you stopped and for how long."

"This question sounds ridiculous under the circumstances but is all of that legal?"

"So far it is. Marketing people can use it to see what's effective and when you get near their product they could send you an email or a coupon," said Ned. "Okay, here's the first bit of metadata."

Wallis and Norman leaned over Ned's shoulder to get closer to the computer screen. There were lines of data listing all of the children in the Circle program with a list of which orphanage and what their plans were for the future.

"No wonder everyone wants this. It has thousands of names on here," said Wallis.

"If someone had this information they could forecast where the Circle was headed and even manipulate things without being seen."

"Tell me again how this list differs from the other team?" asked Wallis.

"You are free to change your plans at any time," said Norman. "There's not only an out clause, there's a 'we can work with you' clause. Big difference."

"What about the original twenty?" asked Wallis. Norman looked surprised and he quickly looked down at the floor. "Between Esther, Helmut and Pastor Donald I kind of have the basics of the story," she said.

"What story?" asked Ned, but before anyone could answer, something caught his attention and he hunched closer to the screen. "Hey, wait a minute, there's another layer here. I've never heard of multiple layers of metadata. There's something else. Hold on, I think I can manipulate the search engine to ask for the deeper tags."

"Do we bother to ask how?" asked Wallis, glancing at Norman.

"Only if you'd like that feeling of dread in the pit of your stomach about how little you grasp to grow and grow," said Norman giving her a small smile.

"Quit kidding around, Dad," said Ned. "We're working as a team here," he said, giving his father a serious look. Norman smiled at his son and said, "You're right. Pardon my indiscretion. We're Weiskopf men after all."

Wallis looked at the two of them and suddenly felt a little better. Maybe there was a way out of all of this where they could find a place to live in peace.

"What does all of that mean, Dad?" asked Ned, "It looks like a plan for increased GPS Marketing. Hey, that's the thing I was telling you guys about and there's even something here about individualized information marketing. But why do they mention China?"

CHAPTER

IT was a beautiful Sunday morning and the kind of winter day that only Richmond knows how to provide. The air was just warm enough to remind everyone of spring even though it was still at least a month away. Everyone would be out walking today after church with their coats open, smiling and waving feeling good about their prospects in life.

The Episcopalians would already be filling up the tables at the local Red Lobster and the buffet line at Joe's Diner by now, trying to get ahead of the wave of Baptists who'd be along about an hour after them. All of the different denominations in Richmond knew the schedule and when they'd be most likely to see their own people. Anyone who had skipped church that day to sleep in knew better than to show their face at a local restaurant before suppertime. They would be settling in for some Ukrop's chicken at the local Martin's instead.

Tom slipped into the back door of Book People and wove his way into the reference section just as Esther had instructed him to do. He had turned on the necessary apps in his iPhone at the airport parking lot to make sure he would elude detection until he arrived at his brother's doorstep.

He settled into the Queen Ann chair and opened a book on marketing with social networking just as Esther came around the corner.

"Eck, social claptrap," said Esther with more than a little feeling. "Everyone thinks they're in business for themselves these days because of all of that nonsense. Too much selling all the time smoothed over with inspirational quotes." She held out her arms wide as if she was going to be able to hold Tom aloft.

"Esther you're still keeping inventory in a notebook. You may have a certain bias," said Tom, smiling, as he rose to give Esther a hug. "How are you old friend?"

"A bit weary of all of this cat and mouse but you know, it's all I've ever known. Perhaps, I'd be bored if there weren't secrets to keep or people to hide. My, you're growing a little round around the middle. Living in that tiny town must be agreeing with you."

Esther had been a good friend to Tom's parents and a second mother to the three Weiskopf boys from the moment they were born. Tom knew she saw them as her own.

"Having you fuss over me has always made me feel a little safer in this world," he said, hugging her tighter.

"Be careful with an old woman," said Esther, smiling as she tried not to tear up. "I only wish you could live closer."

"So you could mind my business a little more?" asked Tom, smiling.

Esther batted at his shoulder and laughed, "Exactly, you see right through me. Ah, if it weren't for all of this trouble I might see this all as a blessing. Two Weiskopf boys in my midst."

"Have they found the missing operative yet?"

"No, but there's been no mention of him on the other side as well, so at least there's that," she said.

"Why did they kill his wife? Do you think they knew who she was?"

"I don't know. We can't be sure that her death was a calculated move. If they did then something is very wrong within our midst," she said, looking at Tom.

He didn't want to think about what she was saying.

"There has been a lot of destruction lately and not all of it was with Management's approval," she said. "I'm sure of that. That despicable Richard Bach, I knew they wouldn't be able to control him. Can you imagine?"

"What's he done?"

"There have been several unexplained deaths here in our quiet suburbs that seem to be a warning but they don't look like Management's style." Esther shook her head, weary from all of the years of having to calculate what others were doing. "I was actually glad when Management took that one in as a boy. Richard was such trouble even then. I was hoping that fear would keep him in line. I should have known better."

"What kind of warning? What is it we need to be warned about aside from the usual machinations?" asked William.

"That is a good question and I've been rolling that one around in my head. You know, there seems to be some concern about what we might know. I think there's information floating out there about Management that could be very bad for their plans."

"What plans? You think it's on that drive?"

"I don't know but the way they're behaving reminds me more of someone who is angry about something precious being lost than someone who is trying to get one over on their old opposition," said Esther. "Like I said, maybe I have been playing this game for far too long and imagine more than what is really there."

"Esther, you're the reason my brothers and I are still alive at all. Your intuition has kept the wrong side from figuring out our identity more than once."

Tom felt a shudder as he thought of the time when he was sixteen and had been awarded a National Achievement honor for his work on the robotics team. Management had briefly considered him as a potential candidate. It was Esther who quickly realized that they were digging into his background to check his lineage for any major fault lines.

A top cell of the Circle had been able to double back to all of the

Weiskopf connections that had been so carefully arranged to make sure everyone would give the same well-rehearsed story. Tom had turned down the scholarship to Sutler without any lasting affects.

"This time is different. Back then all I was doing was confusing a handful of locals away from my precious schmetterlings. Something has changed and they're focused on our little hamlet. Bigger forces are gathering here. Why is that?"

"What do you mean, bigger? What have you seen?" asked Tom.

"Robin Spingler is in town. She's been here for the past two weeks. I passed her in the Target and it was all I could do to not look back and see what she was doing."

"Maybe that's a good thing. They want to pull Richard back into line, keep a close eye on him."

"Maybe, but something's wrong. I keep thinking of a momma bird when a predator gets too close to the nest. They flap their wings and crow just off to the side to try and distract but they also never venture too far away."

"Esther, you're talking in circles."

"I think there's something here that's become very important to them. There's something about Richmond in particular but they're trying to distract us from seeing it."

"Do you think the missing drive has anything to do with it? Can an OTP mean that much to them?"

"No, it really shouldn't," said Esther.

"I haven't been able to ask my brother. Does Wallis still hold the thumb drive?"

"Yes, but last I was able to connect with Norman no one had seen what else might be on it."

"You mean, besides the Schmetterling Project," said Tom. He felt a shudder move through him.

"It makes me nervous to even say those two words together out loud," said Esther, gently shaking her head. "The horror of what happened the last time."

"How would they ever pull off something like that again?" asked Tom.

"That's not a storyline I let myself contemplate. Better to keep going and hope there's enough time to fully enact our program. Then, maybe we'll all be safe for at least a little while."

"Esther, we're talking years before that can happen. The first generation of children from those homes are just entering the workforce in waves. It's another ten years before they really hold any positions of power. Once that happens, then we'll have something."

"Well, then we'll have to make sure that can happen. Gott, please make it so."

Outside, a white Volvo that had seen better days was pulling out of the Book People parking lot and turning right onto Granite where there would be fewer cars to note any coming or going. The front end of the car looked like it had recently been in some kind of collision with a sound object but the car was rolling along nicely despite the damage.

Oscar leaned forward in his seat, adjusting the seat belt till it slid comfortably under his belly. "No one will know it was me," he whispered. He made a mental note to replace the road flares he'd used from his trunk.

He was working without orders and taking out a small revenge on the old woman. Oscar knew the owners of the bookstore were with the Circle. He had caught a glimpse of their pins on more than one occasion. He was sure they had been harboring Circle operatives on more than one occasion but Bach had always told him to stand down and leave her alone. No explanation and as far as he could tell, nothing was ever done about it. But this past week had been too much for him. He couldn't stomach just sitting by quietly while everyone else got to run around just as they pleased.

He saw Wallis Jones enter the bookstore and was about to rush in when he caught a glimpse of Richard sliding in the back door. For just a moment he had felt a surge of pride that his people were going to finally do something. But he watched as a tall, thin man left in a hurry and then Richard followed not too long after that. Wallis didn't stay too much longer but she still looked calm and in control. He hated that about her. Richard must have done nothing, once again.

At least he had never seen Oscar standing back in the shadows of the gas station across the narrow street watching all of them.

Oscar felt the wound across his cheek. It was healing nicely but the raised skin made his stomach churn with anger. Nothing was going right for him.

He made himself focus on what he had just put in motion. It wouldn't be long now. He turned right onto River Road and headed for the other side of town. He would need an alibi he could tell Richard, just in case.

Tom missed what Esther was saying. He stood up slowly and turned his head just slightly as he tried to pay attention but at the same time catch a better whiff of something new in the air. He had always had a heightened sense of smell. He even knew when someone was smoking through two closed doors on another floor. Esther was talking about something but that smell was distracting him.

"Maybe there's a way we can all have dinner together while you're in town," said Esther. "Are you paying attention? What is it?"

"Do you smell that? I can almost place it," said Tom. The aroma just barely burned the inside of his nose and made him think of burning metal. That's it, he thought as he jerked his head around to try and get a stronger whiff of the telltale odor. He jumped to his feet and a sickening dread came over him. The maze Esther had so carefully built was between him and the back door and he began shoving at the stacks of books in a desperate search to find a shortcut before it was too late. "There's still time," he called back.

"Tom, Tom! What are you doing?" yelled Esther, who was close behind him. He turned and shoved her backwards.

"Run! Run! Do it!" he barked at her. Esther looked puzzled for just a moment until the smell grew stronger and panic grew over her face. It was the last moment Tom had before he turned his head and saw the back of the bookstore peel away as it seemed to spit out a stream of books in a violent cresting wave all around them.

A bomb, a bomb, he thought, as he felt himself gently rise off of the floor.

It's amazing, he thought, how little it doesn't hurt at all. All that changed as he covered his face with his arms while the hard edges of last year's best sellers on how to manifest your dreams catapulted into his gut, knocking the wind out of him. He tried to twist and find Esther as he blew backwards but before he could turn at all he was hitting the floor. The pain rushed through his body and just before he closed his eyes for awhile he looked up and saw a clear blue sky where there had just been a roof. It's a nice day, he thought.

Norman's phone rang only a few minutes later with word from a Circle operative in the fire department. There had been some kind of explosion at Book People. Norman knew Tom was stopping by there first after he got in from the airport.

Wallis was just coming in the door with Ned and Harriet who had wanted to take them to church that morning. Wallis told Norman she wanted to go to see if she could get Harriet to let anything slip about what was going on in Richmond. Norman knew that Wallis still wanted to believe that Harriet had limits that didn't include murder, at least, not killing anyone other than close family members.

Wallis was still rattled by what they had found on the computer. Fortunately, Ned had not been able to comprehend what it all meant.

He didn't have time to make any of it look seamless and pulled Wallis into the kitchen, the words coming out in one long stream.

"Something's happened at the bookstore, at Book People," he said quickly. "An explosion."

"Esther," said Wallis, her face turning ashen.

"I don't know anything yet but I think Tom might be there too. I have to go. Are you alright here with your mother?"

"Of course, go, go. Ned and I will distract her but call me as soon as you know anything." Norman saw the worry in her eyes and leaned in to kiss her, first on her forehead and then on the lips. He knew that he wasn't the cause of any of the mayhem swirling around them but he still couldn't help feeling a little guilty.

"I know what you're thinking, Weiskopf and you aren't that powerful," said Wallis. "And you're coming up with scenarios in your head based on what you think might have happened if we'd never met. How do you know that you didn't save me from marrying some Management stiff who would have drawn me further into the organization?"

"I kind of doubt that would have been a marriage that lasted and that's if someone like that would have ever been able to convince you to walk down the aisle in the first place," said Norman. He felt himself relax just a little.

"Exactly," said Wallis, "Go find your brother. Please let them be alright."

"Wallis, I think you just said a prayer."

CHAPTER ③③

WALLIS' last words had made Norman think to call the Reverend and ask him to meet him there. Pastor Donald was just finishing up his last service and said he'd be right over.

Normally, he'd have thought twice about calling Pastor Donald to the scene of an explosion that was probably set by someone in Management. It was too easy for anyone watching from afar to start to connect dots.

But Norman was tired of always having to weigh whether or not it was alright to be seen in public with anyone in particular. He just wanted everyone he loved to be alright and short of that he was going to need some support.

Pastor Donald was already waiting there when Norman arrived.

"The bookstore took the worst of it," said the Father. "Tom and Esther are both still alive and relatively in one piece."

"Relatively, what does that mean?" said Norman rushing past the Reverend to get to the ambulances still idling in the back. Pastor Donald lengthened his stride to keep up with him.

"They both got pretty banged up. Those towers of books became pretty heavy missiles, like literary shrapnel. Tom has a broken leg and a really nice concussion and Esther may have some internal damage. They're about to take them both over to Doctor's Hospital."

"You're sure of that?" asked Norman. Pastor Donald knew what he was really asking.

"Yes, I checked. Those are Circle people in the ambulance with them. I made sure of it. Louie's riding along with Esther and he'll make sure nothing bad happens. He's agreed to wait until they're safely in a room."

Norman worked his way through the small clot of people standing around near the back of what had been the bookstore. Two large fire trucks and two ambulances were forming a semi-circle around the back of the store near a gaping hole where there should have been white clapboard and a back door. The overgrown grass was singed in places and matted down from all of the water the fire company was still pumping onto the smoldering embers.

Books were strewn everywhere mixed in with jagged pieces of wood painted white. Several of the neighbors were quickly picking up the remains of Esther and Herman's inventory and carefully putting them in a pile off to the side before more boots could trample across them. Esther was well thought of by almost everyone.

Norman stopped at the first ambulance and glanced inside. He saw Esther lying prone on the gurney and wondered for a moment if her status had changed.

"Esther?" he gently called out.

Esther lifted her head for a moment and her eyes slowly opened. He immediately regretted making her work so hard to make him feel better.

"Norman, is that you? Have you seen your brother yet? It's okay, it was only the remainders." Her voice sounded raspy as she tried to make a little joke to ease Norman's worry. She knew him better in some ways than Wallis did and always easily saw through all of his calculations.

"Esther," he said, climbing into the ambulance, "did you see anyone? Do you know what happened? Hi, Louie," said Norman, nodding at the large, blonde, muscular EMT who was sitting on the other side of the gurney.

"Norman, she's been given a sedative for the pain. She's not going to be able to tell you much. Go check on Tom," said Louie.

"Come on, Norman," said Pastor Donald, who was leaning into the back and grabbed hold of Norman's hand. "Right this way."

Tom was in the second ambulance and was sitting up. His eyebrows were singed and his leg was immobilized in a large blue splint but he looked alert.

"Can you give us a moment?" asked Pastor Donald to the paramedic sitting in back. "Sure," he said, "but only a minute. We need to roll," as he slipped out the back to stand guard by the door. The Pastor had known him since he was a small boy helping out as an altar boy on Sundays.

Pastor Donald crawled into the ambulance and sat across from Norman.

"What, no rabbi? Why is there never a rabbi?"

"Because you're not dying, just yet," said Pastor Donald. "Good to see you again. It's been too long."

"Hello, little brother," he said. "Sorry about the voice, my throat is sore. The paramedics said that's from the blowback and the smoke. I was lying near the middle of it for awhile."

Norman was trembling as he took his brother's hand and tried not to squeeze too hard.

"Hey, little brother, it's not that bad. We're all still here. Remember what Dad used to say? That's our bottom line. If everyone's alive and has their parts then no fussing around about it. Today's a good day," said Tom.

"What about your leg?" said Norman, swallowing hard.

"It's seen better days but it was a pretty clean break."

"You see anything?" asked Norman. "You know who did this? Or even better, do you know why?" He was thinking about what he had seen on the drive, the hidden metadata Ned had called it. He wanted to tell Tom what was found but not till he was off the painkillers and wouldn't accidentally mumble anything. One word of the information they had mistakenly gotten their hands on would surely get them all killed.

"No, I smelled something, though. Road flares." Tom gave a crooked smile. "My nose wins the day again even if I didn't have enough sense to run in the other direction. I actually thought I could pull a Batman and throw the things clear in time. I knew the bomb had to be a slow-burner and thought there might be another minute to go."

"Your nose must be a little off," said Norman, relieved his older brother was here next to him. "Did anyone call Harry yet?"

"No, my phone took a direct hit from a Grisham first edition. I haven't been able to get it to work."

Norman leaned in as if he was going to kiss the top of his brother's head and quickly whispered, "We have to talk and soon. I found something," before kissing the top of his head.

Tom gave him a long look and turned toward the minister. "Goodnight everyone, I could use a little rest now. Father, please watch over my brother and his family here." He shut his eyes for a moment and then opened them again, "Norman, don't let them keep me overnight. Just come get me in a few hours. Make them let me go. I can rest just as easily at your palace as in some hospital room, okay?"

"Okay, I'll be there."

Louie leaned into the ambulance. "Just thought you would all want to know. They found a thin fire trail up to the blast point. Looks like someone made a line with toner up to a pile of road flares."

"You mean like copier toner?" asked Pastor Donald.

"That's right, very combustible when mixed with oxygen. Might have been from that old relic Esther still used in the back. Makes a nice explosion. Clever but very simple stuff. Picture an old western movie and a trail of gunpowder leading to the dynamite."

"Thanks, Louie," said Norman.

"Any time," he said, walking away.

"Come on, let's let them do their work," said Pastor Donald. "Time to go. Mind a blessing from an old Episcopal priest?"

"Same God, right?" asked Tom.

"I have it on good authority there's only the one," said Pastor Donald as he bent his head in prayer. "Lord, keep your faithful servant, Tom safe from any further harm. Please ease his suffering and let him know You are by his side. Thy will be done, amen."

"Mazel Tov," said Tom.

Norman stepped back out of the van and waited by the ambulances till they began to drive away. He turned to watch them pull out onto the road and saw Richard Bach lurking on the other side of the street. Richard raised his arm and waved frantically back and forth at Norman.

"What do you suppose that means?" asked Norman.

"I don't know," said Pastor Donald. "I don't know much of anything, though, these days." He looked at Norman's haggard expression and was worried about his old friend. "You headed home?"

Wallis sat across from Harriet in the living room that was rarely ever used. It was Harriet's favorite room in her daughter's house. Wallis was trying to make small talk. She was running out of topics. Ned was up in his room working on his War Hammer collection. Wallis had quietly asked him to stay off the computer and fixed him with a look she rarely handed out. He held her gaze for a moment without expression and then nodded slowly. "Okay," he said, "I'm going to go paint."

Wallis was left to sit with her mother.

"Harriet, Norman will be home soon and he's going to bring Tom. Do you want to stay for dinner?" Wallis knew the mention of two Weiskopfs in the house would probably make her mother find other dinner plans.

"No, I've got to be going soon," said Harriet, "I really wish you'd call me Mother."

"That ship sailed awhile ago," said Wallis. It was all she could do to keep herself from peppering her mother with questions.

"You think Tom is going to be in any shape to come home that fast?" asked Harriet. Wallis startled, "You knew about the explosion?"

"Of course I did. It's all over the news. What, why would you think I wouldn't know?" Harriet fixed Wallis with a stern gaze. "What's going on?"

"No more than the usual bombing of a Richmond bookstore," said Wallis, feeling her anger get the better of her, "with my family in it."

Harriet let out a snort. "Your family. Your family only by marriage." She stood and looked around as if she was trying to find a way to leave without looking rude.

Wallis felt her temper flare. "My family connected by blood to my son."

Harriet turned her head away. "I see you're trying to make some kind of point here. I care less than you think I do."

"What do you care about?" asked Wallis. "No, really, I'd like to know."

Harriet turned back. "You're not usually this direct with me. What's happened? What do you know?"

"Answer me first."

Harriet hesitated and took in a deep breath and let it out slowly. She narrowed her eyes and looked at Wallis. "I see, you've discovered a few things, haven't you." She smoothed out the front of her dress and carefully sat back down. Wallis was struck once again at how carefully her mother made every move. She wondered if Harriet was always on guard against some inner, darker urge. "Well, good, it's about time."

"So, it's true?"

"What, that your father's family was special? I suppose so, yes. But I want to make it very clear, my side of the family was just as good," she said, lifting her chin. "No one ever remembers that part of the story."

"It can't be easy trying to measure up to some invisible standard. Never mind," said Wallis, waving her hand before her mother could come up with a retort. "Contributed to what?"

"Okay, Wallis. I hear the tone of voice. I know you're a good lawyer. You think you know a thing or two and you have made a few judgments already. I can tell. Probably with Norman's help too." Harriet adjusted her feet in the sensible Papagallo heels and looked down at her hands, pressing her fingers into a small pile in her lap.

Wallis looked at her mother and let some small edge of something painful and sharp sink into her skin. "You love me, don't you," she said. It was painful to think that someone could love her so much and be so bad at showing it. "You see me as proof of some kind of worth for you, don't you?"

Harriet's posture, which was always so stiff and straight, suddenly sagged just a little. "It's very hard to be a mother," she said, "especially when so much is expected and from so many different quarters. I tried, you know."

"Tried what, exactly?"

Harriet looked directly at Wallis, not something she normally did except when giving instructions or pointing out someone's mistakes.

"Tried to do what was right for everyone," she said.

Wallis hesitated, not sure she was ready for the answer. "What was it you were really hoping for me?" she asked.

"I wasn't hoping you'd take over the world, if that's what you mean," she spit out. Harriet looked back down. "To not be invisible to everyone around you, that's what I wanted." She looked up, defiant again. "And I think I did a pretty damn good job of at least that, missie."

Wallis could barely hold back the tears. "You are right about that, Harriet. I have never been good at sitting in the back and I suppose I'd have to say I owe that to you. Was that all?"

Wallis felt like she was playing a game with her mother. If she just kept asking open-ended questions without judgment maybe she'd hear something new that would give her a few more answers. But if she asked Harriet a direct question or let any of her old anger or resentment seep into her tone the game would be over and Wallis would have lost her chance.

"Isn't that enough?" asked Harriet.

Wallis chose her next words very carefully. "I have to know something. Is Norman or Ned in any danger? I need your help, Mother and I'm asking for you to be honest with me. Are any of us being targeted by Daddy's people?"

"Your father's people are your people. You can't escape that, and as for the rest, I don't know," said Harriet, "and that's the truth. No one has really trusted me for a very long time," she said, as she fingered the pearl choker at her throat, "as you might imagine. But I could find out."

"You would do that for me? For all of us?" asked Wallis, not sure if she should believe her.

"There is a greater good, you know," said Harriet. Wallis felt a cold chill run across her back at the thought of what that meant to anyone in Management. "However, I've made a few things clear over the years. Leave the child be and kill anyone with my bare hands who would dare go near you."

Wallis gingerly picked up her mother's hand and held it between her own. "I always thought you were waiting for me to become something else," she whispered.

"I was," said her mother. "I was trying to give you appropriate guidance and remind you of something better. However, it never really worked, did it?" Harriet pulled her hand out of Wallis' grasp. "I'm not waiting for your forgiveness for anything, Wallis, if that's what you think. I've made mistakes but I always did what I thought was right."

"So much for a moment," said Wallis, standing up and backing away.

"Why do you need one at all?" asked Harriet, sounding annoyed. "Can you not see that it's just a distraction? Even Norman seems to know that one."

Wallis took in a deep breath. She wasn't sure Harriet could really be trusted at all but she had no choice. "What do we do next?"

"The first thing we all do is get our emotions in check and go back to some kind of routine. Everyone else is up in arms searching for some lost piece of computer equipment, I don't know. It's too much. That's how mistakes are made and people get hurt. That must have something to do with that bookstore." Harriet's voice rose into a high-pitched whine.

Wallis tried to hide her surprise. She could feel her anxiety rising and wondered if Harriet was setting her up. "What kind of equipment?"

"I told you, computer. I overheard that nasty man, Richard, say they had to get it back."

"Where did you see Richard?"

"At a meeting, of course," said her mother.

So that's how it is, thought Wallis.

"They think someone named Robert has it on him. Do you know him?" asked Harriet.

"I know a few Roberts, Harriet, but I wouldn't know which one to offer up as sacrifice. I'll need a little more before I set the dogs loose on someone."

"Well, I see you're back to some version of yourself already," said Harriet, harshly. "Don't be ugly, Wallis. I raised you better than that. Go find Norman, I'm sure he's fine. I will see to a few things in the meantime. Not to worry, there are a few advantages to everyone wanting to avoid me."

"Where do your loyalties lie, Mother?" The question had slipped out before Wallis could stop herself.

Harriet drew her mouth into a thin line. "I suppose the same place as yours, with my family."

Wallis saw her mother to the door and pressed the door firmly shut, carefully locking up behind Harriet.

They may not know I have the drive, thought Wallis, feeling relief for just a moment. Then they can't know that I realize what they're really up to either. Poor Robert, whoever you are. Please, Norman, tell Pastor Donald, thought Wallis, sending up a prayer. Her phone buzzed and she pulled it out to look at the text. It was Sharon wanting to know if Paul could spend the night with Ned. She wanted to say no, but it was a small piece of normalcy, thought Wallis, in the middle of all of this insanity. She quickly answered, 'Sure, you can drop him off anytime.' She thought about the image of David yelling at her office and shuddered.

"David was crazy before I knew what was going on and so I can't say that changes anything," she mumbled. "Now, I'm talking to myself, great."

"Hey, Mom, who was that?" asked Ned.

Wallis startled and tried to smile.

"Why do I have the feeling you already know who that was?"

Ned cocked his head to one side and arched an eyebrow.

"That makes you look like me," she said. Ned gave a small, begrudging smile before he said, "Well?"

"It was Paul's mom and yes, he's on his way over here for the night."

"Yes," said Ned, pumping his arm in the air. He danced around the kitchen stopping at Wallis and grabbing her by the arms. "Pizza?"

"Absolutely," she said and squeezed her son as he tried to wriggle free. He pulled away just as she tapped him on the arm.

"Got you last," she said, laughing. Ned smiled at her and lunged forward tapping her lightly before running for the stairs. "Got you last," he yelled, his laughter trailing behind him.

Wallis shut her eyes and said a small prayer. She asked God to help her hold on to his version of her life. "Make it real, make it real," she said, as she started to cry.

CHAPTER

"I NEED YOU TO GO TO WILLIAMSBURG," said Oscar, "and take care of a little something for me," Oscar sucked in a wad of spit loudly and shot a warm, thick stream just past Parrish' leg.

"I don't take orders from you," said Parrish, looking bored, "just bets." He looked down at his pants to make sure none of the backwash had hit his leg. It mattered to him to always look impeccable.

"I'll pay you," said Oscar, his hand resting on his holster. "It's a private job."

Parrish raised his eyes and looked at Oscar. "You in trouble?" he asked, casually.

"Nothing that can't be fixed," said Oscar. "I'd do it myself but this is your particular expertise."

Parrish gave a good long look at the new red scar on Oscar's face. "And you haven't exactly fared well at your job lately, have you?" he asked in a mocking tone.

"You want the job or not?" said Oscar, getting angry.

Parrish let out a deep sigh. "I'll do it, but it'll cost you. I'm getting a little tired of cleaning up after you lately, dude. But I know if I don't there's only going to be more of the tight-lipped whiny-sort like Robin Spingler messing in my business. Can't have that."

"Best not say that too loudly," said Oscar, looking around to see if anyone could hear them. "She does not take well to criticism."

"What kind of mess is this one?"

"It's all related," said Oscar, "to the Ray problem. I need you to find Alice Watkins, his old coworker and make sure she doesn't have something that we need to get back. A thumb drive."

"What's on this precious drive? This is the second woman you've had me run down."

"Never you mind, Parrish. If you find it you just bring it back here, y'hear?" Oscar tapped his badge hanging at his belt.

Parrish snorted in contempt. "Yeah, that means something," he said.

"You listen here," said Oscar, "I made sure no one found out about your little side business quietly robbing lonely women who are later conveniently found dead, you son of a bitch. You think that was easy to cover up?"

"You were more than happy to cover it all up once I explained to you that I could make sure you got charged right alongside me," laughed Parrish.

"I didn't lose the damn drive in the first place. Those morons in Richmond couldn't keep their hands on it but somehow it's all boiling down to me to put everything to rights, again." Oscar mopped his forehead with a handkerchief.

"You sweating in the middle of a cold snap? You must be worried. Alright, I'll do it, after I have my money and not before. But you better get a grip white boy. Why do you think this Alice has your precious thumb drive?"

"I don't but I need to cover my bases. Besides, I know she saw something in the accounting files at the city when she worked there with Billings. She knows about the money we've been passing through receivables.

If Richard ever finds out about that you and I are both dead. Even you won't be able to get ahead of that one. Robin Spingler will call in outside help."

"You stupid, fat waste of my time," said Parrish, choking out each word in anger. "I knew better than to get involved with you in the first place."

"Right, because you had so much going for you in that run-down apartment where I found your poor, sorry self. You have a little problem, Parrish, with keeping your hands from around old ladies' throats." Oscar kept his hand near his gun. Parrish saw how nervous Oscar was getting and grinned. He wanted to keep their other arrangement going just as much as Oscar.

"Where do I find this Alice Watkins and what is it that I need to find out?"

"We don't need to know anything from her," said Oscar. "I just want her to go away forever and without anyone else finding out."

"That I can do," said Parrish, "soon as you pay me, in cash." He held out his hand and smiled.

Parrish waited outside of Colonial Power and Lighting down by the Warwick Marina in Williamsburg, Virginia. He had been patiently biding his time till he saw Alice.

Alice Watkins lumbered out of the back door and walked toward her car. She looked like she was lost in thought, balancing several bags and a large purse in her arms.

Parrish sat back and waited for her to get settled into her car. He was in no hurry.

He had been watching Alice's movements for a few days and knew she was always one of the last employees to leave on Thursday nights and would soon be all alone.

He could hear her trying to start her old car. However, he had already made sure that there would be plenty of noise but the engine would never turn over and catch. He watched as she put her head down for a moment on the steering wheel before looking up and digging her phone out of her purse.

Someone came out of the building after Alice and went over to her showing concern and asking something but Alice always shook her head firmly, no, and didn't even watch as they reluctantly left her sitting there in her front seat with the car door open.

Parrish made a careful notation of how many people had already left till he was certain that there was no one else. He had been paid well by Oscar to clean up the rest of this mess and find out what had happened to the missing information before it fell into the wrong hands.

Parrish' reasons were a little more self-serving. At the very least, he wanted to stop her from telling anyone about the little side business they were running through the city books by way of the utility department. It was too much money to just walk away. Alice needed to go.

Besides, Parrish always prided himself on being able to do a good job whether it was running numbers or cleaning up after himself.

By his calculations he only had about twenty minutes left before the tow truck would appear. He needed to make his move.

He got out and walked swiftly to the car, making a straight line between the two points. He came around to the back of the car, his hand already wrapped around his favorite small switchblade. He reached in and placed a heavy hand on her shoulder to hold her at the right angle as he brought his other hand up to slit her throat in one clean motion. Alice felt the pressure on her shoulder and lunged first, spraying him with pepper spray and shoving a very wide foot into his groin. Alice had never been a people pleaser. She was not about to wait and find out what he wanted.

Alice had never learned to trust anyone and had lost more than one job from jumping to conclusions without asking questions first. However, when she saw the knife roll out of Parrish' hand as he tried to quickly catch his breath she realized it was all worth it. The next time someone called her a cynical bitch she would remember to smile and think back to this moment. She gave Parrish another good hard kick before he could get enough air and she started running toward the building.

It only took a few moments before Parrish was already trying to shuffle behind her. The lost knife had skittered under the car and he had to quickly lay flat on the ground to reach it, but the black was shortly back in his hand.

He wasn't used to anyone putting up much resistance to his efforts, especially an old woman and was caught completely off-guard by this large woman's deliberate attack. He had almost thrown up on his Florsheims.

He could hear her fumbling with the keys and knew he had a chance to get back on track. He was catching up to her as she swung the door wide and turned around with a wild look in her eyes, swinging a large cloth bag filled at the bottom with what felt like a pair of large shoes.

The bag landed squarely against his chin pushing him back a little as he tried to swing out with the knife and knick her, maybe catch her off guard. Alice lifted her leg and put a shoe squarely in the middle of his stomach, shoving him hard enough to land on the ground. She turned and ran into the building but he scrambled to his feet and caught the door just before it could swing shut and lock him out.

He was going to catch this bitch.

She was doing a fast run-walk down the hall, her elbows working at her sides as he kept gulping in air, holding his stomach and clutching the knife, trailing behind her, stumbling from side to side. The pepper spray was making his eyes water and his vision blurred as he wiped his eyes with his sleeve. He lurched against the wall, hitting with a solid smack against his shoulder before pushing off and propelling himself forward as he stay focused on his goal. Parrish had never left without completing a task and wasn't about to start now. It would put a blemish on his record.

Alice took a sharp left toward the end of the long hall and it was a few moments before he could see where she was headed. She was weaving in and out around the low cubicles toward the far wall. Twice he almost caught up to her and just when he thought he was almost close enough to lunge she had lifted a chair over her head and thrown it at him with a force he didn't think she could have possessed.

The last time he managed to dig the tip of the knife across her hand, drawing blood but Alice didn't even flinch. Instead she let out a loud roar, her mouth wide open, as she brought the chair down.

She didn't even wait to see if the chair had slowed him down enough this time as she kept up her fast walk, arms churning to the fire alarm on the wall just above a cubicle that had the name Alice Watkins on the outside. There was a small dish with wrapped caramels near the edge of the desk and a small fern but no framed pictures or memorabilia. Alice didn't even look down as she reached toward the alarm.

She smacked her hand hard against the thin glass plate, ignoring the little splinters as they dug into her palm. She pulled down the lever and heard the loud whooping sound instantly fill all of the space.

Quickly, she climbed on top of her desk, huffing with the effort, and pointed up toward the corner of the room while looking directly at Parrish.

Parrish hesitated and wondered if the woman was going to try and escape through the ceiling or hurl herself over the low cubicle walls. He was curious to see if she could do it.

When she stood up tall and straight on her desk, her feet planted in a firm stance and her arm outstretched, Parrish stopped to see what she was telling him.

He saw how determined and angry she looked and followed the direction of her arm till he saw the camera tucked up high against the ceiling. He stopped moving and stood there looking at her.

The alarm had activated a live feed to the security company. The marina had expensive boats to protect. The guards would already be looking at the monitors wondering why some large, white woman was disheveled and bleeding so badly from her hand while pointing at the camera. They would surely be asking themselves what or who she was looking at, just off camera.

Parrish knew he couldn't go any further and if he didn't backtrack quickly he'd get caught coming out of the building. Their response time would be very quick. He looked at Alice Watkins and felt a sense of kinship with her. This was one tricky old lady. He smiled broadly at her and nodded before turning toward the exit. Oscar will not be happy, he thought. I'll have to do something about that.

Alice stood right where she was until the guards broke in and came pouring into the main room. She kept thinking about all of the time she had spent coming up with escape plans and ended up telling herself that she was going to need to learn to calm down.

They were never able to find any trace of the intruder.

Alice wasn't surprised and made them stay till they got her car working again. They said some kids must have messed with it as they replaced the carburetor cap. She didn't even look back as she drove down the road toward I64 West and back to Richmond.

Damn that Wallis Jones, thought Alice.

CHAPTER 35

⌐RICHARD sat in his Explorer along the quiet country road waiting for Robin Spingler to arrive. He was parked along Indiantown Road in King George County just past the bend of the road near the large, old oak tree. The sun was beginning to rise and the sky was already a clear, dark blue stretching above the thick stand of trees. It was going to be a beautiful day.

"This isn't good," he said, as he fumbled for the matches he had just dropped on the floor of the car. He lit a cigarette to try and calm his nerves and tried to think about how he could explain away any of this mess.

He took a long drag and held his breath for a moment feeling a little calm come over him just as he saw Robin's black Lincoln Continental pull around the curve. He blew out the smoke and smashed the cigarette in his ashtray. She always complained about the smell.

He got out of his car slowly and waited by his door too unsure of what to do next. She had barked at him with more than her usual sour disposition when she called him last night.

He had heard stories about what she had done to people in her line. He knew they weren't all legend but he didn't want to find out the hard way if the darker stories of people who had suddenly gone missing were true. She was even the one who had first coined the term apparent suicide for some of their more reluctant operatives from the Circle.

"Stop standing there with your arms at your side like you don't have a clue." Robin spat out the words in disgust. She marched over to Richard and took a whiff of the air. "Still smoking. You have no discipline. That's how the entire Richmond operation has gotten to be the stinking hellhole that it is. Leadership comes from the top down."

She gave the dry, clay dirt around her a kick. "Pathetic."

Richard couldn't stop himself. He flinched as if she had made contact with his leg.

"Did you tell that weasel, Oscar to hunt down that Jones woman?"

"No, I definitely did not," said Richard, chopping the air with his hand.

"That doesn't make it much better. The McDonoughs were your idea as we both know."

Richard felt the sting in his back again from the beating he had taken on just such a lonely road. He had instinctively tried to pull away from her as she yelled at him to stop being a coward and take what he deserved. His jacket had been sliced to ribbons. He didn't dare go to a doctor and had made his wife nurse him with a salve.

"You must have the worst kind of dumb luck to have a clod like Oscar loose in the city at the same time that certain factions way above our pay grade are paying attention to Richmond," she said, letting out a snort.

"I'm very sorry about that. I'll make sure something is done," he said, as he tried to hold his voice steady and failed. He pulled the long, charcoal grey cashmere overcoat closer around him, trying to ward off the chill.

"You had better. Crap rolls downhill and if it starts coming toward me I will offer whoever I have to as a trade. You were only authorized to get the thumb drive out of Ray Billings and instead he ended up dead and no information. That wasn't easy to clean up. A lot of people had to get a bonus last month to make that happen. Then you were ordered to watch the Jones woman's house, that's all and you manage to kill a neighbor."

"We tried to avoid that one. It couldn't be helped," said Richard in a bleating tone. Robin looked him up and down.

"You have caused a lot of mayhem lately, Richard Bach."

"None of this was really my intention."

Robin narrowed her gaze at him. "You really are weak, aren't you?"

Richard winced and wanted to wretch up the contents of the bagel he had eaten on the drive over but he swallowed hard trying to maintain some amount of control. He was still hoping to come out of this with his old life intact.

"Now, this Lilly Billings is dead and it's already leaked that she was murdered. There's not a chance we can make her look like the grieving widow who had to follow her tragic husband into death."

Robin was pacing back and forth in front of Richard. He was doing his best to hold still and not make any sudden movements in front of her.

"You think Oscar was capable of that one?"

"Uh, nuh, no, I don't, I don't," he got out, as Robin's anger seemed to grow. "No, definitely not. He's not that clever. Too clean, no one saw anything, a few pieces of jewelry were taken."

"Then give me a name."

"Parrish, Rodney Parrish," he blurted out. "I'd say it was Rodney Parrish. He's been known to break into places for extra cash when he needed it and he has a thing for violence. Talks about all the neighborhood pets he's done in so that he could sleep peacefully."

"You have a problem, then. You just named one of our better informants," she said as she got closer and closer to Richard's face. He could see where the bright, red lipstick had seeped into the small wrinkles around her mouth. "Mr. Parrish is able to get in and out of places without anyone ever knowing someone was there. I rescued him out of lockup myself before he was ever fingerprinted. There's no record, anywhere. But if he gets picked up for a murder he may start talking and we can't have that, can we Mr. Bach." She slapped her hands together in a loud clap, making Richard's legs shake.

"There are Circle operatives who sit on the bench. They know my name and would love nothing more than to see me put away for awhile. I won't let that happen. You find someone to give to the police for Lilly's murder besides Mr. Parrish and I'll overlook the mistakes you seem to be prone to repeating."

Richard wanted to point out that he didn't exactly make this string of mistakes but he knew better than to ever contradict Robin Spingler.

"I want to make sure there are no illusions about what can happen here. There is a grand opportunity here in Richmond to turn the tide against the opposition for generations to come and the rewards will be great for those who do their part. We have had an unexpected gift given to us by the most unusual source," she said.

"A gift?" said Richard, letting his curiosity get the better of him.

"Yes," said Robin, smiling as she licked her lips, inadvertently spreading a little lipstick to her front teeth. "Do you know something I learned a long time ago, Richard that has turned out to be true? Never failed me."

"No, ma'am. What is that?" he said, feeling relief that the subject had somehow moved on from him.

"Everyone is weak and will try to grab more than they deserve at some point. Oh, they'll have justifications and well thought out reasons why it's for the better good. Such piety. But it's wonderful, really because that's when it's possible to finally strike a deal. It's a form of respect, really."

Richard was a good lawyer. He caught on easily and knew there was an informant. "Your informant must be someone big," he said, out loud, immediately regretting it.

"Oh, it's a once in a lifetime plea for help and it means millions to me personally. Do you understand? But in order for it to all come together I'm going to need the problems in Richmond to stop and a conversation with Robert Schaeffer. You need to break your losing streak. There won't be another chance."

Robin suddenly kicked him hard in the groin. Her pointy shoe felt like the tip of a knife. The pain shot out in every direction as he sank to his knees and let his head fall to the ground. He put his hands on the ground and pushed against the gravel while he tried to get a breath back in his body. He could hear Robin let go of a satisfied sigh.

"That's just a little taste to remind you what you need to do next. Do it well or I'll just cut to the end the next time."

Robin had left him there on his knees and slowly pulled away in her car. It took a few minutes before Richard was able to lift his head and sit back on the ground, still working to get his breathing to normal.

"That bitch has got to go," he choked out. "Another apparent suicide."

The drive to the old tobacco warehouse in Shockoe Bottom took an hour. Richard spent the time thinking about what he could say to Rodney Parrish that wouldn't get him killed by anyone but might make him turn on Oscar. Money is the only thing, he thought, as he slapped his hand on the dashboard. He was going to have to make him a deal.

He walked into the large room and tried to pick out Rodney from the handful of men standing around.

"Mr. Bach, you here to place a bet? We would have taken your combinatings over the phone," said Davey. He was dressed in the uniform pinstripe suit and was busy checking on the morning's payouts. The winners would be by soon to collect. Winners always came in person.

"I'm looking for Parrish."

"Rodney? He's been laying low. Picking up the payouts for his best customers and skedaddling the hell out of here just as fast. Something went south, I don't know."

"Where the hell is everybody?"

"At their regular jobs, Mr. Bach. I just stopped by to pick up a payment from someone behind on their loan or I'd be downtown at my city job too."

"Is Mac here?" Mac ran the numbers business in Richmond and was everyone's boss who worked in the warehouse. He was an affable fellow most of the time as long as money wasn't involved. He took in a few thousand in profit a week and buried most of it in a plastic bag on land he owned in Hanover County but no one ever tried to find it. Mac would have chased them to the ends of the earth. The rest of the money he washed through a couple of restaurants he owned on the edge of the Fan District. Davey was his right hand man.

"No, he won't be in 'til later. He doesn't normally get up this early. You can find him downtown having breakfast at Penny's near the newspaper around noon. Does Rodney owe you money? Let me take care of it for you right now. How much is it, Mr. Bach? You're a good customer. No receipt necessary. We can get it later," said Davey, pulling out a thick roll of bills from his pocket. There was a hundred dollar bill on the outside.

"No, it's not like that, Davey," said Richard, running his hand through his hair. He was starting to sweat. "You know where Rodney lives?"

Davey looked a little surprised and slipped the money back into his pocket.

"Is he in trouble, Mr. Bach, because we can take care of that too." Davey's voice had dropped and he was speaking more slowly, leaning back. Richard realized Davey thought Richard was threatening one of their best runners.

Richard raised his hands in protest. "He's not in trouble, at least not with me. I need to hire him. I have a situation," said Richard, annoyed.

"Oh, why didn't you say so from the start, I understand completely. I'll let Rodney know right away and have him call you. That okay if he call you?"

"Sure, sure, but ask him to find me right away. It's time sensitive and I have to move quickly on it. Tell him there's a bonus for him on this one."

"That ought to make the man move faster. My experience is money always does."

Richard walked out of the warehouse without looking back. All he could think about was what would happen if he couldn't give Robin Spingler a fall guy.

"Uh, Davey," he said, turning back. "Can I hire you to let me know if you hear anything that might be important to me?"

"Everything is for sale in this world, Mr. Bach. You just need to have the green."

CHAPTER 36

THE FEDERAL RESERVE not only set policy for the banking system of the United States, they also acted as a giant bank for other institutions, which gave them the power to cash over-sized checks at a fixed rate or create a discount window to loan money at better rates.

No one really knew what the actual size of the Fed Bank was or exactly who they were serving at any given time. Over the years their system had become byzantine with so many layers that it more closely resembled the cell structure of the NSA and held secrets and fortunes equally as well as the Papal City. There was a general sense around Washington that their bank balances were far larger than imagined but even repeated Freedom of Information Act requests from the media or Congress failed to gain outsiders access beyond the uppermost layers.

Outsiders were seen as intruders who didn't possess enough of an understanding of what it took to keep not only the U.S. economy going but an ever-changing world economy. Trying to explain would just take up too much time and the rules would have changed again before the answer was complete making the whole effort obsolete. At least, that's what insiders were always saying at cocktail parties in D.C.

Control over the Federal Reserve wasn't completely held by either Management or the Circle. The technology division, situated in Richmond, was mostly Management and had changed hands only a few times since the 1980's when computers started to play such a significant role in keeping track of everything.

Mark sat in his office looking at the spread sheets on his screen. He was doing his regular monthly check of a sampling of the Federal Reserve's accounts' transfer activity to see if there was anything unusual. His boss would need the data to prepare the regular report.

At exactly eleven a.m. when almost everyone from his division was taking their first break he was planning to take a moment and plug his iPhone into his computer's USB port to check on his own accounts. The iPhone acted as his keyboard, bypassing the software that could detect his keystrokes, which could spell out what he'd been doing on the side.

Then he could start a little program he'd developed on his own to make sure that his activity was proceeding smoothly and undetected. The entire operation took two minutes from start to finish to download to his phone. He could analyze the data later when he was home and away from prying eyes.

The meticulous bologna slicing he'd been doing from Management's foreign accounts for the past year had paid off and soon he'd be able to leave everything behind. He was planning to head for a part of the country that no one from the Circle or from Management really cared to control. The small town he'd found in Montana really did fit the bill, perfectly. He had found the property last year but had wanted to be sure and took his time doing a background check of the people and the area.

Just getting a first look at the property had been tricky. Mark knew there were people constantly monitoring him to make sure he wasn't doing anything like looking for a soft place to land.

He had been careful to use a throwaway cell phone and different email accounts with masked IP and MAC addresses to contact a local realtor who'd never realize what was at stake. He had even set up a corporation called Rosecroft Investments to act as the buyer and hold the title.

There was a nice thousand acre spread on the side of Haskill Mountain with a beautiful view of Flathead Valley. A million years ago the valley had been a place where dinosaurs roamed, some of whom were caught in the Ice Age and became a permanent part of a long-ago glacier. The combination had made the soil fertile and the land was still full of natural wonders and yet very little humanity. It was exactly what he wanted for his family.

On nights when he couldn't sleep he lay in bed and pictured his children hunting for fossils without having to imagine satellites zooming in on their location or lost operatives suddenly passing coded dollar bills.

Mark had managed to take the boys and his little girl on a fly fishing vacation nearby last summer that gave him the chance to check out the property. The acreage sat right near a trout stream and made it possible for him to scope out the perimeter without having to formally meet anyone or explain what he was doing.

There was even a pristine creek that wound through the entire property and a thick stand of aspen trees all along the northern boundary. That made it just big enough to melt into the scenery without being so big that it'd draw attention in town as the new wealth from the east coast. Only one family had owned it since the original homestead.

The money he was going to use was routed through a chain of shell companies Mark formed in Panama, Cyprus, Anguilla and Belize where no one would be looking too closely at who formed the company or requiring too much documentation of any kind.

They had been set up as part of the chain that would buy the ranch under Rosecroft Investments. The next step was to funnel smaller amounts of money that he could live on for years into several American commercial bank accounts in places like Bartow, Florida and Rockford, Illinois where there were no laws on the book concerning multiple electronic transfers.

Most places in the States were concerned about money laundering but some were owned by banks in other countries and were happy to be able to still find someone they could charge with fees. Those banks didn't question the number of transfers or where they originated.

Mark had carefully chosen banks whose governing boards were based in

Montreal, Canada. He knew from his time in the Circle and Management that Canada had done a better job of holding off the tentacles of either side and that gave him a slightly higher degree of invisibility.

Locals would just see him as a rich guy living on a ranch with his family.

As long as the cash remained outside of the traditional systems he knew the amounts and values would never be logged. There'd never be a trail and he would finally fall off of the grid. If there were times he had to bring money into the system he would be able to gently supplement any legitimate holdings that were visible to everyone by claiming small windfalls from odd jobs from someone who paid him in cash. He knew could even say he had sold some personal items if he had to, or gotten a fictitious repayment of some small, personal loan to an old friend. The basis for each of the transactions would always be cash. It was just the excuse that was being used that would change. But as long as he had a cache of funds that didn't need emergency supplements beyond what he'd planned for, his family's lifestyle would appear to be modest and not raise suspicions.

The permanent risk would always be not being able to control what he couldn't see coming that could require a faster access to large parts of the funds. That would be when the fun could begin.

He put that out of his mind. A good operative looked for what they could change and then knew when to let go of the rest, throwing themselves into the hands of fate.

At some point, when dealing with people who manipulate for a living it became necessary to recognize that death was always a possibility in order to stay sane. Ultimately, there was nothing to be done about it.

In the past that's what always made it possible for Mark to get through a day but he wasn't willing to resign his children to the same fate.

He had sped up his plans by a few months and instead of the fall he was moving ahead in just a few short weeks when the children were scheduled to be on spring break from school. No one would miss them for a little while.

His plans could still roll out like he planned but with a faster, more urgent schedule.

Timing was everything, especially now that so many things seemed to be going wrong for both sides. Violence was always a last resort to save someone's ass and even then it was quick and limited. But something had changed. There were too many bodies dropping to predict who was next or what had everyone so panicked.

He knew that neither side would protect him once he bailed out of the system completely. At best they would leave him alone.

He already had a set of paperwork drawn up to show that he was renting the property from Rosecroft and had never met the owners. Every step would be taken care of just in case he ever had to show someone. Rosecroft would be responsible for furnishing the place and setting up all of the utilities. Mark would just move in and set up residence.

He had sent the realtor an email from Rosecroft under the guise of a foreign executive, saying the corporation was looking at several investment properties and someone would get back to him shortly. But he knew that the Haskill property was going to be it and he was done looking for a new home. He was planning to put down a deposit in the coming weeks. Soon, his family could finally live in peace.

Lately, though, he was exhausted and he hadn't been sleeping well ever since Robert's disappearance. Robert had been missing for two weeks and Mark had heard nothing from either side. He didn't know if Robert had come in from the cold and the Circle had kept it quiet or if he was already being tortured by some Management operative. He tried not to think about Robert's sons.

The transmissions from the Circle had become mundane again with no mention of anything unusual. Mark knew his cell level wouldn't necessarily warrant a heads up from anyone with updates on Robert's whereabouts. They'd expect him to go back to his routine.

Fred had been no help at all, although Mark didn't learned a long time ago not to expect anything different. He had kept his questions simple and never used Robert's name directly but Fred was fidgety as usual, talking too much about his wife's friend, Yvette suddenly dying in her kitchen. He said Maureen was too distraught. Sometimes Mark really wished Fred could get assigned to some other cell. Thankfully, soon it wouldn't matter anymore.

Twice Mark had placed ads for an intern on Craig's List using the old OTP short string of numbers that Robert had left on the dollar bill. He had searched the work-for-hire listings to see if Robert was trying to reach out and thought he saw some inquiries that may have been a lead but still, nothing panned out. An ad for low interest loans looked especially promising but when someone answered there was something about the background noise that told him he'd made a grave mistake. He started asking questions about the rate of payments to cover his surprise.

The line had a slightly muddied sound quality to it, which let Mark know he'd stumbled into a secure line. The data was being compressed, encrypted and subsequently decrypted and uncompressed between the two parties. That made the quality sound like a call using Skype. He'd run into the problem before and recognized the change in tone quality like a fingerprint. A cell in Management was looking for Robert too and had set a trap.

It seemed everyone was out looking for Robert.

"Why are you so important?" asked Mark, rubbing his face. He felt exhausted. He hadn't slept well since that day at the soccer fields. Two weeks was beginning to feel like forever.

"What's that?" It was Frank Belmonte leaning into his office. "Were you trying to catch me?"

Frank was a second generation Management operative and Mark was sure he drank the Kool-Aid on a regular basis. Mark had heard Frank expound on how it was possible to be a part of the large organization and still create good for the greatest number acting from within. He drop hints like he was sure he could eventually wheedle that into Mark as well. Mark did his best to avoid him but Frank's office was at the far end of the same hall.

"No, just talking to myself. New technology, that's all." Mark kept typing, trying not to make eye contact with Frank so he would move along.

"Can I be of any assistance?" asked Frank as he stepped into Mark's small office.

MARTHA RANDOLPH CARR **313**

Mark looked up and stopped what he was doing for a moment. He knew he could only push Frank so far.

"No, I'm good. It's the same drill every time. I take my time with the process and eventually it all works itself out."

"Excellent philosophy, Whiting. Doesn't hurt though to occasionally ask for appropriate help too," he said, tucking his tie into the front of his shirt and leaning forward to get a glimpse at the screen.

Mark could never be sure what someone's true motives really were and he was always careful not to leave himself in the position of having to hide anything at work. He didn't want his body language to ever look defensive.

However, there was still something about Frank that always managed to get under his skin. He tried not to show any annoyance and slowly breathed in and out.

"Absolutely, good point. Thank you, Frank. If I hit some roadblocks I'll make sure to ask you."

Frank stood up straight and adjusted his tie. "Okay, then, I'd better get back to work. Don't want to get caught playing on company time."

"Oh, Frank, could you do me a favor?" asked Mark.

Frank ducked back in and looked relieved to somehow be of service. Mark pulled out the dollar bills closest to the outside of his wallet.

"Would you mind grabbing me a cup of coffee from the Gourmet on the Go cart? A large black coffee?" asked Mark.

"Sure, no problem," said Frank. He took the money and folded it in half as he left Mark's office. Mark couldn't be sure he'd turn over the dollar bills to Stephen but he'd know soon enough. He had arranged the money in his billfold this morning so that if the opportunity presented itself he'd be able to ask for direct updates on Robert. Always be ready. That one had saved his butt more than once, he thought.

At the very least, though, it'd keep Frank busy for the next ten minutes and that was just long enough to complete the download. Mark quickly took out the cord from the small pocket sewn in the lining of his jacket and plugged in the phone.

Once he started the download he never hesitated in his motions, knowing that was the easiest way to get caught. It was one of the first things that Management had taught him when they still thought they were grooming him as one of their future linchpins. The program started searching and was retrieving data but after two minutes was still rolling through the accounts downloading information. Something was wrong.

The only explanation was that there was activity on the accounts that wasn't his and was also invisible to the regular Fed software. His rogue program was asking a different set of questions than the Feds and it was getting back data he didn't expect.

There was no time to find out if it was detection software that was following his money trail or something else altogether. Even if he did know, it'd be impossible to tell what cell and at what level had implanted the software. There was also no way to know if they were already on to him and he was about to join Robert in some hellhole. He suddenly wondered where his own children were right at that moment.

The minutes zoomed by and he knew he was in danger of getting caught with his phone still attached to a Fed computer if Frank reappeared with the coffee but he had to know if he was in danger and he was determined to get all of the information. He nervously tapped his finger on the connection, ready to rip it out and drop the phone into his lap at the first sound of footsteps outside of his door. His stomach churned from the anxiety as he watched the screen on his phone trolling through the records.

Something is definitely wrong, he thought. This is way too much information and it's finding streams of money that didn't exist as early as two weeks ago. His jaw relaxed just a little as he began to realize that the passing numbers weren't encryptions meant to search for what was already there but new avenues for money to fall out of Fed hands and into someone's pocket. Someone was mimicking him but he could already tell it was on a much grander scale.

He heard the door at the end of the hall slam shut and knew Frank had taken the stairs back to their office. The iPhone was still blinking as the new account numbers downloaded into his phone.

He hesitated, fingering the cord that connected his phone. He wasn't sure that interrupting the transmission in the middle wouldn't leave a trace that was visible to whoever had created this infrastructure in the first place. The design was done through a backdoor and subtle enough to escape the Fed's detection. Whoever they were, they were good.

Mark listened for Frank's footfalls and knew exactly how many seconds he had left before being found out. He had counted the number of footsteps to his office every time he came back into the building. It was standard training for everyone in the Circle and he knew exactly how many steps it took a man of average height to reasonably move from that door to his office. He had been counting with Frank ever since he heard the door.

Fifteen, sixteen. He could feel his heart keeping tempo.

Just as Frank was about to reach Mark's door the transmission ceased and he pulled out the cord with his left hand, shoving his phone into his pants pocket. He never looked down so that his focus would be toward the door and not directed toward anything else. He tried not to wonder if the cord was hanging out at all.

"Here you go," said Frank, as he set the cup down. Frank started to shake the change in his hand. The coins made a gentle rattle.

"You keep that," said Mark, holding up his right hand. "Consider it a delivery charge. I appreciate the help. You gave me a chance to keep thinking through my process. See, you were appropriate assistance, after all."

Frank smiled broadly and winked at Mark as he turned and left the office. Mark made himself keep breathing normally until the tension passed on its own. No one could hear him suddenly let out a deep sigh of relief. He couldn't remember a time when he had been so tense so many times in one day.

He would have to wait hours until he could be sure that everyone he loved was okay. At least he could duck out for an early lunch and take a quick look at his iPhone. That would confirm whether or not anyone was on to him and calm his nerves enough to make it through the day. The glimpse he got before he had to put the phone away told him that there was someone operating a large structure within Management. Millions of dollars at a time appeared to be flowing into hidden accounts and apparently without detection by the uppermost cells.

Someone was taking even larger risks than he was. If accounts like these were ever revealed there would be a lot of necessary maneuvering to contain the scandal and make some key figures pay in order to stop the appearance of embezzlement of taxpayer dollars and minimize any cry for further investigations.

It will be interesting to see if I can tell, thought Mark, which side is stealing the money. It wasn't possible to know without a little examination if the money was for a covert operation or just flowing into someone's pocket. Not everyone at the Federal Reserve was a part of Management.

"Hello, Fred. I'll take you up on that lunch offer. Let's meet by the benches but I have to eat early today, say around eleven, okay?"

"Sure, sure, that'll work. See you then," said Fred. He sounded hesitant but Mark knew he couldn't refuse. He had used key phrases that were a request to meet in order to exchange information. Fred was obligated to appear and complete the transfer.

Mark hung up before Fred had the chance to ask any questions. His expertise as an attorney with a forensic accounting background would come in handy. He'd recognize the reasoning and motivation behind the pathways and be able to answer what really mattered to Mark.

Fred was particularly good at piecing together what someone's intentions were with money. Mark knew that's why the Circle saw him as invaluable despite his nervous temperament. It was like he was a savant when it came to numbers and patterns and human behavior.

A chill went down Mark's back when he realized that if there was a group out there smart enough to hide large assets flying out the door, they were probably smart enough to realize there was someone else in there with them. Were they tolerating his presence because he was only the mouse to their elephant and they couldn't be bothered?

A worse thought came to him. Any cell knew it was standard procedure to have a fall guy in place in case there was ever any kind of exposure. They would need someone to throw to the media who would then whip up the case for them that this was their culprit.

Someone may have seen him as an added blessing to their scheme.

CHAPTER
③⑦

MARK walked out of the door ten minutes before the appointed lunch time to avoid any unexpected offers from Frank to join him. He walked down the stairs quickly, as he always did, and tried to appear as if he was showing off his stamina instead of his anxiety.

Fred was already waiting for him at the wrought iron benches that was off to the side of the large statue of men near their building. He looked to either side as Mark approached him.

"Stephen said he made your favorite today and he'd be hurt if you didn't stop by and try some," said Fred.

Mark stopped short and looked back toward the Gourmet on the Go cart. "Sounds good," he said. "Makes my choice easier today. Be back in a minute." So much of his life was being dictated lately by some short amount of code or direction that told him what to do next. This was no different. Many different patterns had been set up a long time ago to make the request seem invisible. Stephen pointed out the chicken curry to Fred so he could let Mark know he was needed over by the cart and Mark obeyed the order.

In just a few short weeks his life would be his own at last. Until then, he was going to keep following protocol and he was going to try and take comfort in just following the rules.

He turned and walked toward the cart. There was already a short line of people waiting to buy lunch chatting amiably with each other. A man suddenly strode quickly past him and got in line ahead of him, craning his neck around the others in front of him trying to see what Stephen was doing, as if he were in a great hurry. The man turned back for a moment and looked at Mark.

Mark nodded his head at the man who was young and well dressed but still within the usual parameters for clothing in downtown Richmond. He looked Mark up and down but said nothing and turned back to face the front, checking his watch. Mark rolled his eyes.

The man took out his wallet and pulled out his money, checking his watch again. He took a step back, bumping into Mark and trod heavily on his foot. Mark winced as he pulled his foot back and tried to smile at the man to let him know he wasn't going to start a fight.

The man grumbled, "Sorry," as he stepped back into line. Finally, the line moved forward and he got to the front. "I'll take a dill tuna salad sandwich," he said.

"Dill tuna," said Stephen. "Have it ready in just a minute. Sorry you had to wait."

"Keep the change," he said curtly to Stephen, as he grabbed the sandwich out of his hands and walked away briskly. "Only have a few minutes," he said, his back already turned.

"Guy's a little overworked," said Mark, watching the man walk away.

"There are more regulars like that than you'd imagine," said Stephen. "It's okay, all green is good here. You here for the special? I know it's your favorite, chicken curry."

"Absolutely, no bread though," said Mark, patting his stomach. "Need to watch the middle." He looked back at the short line still forming behind him. "Hi, how are you?" he said to the man behind him. Usually everyone was polite in Richmond. It didn't matter if you'd never seen the person before or not.

There was an entire system of rules that let locals know how long someone had lived there by how many of the subtler commands they followed. No one who was from around these parts ever honked at a light, no matter how long it took for a driver to move forward, and long-time locals gave a two finger wave without ever taking their hands off the steering wheel.

It was always necessary to acknowledge everyone's existence when out in public. A quick nod or short hello occurred between every warm body even if the passerby was wearing a pin from the other side. Some semblance of civility was expected.

If somebody didn't bother it would be assumed they weren't raised right and was sure to be a tidbit of gossip around the supper tables later that night. The older families that lived along River Road would understand completely and gently nod their heads in recognition of what can't always be taught. There would be some speculation about whether or not the offender was a Northerner and therefore some leeway allowed and a short prayer offered for their salvation.

The newcomer who had only arrived ten years ago may not know any better.

Members of either the Circle or Management knew there was another, simpler reason. Making the effort to be polite, at least on the surface, made it possible to get on with some semblance of a routine life. As long as appearances were kept up for the masses who weren't in on the game there could be some moments in the day when it was possible to forget.

Besides, Richmond was a small town and under the more normal, mundane circumstances everyone realized they had to work and play around each other for years. No one could be avoided completely and it was too exhausting to be rude for such a long stretch of time.

Many locals, both inside and out of the organizations, were cousins of some sort and that also mattered in this small southern town. A slight could ripple out and cause hurt feelings to spread and resentments to take root. It was better to just nod and wave and show a little extra patience.

"Where do you think that guy had to get to?" asked Mark, gesturing behind him.

"Don't know. This economy has people a little more worried about their jobs than usual. They want to show the boss they're willing to eat at their desks," said Stephen.

Mark got out a twenty to ensure that there'd be bills in his change just in case there was an answer from his earlier inquiry.

"Thanks," he said, taking the dollar bills. They were turned in every direction. It was a routine signal that there was nothing to report. Maybe Frank didn't pay with the ones Mark had given him after all.

Mark would have to let it go for now. He went back and joined Fred on the bench.

"You get the curry?" asked Fred. "Don't care for it. Makes my stomach churn. I like the hummus and tabouli. Get it everyday."

Mark knew from observing him over the years that Fred felt comforted by patterns. It was why he was so good at his job. He could easily spot sequences and in the past had even been able to tell when there was something or someone that had moved outside of one.

The two men carried on like old friends and ate their sandwiches, talked about their families, the basketball league they played in and what was going on that weekend. It wasn't until Fred was thoughtfully chewing his pickle that Mark started to set up a way to transfer the information he had downloaded earlier.

"I need to check my messages," he said, and picked up his phone. He had been careful to separate out the information about his own bologna slicing from the Fed from whoever was building a war chest that could reach a billion dollars.

Fred hesitated a moment and then raised his own phone, switching on the Circle application to transfer large files. He started texting someone in the office to cover the few seconds it would take for the application to be ready.

Fortunately, everyone around them was distracted by their own phones.

"There are some banking patterns that require an analysis," said Mark, trying to keep it as brief as possible.

He lightly held his phone, wrapping his fingers around it and gently bumped fists with Fred as if they were agreeing on some finer point of a basketball game. That was all it took for the file to transfer to Fred's phone. He saw Fred briefly glance at his phone before he slipped it into his pocket.

"Got to go," he said. "Maureen's making pot roast and red potatoes in the slow cooker and I want to leave the office on time." He shrugged his shoulders and put his hands in his pockets, jingling the coins. "Funeral for Maureen's friend is in a couple days. I said I'd go with her."

"I take it you didn't really know her friend," said Mark.

"Don't tend to hang out with the hens," said Fred, the sounds of the coins rolling around in his pocket picked up just a little. "Catch you Friday," he said and walked away.

Mark sat back for a moment and tried to do a slow swivel of his head as he took inventory of who was outside on a raw day eating their lunch and might look a little too disinterested. Just as he turned he caught a glimpse of someone walking toward him with a determined stride. It was a lawyer from Fred's large practice, Richard Bach, a Management operative. He was taking long strides up the slight hill to where Mark was sitting, finishing the last of his carrot sticks.

Mark had never cared for him. He seemed to always carry such an air of entitlement.

He stopped right in front of Mark and seemed to want to say something urgent.

"Well, I uh, you know," he said.

Mark could see that he was sweating even though it was an unusually raw, cold day, especially for the beginning of April. Most people were buying their lunch and taking it back inside. He watched as Richard took a deep breath as if he was trying to steady his nerves.

"You alright?" he asked in a calm voice.

Richard looked pained and said in a low voice, "I know you have him."

"Have who?" asked Mark, slowly.

"I know you've put him somewhere for safekeeping," he hissed. He looked around nervously, his eyes darting to the different clusters of people.

"Who are you looking for, Richard? It's Richard, right?" Mark had never seen a director from Management approach someone out in the open. He wasn't sure how to react but he knew better than to admit to anything.

"I don't have time for this," hissed Richard in an angry tone. "Where is he? Do you think I've survived this long by just letting things slide?"

"You seem a little overwrought," said Mark in an even tone. "Maybe you should sit down."

"I'm not staying," said Richard, straightening his coat. He shook his head. "You know, I don't get it. We offered you everything and you turned your back to be a part of some second-rate place that has failed miserably more than once. You could have had such an easy ride."

Mark stood up slowly and leaned in to whisper, "As long as I didn't mind who the devil was driving the bus."

He took a short step back and felt a slight tremor go through his body. He tried to hide the panic as he saw Robert emerge from the shadows of the parking deck across the street. He looked thinner and tired and was wearing a baseball cap but Mark knew it was him. The boys weren't with him.

He was trying to make contact.

"I'm going back to work now," he said. He was yelling in Richard's face as everyone around them turned to look. "You feel the need to report something I suggest you do it."

He caught a glimpse of Robert startling and quickly turning back toward the shadows. They had missed their chance.

"This isn't over," said Richard, calling after him. "I'm not taking the blame for this."

Mark kept walking. He could feel his heart pounding and he was glad for once he had a brief excuse not to look calm and steady in front of people. He dropped his phone into his coat pocket and felt something brush against his hand. As he climbed the stairs two at a time he pulled out the neatly folded dollar bill in his pocket. The man in line, he thought. He must have slipped it in. He didn't like how important he was becoming in this game. Too many people from both sides were approaching him.

He walked back to his office and nodded at Frank in the hall, who looked like he wanted to say something. He was in no mood. He quickly shifted a few files to the chair near his door just in case and waited a few minutes before he pulled out his phone and fed in the last three numbers.

'Robert is still missing. Priority. Find him,' said the message.

"Easier said than done," said Mark. He would have to search Craig's List again tonight. He wasn't sure what else there was to do except try and make sure his family survived intact.

He sat down and sent an email to the realtor, telling him that Rosecroft wanted the land and was making an offer of cash. They would need the paperwork back as soon as possible.

He needed to get out of this mousetrap.

CHAPTER

THE TREASURY BUILDING took up the entire block of 1500 Pennsylvania Avenue and was located directly next door to the White House. Fred knew a car would attract too much attention near the building ever since the new anti-terrorism measures were put in place. He had taken the Metro into town instead and was walking swiftly up the sidewalk keeping pace with everyone in their dark blue or grey suits and unadorned overcoats as they bustled off to work.

The original Treasury building had been burned to the ground first by the British in 1814 and then again by arsonists nineteen years later. The current, massive fire-resistant granite structure was started only three years after that and was one of the largest office buildings in the world for awhile. The black marble tiles used for the main floors even had ancient fossils embedded in them, here and there, that amazed schoolchildren from all over the world.

America had wanted the world to know that the country may have been young but they were a steadily growing force. Management was in charge at the time and had drawn up the original plans but even the Circle directors who came into power during the construction felt awed by the structure.

Nothing was changed to the main plans. However, there was one secret addition.

On the building's southern side facing the Ellipse near a statue of Alexander Hamilton, the first Secretary of the Treasury, stood a hidden, private entrance no one ever seemed to notice.

Fred walked swiftly by the statue and up the stairs toward the door that was out of the line of sight of tourists who would all be gathering on the northern side along Fifteenth Street.

Fred had left before dawn so that he could easily mix in with the commuters on the D.C. streets. Maureen got up with him as she always did and took care of some of the details for Yvette's funeral that was scheduled for the next day.

Occasionally, back in Richmond, he ran into Alex Hamilton, a descendant of the original, who still lived in the old southern city along with the current Robert E. Lee, who went by Bob and Patrick Henry, who went by his middle name, Gilbert, given to him by his mother. He was the first male Henry to have a middle name in over two hundred years.

They could be seen running errands at the local Home Depot, walking down Cary Street or sitting in one of the front pews at St. Paul's Church down near the Governor's mansion. Fred had been to church there a handful of times and sat in the back on the Gospel side of the church near the Tiffany window that depicted Moses on one side and Lee on the other. It was explained to every generation of Circle children in Richmond that both men had chosen to lead their own people.

It often took outsiders generations to really understand how Richmond worked but it became innate for anyone who could trace their roots there.

He parked the car at the Van Dorn station in Alexandria by seven and rode the blue line in the rest of the way to the Metro Center stop. Fred was making an unscheduled visit to the President with news that could change the Circle's plans. Mark had inadvertently found the money trail that exposed what Management was planning to do in the coming years. Some of it the President's team had already speculated about but didn't have the confirmation and the rest made the discovery breathtaking in its scope and could alter the balance of power far too much.

The Treasury Building was just a short walk for Fred after he got off the train. He joined the flow of people headed in the same, general direction. It was still too early for most tourists but that would change in just a couple of weeks. The cherry blossoms would begin to bloom along the Tidal Basin and the city would become crowded from the early morning until dinner time. As the sun set most of them would leave the city for the relative safety of the cheaper hotels in the nearby suburbs.

The White House was Fred's final destination and sat on the western side of the Treasury building where there was also a reproduction of the Liberty Bell, minus the famous crack. He would need to move unseen between the buildings so that no one would begin to wonder who he was and begin a background check.

Fortunately, deep, underneath the ground was a tunnel that connected the two buildings and was only used by the sitting President and his closest staff. Both sides knew about it but had been unable so far to place any kind of detection devices that went unnoticed by whoever was occupying the White House and therefore controlled the tunnels.

The tunnels had been put in place after the British tried to burn down all of Washington and it became apparent there was the need for safe exits.

Other tunnels were added later including a shorter one that could take the President and his family from the private headquarters on the third floor of the West Wing down a fire proofed passage to a secure section in the basement. There was even a newer tunnel that linked to the nearby Metro Center station but was rarely used and never during the day when it would be impossible to guarantee moving about undetected by commuters.

All of the tunnels had been built using the simple cut-and-cover method from the bottom up with an excavated trench that was covered over by a clay roof. The oldest passageways were still lined with rows of large, handmade bricks and had initials etched in some of the stones by past presidential children starting with Theodore's rambunctious brood.

A clay-kicker had been used by the early nineteenth century construction crews to quietly remove the hard clay soil by hand without attracting a lot of unwanted attention. The method made it possible to build the system of tunnels without disturbing any of the properties above or making a lot of undue noise.

Every tunnel originated from somewhere within the White House and there were even rumors that there were a few that had been boarded over and forgotten that at one time had lead to less reputable parts of town.

The current president was known to use the passageway that burrowed under Lafayette Square in front of the White House to the Hay-Adams hotel with a side shoot that ended at the rector's office in St. John's Episcopal Church. It was necessary to meet with Circle operatives within the Episcopal Church from time to time who were known to wear vestments rather than a pin. Many of the ministers and bishops had managed to go undetected by Management or lower level Circle members for years and were seen as neutral mediators. Occasionally, it was even necessary for an operative to be spirited through the tunnels to the Hay-Adams where a safe room would be set up to keep them secure from harm in rather expensive surroundings.

The short tunnel to the church had been covertly put in by the Circle over a century ago to connect one of their main seats of early power back to the White House. However, when Management was in the White House it was barricaded from the St. John's side and left to look as if it had been undisturbed for decades. None of the zwanzig knew anything about it except for the uppermost holder of all the cell information, known as the Keeper. Besides that one person there were only a handful of additional Circle officials were aware of the extra passageway.

President Haynes had already used it more than once late at night to consult with the Bishop of Virginia, Lionel Crane who had been his friend in the Circle since they were young men at Episcopal High School just across the river. The President knew he could rely on Crane to not only tell him the truth but also help him to keep his integrity intact as much as possible.

Over time, the church had come to be known by the populace as the Church of Presidents but for a very few the congregation was more of a clue about who was moving within the top levels of the Circle.

The Hay-Adams had become the place where newly elected Presidents from both sides stayed with their families during the transition between election and inauguration. The stately hotel's underground tunnel gave easy access to the team coming into the White House without raising uncomfortable questions from a prying public.

During large receptions the Secret Service set up cots inside the Hay-Adams tunnel so they could take turns catching quick naps. Rats were an unending problem inside the tunnels and large ones were known to prowl inside the passageways, waking the sleeping agents with a jolt from the sudden weight on their chests as the oversized rodents leaped from place to place. They rarely bit anyone.

Andrew Johnson used the tunnel that connected to the Treasury all of the time after Lincoln was first assassinated. He couldn't be sure if Management would try to strike again and had set up a temporary office on the third floor of the Treasury. The windows overlooked the black bunting that had been draped across the buttress of the White House.

Fred and Maureen had stayed at the Hay-Adams together a few times, always requesting a room overlooking the White House where he could see the Secret Service on the roof quietly keeping track of who was watching them. It was one of the few times when he let himself give into the luxury of his surroundings and the high, antique bed with Egyptian linens, the ornate plaster ceilings, the rich wood accents of the walls and the elegant furniture.

Very powerful and fascinating people over the years who had come to town to take in a play at the nearby Kennedy Center or had business along K Street made a point to stay at the Hay-Adams. Their true intentions were never suspected.

For these few unique visitors there was always an unwritten appointment in their schedule when they slipped away to take the short walk two stories under the ground to the White House at the behest of the President.

Fred slipped down the old stairs to the windowless basement past the offices taken up by GS-12 and GS-13 government employees who worked under the constant glare of fluorescent lights all day and emerged after five o'clock to a dark sky. It would be well into April before the horizon would still have a tint of orange at that time of night that would gradually disappear by the time they'd made it to the Metro.

As he passed by the last of the cubicles he saw the impressions that were still visible in the basement floor where the old printing presses used to stand alongside large tables where employees had signed, separated and trimmed the sheets of demand notes by hand. They were some of the first government employees to have background checks even though they were regularly searched before leaving the premises.

Now, there were just neat rows of short cubicles with treasury employees hunched over their desks typing away at computers.

Everyone who worked down here was a junior executive but still had to have the TS-Delta clearance in order to ensure they would ignore the comings and goings through the wide doors on the far western wall. The first rule about working in that department was to never gossip about the door. One short conversation was a guarantee to not only get fired but endure a long interrogation.

Two Secret Service agents stood guard by the door at all times, one on either side, checking paperwork. Only someone who had a clearance of TS-DeltaTau was allowed to pass while the tunnel to the church was visible.

Fred walked through the last of the short maze of desks toward the door that was the entrance to the Treasury tunnel without making eye contact with anyone. No one was paying any attention to him. They all knew not to note anything about the visitors who passed briefly through their midst from time to time.

He walked toward the entrance as the agent swiftly unlocked the door and held it open. He never had to break his stride. He emerged in a narrow, short hallway of the West Wing and was greeted by another agent who said nothing as he went up the small back stairs to the private quarters. Someone had already informed the President he was en route.

"Mr. Bowers, so good to see you again," said the President. He had moved to his favorite chair near the window and was waiting for Fred to enter.

"At your service, sir," said Fred, as he waited for further instructions.

"Please have a seat and tell me what has you in Washington the day before a funeral. I assume this couldn't wait."

"No sir. We've taken possession of new and unexpected information."

"Let's have a look at it," said the President, waving at Fred to sit down. Fred opened the report on the coffee table and pointed to the first row of numbers.

"These are Management bank accounts in Somalia, South Africa, China, Panama and Anguilla. They represent only a few of the accounts that were set up in recent months to move large amounts of money unseen by anyone else," said Fred.

"How large are we talking?"

"Billions of dollars have been moved around. Much of it appears to be payments to China. Those were harder to trace but we were able to track the funds until they disappear into Beijing. There are smaller payments in the millions sent to different parts of the Middle East and Africa, which are most likely payoffs."

"For their natural resources," said the President.

"No sir, they've been making agreements for gold, copper, diamonds and oil along more traditional lines where they knew we'd detect them. Not exactly visible but we knew what they were doing. That may have been more of a distraction for our benefit."

"Then what is it?"

"Sir, we've been able to tie the funds to a network of terrorist organizations. They're all relatively small and loosely connected around a radical view of Islam but they don't seem to have any real connection to each other. The money has been used for arms and to boost certain local officials."

"Can we tell what part of Management is controlling this money? How high does it go?"

"That is even more interesting, sir. Authority for the operation is coming from a self-contained cell buried near the top. We have someone in place in the structure but they were unaware of the plan. A new power structure appears to be coming to prominence and they have a more violent take on things," said Fred.

"So the question becomes how do we deal with them," said the President, as he sat back in his chair. "Is it possible to tell how long this has been going on or how many places they've managed to get their hooks in just yet?"

"No sir, not completely. Our best estimate is this has been going on for at least twenty years. We have integrated the intel reports on terrorist groups from 1970 to the present and we were able to detect similarities in a hundred different groups, some within the U.S. or North America."

"Best estimate," said the President, shaking his head. "Are we too late?"

"Too late for what, sir?"

"Too late to stop them without starting a widespread war."

Fred pulled out an iPad and brought up a slowly revolving map of the world that had different areas all across the globe highlighted in blue or red with dotted lines and a progression of arrows connecting them.

"This is what we've been able to put together so far, sir. As you can see, a pattern emerges. War is actually their endgame. Not one large war but many, smaller wars that keep pulling different stabilized and independent governments into them. The governments use their resources of money and manpower to put out the fires and are too distracted to notice what's going on in their own countries."

"They have figured out how to get us to step out of the way voluntarily," said the President.

"Yes sir, on the world stage and in our own infrastructures. We were able to detain one of their operatives who has since been reported as dead and question him on the operation."

"Is he dead?" asked the President.

"Yes sir, he did not survive the interrogation."

"This was necessary?"

"It was an unintended consequence. He was able to tell us, however, that the real intention was to foster a sense of frustration within these more stabilized governments by raising the general level of fear through a long series of small, unpredictable wars. Then, they introduce a roster of candidates for elections in Parliaments or Congress that have more radical ideas about how things ought to be run."

"And they get actual air time because the powers that be look so ineffectual."

"Yes sir, and because the voters they're really courting have more comfortable lives than where the wars are being fought and have more to lose."

"Is there any kind of response being put forth?" asked the President.

"Yes sir, we are working on that but its long term."

"What does that mean?"

"They are too entrenched to stop head on and their plan is working. Millions of people believe the world is a more dangerous place. They have been very thoughtful about how to build their plan. There may be even more than we know about, just yet. But we can expose certain elements of the plan and draw connections to key figures we'd like to see step back without exposing that we are aware of the bigger picture."

"And what is the longer range part of the plan that's being developed?"

"The Schmetterling Operation, sir. They are still our best hope to splinter apart the Management," said Fred.

"How many years till that takes root?"

"Our first children from the orphanages have already graduated and are placed in various industries, including politics. They remain undetected and are seen as neutral by Management."

"We are playing a very dangerous game, Mr. Bowers."

"Yes sir, and there is one more piece of related news. We believe that that dead Circle operative in Georgia had found out about Management's grand plan and downloaded the information onto a thumb drive. The same thumb drive that's now in the hands of the Jones woman," said Fred.

"The same thumb drive that also contains the list of nearly every child in every children's home that we've placed around the world," said the

President.

"There may be further useful information on there as well. But we have been unable to see what's on the thumb drive."

"The Jones woman has refused?"

"We have not approached her to ask, sir. We need to be more certain of her answer."

"You mean to determine which side she's been on all along. All of those children," said the President, letting out a deep sigh.

His chest felt a little tight as he tried to take back in a deep breath.

"Mr. President, are you alright?" asked Fred, concern in his voice.

"Can you get me a glass of water? How did it happen that so many year's of effort is now resting in one person's pocket? It is amazing that Wallis Jones and her entire family isn't dead."

"Not really, sir. We think they're still alive because the top ranks of Management don't know about the operation. The flow of money never reaches the top. If someone were to murder Wallis there would be a lot of inquiries within and not only would it put their plan into jeopardy it would interrupt their stream of income."

"So how do they hope to get the information back without exposing their plan," said the President, sipping the water.

"That is a good question, sir. We believe there may be a mole within our ranks who is close to the family and has gone to Richmond to take the drive and all that is on it."

"Inadvertently exposing our network of children as well." The President mopped his face with a handkerchief. "Do we have any idea who it is?"

"We have an unconfirmed report, sir. A zwanzig has been turned."

The President turned ashen and loosened his tie. "Where did we get this information? Can it possibly be reliable?"

"Yes sir, the captured operative told us, shortly before he expired."

CHAPTER

③⑨

AN entire week had passed with Wallis having to wonder what might happen next. Yvette had died as a result. Wallis was tired of doing anymore waiting.

She sat beside Tom' bed in her guest room waiting for him to finally open his eyes. He was propped up on pillows in the center of the antique sleigh bed. It was still early and no one else was up in the house. She heard the paper hit the driveway and looked up just as Tom' eyelids fluttered open and he realized someone was sitting by his side.

"What?"

"It's me, Wallis," she whispered.

"What's going on? Is everyone alright?" He tried to prop himself up on his elbows.

"Yes, lay back, its okay. I wanted to get you alone so we could talk."

Tom looked at his sister in law. "You look pretty determined. What exactly are we going to chat about?"

"Norman said you were going to be a pleasant surprise and considering that so far three people I know have been murdered that's got to be significant. So, I have to know, why are you here?"

Tom took in a deep breath and laid his head back on the pillow.

"You're buying time, why is that?" asked Wallis.

"You know, I've always appreciated your directness. I'm hesitating so that I can give you as much of the truth as possible. How do I explain this?"

"Just try honesty and see how far that gets us. Did it ever occur to any of you that a large part of what may have gotten you into this mess is an inability to rely on the truth and then let it do its own work. I know, I know," said Wallis, holding up her hand in protest. "Honesty appears to have had horrible consequences in the past but I've watched enough clients build entire lives on half-truths and it isn't long before none of them are sure what to do anymore. They always end up miserable." Wallis looked down at her lap. "I'm not sure I can live like that."

Tom reached out and took her hand. "That's why I admire you so much. Okay, let's try pushing the envelope and go for a little more truth telling than normal. It's a concept." He hesitated and searched for the words. "I was called back, ordered here because what at first appeared to be a set of remarkable and tragic circumstances started to come together in a pattern. The only explanation for everything that's gone on is that there's someone from the Circle who's been leaking some of their own truth to Management."

"What does that have to do with you?"

"I am the current zwanzig that the highest cell in the Circle could trust, or so they hope. Let me explain. You see, all of the different mechanics of how we operate in the Circle and all of our plans for the future were broken into pieces and given to different cells that don't communicate with each other. They aren't even aware of who might be in the other cells or the numbers of cells like them that exist. It was the only way we could prevent a widespread failure like the one that happened to my grandfather and all of those people."

"So you're part of a cell."

"Not really. In any organization there still has to be somebody who gets the big picture and can communicate somehow with the others when it's necessary. Otherwise there really isn't an organization. In every generation there is one person, known as the Keeper. But that's where it can get very difficult."

"If everyone knows who is the one keeper of all of that information then it becomes simple to cut off the head of the snake," said Wallis.

Tom smiled and rubbed his neck. "Exactly, dear sister in law. A fate no one wants to experience. But how to communicate with the cells and not reveal the identity? How to even set it all up was an undertaking. The original twenty agreed that one of them would choose the first guardian and take that secret to his grave. Then that guardian would choose a successor from the descendants but never in his own family and he would keep their name a secret forever as well. The original twenty had no problem with the plan because they remembered the original horror and could be trusted to keep quiet. Then over time there were more descendants and it became increasingly difficult to guess who it might be. Plus, I suspect that some descendants were never even told about this part of the Circle and therefore never knew to speculate. That would have been a better idea for all of us."

"You were chosen," said Wallis, her eyes growing wider.

"Yes, a few years ago I had a visit from an elderly woman who I adore. She knew that I would find it very difficult to turn her down."

"Esther," said Wallis.

Tom lay back and let his body relax into the pillows as he shut his eyes. "You are a quick one, Wallis. But there was a catch this time."

"A catch?"

"Yes, Esther was only the messenger. She was preparing the way for the next Keeper in case the line of succession has to change quickly."

"They were worried about the Keeper dying," said Wallis.

"More like murdered but that's just a word. Dead is dead and it was the need to create just the slightest added bit of structure at the top. Only the Keeper still held all of the names but it was decided that someone would know who was the present guardian and who was yet to come. The last remaining original zwanzig entrusted Esther but told no one else. It's probably the only reason Esther is still alive."

"Why are you telling me so much? The Circle keeps a secret for generations and then you tell me?"

Tom opened his eyes and looked at Wallis. "Every good plan has moments where it becomes necessary to think on the fly and make decisions more quickly or risk losing everything. There isn't enough time to reason everything out and we need to get a handle on things before it all really gets worse."

"You have to discover the liar."

"Yes, I have to figure out who is like a brother or a sister to me that has a connection to Richmond and cares so little for the rest of us that they're feeding information to Management. You know, on the surface their organization looks like a good idea. Give the masses a better life, feed them, clothe them and give them a decent job. But it never works. Either someone just wants to choose something different for their life that doesn't benefit the machine or someone gets invested in the idea that the power structure is their Higher Power. Then anyone who threatens that has to go by any means necessary," said Tom.

"And then the killing begins."

"Yes, then innocent, decent people die. So, Esther has called me back in order to ferret out the one person who knows just enough to get Management's attention and leak names. Whoever it is, they started this by getting Carol killed."

"That woman in Georgia, right?" asked Wallis.

"Yes, that happily married, mother of two. She suspected someone was getting ready to expose her. That's why she sought out this Ray Billings. It just so happened that she had a little more information than we knew." Tom rubbed his face. "Carol was a banking regulator in Georgia. She had been groomed as someone that Management would never pay attention to and was viewed as an outsider. Not a member of either group. It gave her the ability to be an effective watchdog over the coming and going."

"But someone exposed her real background?"

"Yes, Carol was a zwanzig, just like me and just like Norman and now, just like Ned, whether he knows it or not," said Tom.

Wallis sat back in her chair, her jaw clenched.

"You don't like any of this, I get that, but there are a few facts in this life that are hard to change. People made decisions a long time ago and the affects are still rippling out to the rest of us."

"Tom, if you and Esther had both died in that explosion. What would have happened to the Circle?"

"We would have been many little groups with no real central focus. That is, if I didn't have such a hard time with keeping secrets all by myself." Tom gave a sheepish smile. "I'm not very good at suffering alone. I like to make sure there's someone to commiserate with."

"You told Norman, didn't you?"

"I told Norman, who is the master of keeping secrets, as you know."

Wallis smiled. "My dear husband has raised it to a fine art."

"You know, I finally prodded Esther once into telling me that he was her original choice for next in line but he had already fallen for the one woman that would make that impossible. I think Norman is a very wise man for a number of reasons," he said.

"Do you think that someone does know about the two of you? If that's true, it's almost too much." Wallis stopped speaking and thought about what it could mean to her family.

"I've had a few days to think about that one and no, I don't. It was too amateurish and in your face. Sure to draw too much attention. If someone really knew about me or Esther we'd have died of apparent suicides or some kind of accident out of the public eye. An explosion is not Management's style."

"Someone started this ball rolling but it's gotten out of their control, hasn't it?" asked Wallis.

"Yes, that would seem to be the case. But still, if we follow all of the pieces it still makes a pattern of sorts."

"I don't see it," said Wallis.

"I know and that's where I'm afraid I have to stop talking. I can't be sure yet and wild speculation will make things worse. Plus, I hope I'm wrong. Someone exposed Carol Schaeffer with the idea to pull down the Circle. They knew she had a piece of our puzzle."

"The information from her cell."

"Yes, the list of children in the homes. But they didn't know she had also come across something inside Management. We didn't have confirmation of that until forty-eight hours ago and I take it by that look on your face, you already know what I'm talking about. So there is something on that drive. I'd like to see what's on there."

Wallis hesitated. She wasn't going to give up what Ray Billings had died to keep hidden until she was sure.

"It's alright, check with Norman," said Tom. "But make it fast. We don't have a lot of time. We believe that there's a cell operating within Management to try and take over from within the organization. A quiet coup of sorts and they're raising funds to do it. Up until now, they've managed to keep everyone at bay from this house in order to hide their plan but they won't wait forever. Someone will figure out that you have the thumb drive by process of elimination and they won't wait long to wrest it away and then do away with all of the loose ends."

"All of us," said Wallis, feeling her stomach churn.

"Yes, but we're going to move before any of that happens. However, there is one idea I'd like to set loose in that lawyer brain of yours right now. Who would be the most likely to lose in this town if Management clamped down?"

"I have a few candidates. There's a fat little man named, Oscar, I'd like to nominate. But he seems too far down on anyone's ladder to be the brains behind anything. I don't know."

"Yeah, I heard about what happened. The attempt on your life had to be another in a series of panicky move by someone. This is what happens when you rule by force. That idea tends to trickle down and it becomes hard to shut down. Norman suggested a man named Richard Bach."

"He's slick enough and just smart enough to think he ought to be in control of something," said Wallis.

She got up to leave. "Everyone will be getting up soon. You should rest." She stopped at the door. "Tom, if you're the current guardian and you keep all of the information on the cells then you know who else was in Carol's cell and how they might connect to Richmond, don't you?"

"Yes, I do," said Tom, grimacing.

"And Norman must have asked you."

"But I didn't tell him," said Tom. "There are limits."

Wallis hesitated but didn't ask anything else. She wanted to ask Tom if she might know the person too but she wasn't sure she could handle the answer. Tom listened to her footsteps disappear down the hall and felt the wave of grief come over him again.

"Harry, my brother, what have you done?" he said, quietly, as he slammed his fist into the bed.

CHAPTER 40

THE rain came pouring down in Richmond the next day making everyone huddle under a variety of umbrellas as they tried to swiftly move from the parking lot of St. Stephen's and into the vestibule. The mood was dampened along with the weather as everyone quietly chatted about what was the real cause of Yvette's death.

The coroner had finally signed off on heart failure and released the body for burial after the toxicology report came back clean. "These things happen sometimes," he had said to Yvette's family, "and we never know why."

Her husband, Bob and their three children sat huddled in the front row surrounded by immediate family members. The youngest, Lance kept craning his neck around watching who was coming and going and wondering if maybe his mother might show up after all. Maureen and Fred slid into the row right behind them as Maureen leaned forward to squeeze Bob around the neck. Yvette had been her best friend and someone she could hang around with without having to talk too much. It had made life easier.

The night before after Fred had returned quietly from Washington the two of them had sat up watching TV in bed without saying a word. Maureen was bristling with anger and had wanted to scream out in rage at whoever had seen Yvette's life as so easily expendable just to make a point. Fred was the one who had been able to divert the blood and tissue samples so that no one would ever realize she was poisoned and perhaps start a manhunt for a serial killer who didn't really exist.

But Maureen had insisted on knowing and the grief she felt in the center of her chest felt like a sharp rock that wouldn't diminish. There was so little in this life that was hers to claim but this precious friendship had been one corner that was her safe harbor and now it was gone. Arbitrarily stolen away in the middle of some petty fight over power or land or riches, she kept thinking.

"They had no right," she had whispered to Fred in the middle of a loud commercial. He had turned to her but said nothing. He had never seen her in such pain and had no idea how to comfort her or take any of the misery away. The tears had poured down her cheeks and her shoulders shook but no real sounds escaped. She was a good operative even in the middle of her grief. He had never felt so helpless and for the first time he found himself questioning the point of any of it.

"If none of us can just get through a day and be happy, what's the point?" she had said to him. He had reached up and brushed away a tear on her cheek to stop himself from thinking about that question too much. She had a point.

He had taken her in his arms in an uncharacteristic movement and enfolded her as she wept. His shoulder muffled the sound.

"I love you," he had whispered, and he knew he meant it in some deep and abiding way. Maureen cried harder.

The church was crowded with people who had known Yvette. Maureen and Fred sat directly behind Bob and the three small children. Maureen couldn't stop looking at them without thinking, they have lost their mother for no real reason and will never have any answers. Fred reached over and took Maureen's hand and gave it a squeeze.

She looked up at him a little startled and gave him a small smile.

In the back Wallis and Norman were taking their seats. Tom had stayed at home still resting from the after-effects of the explosion at the book store. His leg had pins in it and was in a cast propped up on pillows. Esther had insisted on getting out of the hospital as well and was already calling contractors to talk about starting work and getting the store reopened.

Ned had tried to stay home but Wallis didn't feel comfortable letting him out of her sight. He asked if he could at least sit with Paul and his mother, Sharon and Norman had said, "Let the boy. It'll be okay," as he placed his hand gently in the small of her back.

"Nothing is the way it should be," she whispered as she laid her head on his shoulder.

"Unfortunately, it's the way it's always been only now you see it. It'll be okay, Wallis."

"How do you know that?" she asked, lifting her head to be able to look at him and see if he meant what he was saying.

"This one may throw you but I know it'll be okay because I believe God is actually in this whole mess that we humans have created," he said. "It's the way I've survived at times over the years. Every time it's gotten to me I try to remind myself that none of us are really in charge and all I can do is try to keep my own integrity intact."

"Weiskopf, you never cease to amaze me," she said, tearing up. "Is this a new realization or have you been holding out on me?"

"Holding out a little, which should come as no surprise. As I've always told you, a good marriage should always keep a little mystery going."

"I'd laugh at that one but it's just not so funny today," said Wallis.

Norman pulled his wife back into the crook of his arm and said, "Yeah, I know."

"Pastor Donald has been a good influence on you," she said, settling back into the pew and opening the bulletin for the funeral. A picture of a smiling Yvette with her family was on the back cover.

"I'll let him know you feel that way."

The service was beginning and Pastor Donald began to recite from the Book of Common Prayer. Maureen had brought her own white leather bound prayer book she had received as a young girl. She turned to the Burial of the Dead, Rite One and closed her eyes to let the words wash over her. At least here she could still find some comfort.

"Oh God, whose mercies cannot be numbered. Accept our prayers on behalf of thy servant, Yvette, and grant her an entrance into the land of light and joy, in the fellowship of thy saints, through Jesus Christ our Lord, who liveth and reigneth with thee and the Holy Spirit, one God, now and forever. Amen."

The rain could be heard hitting the roof far above their heads as everyone bowed their head in prayer.

"I will lift up mine eyes unto the hills," read Pastor Donald, "from whence cometh my help? My help cometh even from the Lord, who hath made heaven and earth. He will not suffer thy foot to be moved, and he that keepeth thee will not sleep." The minister's voice carried easily over the rain and he said each of the words with tenderness.

"God, I hope so," whispered Wallis, as she glanced over at her son giggling over something with Paul. She bowed her head and prayed for only the third time in years.

Pastor Donald ended the prayers with a plea that made Wallis wonder if it was chosen to give comfort for more than one reason.

"Help us, we pray, in the midst of things we cannot understand, to believe and trust in the communion of saints, the forgiveness of sins and the resurrection to life everlasting. Amen," said Pastor Donald as the congregation echoed "Amen" back to him.

Wallis felt some of her anxiety from the past few weeks start to lift and her first feelings of relief come over her.

"Maybe everything will be alright," she said, as she rose to walk up to the altar rail for communion.

"I'll wait here," said Norman. "Best not to press my luck with God or with Pastor Donald." Wallis smiled and squeezed his hand as she went and joined the line waiting for their turn to kneel at the rail. Sharon came up and slid into line behind her.

"Wallis," she whispered. "How are you holding up? Are you going to the other funeral tomorrow too?"

"What funeral?" said Wallis. She had been moving slowly forward with the line but froze at the word funeral and turned around to face the people still in the pews, a sense of dread growing in the pit of her stomach.

"Didn't you hear? I'd have thought for sure someone would have called you. She was your client, after all," said Sharon, her voice growing higher. "And it was all over the news, so horrible. Richmond is just not what I remember as a little girl."

"Sharon," said Wallis, in a firm voice, not looking at her but searching for Norman still sitting in the pews. "Who died? Who is dead?"

"Why Lilly Billings, Lilly Billings is dead. She was murdered in her own home. Throat slashed they said and not a single clue about who did it."

Sharon kept talking, giving out more details as the communion line moved around Wallis who stood still in the middle of the aisle, frozen right in front of the choir. Every little bit of calm she had found was gone and she couldn't seem to catch her breath. She wasn't sure if she should turn and go up for communion or run back to Norman and pull Ned along as she went. Wallis searched the back of the church and saw that Norman was half-rising out of the pew with a look of concern on his face.

She looked at him and shook her head as if she was trying to let everyone in the church know that she was done. Norman stood up and swiftly moved up the aisle. Sharon was still talking when he got there.

"Thank you, Sharon, I've got it from here. Yes, thank you, okay, you can go on," he said, pulling Wallis toward the front and the other side of the altar rail away from Sharon who was mumbling, "I'm sorry."

"Lilly's dead," said Wallis, as she kneeled down, not even trying to whisper. Pastor Donald stopped in midsentence as he was blessing a wafer and glanced over at Wallis. He caught himself and said, "Feed on him in thy heart, with thanksgiving," in an even calm tone as he moved down the line. Norman would have thought Pastor Donald was unmoved if he didn't see the slight tremor in his hand as he placed the wafer in the person's outstretched palm.

"Murdered, Lilly was murdered. Her throat cut," said Wallis, still talking at a normal volume. Others at the rail looked up and turned their heads toward her. Pastor Donald kept moving down the line. "Preserve thy body and soul into everlasting life," he said as he reached down and gently turned over Wallis' hands, peeling them away from the rail. He placed the wafer in her hands and stopped for a moment to place his palm heavily on the top of her head.

"Bless thy servant, Wallis, Lord as she struggles to feel you close by her side, offering support."

Wallis put the thin wafer in her mouth and let her head fall on top of her folded hands as she clutched the rail. Norman grabbed her around the shoulders and helped her rise to her feet as they moved back down the aisle. She looked first at Bob and Yvette's children as she passed by the front aisle and said, "I'm sorry." Norman gave her a gentle nudge to try and keep her moving as Maureen reached out and squeezed her hand. She stopped to grasp Maureen's hands for just a moment and return the gesture.

People continued to move around them toward the altar to receive communion or tromping down the aisle, back to their seat. The choir was singing a Latin hymn and had just reached the build-up to the chorus as Wallis heard someone sneer, "Black widow."

She turned to try and see who it was but no one was looking in her direction. Someone had come to Yvette's funeral to gloat, she thought. There's no end to it.

"Did you hear that?" she whispered to Norman as they finally made it back into their pew.

"Yes," said Norman, looking straight ahead, his mouth pulled into a thin line. Wallis glanced over at Ned who was staring at her with a worried expression on his face.

"I'm okay," she said, even though she knew he couldn't hear her. She smiled and did her best to let her body relax. My son, my beautiful son, she thought. They think he's some kind of prize.

There was a short reception in Peyton Hall after the service. The body wasn't being interred until the next day with only the immediate family at the grave site. As everyone filed out Ned ran up and wrapped his arms around his mother as if to comfort her. Wallis rubbed the top of his head and felt some measure of strength return.

"This is what matters," she said to Norman. "As long as I can remember that I'll be okay."

Ned looked up and smiled at her before letting go and running off to find his friends.

Wallis and Norman said their goodbyes and Wallis made a point to put herself on the list to make dinner for Bob. She put down something she knew Norman liked to make knowing full well who would end up doing all of the cooking. Lasagna was always a good comfort food.

They walked in the house and greeted a barking Joe who danced around in circles wagging his tail, happy to see them again. Ned patted his head and dropped his coat in the front hall as he took the stairs two at a time.

"Ned, get your coat," Wallis called after him. "He can have very selective hearing when he knows I'm too tired to run after him."

"He has a new video game. I took a look at it. Even his games are more complicated than my high school math class."

Wallis leaned over and picked up the coat and felt a twinge in her shoulder. Joe ran over to her and licked her face and her hand, running back and forth across the coat until Wallis had to smile.

"This is why we have a dog," said Norman. "Really happy to see us and with very few expectations. Aren't you, Joe?" he asked, as Joe rolled over and he rubbed the dog's belly.

"Norman," she said, as he took off his tie and threw it on the banister. "I can't believe I'm going to say this, but Harriet is right. We have to go on with our normal routines as much as possible. I can't do this to Ned. I can't let him think he needs to watch out for me. That's even worse than having him look at those files."

"You're a good mother," said Norman, as he pulled off a shoe.

Wallis picked up his tie and started up the stairs with Norman and Joe right behind her.

"Yeah, well," said Wallis, "I'm still figuring out what that means."

"I think," said Norman, "it's wanting to stay in the struggle that makes you into one."

"Kristen McDonough was struggling to do the right thing for her family and look what happened to them," said Wallis, as she turned and whispered, "All of them dead."

"We have a few things going for us that the late McDonough's did not. Chief of those is we still possess this thumb drive and we now know what's on it."

"What else?" asked Wallis.

"I've been playing this game my entire life and I know how to bend a few rules."

They both turned and looked downstairs at the front door as someone began repeatedly pushing their doorbell.

"Who could that be?" asked Norman.

"The list is growing too long to guess," said Wallis, as she turned to go back down the stairs.

"No, no, let me go," said Norman. "I'd better get down there before whoever it is wakes up Ned and Tom."

"I should go check on Tom, anyway. See if he's okay."

Norman hurried down the stairs in his stocking feet and looked through the peephole to see an angry, older woman standing at his front door holding several cloth bags that were filled to overflowing. He slowly opened the door not sure what to expect.

A faint odor of mildew wafted off of the woman every time she shifted a bag.

"Can I help you?" he asked.

"I'm here to see Wallis. Tell her Alice Watkins is at her front door and we have a few things to get straight."

"Wallis," Norman called out without turning away from Alice. "I think this one is for you." He opened the door wider. "Would you like to come in Alice?"

"About time," she said, as she stepped inside and dropped her bags.

"This way to the kitchen," he said.

CHAPTER 41

IT was late Friday night and everyone in Wallis' neighborhood was in for the evening watching TV or already tucked into bed. Richard Bach had been sitting in his SUV down the street from Wallis and Norman's house keeping watch for hours. The orders were to watch the house till he was relieved but make no contact.

He was still hoping an opportunity would open up to get Wallis Jones alone. He needed that thumb drive in order to get back in the good graces of his Management elders and he suspected Wallis might be in possession of it. He had to find out and try to get it back. It was starting to look like his only option. He was picking up no traces of Robert.

Rodney Parrish appeared in his rear view mirror, walking toward the car as he straightened his tie with one hand and swinging his briefcase by his side in the other. He was humming to himself as he got in the front seat next to Richard and shook his hand before sitting back and letting out a low whistle. He seemed so relaxed. It was annoying Richard.

"Well, well, nice ride, Mr. Bach. I have something very similar."

Richard was about to interrupt him. He was in no mood for a conversation and he hated being in Rodney Parrish' company wondering how many old women he had killed with those hands. "It's okay," said Rodney. "You're in a hurry. I got the message from Davey. What can I do for you? I understand you're looking for a solution."

Richard rested his hands on the steering wheel and looked at the front of Wallis' house. "I have a special situation that I need you to fix."

"Absolutely, I am your man for all kinds of situations. You need me to get something for you out of that house?" He smiled at Richard and turned his attention to the house. Richard wondered if he was already figuring out the best way to slip in unnoticed.

He could feel his anxiety rising. "No, no, at least not yet. It's the Blazney guy and that Billings woman, I need to give the cops someone."

Rodney's face took on a scowl and he sat back and waited for Richard to speak. Richard knew he never took complaints about his work very well.

"I'm not saying anything in particular about what was done and I don't care who was involved in any of it," said Richard, putting out of his mind the old man asking him if he needed to use a phone. "Look, there's ten grand in it for you and the gratitude of some very important people above me if you can plant some evidence that'll stick even in court."

Rodney pursed his lips for a moment before answering. "Not a problem but I'll need half of it upfront."

"I have it right here," he said, patting his coat. "But you have to have it done before the sun rises tomorrow. Is that going to be a problem?"

"I don't have problems," said Rodney, smiling broadly. "Where am I leaving this evidence?"

"That's up to you, Parrish. Just make sure the trail leads to your pal, Oscar. That going to be a problem for you?"

"This is your lucky day, Mr. Bach. I'm able to say, no, not at all to that too. Oscar is not too happy with another situation right at this moment and we are on the outs. Besides, I try not to get too attached to anyone. That becomes a problem when you can't do your work over some feelings this way or that for someone else."

"Just make sure the police can't ignore it or shove it away and get it done by morning. Do that and I'll be by the counting room this time tomorrow with the rest. Everyone has to be looking for Oscar's head before then."

"Like I said, not a problem at all. Just so happens I kept a few trinkets that should work nicely."

Rodney smiled as Richard handed him a fat, large brown envelope. "It's been nice doing business with you, Mr. Bach." He opened the door and slid quietly out of the front seat, humming another tune and swinging his briefcase. Richard watched him in the rearview mirror till he disappeared from view. The tightness in his chest seemed to only grow as he turned his attention back to the front of the house.

There were moments when he lay in his bed in the middle of the night listening to his wife quietly snore and he would wonder what had happened to him. This wasn't where he had expected to end up when he had started at Sutler. He had pictured himself leading hapless men who didn't understand what it took to keep a community growing and thriving. He had thought there was going to be a grand purpose. There was very little of that in his job description anymore. He looked out at Wallis' house and whispered out loud the word that best described himself these days. "Thug," he said, feeling the tightness spread.

Wallis sat in her kitchen across the island from Alice Watkins waiting for her to say something. Norman was starting a pot of coffee and rooting around in the tall pantry for something in the way of food to offer their late night guest.

Alice looked uncomfortable perched on top of one of the bar stools but she had firmly turned down Wallis' offer to move to the dining room. Wallis had smelled the distinct odor of damp mildew and had started to offer a towel but thought better of it.

"Alice, I'm a little surprised to see you," said Wallis. "I thought you had left Richmond in your rear view mirror forever."

"So did I," said Alice, "until someone showed up at my new job and tried to kill me. I'm thinking that's somehow connected to you."

Norman was struggling with a bag of chips and jerked the sides open too fast, sending a few flying through the air. He tried to gather them up quickly as Wallis took in a deep breath.

"Do you know who it was?" asked Wallis, wondering if Oscar had spread out his territory to Williamsburg.

"No, it was a black fellow. He seemed young and determined. But not many can put one over on me, including him. I was ready for some such nonsense."

"Ready?" asked Norman who put a plate of chips and cookies in between the two women. "It was all we had," he said, looking at Wallis.

"Can't you make a sandwich?" asked Alice. "There's no real food here," she said dismissively, moving the plate away from her.

"Absolutely," said Norman, opening the refrigerator. "Of course."

"How could you be ready, Alice?" asked Wallis.

She let out a distinct tsk and spread her fingers out, pressing down on top of the wooden island.

"I'd sit at my desk and every now and then think about what I'd do if somebody ever showed up there. I'd plan out how to put a crimp in someone's day, just in case. It passed the time. I did it at home too. Good thing because that fellow must have been watching my place of business and waited till everyone else was gone. He seemed to know a little bit about what he was doing."

"Do you mean a professional?" asked Wallis.

"Maybe. Until a few months ago all I knew about any nonsense like this was from watching TV. I'm not sure I'd know the difference between a psychopath and a professional hit man."

"I'm not sure there is one," said Wallis.

"Except the hit man has enough sense to at least get paid," said Norman. Wallis looked at him and Norman shrugged his shoulders.

"It's okay," said Alice. "He's right. But I also have to figure that either way that's probably not the only attempt that's going to be made. Now, I'm going to need a way to start over, again," said Alice, giving a pointed look at Wallis. "But I'm going to need help this time."

"You're thinking we may know how to help with that?" asked Norman.

He put a peanut butter and jelly sandwich in front of Alice, cut into quarters. "That's all we have at the moment. Need to make a run to the store."

Alice let out another distinct 'tsk and bit into the sandwich, still talking. "I don't know everything that's going on but I saw enough of what was on that thumb drive to get that there's some real organizations behind all of this. Someone is going to know how to help me disappear."

"I may have an idea," said Wallis, "but I'll need to make a few phone calls first. Do you have a place to stay?"

Norman stood behind Alice shaking his head, no but Wallis made a point not to make eye contact.

"I believe I'll stay here till we figure this out. For some reason no one wants to hurt you," said Alice, looking directly at Wallis. "That's some mean reputation you must have."

"I wouldn't go that far," said Wallis, feeling the dull ache that was still in her shoulder. "Let's go get you settled. You can take the sandwich with you."

Norman carried up the bags as Wallis followed and made up a bed for Alice who was getting settled in the one remaining bedroom that wasn't occupied. Alice sat in a chair watching them work.

"Alice, there's one thing I haven't been able to figure out at all. How did Ray Billings get involved in the first place?"

"Ray didn't always work at the Utility Department. He started out as a social worker further down South in Georgia. Spent about six or seven years living on the grounds of a children's home. That's where he met that woman that died. Her name was Carol. Hold on a minute, I have her last name here somewhere." Alice opened her large purse and unzipped a little pocket on the inside. She pulled out a small notebook and thumbed through the pages. "Baumann, she was a Baumann. What, that mean something to you?"

Norman had stopped helping Wallis stuff the pillows into pillowcases and stood up straight.

"You know her?" asked Alice. She let out a throaty chuckle. "Ray had a nickname for her. Called her his little butterfly. He said that's what he called all the children."

"Norman, are you alright?"

"The name sounds familiar," said Norman. "Would you excuse me?"

Wallis thought about following him but she needed information from Alice and she couldn't take the risk that Alice might decide to stop talking at all, again. There were still a few more questions and fewer people every day who might have the answers.

"It's been a long day for us. We just got back from a funeral for a good friend. Did you know anything else about her?"

"She's married now. Ray told me that too. I think it was Schaeffer."

"She was another social worker, I take it" said Wallis.

"No, she grew up there. She was a resident, you know, an orphan."

"Why would she give this information to Ray? Were they close?"

"Not particularly. Maybe they were when he had worked at the home but that was a long time ago. No, Carol told Ray that she needed someone she could trust to hold onto all of it until she could figure something out."

"Figure out what?"

"Who was the turncoat. There is apparently a rat in the woodpile. Carol suspected someone out there in her group was telling tales, especially about that place she grew up, about the orphanage. She was worried that someone was going to end up dead. Boy, was she right about that."

"Do you think she knew who it was?"

"No, I don't. That's what she was trying to find out when she suddenly turned up dead from a drowning. Drowning, my ass. That's when Ray started to panic and look for someone else to hold the information, just in case. He dragged me and Stanley into it and then he ended up dead. Now, someone's come after me. Who knows where Stanley has gotten to. I hear he's stopped showing up at work." Wallis knew better than to offer any information and let the comment pass.

"Lilly Billings is dead too. Murdered in her home. Her throat was slit," said Wallis.

Alice shuddered. "That's what that black fellow did just before he left. He smiled and ran his knife along his throat. It was like he was telling me what he had planned."

"Alice, do you think it could have been the same person who murdered Lilly?"

"Anything is possible these days. You know, Ray showed me some of the information on that drive the night that Lilly caught us at the diner. I know about all of the accounts and I know it was a lot of money moving around between a lot of countries. I don't know what it's for but I know payoffs when I see them."

"There only seem to be more questions. There doesn't seem to be any clear connection to Ray that someone could have picked up on from Georgia," said Wallis.

"I don't know. Phone records, maybe they realized the connection at the orphanage. Ray knew but he never got the chance to tell me." Alice let out a sigh as her shoulders sagged forward.

"I'll let you get some rest," said Wallis. "That's enough for one night."

"It's a strange thing, Wallis Jones. We have all of this dirt on people, good dirt. But there's nowhere to take it and knowing it is actually more dangerous."

"Yes, I've noticed that too." Wallis turned to leave. "Alice, how did you get here? Is your car parked outside?"

"No, I'm not that stupid. I know that just getting all of the way to your front door is a triumph. I left my car in Ray's garage where no one will think to look for months and I took a bus as far as I could and then walked the rest of the way."

"There's still a chance someone saw you walk in here."

"Yes, there is, but like I said before, for some reason very powerful people want you to stay alive and I'm counting on that for at least a few more days."

CHAPTER

WALLIS was brushing her teeth the next morning when she noticed it. Her hand was shaking ever so slightly and she couldn't get it to stop. She was having trouble eating much of anything as well. Norman had noticed but she had said she was doing the best she could and he dropped it.

"Hello, Laurel? I have a favor to ask."

"It's about time. I'm on standby lately and I'm not getting nearly enough updates," said Laurel.

"I noticed the phone only rang the one time," said Wallis, taking in a deep breath.

"Your nerves are on edge. I can hear it from here. If you don't start leaning on me more I'm going to have to come over there and figure out how to help on my own."

Wallis smiled despite how she felt inside. "You may regret this one. Can you come with me to the Sutler tea this morning? It's short notice but I can't say I've had much time to think about it in the past few days." She could hear Laurel let out a laugh.

"What with someone trying to kill you and everything," said Laurel. "Of course, I'll come. Are we spying on anyone?"

"As a matter of fact, we are. Did you hear Lilly Billings is dead?" asked Wallis.

"I did and it doesn't take a genius to start to see there are dots to connect. I can be ready in an hour. You can bring me up to speed in the car and tell me what we're looking for at the tea. Should be an interesting afternoon."

"Very grateful you're my friend, Laurel. Between you and Norman I actually feel a little better. You know, I want to offer you a raise or a bonus."

Laurel cut her off.

"Look, I love the idea of more money and if you're doing it because of the bang up job I've been doing all along in the office then bring it on. But don't even try to pay me for being your friend. You'll just insult me."

"Thank you, Laurel. I can see that I'm going to have to just let you lead for a little while."

She hung up the phone and saw her hand was still trembling. She closed her eyes and tried to think of a short prayer for just a moment. Nothing was really working. "I am so afraid, Lord," she whispered. Maybe that was enough for now. She put on her shoes and headed downstairs to the kitchen.

"Where are you two headed?" asked Tom.

He was hobbling around the kitchen on crutches, trying to carry a plate with two pieces of toast that kept sliding from side to side. Wallis had already found a trail of oyster crackers across the kitchen floor from where he must have dropped them and had to let it go. She bent her usual rule of leaving all the housework to Norman and went hunting for a broom and dustpan. It took her three tries before she found where they were kept.

"Can I go," said Tom, as the toast went sailing off of his plate. Joe caught the first piece before it even hit the ground. Norman caught the second one and put it back on Tom's plate.

"Thank you, little brother."

"Anytime," said Norman, who was dressed in a sport coat and tie.

"I promised I'd attend a Sutler tea," said Wallis.

"Oh, gathering info on the other side," said Tom. "I'm impressed and thank you. And you, little brother? How are you going to go out there and fight the good fight? What's with your version of casual wear?"

"Don't remind me of why I'm always so glad we live far apart, Tom. Wallis told me you shared your legacy with her."

"Pillow talk, I take it. It seemed prudent," said Tom, smiling at Wallis. "It's refreshing to see you two don't keep any secrets."

Norman blushed and said, "I gave my word about that one."

"And I managed to point out another secret. Sorry about that little brother."

"Yeah, well, next time let me know first so I don't stammer quite so much. I am headed to a shad planking, if you must know."

"How did you get invited to that?" asked Tom.

"What? It's not that hard. Make a donation and you're invited. I've been going for ten years now."

Tom made a face and looked at Wallis.

"It's true," she said. "I used to think he was doing it to find some new business clients but now, I'm thinking it's a different kind of networking," said Wallis. The anxiety rose up in her chest again as she tried to ignore it. "Tom, you said you have a plan to end of all of this and get everyone to start playing nice again. Does that plan start today?"

"It's already underway. No worries, just go about your business," he said, as he turned on his iPhone to get the daily signal.

"Keep our other house guest happy," said Norman. "She is officially your responsibility for a little while."

Tom grunted and waved them away as he kept his focus on the phone.

"Do you think he knows there is someone else in the house?" asked Wallis.

"He's a Weiskopf. He's aware," said Norman pat-patting the back of his head.

Wallis smiled at her husband and kissed him on the cheek.

"It'll be okay. It has to be. Remember what we agreed. We go on with our usual routine and give Tom a chance to do whatever it is he's doing. We don't have much of a choice unless you'd rather sit in this house with Alice, Tom, a kid and a dog and make small talk. Harriet might come by, too," said Wallis.

"I'm out the door," said Norman. When he got to his car he turned around and looked at the house and saw Wallis watching him from the window. He knew she couldn't handle much more and was trying to hide how anxious she was becoming. He gave her a smile and a wave. He couldn't remember if she had ever watched him leave before in all their years together.

Just as he got in the car he looked up and saw Alice Watkins watching him leave as well.

"Have to get my damn house back soon," he mumbled. He noticed there were police cars gathered down by the Blazney house as he pulled out of the driveway. He drove by slowly and rolled down his window.

"Hey Arnold," he called out. The officer walked over to his car.

"Norman, how are things at your house? Heard about your brother. He doing okay?"

"He's on the mend. His leg will probably give him trouble every time it rains from now on but he's lucky to be alive, which I'll remind him. What's going on here?" asked Norman, trying to look calm. "Something new happen?"

"Maybe. We got a lead on a suspect and we're back over here looking for evidence. Might be tied to something else."

"Really? Can you say who?"

"No, we have to keep it under wraps for now. I'll tell you though, it's a big surprise if it really pans out. Would have never seen it coming," he said, scratching his head. "Just goes to show you never know." The officer took a step back and directed a car around Norman. "Well, have to get back. We'll catch up later. You headed to the planking?"

"Yeah, I am," said Norman. He felt relieved that no one else had been harmed in the neighborhood because of their proximity to his house. But he wondered what Arnold had meant about the suspect. Norman had a pretty good idea that whoever it was, if he was involved at all, he was taking a fall for somebody else.

Wallis picked up Laurel on the way to the Sutler tea. She was driving a rental while the mechanics went over her Jaguar to see if there was a way it could be salvaged. Wallis was pretty sure she already knew the answer to that question.

They pulled up to Tina Behren's large house that was tucked at the top of the curve of Rounding Run in a small subdivision of more expensive homes. They looked like a short series of McMansions on tiny lots all along a stretch of Pump Road. Tina's house was a large Colonial that sat on a hill with four other houses right in a row on the same hill before dipping down to what Tina always referred to as the valley.

All of the McMansions were separated from the busy road by a tall, continuous wooden fence with fir trees in the backyard to muffle the noise and help the wealthy owners feel like they were in a more exclusive enclave. Wallis could have walked the mile and a half from her house but it was all uphill and she had put on her good heels for the tea.

Just down the street was the large, public high school, Godwin where most of the neighborhood children went to school. It was considered one of the best in the state and regularly sent most of its graduates to college. Volvos, BMW's and shiny SUV's dotted the student parking lot and the football field was as nice as any college.

But there were still plenty of parents who were fighting for more. They tended to be the ones who had started with far less and fought their way to the solid middle class life. They knew what a toll all of the scrapping and saving had done to their lives and they couldn't help wondering if maybe something different, something better were possible for the next generation. A private school education like Sutler could offer would open more expensive doors for a lifetime. That'd be something any parent could be proud of no matter what happened next.

However, for generations Richmond had offered only a small selection of private schools to choose from and almost all of them were run by the Episcopal Church.

Sutler Hall had been founded in 1975 as an answer to all of them just as Richmond became more of a hub for corporate headquarters and the Federal Reserve chose the location to house all of their new technology.

Management had needed a place to send all of their children without having to constantly deal with the Diocese's influence.

There were other advantages to basing more operations in the former capital of the South. The good old boy network was a longstanding tradition all across the area and it was easier to sell the idea of a lifetime of service to a cause in exchange for a few economic certainties. The Management's program easily took root and by the 1990's they had to turn more children away than they could accept. It was all working perfectly.

Wallis and Laurel walked up the steep driveway to the front door and was about to push the doorbell when the door opened.

"Oh, Wallis." Julia was standing in the doorway in an ill-fitting suit that made her look pinched and uncomfortable. "How long have you been standing here?" she asked. "Come on in," she said, as she stepped back from the door. Wallis stepped in and waited for Laurel as she slipped out of her coat and looked around for a closet.

"Julia, this is Laurel, a good friend of mine. She has two young sons who would make good candidates for Sutler."

"Nice to meet you," said Laurel, holding out her hand.

They had gone over a short plan in the car and Wallis had told Laurel everything she knew. She had thought about holding back what Thomas and Esther had told her but she was done with trying to keep other people's secrets at least around Laurel. She was going to have to trust someone besides Norman and she needed a friend.

She was already uncomfortable just being at the tea but with Yvette being gone it felt like nothing could be the same again. There was far too much to ignore.

"We almost cancelled after what happened to Yvette," said Julia. Her voice trailed off and she looked away for a moment.

"This is a lovely home you have," said Laurel. Wallis smiled. She knew Laurel was aware who Julia was and who lived here but she'd found a way to change the topic.

"Oh, no, I'm just a guest," said Julia. "Tina Behrens is the host. She's in the kitchen," said Julia, pointing. "Wallis, could I talk to you for just a moment?"

"Just one second," she said as she walked toward the kitchen with Laurel.

Laurel squeezed her hand and whispered, "You'll be okay. I'm going to go scope out the enemy and I'll be back before you know it. Go on, divide and conquer."

"I think they meant divide the enemy," said Wallis.

Wallis swallowed hard and tried to conjure up what Harriet would do in a moment like this. Surely, some of those old Southern manners she was always touting would be useful right about now. She walked back toward Julia who was still waiting by the front door. She looked like she was hiding there.

"That's a lovely set of pearls you're wearing, Julia. Anniversary present?"

Julia fingered the choker strand. "Yes, Sam surprised me with them last month." She looked like she was still thinking about tearing up as Wallis took her firmly by the elbow.

"Let's go see what everyone else is up to in the other room. We haven't had a chance to catch up on what our children are doing for at least a month. Boys grow so quickly in middle school that it seems like Ned is somebody new every time I turn around," said Wallis. She had seen Harriet maneuver a conversation around for years by denying the obvious until the other parties gave up and followed her lead. Until now Wallis had always thought it was a little too manipulative and she just preferred some kind of honesty. But everything had changed over the past weeks.

It was so much easier to be honest when she wasn't worried about the consequences.

Wallis came into the family room and tried to scan for a seat where they could all fit. She wanted to find a spot without having to do a lot of the social niceties and get heart felt hugs all around, especially after yesterday. Her nerves were so raw she couldn't be sure that she was going to be able to keep herself in check. A teary display would only bring more sympathy and then gossip. She wasn't sure she could stand that right now and if anyone was watching her, she didn't want to give them the idea that she was cracking.

"Wallis!" It was Maureen, waving her over to sit next to her on the dark blue folding chairs set up in short rows in front of the over-sized flat screen TV. She was balancing a porcelain coffee mug decorated with butterflies on a small, matching plate that held two shortbread cookies. "Sit here," she said, patting the seat next to her.

Wallis glanced toward the kitchen for Laurel and saw she was busy chatting up the hostess. She's really taking this whole assignment seriously, thought Wallis.

"Sit here, Julia. I'll get us some coffee. You want anything in it?" asked Wallis. Julia shook her head, no and sat down, looking straight ahead like she was hoping no one would try to start up a conversation. Maureen stood up and hugged Wallis tightly, some of her coffee sloshing onto the cookies.

"You know, I'm sorry we've never got together more often," said Maureen. "I'd like to change that. Fred and I never have anyone over for dinner but I was wondering if maybe you and Norman could come sometime. You can bring Ned. We'd love to see him. There's never the sound of children in our house."

Wallis hesitated, unsure of how to answer an invitation in the middle of all the chaos. "That is a good idea," she said. The words stumbled out. "We have a houseful right now with Norman's brother who's getting around on crutches right now." And Alice Watkins and Who knows who else might show up next, she thought. "But maybe in a few weeks."

"Of course, I heard about the accident at the bookstore. An explosion, right? Your brother in law doing okay?"

"Yes, he's in one piece with a couple of pins. Would you excuse me? I want to get some coffee and say hello to Tina before they get started," said Wallis.

"Sure, sure," said Maureen, sitting back down and patting Julia on her knee. Julia startled and turned to smile briefly at Maureen before returning to studying the books along a nearby shelf.

Maureen had wanted to tell Wallis that they were on the same side but she knew that was impossible. She was weary from not being able to openly take sides.

She had startled Fred this morning when he caught her taking out her Circle pin from where she kept it hidden. The commonly held view around town among Management and the Circle was that Fred was a low-level Circle operative but Maureen was just a housewife with a garden, a Bunko group and a few volunteer activities. If they were found with two pins it would quickly become evident that Maureen had more training than anyone realized and the obvious question would then be, why.

"I want to wear it," she had said, anger rising in her throat, making it hard to speak. Fred had knelt down beside her and taken her hands into his.

"You know you can't. It would put us both in danger and have very significant consequences for so many people," he said.

"I'm sick of this creeping around and I'm angry. I feel useless and all I do, year after year, is observe what's going on around me without ever getting involved."

"I know, I know," Fred said.

"You don't know. How could you? And now my best friend is dead. My friend who was not a member of either side!" She spit out the last words. "I played by the rules because I believed it would keep everyone safer," she cried out.

"Maureen, you did make everyone safer," he said, pulling her closer, "you did. As horrible as these past few days have been, these past years would have been a lot worse if there weren't people like us holding them back as much as possible."

"How can you say that?" she said through clenched teeth.

"It's not always about what we can see. Sometimes the victories are about what hasn't happened and that's harder to quantify." He had sat back on his heels and gently tilted up her face so he could look into her eyes. "Look, I've been thinking about a few things, lately and I've realized I've made some mistakes. This marriage may have been arranged but it's still a marriage. It's still ours and we can treat it more like that than I've really left room for in the past."

"You mean that?" she said. She had sat back, still holding the pin tight in her grasp.

"Maureen, my wife, when have you ever known me to say one word without first thinking about it from every angle?" He had managed to get the beginning of a smile out of her. "But we have to dispose of this pin and we have to do it the right way. You know that, right?"

She had looked away for a moment and then slowly opened her hand. "Take it," she said. "It won't bring back Yvette and it won't make anyone at Management back down. But if you can be here more, if I can find more balance, then maybe together we can figure out how to at least chip away at them a little more. Maybe I can be the constant paper cut in their giant backside."

Maureen blinked a few times trying to stop herself from tearing up as she sat in Tina's family room remembering the first tender moment she had ever had with her husband. She sipped her coffee and realized it was getting cold. "I'll be right back," she said to Julia, who was sitting back glumly in her chair.

Wallis had gotten coffee and was standing next to Laurel listening to her gently grill Lois. She wasn't in the mood to go and coddle Julia anyway. Maureen apparently didn't want to either, she thought, as she watched her pour herself another cup of coffee from the percolator and came to stand nearby.

"So, you said this is the third tea you've thrown for Sutler? It's becoming like a tradition," said Laurel, smiling.

"Oh, yes," said Tina, "ever since our son started in middle school there we've been hosting a tea for prospective parents. We love it so much and want to help spread the word."

"I have two young boys of my own," said Laurel. "So full of energy and I have big plans for them. What do you think Sutler has done for your boy?"

She's as good as Harriet at this, thought Wallis. If I didn't know any better I'd think she was really one of the pushy parents who Wallis saw bleating in the halls of the courtroom every day about their entitlement. They always needed more money for yet another activity to make sure their child would succeed.

"He's really blossomed," said Tina, smiling widely. "This year he ran for student treasurer and has gone out for track. We're very pleased." Wallis noticed Tina wasn't mentioning what the boy actually succeeded at just yet.

"But how is that any different from Godwin? They have all of those things and for free. Even bigger stage to succeed, isn't it? More children, more activities? I don't know, am I wrong?" asked Laurel.

"Well, it's not just about what the children are doing now but where they will end up, as well. You know, the connections they become," said Tina, smiling harder. "Excuse me, I'd better check on our guest speaker," she said, and turned her back to the small gathering. Wallis watched to see who was the speaker and saw a woman she recognized from Harriet's church. The woman looked up and smiled at Wallis, giving her a thumbs up. Wallis nodded back, wondering what exactly that meant.

"I don't believe you got a really good answer," said Maureen, smiling at Laurel. "Ask that one again at the presentation."

Laurel laughed and said, "I had a few more but she got away from me. I hope it didn't hurt my chances."

"Okay ladies, it's time to start," said Tina from the other room, clapping her hands sharply. Wallis hastily poured two cups of coffee and brought them back to her seat, handing one to Julia. Laurel found a seat closer to the front and sat up primly like she was going to soak in every word. Wallis wanted to hug her tightly for what she was doing and at the same time remind her of how deadly these people could be at times. Better to annoy them enough to put a little doubt in other people's minds but not so much they would want to put Laurel on any kind of list. What had Norman called it? A Watcher's list, thought Wallis, and shuddered slightly. She tried to cover by pulling her jacket closer and taking a sip of coffee.

Tina stood in front of the small gathering and said excitedly, her arms moving, "Today we're very fortunate to have Mimi Blanchard from the board of regents of Sutler School. Mimi has had four children graduate from Sutler and has been tirelessly working for the school for almost twenty years. I could go on and on about all of Mimi's service to our community but I'd rather not take up too much time and instead get on with the reason everyone is here. So, I will concede the floor to Mimi," said Tina, to polite applause as she took a seat in the front row.

Mimi Blanchard stood up in front of the women and immediately launched into a long story of how many families who had come from nothing had watched their children grow and thrive at Sutler. "It's such a privilege to be a part of their success story at breaking the chain of poverty as they struggle to reach for bigger dreams," she said. The women applauded again. Mimi brushed back an imaginary blonde hair into place. Her upturned hair was held neatly in place and there was nothing about the wool suit or simple jewelry or anything else that needed to be adjusted or fixed. Even the flag pin was turned at just the right angle.

Wallis made herself keep breathing deeply. She knew that the sales pitch was working because without the rest of the details on Management's plans everything sounded so wonderful, and very few would believe the reality if they didn't see it firsthand.

The women took a short break and Wallis moved her knees to the side so that Julia could run to the bathroom. Maureen offered to get her more coffee but she said no, and handed over the mug. She was jittery enough without the added caffeine.

Mimi came over and said offered her hand to Wallis. "I'm so glad you came after all," she said, giving her best Southern smile. "We heard you were thinking of joining us. It's about time. I've been telling your mother for years we needed to get your more involved."

Wallis was struggling for something to say when Tina gave another sharp clap, clap of her hands and the women came rushing back to their seats. Mimi gave her a wink and went back to the front of the room.

Wallis struggled to stay calm and wondered what the home life was like for the rest of the family with Tina clapping everyone to attention like they were trained dogs.

Mimi launched into the next part of her presentation telling everyone what to expect as they moved through Sutler and what kinds of scholarships were available. There was a chart listing all of the colleges and universities that Sutler graduates had gone onto and a list of professions with a breakdown of how many ended up where and how they had ended up helping each other over and over again throughout their careers. A real network. Laurel twisted around in her seat and made a face at Wallis like she was saying it was all a little impressive. Wallis smiled at her. They made a good spy team, she thought.

Mimi finally wound down and asked for questions just as Laurel's hand shot in the air. Wallis tried to look nonchalant and glanced over at Maureen who was leaning forward to catch the question.

"How old does a child have to be before you can apply?" asked Laurel.

Mimi looked over at Tina and they smiled at each other as if they had finally won over even the most recalcitrant among the ladies. "One full year prior to entering the school," said Mimi and looked over Laurel's head to see if any other hands went up in the air.

"What could we do in the meantime to better ensure their acceptance," Laurel quickly added.

"A strong academic, service and athletic school portfolio certainly helps," said Mimi, glancing at Laurel before looking around the room and opening her arms wide.

"Just one more, Mimi. What would we owe Sutler if we decided halfway through their high school career to move them say, into Godwin and public school?" asked Laurel.

Wallis held her breath and waited. Mimi's smile pulled into a shiny, thin, lavender line for a moment before the large smile was plastered back into place.

"All of that is discussed at the time of admission. Does anyone else have a question or concern? We'd like to hear from everyone," said Mimi, looking around the room.

"Well, give us some idea of what that might look like," said Laurel, no longer asking, "You know, an example. Like the stories you told of the families who broke the chains. There must be a few who changed their mind."

Mimi's smile was still frozen into place but her eyes gave her away, thought Wallis, watching the woman grow angrier with every word out of Laurel's mouth.

"You know, you'd be surprised. There are really very few. We have a very careful screening process and we have found that with the right questions we can make a good match between Sutler and their students. Very few young people ever choose to leave."

"Now, that's impressive," said Laurel, with just as much enthusiasm as she sat back in her chair. Wallis noticed Maureen watching Laurel and smiling, as she slid back in her chair and crossed her arms over her chest.

CHAPTER 43

THE shad planking was always held in Wakefield, Virginia on the first Saturday in April by the local Ruritan Club as far back as 1949. Norman pulled up to the open field that was turned into a parking lot for the day just as people were starting to gather. He wanted the chance to shake hands and meet a few people before the good Virginia bourbon that got passed around could take hold and the speechifying started. The drive up to the clearing in the woods was dotted with thousands of political signs for both sides of the Republican and Democratic aisle. They had been planted by dutiful interns the night before and would disappear just as quickly that night after the revelry was over.

The event had started out years ago as strictly Southern Democrats who were almost all good Baptists with some old family Episcopalians mixed in and all the complexities of what those combinations meant in Virginia. However, just as many Republicans were now attending the event and trading campaign buttons and pins with anyone who would haggle and trade. There still were only a handful of Jews, Catholics, blacks or women but just enough to count as integration in the South.

The original celebration had started fifteen years earlier in Smithfield, which was still more famous for its peanuts and ham than the oily, bony fish that used to run in large numbers through the rocky James River. The very first gatherings, before even the Southern Democrats joined in, were made up of local hunters and fishermen as a way to pay tribute to the shad and were the male equivalent of a Southern ladies' Junior League tea. Instead of the expected pearls and good silver, there were tan khakis and good silver flasks.

Men could tromp around in the woods, smoke Marlboros and Camels from nearby Phillip Morris and tell off-color jokes without upsetting anyone. Eventually, they got around to the reason they were there, which was smoking the shad on hickory planks over a large open flame while still trading tall tales around the large fire.

Every year there were stories about the antics at the event that grew more colorful with every telling and soon enough, more men wanted to join in the next year.

However, like any good time in the smaller counties of Virginia that involved food and a few voters, the politicians soon started showing up in ever larger numbers supposedly just to shake a few hands. Since then, anyone interested in running for any kind of state office for the past fifty years had made a point to attend and look like he was having a hell of a time.

As the numbers grew a few of the organizers saw an opportunity to raise some money for a good cause and make sure the event wasn't a drag on any of the attendees' wallets. It was a rousing success every year.

The shad planking was also unique in these parts because it was one of the few social events where there was an even mixture of Circle and Management team members shaking hands and telling jokes. They were bound to follow like a bead on an invisible string tied to first the voters and then the politicians. Most of the Ruritans who organized the event were aware of their presence but had made it a rule that no one could bring that into their planking.

"We don't have a dog in this fight," was the message that was passed back.

Once or twice someone in Management had tried anyway and had been told to sit at home for a few years till they had learned how to listen and play nice. It was pretty much the only rule the event enforced.

Norman parked his Jeep and made his way through the field shaking hands and taking pats on the back as people asked after Wallis and his brother, Tom.

"Norman, how's Tom getting along?" It was Louie, changed out of his EMT uniform and into the more casual uniform of light tan khakis and a starched, white button down shirt with the sleeves rolled up to the elbows.

"He's up on crutches and bothering everybody," said Norman. "I'd have brought him with me but he's been too heavily influenced by all of that Yukon politics that comes over the border where he lives and I knew it would just annoy everyone."

"Maybe even earn you a time out for next year's planking," said Hank, a Circle operative who ran a veterinary clinic in the West End.

"Exactly," said Norman, as he moved into the crowd. "I'm going to go see what kind of good bourbon I can lawyer out of somebody before it's all gone. I'll catch up with y'all later," he said, nodding as he quickly blended into the crowd.

He saw a few of the local deputies from Wakefield in uniform wandering through the crowd and thought of Oscar but he was nowhere to be seen. Norman wasn't sure what he'd do if he was to cross paths with him. He felt certain he'd probably earn the first lifetime ban from the shad planking. The thought made him smile until he spotted Richard Bach taking a swig and leaning in to make some point among a group of men Norman recognized as all Management operatives. Of course the man wore a tie to a shad planking, thought Norman. "Not even Pastor Donald wore his collar to this event," he said.

"Calling my name in vain," said the Reverend as he offered Norman a small, fluted drinking glass with two fingers of bourbon in it. The minister was wearing the required khakis and a pale blue button down shirt.

"It's so strange to see you out of uniform," said Norman.

"Besides the shower or bedtime it's really the only time of year that I am."

"You just get here?" asked Norman.

"I've been here a little while. No sign of Oscar or any of his cohorts. They're probably not coming this year, which is a very good idea. I imagine Mr. Bach over there had something to do with that or his boss, Robin Spingler. You see her? She's over there telling jokes that even managed to embarrass me," said Pastor Donald.

"That is an achievement," said Norman.

"I've noticed that Richard is making more of a point than usual not to be in her orbit. Makes me wonder if he's the cause of a lot of our problems lately. I haven't said anything directly to him other than hello, though. I thought I'd save that for you. Seems like you've earned it."

"Maybe after I've had a drink," said Norman. "I'm not sure I could handle a conversation with him much better."

"You know, I appreciate that you're really not a Circle operative. You don't just suck it up and bury the feelings to get on with the mission. It's kind of refreshing considering what I have to listen to for a better part of every day."

"Makes the more mundane confessions of adultery and lying seem like a slow day," said Norman, taking a swig.

"Amen," said Pastor Donald. "You know there's chatter up the line that's very troubling," said the minister looking down into his glass. "Apparently, there's a strongly held belief that there's a liar amongst us. Someone who goes way back that's crossed over with the express purpose of spilling secrets."

"I know, Tom has been hinting around at the same thing. I take it that's why he's in town and was meeting with Esther in the first place," said Norman, finishing off the drink in a large gulp. Pastor Donald poured a little more into his glass.

"This is probably enough for you today. Calm your nerves, what with everything that's going on around you but keep your wits together. I'm glad Tom didn't come with you. Everyone can see that you're not home with Wallis and after what happened on that bridge I don't like the idea of her being home alone with that drive still in her possession."

Norman looked around as a warm breeze blew against his face. It did nothing to warm the feeling he had inside.

"You haven't heard," said Norman, "but we have another houseguest, Alice Watkins. She worked with Ray Billings and knows what was on that drive. Knows about all of it. Turns out Ray was able to figure out how to see everything."

"I know all about Alice. The last I heard she had left town. Did she say why she's back?"

"Someone tried to kill her. The last of the cleanup I suppose. But Alice is a very tough old bird. I've only known her for a couple of days and I'm not surprised they failed. I'm more surprised she didn't inflict some kind of pain on them," said Norman.

Pastor Donald smiled as he watched Richard Bach carrying on nearby. "They're not going to stop until they have that drive in their hands or are pretty convinced it's been destroyed. That brings me to my big question. Given how you feel about being involved in all of this, why haven't you just destroyed the thing? Could it be that your grandfather's legacy is a little harder to shake than you imagined?"

"If you mean common decency was his legacy, then yes. There are thousands of children's names on there, including my son's and they need to be protected. I suppose just destroying the drive would do that for the short term. But after what I saw buried underneath all of that I realized that there are thousands of other innocent people out there who are in harm's way because of Management and maybe there is something I can do after all. The problem is figuring out just what that is without getting anyone in my family harmed and still being able to go back to a semblance of the life that I've had."

"Any ideas at all?" asked Pastor Donald.

"I showed it all to Tom and I suppose that's doing something. Maybe he has a better idea of what to do with the information than I do. There's one thought but I'm not sure how effective it would be," said Norman, hesitating.

"And that would be?"

"Helmut Khroll. Give him the information and let him leak it in whatever way he sees fit," said Norman.

"That may get in the way of some Circle plans that are in motion. You know that, don't you?"

"I realize that but I've never been a big fan of letting human beings do all of the manipulating. Why not set some of the information loose and let the cards fall where they may."

"Now, you see that's really your family's legacy," said Pastor Donald. "Looks like all of the candidates have gotten here. Look there's Matheny. Heard he wants to run for governor."

"Where is Khroll?" asked Norman, looking toward the parking lot. "I thought he'd be here with you."

"He's here. I saw him talking to a group over there about their votes in the state senate. He's going to get himself banned but I suppose he wouldn't be doing his particular style of journalism if he wasn't by the end of the day," said Pastor Donald. "He may have gone back to the car for something, check there. If you can't find him, let me know. There are more than a few people here who know him by reputation at the least and don't care for him. Any other year and I'd say that he'd only be risking a good bruising but I don't know."

"I'll let you know," said Norman. "You hang onto this for me?" he asked, handing Pastor Donald his glass. "I'll be back in time for some fish and a few handshakes. Might try focusing on more normal reasons to be here. Has to be at least a few nervous business owners who could use a good lawyer."

"Hurry back, you don't want to miss the main speaker. It's Senator Stanford this year, one of my own," said Pastor Donald, smiling. "Good Episcopalian."

Norman walked back toward the parking lot and scanned the line of port-a-johns but didn't see Helmut. He ducked back into the line of trees to see if Helmut was anywhere to be seen. The fallen leaves crunched under his boots as he wove in between the large stand of walnuts and the pines that could be found everywhere. He could smell the hickory planks over the fire from where he was and it brought back memories of a better time. He stopped walking and breathed in the scent, shutting his eyes for just a moment. He remembered the first time his father brought him and his brothers to the shad planking. Norman was only thirteen and Tom and Harry kept telling him that he had better be cool so they could come back the next year.

Norman had felt like he was being let into some kind of club. He had spent the entire day not saying much of anything and just watching all of the men he regularly saw at church or hanging out in his house laughing and carrying on in ways he'd never imagined they even knew about. Mr. Palmeroy had given him one of his cigars and the men had laughed and slapped his back when he breathed in too deeply and started gagging. Tom held the flaps of his coat back when he puked into the leaves. Harry had complained, saying Norman was such a kid, even though they were only separated by a few years.

Norman stood there breathing in the familiar scents, trying to remember the sound of his father's voice when he was distracted by a heated conversation going on in hushed tones deeper in the woods. Something about the voices seemed familiar. He opened his eyes and slowly looked around trying not to shift his weight and crunch any of the leaves. Suddenly, he felt exposed in the thin part of the clearing where he stood.

"What the hell are you doing here?" asked a man, a little distance from Norman.

"I came to see my brother," said the other man. "I need to make sure he's alright and this is the one place where I knew I could see him without being detected."

"You had better be damn sure of that."

It was Richard Bach, Norman was sure of that and he was talking to someone who was supposed to be over eight hundred miles away looking after senior citizens. Norman risked being heard and walker closer to the men, stopping behind a large oak that had several large sucker trees growing off of the base giving him some cover.

He was able to just make them out and when he saw the older man standing next to Richard Bach he doubled over and placed his hand against the tree to steady himself but he never took his eyes off his older brother, Harry for a moment.

"Things have gone too far for you to suddenly have any ideas about just going home," said Richard.

"I fully realize that. I'm not a simpleton. But I never expected things to get back to my own family. I received assurances that this would never happen," said Harry. "You gave many of those assurances yourself and now, you've managed to threaten my brother and his family."

"That wasn't me," said Richard, bending toward Harry till he was only inches from his face. "I did not have anything to do with what that idiot deputy has been up to."

"He's under your command," said Harry, who didn't even flinch.

"It doesn't matter anyway," said Richard, backing up and waving away the concern. "I've taken care of it."

"More violence," said Harry, rubbing the bridge of his nose.

"No, no violence. A little justice, maybe," said Richard, looking annoyed. "Look, get the hell out of here. If anyone sees you, and I mean anyone including Robin Spingler then more hell will be set loose. You're supposed to be back in Florida, anyway where everyone can see you going about your normal routine. That's what you said you wanted, isn't it? A chance at a normal life with no one bothering you? How are we supposed to deliver on that if you come up here right in the middle of the mess?" said Richard.

"No one was supposed to die," said Harry.

"Yeah, well, next time don't dangle such a large carrot in front of our noses without having the goods already in your hands. Look, you gave us Schaefer's name and we went to get the drive. Things got a little more complicated from there."

"You murdered her," said Harry, the anger rising in his hushed voice.

"She didn't give us a lot of options."

"And you let the damn thing slipped out of your hands before you even saw what was on it," said Harry.

Richard let out a low growl and kicked the nearest tree. "None of the Georgia operation was in my control! You know what I've never understood? Why you don't know what was on it. You claim you were pretty high up in the organization and yet you can't give us anything beyond the name of a woman you claim held the secret to the Circle's grand plan and then some guy in a utility department that took the drive from her. I've never really bought any of that."

"I've told everyone already a thousand times. The Circle is broken up into hundreds of individual cells and only one person knows who is in all of the cells. They keep that name a secret from everyone but the previous successor. That woman was the most likely candidate but your thugs killed her and then let the drive she always had with her slip away. If it wasn't for me following her, you would never have known it was in Richmond in the first place." Harry sounded like he was whining.

Norman realized what his brother had done and he leaned his head against the tree willing himself to not wretch in the woods. His head was spinning as he listened to Harry pleading his case with Richard Bach about all that he had missed in this life because he was saddled with a lifetime membership in the Circle. No wife, no family and always having to look over his shoulder.

"Coward," Norman whispered, swallowing the bile in his throat. His foot slipped on a wet leaf and he caught himself just in time, making only the slightest of noise. But Richard Bach was on edge and heard the sound, turning in Norman's direction as he hid behind the wide oak, his chest heaving from the mix of anger and grief.

"Enough! Enough of your whining," said Richard, throwing up his hands. "I can't keep doing this. If you want out, then do it. Tell Spingler you want out and see how she handles it. I'm done with you," he said. He strode off toward the revelers breaking small saplings as he tore through the woods. Norman could hear Harry's muffled crying but he felt no compassion for his brother.

He stepped out from the stand of trees.

"You could have come to me," he said, quietly. Harry's face jerked up and he quickly wiped his faced on his sleeve. "You never even tried."

"Norman!"

"You aren't a stupid man, Harry. You had to know what they would do with the information you were turning over."

Harry took a couple of steps backward, his body shaking. "It was better than going through my entire life trapped in that day to day boredom."

"So your dissatisfaction was worth a few lives? Were you always such a coward?"

Harry reeled back like he had been slapped. He made a gurgling noise as if he was starting to choke.

"Your stupidity almost got my wife killed. My neighbor, a nice old man was found dead in a field. He had nothing to do with any of this. Was his life worth it? And that woman you offered up, did you even know her?"

"Carol Schaeffer. Yeah, yeah, I knew her. She was in my cell. She never really liked me," said Harry.

"Is that still what's important to you, even now?"

"I told her what I was going through and she said I should get a hobby. A hobby! So imperial and acting like she had it all. I knew she had to be the Keeper," he cried out, snot from his nose running down into his mouth. He had turned his shoulder to Norman, cowering as if he was trying to protect himself from a body blow.

"Who's out there?" It was Robin Spingler moving through the woods with a couple of men from Management.

Harry looked back and forth between Norman and the sounds of the approaching people. He ran closer to Norman grabbing his arms tightly and quickly sputtered, "They're watching your house around the clock. They're planning something to happen tonight. I'm sorry, I'm sorry," he said. "They know Wallis has the thumb drive."

Norman saw all of the pain in his brother's face and how tortured he was but the image of Mr. Blazney greeting everyone as he walked his dog flashed in his head. He jerked his arms away and turned his back working his way back to the field. Let them have him, he thought bitterly. Let them do what they want with him. He turned his back and quickly trudged out of the woods.

He found Pastor Donald and said, "I'm going to need another drink."

"What's wrong? Helmut came back a few minutes ago and said he never saw you. You look like what I've always imagined hell would be like," said Pastor Donald. Norman pulled him away from the small clusters of people to the edge of the party.

"I know who betrayed us. I saw him in the woods. It was Harry," he said, his hands trembling as he tried not to cry. He took the drink from Pastor Donald and drank it down quickly, pressing his eyes shut for a moment as he felt the slow burn down the back of his throat.

"He thought he could break apart the Circle and find a new life for himself. He gave them Carol Schaeffer because he thought she slighted him. It was a calculated guess that she was the Keeper. He is just as responsible for killing her as if he had held her under the water."

"You need to get a hold of yourself," said Pastor Donald, firmly grasping Norman's arm. "If that means you need to leave early then I suggest you do it. Go home and tell Tom you've seen Harry in the area."

"Wallis almost died," he said, "Harry did that."

"Go home," said Pastor Donald.

"No," said Norman. "My brother started all of this and he's managed to hurt a lot of people. I can't stay on the sidelines anymore. I'm going to try and make some of it right if I can. Where is Helmut Khroll? I'm going to tell him what I know about Management."

"That's a very dangerous game, Norman," said Pastor Donald, "and is it really all that different from what Harry was trying to do?" he said gently.

"Harry was trying to save his own pathetic ass. I was more like him when I was trying to do nothing and ignore that any of this was going on right outside my door."

"Hey, you don't look so good," said Helmut, walking up. "People are starting to notice."

"Take him home, Helmut," said Pastor Donald. "That's what you want, isn't it Norman? There's your cover."

"Sure, sure, I wasn't really making any headway with any of these guys anyway," said Helmut. "No one would give me anything."

"My friend, that is about to change. Drive Norman home to Wallis."

CHAPTER 44

MARK got up early to scan the internet again for the sites Circle operatives were known to use most. He was searching for Robert. Later in the day, he was planning on heading out to the shad planking to at least make an appearance. His neighbor was coming over to watch his children.

The boys were already up and doing their chores. The youngest, Peter was fussing about getting stuck with trash duty two weeks in a row. Mark reminded him that's what happened when you make bets with your older brother over who can make the most hoops. Peter harrumphed and insisted on holding his nose as he dragged the bag the entire way.

"You're going to end up cleaning the kitchen floor too if that bag tears," he called after him. Jake came in the kitchen and said, "I'm done cleaning my room. Can I go over to Lexi's house now?"

"No, remember, we talked about it. You're helping the neighbors watch your brother and sister for me while I go to the annual shad planking."

Jake groaned and swung his arms around in frustration. Lexi was a girl he liked in school. It was going to be hard to suddenly move him across the country but there was no other way. Just a little longer, he thought.

Then we'll be free of all of this.

He went outside to the deck to get the early morning encrypted signal on his phone. The words started playing across the screen, 'Neither slavery nor involuntary servitude, except as punishment for crime whereof the party shall have been duly convicted shall exist within the United States, or any place subject to their jurisdiction.' It was the thirteenth amendment ratified in 1865 telling Mark that his worst fears were rapidly coming true. Management was planning to use him as their scapegoat.

For a moment he couldn't catch his breath. The panic was taking over and he wasn't sure what to do next. The message didn't say how long he had or what they were going to falsely accuse him of but he had a good idea. It didn't matter anyway. Once Management decided to put someone in prison it was hard to reverse the process. He was out of time.

The words kept spilling across the screen and he had to force himself to hold the phone steady and read them even though his head was spinning. A short series of numbers appeared after the rest of the amendment and just as quickly he decrypted them. It was instructions to download two songs, Wayward Son and Sympathy for the Devil, from the Apple Store at exactly ten that morning. Everyone who bought the songs at the same moment would get a version with metadata tucked underneath the tune. The few hundred who bought the altered songs would never notice anything except for a slightly reduced quality in the tone.

Things were coming apart. He couldn't be sure what he was going to still be able to do for Robert if he had to quickly leave town. His own family was in jeopardy.

Robert had looked drawn and tired when Mark caught the brief glimpse of him coming out of the parking deck. At least Mark knew that Management didn't have him or the boys.

"Jake? Jake, can you come here?" he yelled upstairs, trying to keep the rising tension out of his voice. Jake appeared at the top of the stairs.

"Yeah?" he said, still looking a little sullen over not being able to see Lexi.

"Something's come up and we're hitting the road. I need you to help your Peter and Ruthie pack a few things. We're taking a short trip," he said. He couldn't risk upsetting any of the kids and giving away what they were really doing to anyone watching him, including the Circle operatives.

"What? Why? I have a test coming up. I can't go anywhere," said Jake.

"No arguing, I just need you to do this. I need you to take the lead," he said, pronouncing every word very clearly. Jake looked at his dad like he was expecting him to say something else and clear up the confusion. Mark had told his son the phrase and had him practice it ever since he turned thirteen with the express directive that it was to be used only in case of an emergency. He was to take the lead. They were now operating under protocol and there wasn't a lot of time. Jake needed to get moving.

His mouth fell open but Mark shook his head hard just once and pointed toward Peter's room. "Go help him. We can talk later."

Jake looked frightened for just a moment and looked back toward Peter who had come out of his room. "What's up?" asked Peter. "Why is everybody standing in the hall?" Jake straightened up and said, "Come on, we're going on a road trip, Whiting family style. We have to get packed if we're going to make the first surprise."

"Surprise? What is it?" asked Peter. "Can you tell me a little?" he said, poking his brother. Jake gently pushed him toward his room.

Mark found Ruthie sitting in front of the TV still wearing her Hello Kitty pajamas and sent her upstairs to help the boys. He sat down on the edge of a chair at his kitchen table and tried to calm down enough to think about how he was going to do this.

At precisely ten o'clock he made sure to spoof his MAC address and went to iTunes to purchase the songs. It wasn't long before he had the metadata with the longer instructions that were coming from an unknown cell above him.

Robert had made contact and needed to be met. The safe house had been compromised and it was going to take personal contact. He was to drive to a parking lot at the Short Pump Town Center in front of Macy's and switch cars. The new car would have a license plate with the first three numbers from the current OTP and the keys would be in the driver's side wheel well. The GPS would have directions to Robert's location. Get Robert and his boys and drive them to an address in Northern Virginia, switch cars again and keep going. The second car would have details about their next destination. He was to leave immediately. He had been compromised.

He knew there was hardly any time and if he foolishly waited too long Management drones could come in his front door and it would all be too late.

There were things that had to be done first. He made himself sit down and call the realtor from a throw-away cell phone. Mark gave the false name he'd been using as the contact at Rosecroft and said he was returning the signed contract to the realtor with the full asking price in cash but he would need a signature from the owners within 24 hours or the entire deal was cancelled. He told them Rosecroft already had a renter interested in the property and needed to move quickly.

The realtor said the owners were anxious to sell and were already aware of the investment company's offer. As long as there was no problem with signing the codicil that prohibited commercial use, dividing the land or harvesting the timber on the land there shouldn't be a problem. He'd get back to Mark within the hour.

Mark hung up and transferred enough funds so that the full amount would be ready to go and he could finish the operation from his phone. The entire transaction had taken only fifteen minutes but he knew it was far too long. Circle's message had been marked imperative and there was no time. He was expendable to everyone even if Robert was not and they wouldn't go to any extraordinary measures to save him or his children. That had its advantages when it came time to disappear but not if Management got them all first.

He ran upstairs to his room and pulled the emergency suitcase out of the back of his closet. It was packed with the essentials and always ready to go. This way, anyone who came along later and looked in his closet would think he was still somewhere in town instead of making a run for it. He checked to make sure the cash was still in the bottom. There was more than enough to get them where they needed to be. He would have to cut up his credit cards and use the cash until he was safely in Montana and could access the new accounts.

"Dad? We're ready to go. What do you want me to do next?" It was Jake trying to sound calm but Mark could see him tapping his fingers nervously against his thigh. "Get Pete and Ruthie in the car with their bags. I'll be right behind you," he said. "Thank you, son," and hugged him tight around the neck, kissing his head.

He went through the kitchen and pulled the vinyl bag out of the back of the pantry that he kept filled with small snacks and juice drinks and carried it all out to the car. His neighbor, the Harkins were standing out on their front lawn.

"Too nice a day," he yelled. "Decided to take the kids out instead of hanging around a bunch of guys in the woods eating smoky fish." The neighbors smiled and Mrs. Harkin yelled back, "Sounds like a much better idea. We'll do it again some other time."

"We'll be back late tonight. Maybe we can do something together tomorrow," he said, giving the Harkins the story he'd want them to tell whoever was stopping by later. He had a momentary thought about what lengths Management might go to in order to get information, but he put it out of his mind. There was protocol to follow for just a little longer.

They pulled out of the driveway and drove through the smaller side streets till they got to the mall where he saw the car tucked in among a row of cars, facing out. The first three numbers on the license plate were nine, six, seven, which was the right code for car until the month was over and the OTP would change again. He parked nearby and turned around to his children.

"Alright, Jake, I need you to follow me and quickly switch everything over to the dark blue Dodge Grand Caravan. We're taking a newer car on our trip with all kinds of gadgets. Peter, go see if there are any DVD's under the backseat. If there aren't we'll stop somewhere and get some new ones, okay?"

"Can I get some too?" asked Ruthie, halfway out of what was rapidly becoming their old car.

"Absolutely, I'd never leave you out," he said, grabbing bags out of the trunk. He took the old keys with him and left the car looking like they were hanging out at the mall. All of his old identifications and keys would be disposed of later.

The children climbed in the back as he felt underneath the left side of the wheel well and pulled out the small magnetic box.

"There are DVD's," yelled Peter, waving a couple of them around in the air.

"Get your seatbelt on, Peter," said Jake, as he helped Ruthie get in her seat.

Mark got in and smelled the new leather. It always took him back to his childhood for just a moment. His father had insisted on turning in his car every three years and driving something new off of the lot. He started the car, plugging in the GPS. The destination was on Lady Street in Oregon Hill. He headed for the highway as he docked his iPhone in the pad that was already in the car and put in his blue tooth. Further instructions immediately downloaded and a woman's voice told him to get the baseball hat, sunglasses and jacket out from under the front seat and put them on immediately. Proceed to the alley behind the address and knock sharply on the door four times. Once all of the Schaeffers were loaded into the minivan they were to get back on the highway and drive to the Virginia Seminary in Alexandria, Virginia where they'd find another car and instructions for where they were heading next.

Mark was hoping that destination would at least be in the general direction of out west where he was planning to stop for good.

Ruthie got to pick the first DVD and Jake started One Thousand and One Dalmatians for her as Peter groaned. "Your turn will come next," said Jake. Mark felt a twinge of regret at making Jake let go of just being a kid but he knew there was no choice until they were safely in Montana. He was just hoping that when Jake realized the full extent of what was changing he'd forgive his father some day.

Mark put on the jacket and sunglasses while he drove. The GPS told him to take the exit that was marked 'Hollywood Cemetery' where most of Richmond's famous was buried. He pulled the baseball cap down snugly and tried to steady his nerves. They were almost there.

He easily found the alley and pulled up to the back door.

"We're taking a few people with us on our road trip," he said, looking in his rear view mirror at his kids. "Everyone welcomes them and stays put while I go collect them. We understand each other?"

Ruthie was absorbed in her movie and ignored him. Peter nodded his head and looked out the window with a worried look. He didn't take to strangers very quickly. Jake leaned over and whispered, "It'll be okay, I'm here."

Mark walked up to the back door and knocked four times, standing back just a little. He heard a small commotion and wondered what he'd find when the door opened. He should have told Jake to take the wheel and get out of there the best he could if there was suddenly trouble.

The door opened slightly and he saw Robert looking more exhausted than before with his two sons standing close behind him. "We have to move," he said quietly. "What can I carry?"

"Nothing," said Robert as he moved past Mark toward the car. He opened the sliding door and said, "Trey, you get in the far back with me, come on."

Management was now hunting both men and it would have been stupid to sit them both up in the front seat for every camera to scan as they passed through stoplights or toll booths. It was possible to fool them with a small disguise with one man but both would have been impossible.

Mark noticed how Robert's boys followed orders so quickly. Trey threw the sleeping bags in back and quickly climbed behind Jake. He didn't even make eye contact or say hello. He put on his seatbelt and curled up against the side and shut his eyes.

Will got in the front seat and leaned his head back against the headrest and shut his eyes. Mark slid in behind the wheel and said, "Look under your seat and see if there isn't something for you to put on," he said, tapping his baseball cap. Will opened his eyes and gave Mark a weary look.

"Look under your seat," said Mark.

Will pulled out a sweatshirt from Georgetown University and another cap and put them on. He did all of it without saying a word, crossed his arms over his chest and shut his eyes. Mark wanted to pat him on the shoulder and tell him everything would be alright now but he wasn't sure that was an accurate assessment of the situation just yet.

He got to the highway again and was finally able to take a deep breath.

"There is food in the bag just behind your seat. Help yourself to whatever you want," said Mark.

Mark made a point of keeping his eyes on the road when he was speaking just in case there was someone watching the highway cameras that were attached to the top of the oversized green highway signs.

The drive was uneventful until they neared Springfield and the traffic started to slow down. Mark had done his best not to grip the steering wheel and to carry on whatever conversation he could with Will who never really carried his end.

"Are we getting close?" asked Robert.

"Yes, we'll be at our first stop within the next hour but we won't be staying long," said Mark. Robert had not said much of anything to him yet. At one point he had gathered the sleeping Trey in the crook of his arm and stared out the window as they passed the endless pine trees along the highway. The only break to the monotony was the signs for outlets and the stretches of thick kudzu vines that engulfed the trees leaving only a leafy outline of what was underneath.

Mark kept looking in his rear view mirror to check on everyone but each of them was in their own little world. Only Ruthie occasionally asked Jake a question or laughed at something she saw on the drop down screen. They were already on Peter's choice of Pirates of the Caribbean. Twice Mark heard Ruthie gasp and his heart raced for a moment as he quickly looked up to see her staring at the screen and grasping Jake's arm. There was still a huge smile across her face even though she was gripping Jake tightly. She loved to be scared.

They came to the Seminary Road exit and the soothing female voice on the GPS told him to take a right. They wound down a busy six-lane street and past a large hospital complex on the right that quickly gave way to a much narrower road and McMansions packed tightly against each other on both sides. But after only another mile the landscape opened up and there was suddenly a wide campus with a small white post office on the edge of the road and older brick buildings spaced back and well apart.

"Turn left," said the automated voice, as they neared the middle of the campus. There were two large cement pillars and a stately bronze sign that read, Virginia Theological Seminary and tucked just behind that was a smaller green and white sign that read, Slow, Children at Play.

The instructions were to take an immediate left and head to the parking lot just behind the tennis courts.

"We're here," he said, as he parked the car. He could smell ham and realized he was hungry.

"Where are we?" asked Ruthie, blinking at the bright sunlight. The dark, tinted windows made the interior of the car deeply shaded and the boys were all holding their hands up over their eyes as they got out of the car and stretched. Robert got out and stood on the side of the minivan away from the street even though they were hidden by a stand of fir trees.

"I smell something good," said Trey. It was the first words Mark had heard him say all day.

"Let's go check it out," said Mark. There were no instructions about which building to head into first and he knew they all had to be just as hungry as he was. A door opened on the back of the long, low building and a large woman wearing a white uniform and a hair net leaned out, holding open the screen door.

"We've been waiting for you. Leave your things in the car, they'll be okay there. Come on in, quickly now."

Jake picked up Ruthie and waved to the other boys as they fell in line behind them. Robert followed as Mark locked the car. He passed by the woman as the smile dropped from her face and she said in a low voice, "Someone will switch all of your belongings into the next vehicle while you're eating. You'll be ready to go by the time you're done."

Mark knew he needed to rest a little before the next leg of the journey. He didn't even know yet just how many miles there were left to travel but he knew they needed to get out of Virginia and put some distance between them and the Management cells operating on the east coast.

They were ushered through a large, industrial kitchen full of men and women in similar white uniforms who were busy cooking in large pans and didn't even look up to see the tired group moving through the area.

Ruthie passed by a man who was stirring what smelled like vegetable soup and she took in a deep breath. "Smells good. Boy, I'm starving," she said, looking up at the man as if she was hoping he'd spoon some out for her. He nodded and smiled at her but said nothing. She looked back at her father.

"It's okay, dear," said the woman who had let them in the door. "There's plenty in the refectory. You're only a few feet away from lots of good things to eat."

It was true. There was a long, narrow room set up with a line of steaming trays of ham with circles of pineapple, turkey or pork roast followed by green beans and stewed tomatoes and macaroni with cheese. Mark counted twenty dishes in all.

The children ran to the stack of trays and dishes at one end and started quickly down the line, filling their plates.

"Show a little restraint," said Mark. "You can go back for seconds."

"We knew you were coming," said the woman. "By the way, my name's Elizabeth," she said, shaking Mark's hand. He noticed she was missing a couple of fingers but still had a strong handshake. "I hope your journey has been uneventful so far."

"As uneventful as packing up and leaving everything just ahead of a pack of hounds can be," said Robert.

"Are you okay?" asked Mark. Robert turned to him and said, "No, I haven't been since they found my wife and I've been a little less so every day since that moment." He turned to Elizabeth. "Is this going to be it for us? Are we going to keep moving for the rest of our days?" Robert looked like he was so tired he could barely stay on his feet.

"No, that's not much of a life. There is a destination in mind. More will be revealed in just a little while. I'm sure you don't like all of the bits and pieces of information but much as it might seem like it right now, this is not all about you. We have many people to protect as well so we're going to have to keep following guidelines."

Robert looked like he was about to say something but Elizabeth cut him off.

"You're always free to leave with your boys and take your chances if you prefer," she said. Robert clamped his mouth shut and walked away without another word. He went to the start of the line and picked at the food, barely filling a plate.

"Sorry," mumbled Mark.

"No worries," said Elizabeth. "None of this is easy but occasionally we need to be reminded we have chosen to take the help that was offered. You'd better get something to eat while there's time."

He went and got behind Robert and once he had some food followed him into the large dining hall full of long tables. No one else was in the room besides their little group.

"Follow me, the children are all in Scott's Lounge where there's a little added privacy," said Elizabeth. Mark followed Elizabeth into a small comfortable lounge where a round table and chairs had been set up with the children already seated. There were still two seats left.

"We knew how many to expect. The students and staff won't be in until later. You can eat in privacy without worry," said Elizabeth. "Help yourself to whatever you need." She turned and left them alone to eat in silence.

Food was only making Mark feel more tired. He desperately needed a nap.

"I can drive," said Robert.

Mark looked up and realized he had almost nodded off.

"No, that's okay. I just need to lie down for a few minutes. I'll be okay."

"It's not going to do us any good to get in an accident. I'm still capable of following directions and driving," said Robert.

Mark didn't answer him. He didn't want to tell Robert that he didn't completely trust him with the lives of his three children. Besides, Mark had an entirely different plan in mind and he wasn't sharing the details with anyone.

He got up to go for more food and felt his phone vibrate. He kept walking toward the narrow room that was now empty of people and started dishing up more spoon bread as he pulled out his phone and glanced down.

The contracts had been returned with the necessary signatures. He felt some of the tension leave as he made the transfer of funds and sent a message back to the realtor that new renters would be arriving in two days. They still had a chance.

CHAPTER
45

"ALL UNITS, 1099. Suspect is armed and considered dangerous. Suspect is Oscar Polansky, wanted on felony murder. Last seen at place of work, Henrico County Family Court where suspect is deputy. All units, 1099. Suspect is male, Caucasian, age forty-two, five feet seven inches tall and approximately two hundred and twenty five pounds. Approach with extreme caution and request backup immediately."

Oscar was holed up in the back of his sister's apartment listening to a police scanner growing angrier by the minute. He was dressed in his deputy uniform, neatly pressed, with his hunting rifle, two handguns and boxes of ammunition for both.

He would have walked right into the waiting arms of the arresting officers if it hadn't been for Davey who called to give him a heads up in exchange for not coming anywhere near the combinating room.

Oscar thought about coming in there anyway and shooting up the place. Damn that Parrish and his shiftless lack of any kind of character. First time the jackass manages not to finish a job and it has to be on Oscar's dime. Then he turns around and double crosses him somehow. Davey never said so but Oscar knew it had to be Parrish.

The knife used to kill Lilly Billings was found in a dumpster behind the Bill's Barbeque near Oscar's apartment with Oscar's fingerprint still on it.

Oscar had sped home after the phone call just in time to see the police breaking into his apartment. He saw them carry out bags of evidence and knew that Parrish must have planted more in there as well. Davey said the police had received an anonymous tip.

Oscar didn't believe that either. They didn't need the tip. Someone had decided he had to go. He saw Richard Bach's black SUV parked nearby and Richard and Robin Spingler standing around outside.

"That's who's giving the orders," he said, as he took another swig of Mad Dog that he picked up at the Wal-Mart along with the ammunition. He was on a first name basis with the salesmen behind the gun counter. "Got to change their minds."

He was sweating through his carefully pressed uniform. His sister had checked on him twice and shaken her head at him but he had raised a gun and pointed it at her and she hadn't come near the room since.

He was trying to formulate a plan. There had to be someway out of this mess. All of it had started with that prick, Richard Bach. The man had no idea how to get a job done. Too much waiting and watching and not enough decisive action. If they had torn up Ray Billings house like he had wanted to in the first place they might have walked out of there with the damn thumb drive and then none of the rest of this would have happened. They would have never been outside of that Jones woman's house or cleaning up one mess after another. They'd have been heroes just like Richard said they would be.

But no one had listened to Oscar. Richard had told him more than once to shut up and do as he was told. "Look where that got me," he yelled.

There was still the thumb drive. He knew everyone was hot and bothered to get that back. He didn't know why and didn't much care. Oscar had never had much use for computers. It was just enough for him to know that some very important people in his organization wanted the damn thing and he'd overheard Richard saying that it had to be in the Jones house.

So, Oscar Polansky, good American that he was, was going to go and get the thing back for them if he had to march through the front door of that Black Widow's house to get it. It was about time that someone showed they still had their balls intact.

"Yeah, that's it," he mumbled, spitting just a little. "That's a plan." He scrambled up off of the floor and scooped up his guns and ammunition in his arms, making sure the safeties were on as he stumbled over the small throw rug and stepped hard, dropping a gun. "Damn it," he yelled. He heard his sister running from the living room into her bedroom and the lock turning into place.

He drove to the West End, his resentment building as the houses went from smaller and older to newer and much larger. All those years of watching fancy lawyers run by the metal detectors like they didn't count, not respecting his job and his authority. Enough already, he thought, hitting the horn at a driver who was slowly going through the green light.

"Whole town has lost the ability to get things done!" he yelled out of the window of his Volvo. The front end was now being held together by silver duct tape and wire since his encounter on the bridge. No one had authorized a payment to get it fixed yet and Oscar had surmised that now that they were hunting him down, no payment was probably ever coming. One more reason to get back in their good graces any way he could, he thought, and no time like the present.

He came down the tree lined street with lawns that were obviously tended to by hired gardeners, turned the corner just ahead of Wallis Jones' house and kept going for another block. His car had been his pride and joy but was now bound to garner attention. There were any number of people who would be happy to turn him in or shoot him on sight. He grabbed the duffel bag out of the backseat that now contained all of his weapons and he zipped up his dark blue jacket a little further to hide the oatmeal colored uniform.

"Should have changed," he said, feeling the cold wind hit him in the face. He weaved through the back yards until he came to Wallis and Norman's kitchen door where he calmly set down his duffel bag and pulled out the two nine millimeters, which he'd taken the time to load back at his sister's house.

He looked up the drive to see if he was in view of the Management vehicle that he knew was watching the house but he was hidden from the street by the cars parked at the bottom and the fir tree right by the door.

He dumped a box of ammunition on the driveway and stuffed his pockets with more of the hollow point bullets. The three-o-eight Winchester was left in the duffel bag. Oscar realized it had been foolish to bring a long gun at all.

He teetered just a little as he stepped back to catch his balance and raised his right leg, wavering in the air for just a moment before he gave the door a solid kick, splintering the lock. His head felt like it was spinning from all of the cheap liquor as he stepped into the kitchen and fired off a shot into the air. Gunfire made the average person run in the opposite direction and could buy him time to search some drawers. If he could get the drive and get out he was willing to compromise and not actually shoot anyone.

He could hear the sound of people running in the house and a constant thump, thump against the ceiling that confused him. It didn't take him long to empty every drawer in the downstairs rooms.

"Damn," he said, swaying just a little. There was no office, no computer and nothing that looked like a thumb drive. Not even a cell phone. He pulled the trigger and let out another shot as he marched heavily up the stairs.

He got to the top and came to a guest room that looked like someone had left in a hurry. A suitcase was opened next to a small grouping of cloth bags and Oscar quickly rifled through all of them just to be sure. He wasn't expecting to find his prize there but he was trying to be thorough this time.

Just as he came out of the room his head made contact with the tip of a swinging crutch that sent him marching backwards for just a moment as he tried to regain his senses. Someone was fighting back.

Most people would have been taken down by the solid thwack but Oscar was used to brawling, particularly when he was drunk and it was going to take a lot more than someone's crutch to bring him down.

He fired straight out into the hall and came charging out, ready to shoot again if someone challenged him. He'd had enough with people walking all over him. Tom was sprawled on the floor. His shoulder was bleeding badly and the crutches were tangled underneath him.

"Serves you right," said Oscar, as he stepped over him. His head ached from the booze and the dent in his forehead. He went barreling into the next bedroom where the bed was unmade and there was a little side table set up right next to the bed with tissues and a bottle of pills. He kicked it over out of spite for his throbbing head and started pulling open drawers while he kept a gun pointed toward the door. Still nothing.

"Throw it down here," he bellowed, as he came back out into the hallway. "All I want is what is mine in the first place. I've worked awfully hard for it and I'm not leaving without it. Where's that damn thumb drive?" he screamed as loud as he could, firing off another shot into the ceiling.

He lurched toward a narrow set of stairs that seemed to lead to a third floor and heard someone gasp and hurry up the stairs. He was beginning to think it was going to be necessary to actually shoot someone to get what he wanted.

At the top was a small bedroom but there was no one around that he could see. However, there were several computers scattered around the room and Oscar began to feel like his plan was working out. He searched the drawers, turned over the mattress and checked the ports on the computers but there was nothing.

When he opened the closet he found himself face to face with a boy holding a trophy aloft.

"Graaaaaaaaaah," yelled Ned as he brought the trophy down on Oscar's head and pushed past him. Oscar lunged for Ned more out of anger than anything else as he felt a warm, thin stream of blood trickle down the side of his head. He dropped one of the guns and kicked it behind himself toward the wall. He caught Ned by the arm and pulled him in close, tightening his grip so it'd be just a little hard to breathe. He needed a little revenge.

"I have the boy!" he yelled, blinking his eyes. The blood was mixing with the sweat on his head and was getting caught in his eyelashes. "All I want is the damn drive and you get the boy but at this point I'm getting something!"

Wallis stepped into the room. Her fists were clenched. She held out her right arm and opened her hand. The car with the number three was in her palm.

"Give me my son," she said in a growl.

"Mom," said Ned. It came out in a gargle.

"Oh, Black Widow is finally angry?" said Oscar, mocking her tone.

"Ned, are you okay?" asked Wallis. Oscar had relaxed his grip a little and Ned was starting to cry. Oscar gave him a good shake.

"He's fine. He's the Black Widow's son, after all, aren't you?" asked Oscar, his words slurring. He pointed his gun at Wallis.

"Drop the little race car and kick it over here. Then back out of the room," he said, licking his lips. This is really going to work, he thought.

"I'm not leaving this room without my son," said Wallis. "You have the gun on us. Let the child go and once he's out of the room I'll drop the drive. Not a moment sooner."

"You're not calling the shots anymore," yelled Oscar. "This is my game!"

"Whoever has been watching this house saw how you got in here and they have to have figured out that one of their own is threatening Walter Jones' daughter."

"Now it matters to you," he said, spitting on the Persian rug.

"There is probably only a minute or two left for you to get out of here."

"They'll welcome me like a hero, a savior," said Oscar, waving the gun around in the air.

"Not if the police get here too. I understand you're a wanted man. Think about it, Oscar. They'll take the drive from you and feed you to the dogs. You'll be lucky if you live to even see a trial. I'm thinking just another apparent suicide from a deputy who couldn't face the shame of what he had done."

Oscar let out a roar and shoved Ned at his mother as he raised the gun ready to shoot them both. Wallis shoved her son out of the room and whispered to him, "Got you last," as she let him go and turned back toward Oscar. Tears were running down her face.

She heard the loud bang and was surprised at how loud it was and how she still felt nothing. The noise seemed to fill the room. She looked down and saw no blood and felt no pain. It wasn't at all like she expected.

Wallis looked up and was startled to see a look of surprise on Oscar's face and the gun hanging limply by his side. He was shoved back against the bedroom wall and there was an expanding deep red circle in the middle of his shirt.

It took Wallis a moment to realize what had happened and she turned to see who else was there.

"Mom?" asked Wallis.

"Call me Mother, Wallis. It's much more civilized," said Harriet, still pointing a nine millimeter at Oscar as he slipped down the wall.

"When did you get here?"

"My dear, I've been keeping my own tabs on this place since Management came under the delusion they could decide anything about my child. I told them before, no one comes near my daughter. I could have sworn I had made my point."

Ned ran to his mother and wrapped his arms tight around her waist. Wallis kissed the top of his head, pressing her lips against his soft hair.

"I need you to go check on your uncle. I think he was hurt," said Wallis, trying to get him away from the two people with guns.

"No, I don't want to leave you," said Ned, burying his face in his mother's chest.

"Please, baby. Go check on your uncle. I'll be right behind you, I promise," said Wallis, peeling his arms off of her. "It's okay," she said, stepping out into the hallway.

Ned started to cry harder and moved toward the stairs, backing down them one at a time, watching his mother.

"It's okay, Ned," said Wallis, over and over again, as she tried to stop herself from crying. It wasn't working.

Harriet walked closer to Oscar, peering down at him. Oscar was breathing heavily, holding his bleeding belly.

"I shot you in the gut on purpose, Oscar. I heard what you tried to do to Wallis on that bridge. I was willing to let that one go since you failed so miserably but you were too stupid to take your pass and go home. It's going to take the ambulance a little while to get here but by then you'll be dead. You'll have bled out very slowly and painfully and I'm going to watch you do it." Harriet said it all with the same clipped tone she always used when trying to correct someone's bad behavior.

"Mom, could you kick his guns under the bed, just in case," Wallis said gently.

"What?" asked Harriet, turning back toward Wallis.

Wallis shrugged and pointed toward the two revolvers on the floor. "Kick them under the bed, okay?" she asked.

Harriet shoved them with her toe till they were well out of Oscar's reach. She settled down on the end of the bed with her own gun in her lap and watched Oscar grimace in pain.

"This is the end, Oscar. You'll be remembered as a bumbling killer by everyone, including strangers who will have never heard of you before this. All those years of service as a deputy won't add up to anything. Your sister will have to move to another town. I'll see to that myself. She'll have nothing."

Wallis felt a chill watching her mother calmly explain his legacy to the dying man. But she understood completely. If it had come down to it, she would have killed Oscar to keep Ned from harm. She slid the thumb drive back into her pocket and went to check on her son.

The police were barreling up the stairs when she got to Tom and Ned.

"Upstairs," she said, pointing toward the narrow staircase. "You'll need an ambulance and you take him first," she said, pointing to Tom. "My mother shot the intruder. I think you were searching for him. He's wanted for murder."

Ned was trying to hold his uncle's hand but he was shaking so violently that it was making Tom's body jerk. Tom was gritting his teeth trying to comfort his nephew.

Wallis grabbed Ned and enfolded him tightly in her arms, trying to stop the shaking.

"I'm sorry, I'm sorry, Ned. It's over, we're done. I'm not playing this game their way anymore."

CHAPTER

CRICHARD Bach had heard the sound of the door splintering and ran to the top of the driveway just in time to see Oscar stumble into the house holding the guns. He ran back to his Explorer and called Robin to tell her what had happened.

"Stand back! Stand back!" she yelled. "The police were already called. I heard it on the scanner. They'll be there any minute."

He did as he was told and stood back by his car listening to the loud report of the gunshots. The neighbors started pouring out of their houses taking a few running steps toward the sound of the noise and then hesitating as yet another loud crack was heard. Richard felt his body jerk every time and he pulled back even further so that no one would later remember he was standing nearby during the entire episode.

Finally, the high pitch of the sirens could be heard as police surrounded two sides of the block and yelled at everyone to get back inside their houses. Richard went and sat in his car just out of range of the police who were quickly setting up the neon orange plastic tape.

He was getting ready to leave when he saw Norman Weiskopf's car in his rear view mirror speeding toward home. Norman gave Richard a look as he passed his car that made Richard wonder if Norman was capable of committing murder. A cold thought occurred to Richard that if anyone Norman Weiskopf loved was dead in that house there was no place on earth he was going to be able to hide. He'd have to kill Norman himself or get Parrish to do it to avoid an early grave. Things had gotten so complicated.

The car was too out in the open. He needed to move it so that he could still see who was coming and going but not sit here like a sign post. He realized that anyone coming by might think he gave Oscar a ride.

He pulled the car around the corner and saw Oscar's dented Volvo. There wasn't a safe place for Richard to be for too long in this neighborhood anymore. If Oscar didn't have that thumb drive by now it was going to be a dead issue as far as Richard was concerned. He had done his best.

Just as he turned off his motor he saw Norman come out and hurry up the driveway. He looked toward the direction of where Richard had been parked and turned in a circle, peering in every direction. Richard realized Norman was looking for him. He ducked down in his seat.

Norman ran back inside and took the stairs two at a time.

"Is my brother going to be okay?" he asked Louie, who was applying a pressure bandage to Tom's shoulder.

"Yeah, but we have to keep him out of the way of bombs and guns," said Louie, "or else he'll never be able to get life insurance again. You doing okay, buddy?" asked Louie, looking at Ned who was still shaking, clutching his uncle's hand.

"Yeah, yeah," said Ned. His eyes were wide and his teeth were chattering.

"You want me to give him a mild sedative? It'd probably be a good idea under the circumstances," said Louie.

Norman looked at his son. He had never seen him like that and he was worried that the damage was permanent. He needed to get him out of here.

"Yeah, do it," said Norman. "What have I done?" he asked.

Tom raised his head and reached for his brother's arm.

"You haven't done anything, little brother. You've dealt with the events as they have unfolded, crap and all."

"You don't know who I saw today at the shad planking," said Norman, his face growing paler.

"I'll bet I do," said Tom, putting his head back and closing his eyes. "Did he look alright?" The EMT's lifted him carefully onto the gurney as he groaned from the pain.

"Is it your leg that's bothering you or your shoulder?" asked Louie.

"Does it really matter?" asked Tom.

"As a matter of fact, it does, but you have a point. You need to end this vacation and go home where it's a little safer," said Louie.

"How can you be so calm?" asked Norman. "Do you know what our brother has done? He's responsible for people dying, for you getting injured. Do you see what he's done to my family?"

Tom grimaced and looked at Louie. "Didn't hear a thing," said Louie, "Surprised you even need to ask."

Wallis came down the stairs as Tom's phone started to buzz. Louie was shaking his head, no, trying to get him to relax.

"I have to, I have to get it," he said. There were numbers spilling across the screen and just as quickly translating into a message. Robert was safe and had made it to the first destination with Mark. They were taking a short respite and would be heading out that night for the next leg. Tom didn't like that they were staying in one place for so long. They needed to keep moving.

"What is it?" asked Wallis. "Tell me, Tom or so help me, you'll never be welcome in this house again."

Ned looked up, worried at his mother. His face was streaked with tears. Louie handed him a small pill and a little paper cup of water.

"We're not playing by your rules anymore. This is our life, our family that all of you have invaded and we're taking it back. You tell me what it said or get out and don't come back. Don't Norman," she said, putting out her arm to stop him from trying to comfort her. "I don't need anything but a little information right now. What's it going to be, Tom?"

Tom looked from Norman to Wallis and let out a sigh. "You people could take out Management all by yourselves," he said. "There are some Circle operatives and their children, a couple of zwanzigs amongst them that we are moving through the system to a safer place. At least one of them knows far too much to just leave out in the wind. They have reached the first safe place."

"It's that man, the one whose wife died," said Wallis. "She was the one who died trying to protect all of those children," said Wallis, holding out the little race car.

"Put that away," said Tom. "You hold onto it for now. You have proven to be the best guardian of it."

"Where is he? Where are they now?" asked Wallis, with a determined tone.

"I can't tell you that," said Tom, "alright, alright. I won't make you repeat your speech. But what are you planning to do, go there?"

"Yes," said Wallis, "after we get Ned someplace a little safer. I need to call Laurel."

Wallis turned and looked back at the stairs leading up to the third floor, hesitated and looked back at her son.

"Come on, Ned. Let's go downstairs for awhile. They'll be taking Tom back to the hospital. He'll be okay. You can let go of his hand. Grab on to Mommy's hand. It's okay, sweet pea," she said in a soothing tone. The same one she used to use when he was three and had a nightmare.

"It's okay, Ned. You did a great job," said Tom. "You kept me calm this whole time," he said, as he kissed the boy's hand and let him go. "Go with your mom. It's okay. The grownups are going to take care of everything and make sure this doesn't happen again."

Wallis hugged her son tight, rubbing his back. "Come on, Ned. Let's go downstairs."

Norman watched them go and waited till they were all the way downstairs before he asked the policeman standing at the bottom of the stairs. "What's it look like upstairs?"

"Oscar's dead, bled out. It's definitely a self-defense on your mother in law's part. I'd hate to get her on my bad side. She's a little too calm for me," said the officer.

"I know what you mean," said Norman, as a shudder went through him.

"What in blue blazes happened here?" asked Alice Watkins. She was lumbering up the last of the stairs. "I go to the store finally for just a little while and the place goes to hell in a hand basket."

"Thank goodness you're here, Alice. I need a little favor. Can you make sure my mother in law gets home?" asked Norman.

"I know who she is, you know," said Alice, arching a badly penciled eyebrow. "Sure, sure, I'll do it. It seems I'm in this mess no matter what I do so I might as well help out. Where is she?"

"Upstairs with the guy who shot up this place but he's a little worse off. Dead in fact from a bullet to the abdomen."

"If it makes you feel any better, I believe he's the one who gave the order to try and get you killed," said Tom.

"Well, then this day is looking better and better. Who shot him?"

"My mother in law," said Norman.

"I like her already," said Alice, "What's her name?"

"Harriet, Harriet Jones," said Norman.

"Harriet, you doing okay?" Alice called out, as she headed up the stairs.

"You have interesting house guests," said Louie. "Okay, we're out of here. Ready guys, on three we lift him."

Norman waited until Tom was in the ambulance and Alice had convinced Harriet to leave with her. Harriet seemed to be under the impression that Alice was some kind of help and said, "It's about time, Wallis," as she gathered her purse from where she had dropped it in the foyer. "The police took my gun. Do you have one?" she asked Alice as they headed out the door.

"We're heading out," said Wallis. "We're picking up Paul and dropping both of them at Laurel's," she said, still holding onto Ned. "They're going to hang out at her house and eat pizza while we take a short road trip."

"But nothing dangerous, right Mom?" asked Ned.

"Right," she said, knowing she might be lying.

Norman gave the keys to the house to the coroner and asked him to do his best to lock up when they were done collecting evidence. He called Esther and told her what had happened and she said she'd make sure the broken door was taken care of immediately. He checked his car for any tracking devices before they pulled out and told Wallis to sit in back with Ned. The sedative was starting to take effect and Ned had stopped shaking but he wouldn't let go of his mother. He fell asleep with her arms around him.

Richard saw them pull out and started following them from a short distance. Everything was a horrible mess. He saw the man on the stretcher and then the black body bag but he didn't know who was injured and who was dead. Robin had called three times screaming over the phone about the amazing inability of everyone in Richmond to follow very simple orders. She was screaming at him to meet her at the Holiday Inn on the South Side when he pulled onto the interstate a few car lengths behind Norman. He stopped taking her calls after that. He didn't have any idea what he was going to do but he was sure he was running out of options and getting anywhere near Robin Spingler right now was a very bad idea.

They made several stops as they picked up a child and then dropped off two of them in the east end of town. None of it made sense to him. He began to wonder if they were just out for the day like nothing had ever happened. It's possible, he thought. I don't understand these people at all.

They pulled onto the highway heading north and this time there was no stopping as they drove for an hour and a half, past Fredericksburg until they got closer to the suburbs surrounding Washington and they split off toward 395 heading past the Landmark Mall. He let them get as far ahead of him as possible till he wasn't able to always see them.

He worried about losing them but he could see that they were in the far right lane and were peeling off, onto Seminary Road.

It wasn't long before they turned onto the sprawling campus. Richard saw the sign and realized the seminary must be connected somehow to the Circle. He parked his car across the road and watched them come down the campus road that ran parallel to Seminary Road till they stopped at the first parking lot just behind the post office. They got out and walked toward the two-story red brick building right in front of them. A large woman came out and greeted them and Wallis seemed to recognize her and called out something as they hugged. Norman shook her hand and they all disappeared inside.

Richard was wondering whether or not to hang around and watch what might happen next when he saw the Lincoln Continental from half a mile away weaving in and out of traffic and headed in his direction.

"Not again," he muttered. He could feel the sweat appear on his forehead instantly and he wondered if he should try and run. "What's the point," he said. He shoulders sagged and he smiled briefly as the car pulled up alongside him. He couldn't see through the heavily tinted glass but he knew somewhere behind there was the crimson red smile of Robin Spingler. She had found him anyway.

She threw open her car door and threw out a pale, meaty leg in a black, sensible pump.

"You're lucky, Richard. That's probably the first time I've ever thought that about you and the last," she said, letting out a throaty laugh. Richard stood behind the front of his car to keep a little distance between them.

"You managed to do something that hundreds of Management operatives who actually had a direct order were unable to pull off," she said, standing up and smoothing out her navy blue skirt. "You seem to have found Robert Schaeffer. You may live to see another day just yet, unlike that pig, Oscar. He's very dead, which is all for the best considering all the evidence the police found on him." Robin looked at Richard and pursed her lips. "You may think you have Parrish on a leash for you but you'd be very wise to heed my warning. I know how you feel about me," she said, smiling broadly, "but I only injure. Parrish likes to play for keeps and trust me, you won't see him coming."

Richard felt a little bile rise in his throat. He was less and less sure of what was a worse choice.

"How did you find me?" asked Richard.

"Really, this should all be so easy for you, Richard. You went through all of the training," said Robin, sounding annoyed. "Your car has a permanent tracking device in it. We always know where you are. I get regular reports on all of my staff," she said, preening. "What have you seen? Who's here?" she asked, shading her eyes to get a better look at the campus across the street.

"That's the Weiskopf car right there. They went in that building just in front of it but besides one old, large white woman I haven't seen anyone else."

"I have a feeling I know that old woman and I have a score to settle with her as well. She's a hard one to capture and a pain in my side," said Robin. "Do you think anyone saw you, and don't lie to me," she said.

"No, no, I don't think they have any idea they were followed."

"That's good, very good. You see, Richard, it's possible to work your way back in to my good graces. However, it's always going to be true that you're only as useful to me as the information you carry." She laughed again. Richard felt the bile growing. It was safe to say that Robin Spingler disgusted Richard.

Robin pulled out a thirty-eight Special with a black grip and a pink barrel. She checked to make sure it was loaded and put it back in her purse.

"What are you planning to do?" asked Richard, worried about what his part in all of this was going to be.

"Well, I'm sure as hell not sitting around here waiting for something to happen. We're going to go in and take care of this. We either leave with Robert Schaeffer or kill him where he is and see if we can't find a certain thumb drive."

"There are a lot of people in there. Did you see what this place is? It has to be crawling with Circle operatives. We'll never make it out of there."

"Relax. You are nothing but a big girl," said Robin, looking Richard up and down. "It's a seminary. I can see that, which is why we're going in right now before they leave that building. It's our perfect chance. These morons don't believe in weapons and don't allow them on the grounds. They think God will protect them," she said, rolling her eyes. "Let's see how well that works, shall we?"

She put her purse over her arm and looked both ways before darting across the wide road. Richard wanted to ask her if she was crazy but knew better than to point out the obvious and ran behind her, nervously checking for traffic. She strode up the grass and crossed the little campus road as if someone was expecting them toward the building with the small brass plate on it that said Building One.

"I don't have a good feeling about this," said Richard.

"When have you ever had a good feeling?" asked Robin, the sound of contempt obvious in her voice. They went up to the door Richard had seen everyone disappear through and saw that it had a push button pad. Robin jiggled the handle anyway but it was locked. She dropped her chin and let out a deep sigh as if the world were conspiring against her.

It was a simple cipher pad with only five number buttons which was quite popular years ago and could be broken into within minutes just by punching all of the potential combinations in sequence.

"We use to routinely get into secure spaces this way in the late '80's and '90's as long as you had a few minutes to do it," said Robin, as she continued to methodically punch in the different combinations. The door finally made a loud buzzing noise.

"Aha," said Robin as she pulled open the door and stepped inside.

They strode in the long hall that had doors on both sides all the way down the hall and an opening to a stairwell at the end. It was some kind of dorm.

Suddenly a small girl appeared at the end of the hall stepping out of the stairwell and smiled at Robin. That kid has a lot to learn, thought Richard. An older boy appeared and grabbed her arm, giving them a worried look as he pulled her back and they heard the sound of footsteps running up stairs.

"That's them," said Robin. "They're cornered, it's perfect." She strode down the hall with the confidence of someone who knew they were not only in charge but they were about to inspire fear in a small group of deserving people. Richard followed behind her from a short distance trying to give himself room to run if it became necessary. His phone buzzed and he looked down to see a tweet from Davey.

Robin had paid Parrish to take care of Richard, it read. She was done with him. Parrish was going to complete the job unless Richard came up with an alternate ending first.

Richard almost dropped his phone. It didn't matter how any of this turned out, he was still finished. He was glad he hadn't flinched when Davey had said that it was a delicate job and would cost him a thousand dollars if he wanted to be kept in the loop.

Robin was right, he would never even hear Parrish coming and he couldn't be sure where it would happen. There has to be another way, he thought, his mind racing.

They started to climb the wide, metal stairs to the second floor.

"There are children up there," said Richard. "He wasn't sure he really cared but maybe Robin was a woman after all. She grunted and kept moving.

Suddenly, Wallis Jones appeared at the top of the stairs.

"You came for this," she said, holding out a little race car in the palm of her hand. "Then go get it," she yelled, and threw it over their heads. It clattered against the far wall and slid down behind the stairs. Robin looked genuinely surprised and wavered a moment between pointing her gun at Wallis or running downstairs for the prize.

She chose the thumb drive and pushed Richard out of the way.

"I can't trust you," she spit out, as she planted her pointed red fingernails in his chest. He didn't even think about what he was doing. He reached out and shoved her forward with all of his might letting out a high pitched whine. Her sensible shoes slid against the metal step and she fell forward, head first, taking flight toward the opposite wall.

Her head made a satisfying crack as she made contact with the cement blocks and she slid down, landing squarely atop the thumb drive. She had it at last even if she was never going to know it. There was a slimy trail of blood and brain tissue that marked her descent.

Richard ran down the stairs and felt for a pulse. He wanted to be sure she was dead before he reached under the squishy belly for the race car.

"Ding, dong the witch is dead," he sang, as he grimaced and rolled her back a little to see where the race car was buried. Robin's eyes were still open with a look of frozen amazement. "At last," said Richard. He let her go and watched her flop back into place.

"I'll take that."

He looked up to see the older woman from earlier standing only a few stairs from him holding a gun.

"Does every bitch around here carry a gun?" he pleaded.

"It may be the company you've been keeping," said Elizabeth. "Hand it over or I shoot. Three, two, one." She pulled the trigger and grazed the side of his head. Richard felt his pants warm and a trickle run down his leg as his bladder let go of its contents.

"I'm a damn good shot," she said. "I didn't miss."

"I thought you people weren't allowed to carry weapons," said Richard.

"I've never listened very well. Throw it here or the next one is just a couple of inches to the right."

"Enough! Enough with you all," he said and threw the drive at her. "What now, are you going to shoot me?" he yelled. "I'm going to die with that bitch right here in this stairwell?"

"Why, Mr. Bach, you seem to think this is all about you," said Elizabeth, sweetly. She caught the race car in the air. That's when Richard noticed her hand.

"It's you," he hissed.

"So good to see you again. I'll tell you what, Mr. Bach. They do have a policy about killing people for being overly annoying. You take your pissy pants and go now and we'll call it even, seeing as how you took care of the bigger problem for me."

"This isn't the life I wanted," said Richard. "It's not what I was promised."

"You're telling the wrong being, dear."

He looked down at Robin's still body. "I'm not sure if I'll be seen as a hero or a permanent loser for this one." He looked back up at Elizabeth. "You know, I'd get out if I could figure out something to do."

"Mr. Bach, that is way too much self pity for any one body. Get out of here and be grateful for the second chance you've just been given. If you want to find another way, go home and get on your knees and stay there until you start to think about something other than yourself."

"That's all you people can talk about, you know that? And it's worthless, worthless," he said, shaking his head. "No God is ever going to answer me."

"You have it backwards, Mr. Bach. You need to answer Him."

"You're crazy. None of your proselytizing has ever changed the world. Management will always be there." He started to go and turned back. "If any of you ever had the balls to stand up to Management, to beat them at their own game I'd have joined a long time ago," he sneered.

"It's amazing how you manage to miss the point. Get going, Mr. Bach. My finger is feeling very itchy."

Wallis appeared beside Elizabeth and she looked down at what had become of Robin Spingler and Richard Bach.

"You come anywhere near my family again, Richard and you'll end up paying for this and a few other things," said Wallis.

"That's why you're the Black Widow," said Richard in a mocking tone. He walked out to his car and could feel the constant anxiety already coming back and settling into his chest. Not even the death of Robin Spingler could take away the unease.

CHAPTER 47

"THAT WASN'T VERY NUN LIKE," said Wallis, hugging Elizabeth tightly around the neck.

"Careful, careful let me get rid of this weapon first. Thank goodness that soul is not a bright one. He couldn't tell I didn't know what I was doing. I was really aiming at the wall when I parted his hair," said Elizabeth with a laugh. "I'm afraid I don't have very good balance in this hand anymore," she said, wiggling the fingers she still had left. "Besides, I wasn't a Mother Superior for long, so there you have it. I'll hang on to this, if it's okay with you. I know where it ought to go." Elizabeth was holding the small race car that so many people had been fighting over.

"Consider it done," said Wallis. "I am relieved to let go of the burden. I know what's on it, you know."

"I know," said Elizabeth, "And we're going to keep that just between you, me and that husband of yours. Let everyone think you didn't want to know. Safer that way," she said kissing Wallis' forehead.

"You're like the daughter I never had," said Elizabeth, wiping her eyes.

"What is your real name, anyway? If you're like a mother to me, which is a low bar by the way," said Wallis as she led the way back to the small dorm room, "then shouldn't I know?"

Elizabeth laughed until her whole body shook. "Labels don't matter dear and I'm not sure how much longer I'll have this one anyway."

Wallis stopped, worried and was about to say something but Elizabeth held up her hand.

"Not to worry. I'll make sure we somehow stay connected. But you're going to have to let things unfold. You're powerless over it being any other way, my dear."

"Amen," said Wallis, provoking Elizabeth to let out another hearty laugh.

Everyone was still huddled behind the mattresses they had pulled up to protect themselves. She saw the frightened look in all of the children's faces and thought of Ned.

"I'm sorry," she said, looking at Jake, feeling a wave of guilt. "Someone ought to call the police," she said to Mark.

"We will but all of you need to get out of here first. There would be far too much explaining to do. Tragic accident, that one," said Elizabeth.

"Really?" asked Norman. "They'll buy that?"

"Robin Spingler was very unpopular with just about everyone. They'll want to buy it. There will be champagne corks popping all over the Mid-Atlantic region tonight when they hear that someone finally sent that one to her final reward. Now, Mark, you never got much of a nap but I'm afraid you'll have to be leaving anyway. The Richmond contingent may not be after you and Robert anymore but soon enough, they'll be replaced by others."

"It's you, isn't it?" asked Robert. He got up from the floor, helping Trey to stand and walked over to Wallis. "I heard what he called you. I wasn't sure when Elizabeth introduced you before but there was no time to ask you. You're the Black Widow of Richmond."

Wallis winced. "Great, I'm apparently famous."

"You don't understand," he said. "You were the reason I came to Richmond. Carol talked about you. You and Norman and your son, Ned. It gave us hope. If you two could somehow live in peace then maybe it's possible for our children. We loved your nickname," he said, tears in his eyes, "Carol said it was Management's sign of respect and said so much about your integrity and your faith."

"Robert, I'm not sure I ever earned that moniker and my faith may be a newer addition. It was your wife who worked so hard to change things. I'm so sorry for your loss," said Wallis.

"She would have liked to have met you," he said. "Don't sell yourself short about your relationship with the Lord, either. I've wanted to lately, but without that connection the pain and futility is too much. Carol knew that and it's probably the best thing she was able to leave us. Her faith has saved me in more than one way."

"Do you have pictures?" she asked.

"Yes, yes, I do. No one has asked me that since she died," he said, eagerly, pulling out his wallet.

"I hate to break it up but you all really must be going," said Elizabeth.

"We understand," said Norman. "I'm going to miss you next door. I hope we get the chance to meet again under better circumstances," he said, extending his hand.

"Oh, after all this time you're more like family, Norman. Come here," she said and embraced him in a hug.

CHAPTER 48

"**WE HAVE TO GO SEE HIM,**" said Tom.

"Says you," said Norman. "I don't have to do anything." He pulled up a stool to the island in his kitchen and sat down, propping himself on his elbows.

"Nothing changes in this family. Look, you have to go see him because he's our brother, simple as that. Dad would have wanted us to." Tom was sitting in a wheelchair. The wound to his shoulder had made it impossible to use crutches.

"What he did was unforgivable."

"No such thing and he's paying for it. No family, no job, no place to live. The Circle's not going to let him out of their sight forevermore. A very special kind of prison," said Tom.

"Don't you think that's the least he deserves? He should be in a federal prison for the rest of his life," said Norman, frustrated. "All of those innocent people," he whispered. "And what if that information had become public? It would have been a slaughter, all over again. He had to have known that," his voice was rising with every word.

"I don't think Harry thought any of it out. I don't think he ever does. That's why he was in that Circle cell. We were trying to put him somewhere that he could do no harm but he wouldn't realize he'd been neutered. Harry turned out to be a little more clever than I realized," said Tom.

"Do you think he ever thought you were the real Keeper?" asked Norman.

"No, I don't and yes, I think he would have turned me in. He was desperate to find some kind of life and he thought we stood between him and that rosy picture."

"It's gone forever," said Norman. "They'll kill him before they let him loose."

"Exactly, little brother. Show some compassion even for someone who is without it for everyone else. Go see him."

"Now you sound like Pastor Donald. Very obnoxious."

"Ah, always throwing my name around in vain," said Pastor Donald. "Your wife let me in."

"Did everyone arrive safely?" asked Norman.

"You might say that," said Pastor Donald.

"And what else might you say?"

"That some of the people put a little detour in their plans. I'll explain in the car. Come on, Norman. We're going to see Harry."

"What about Wallis?" asked Norman.

"Nice try," said Tom. "Even I know the answer to that one. She said no."

"She said something a little more colorful than that but that was the gist of it," said Pastor Donald. "She's upstairs playing with Ned. Laurel's up there too."

"It's been hard on Ned. He has a lot of questions that I'm not sure how to answer," said Norman.

"You may not remember but you had a similar reaction," said the Pastor. "It all worked out okay."

"I don't necessarily believe you. I wasn't standing next to my mother wondering if she was about to die," said Norman, choking out the words.

"I'm missing the mark today, aren't I," said Pastor Donald.

"There's no mark to hit today. I did a terrible job of protecting my son and there's nothing anyone can say about it," said Norman, "I can just hope that over time we can help Ned to believe that this was all a bad moment in time and there is a better normal."

"We'd better get going," said Tom. "Anyone care to push the wounded vet?"

"I heard Robin Spingler's funeral was very sparsely attended," said Norman.

"I heard the ground came up and swallowed her," said Pastor Donald, shuddering as he said a prayer.

They drove over to the wealthiest part of Richmond. Harry was being held in a velvet prison. He was locked in a large bedroom in one of the estates along River Road. A well known curmudgeon who was a Circle operative owned the home and had offered up his own bedroom to make sure Harry Weiskopf wasn't going anywhere. The old man said he had known Harry's father and felt he at least owed it to his late friend.

There were two Circle guards just inside the large oak door and two more guards at the top of the curving stairs. Alan Vitek sat in the room with Harry, babysitting him.

"Norman, your family doing alright?" asked Alan.

"Yes, thank you Alan. Thank you for all of your service," said Norman, nodding toward his brother.

Harry was sitting in an antique Morris chair near the window, slouched down against the brown leather. He didn't move when they came in the room.

"Harry, we came to see how you were getting along," said Tom. "Come on, the least you can do after I let those burly guards carry me upstairs is turn around and say hello. I've come a long way."

Harry looked over his shoulder and saw who was standing there. "And you, Norman? You interested in how I'm getting along?"

"It's still all about you, isn't it?" asked Norman, annoyed. Pastor Donald put his hand on Norman's arm but he pulled away. "Enough. He got at least two innocent people killed because of his own selfishness and he was going to let them plot to kill thousands more."

"It's so easy for you to pass judgment," said Harry, quietly, still looking out the window.

"What's that? What's that," yelled Norman, marching over to Harry. "What part of what I just said was incorrect? You know, you've never acknowledged what you've done. No apology, no inkling of remorse. And now, you get to sit in this mansion until they can figure out what to do with you because no one can trust that you won't try just one more time to kill thousands of innocent children. Look at me," he bellowed.

"Norman," said Tom, "he's not responsible for all of it. He's not that powerful. You can't blame him for everything."

"Tell me why," said Norman, clenching his fists. "Why did you risk my family?"

Harry turned his head and looked up at Norman. "That wasn't supposed to be part of the deal," he said, tears in his eyes. "They promised that they'd stay away from you or Tom."

"What about Carol?" asked Norman.

"I didn't know they'd do that," stuttered Harry.

"How could you not?" asked Tom, wheeling himself closer. "You know all of the stories just like we do. You know what they've done in the past."

"In the past, that's all done and gone," insisted Harry, talking faster. "All of those people who did those things are dead. None of us ever saw someone from Management harm anybody," he pleaded. He was sitting on the edge of the chair. "They said that all they were going to do was expose what the Circle was doing, whatever it was, and let the public make up their own minds. I was trying to find a way to live my own life, just like you Norman."

Norman covered his face with his hands for a moment.

"Why didn't you just ask me for help?" he asked.

"You don't make it that easy," said Harry, looking down at his hands. He went back to looking out the window. "It doesn't matter now, anyway. I went too far, even I can see that. For what it's worth, I am sorry. I didn't see any of that happening. I don't know. You made it look so easy, Norman. You did the impossible. You not only stayed out of the Circle, you married one of Management's precious descendants and kept them at bay. It looked like it had to be possible for me."

Norman sat down in the window seat and wept.

"I'm sorry, Harry. I let you down. I was just as selfish. It never occurred to me to try and help you too."

"There's enough blame to go around, I'm sure," said Pastor Donald, still standing near the door. "But we have to eventually forgive and move on. Tom, do you have any idea of what's next for Harry?"

"He's being moved to an estate in Charlottesville where he'll be kept for the foreseeable future. There will be no prosecution because we can't risk exposing the truth about the Weiskopfs. The Circle will see to it that the Schaeffer family is kept safe and we'll somehow find a way to look after the Blazneys and everyone else who was harmed."

"Because of me," said Harry, his lip trembling.

Norman took his brother's hand. "Yes, because of you but also because of us, because of Richard Bach, because of Robin Spingler, because of a lot of people we've never even met."

"Come to visit me?" he asked, softly.

"I will," said Norman, letting out the breath he'd been holding, "once a week. I'll make the drive and we'll sit and talk."

"Well, say your goodbyes. They'll be moving him shortly and we need to get going," said Pastor Donald.

Harry leaned over and hugged Tom. Norman was still holding his hand tightly as he leaned in and embraced his brothers.

CHAPTER 49

MARK was surprised when he got the final destination for Robert Schaeffer and his sons. They were driving across the country to Guilford, a small children's home in Aurora, Illinois. He was even more surprised when Elizabeth said she was going with them.

"It's my next assignment," she said, "and I could use the lift." They all piled into the large white van that was their next transportation.

"I liked the minivan better," Ruthie whispered to Jake.

"I wouldn't have fit in one of those puny seats, dear," said Elizabeth, laughing.

"What exactly do they plan to do with us once we're there?" asked Robert. "I'm not leaving my sons."

"No, no one expects that," said Elizabeth. "But by the time we get there, you'll all have new identities. Think of it as our version of witness protection. There's a packet for everyone," she said, handing brown manila envelopes to Trey and Will. "This one's yours," she said to Robert.

"I don't like it," said Robert. Mark could see him looking at him in the rear view mirror.

"Look," said Elizabeth, "it's a start, a safe start. We've done this before and it's all worked out. Your wife was a beneficiary of this policy, once."

"Mom? She was in the Circle's protection?" asked Trey.

"Yes, she was and she was happy. Look at these," said Elizabeth, pulling out photos from her purse.

"Hey, this is Mom from a long time ago, when she was little," said Will.

Robert leaned forward from his seat behind his sons and asked, "Where did you get these? I've never seen any of them. Who gave them to you?"

"No one had to give them to me," said Elizabeth. "I was the one who took them," she said, smiling. "I tend to get around and I've been around a very long time." She turned around and winked at Robert. "Imagine all of the stories I have to tell. Thank goodness it's a long drive."

Mark drove straight through the night only stopping a few times to let everyone stretch and use a bathroom. They'd pick the nearest fast food drive-through, load up on gas and get back on the road. He was determined to get on with his own plans as well.

"You're awfully quiet," said Elizabeth as they passed through Ohio. Everyone had fallen asleep in the back. "Aren't you the least bit curious about what the Circle has planned for you? Or have you figured out a story all your own," she said.

Mark tried to smile. "You think they'll give me much trouble if my children and I just keep going?"

"Unlike our opposition, we really don't try to take away people's choices. Your life is yours to decide. Besides, there's a little poetic justice to someone from the Circle living off of the fat from Management."

Mark looked over at Elizabeth but didn't know what to say.

"We didn't know until recently. That was a pretty nice set up you had going. If Management didn't have a cell operating from within we would never have known. However, as things sometimes work, that traitorous bunch may just be your cover. They'll never say a word as long as they're trying to hide their own nefarious doings." Elizabeth chuckled, "Ah, yes, God is good, I do believe that."

"I'm not sure what I believe," said Mark, as they passed over into Illinois.

"That's okay. It's not a requirement in order to have God believe in you. Thank goodness," snorted Elizabeth. "Can you imagine how small that pool of people would be, if it were absolutely necessary?"

They pulled onto the grounds of Guilford in the early morning hours and unloaded the van. Robert and his children were shown to a small cottage where they were able to finally sleep in beds for the first time in well over a week. Mark tried to tell him goodbye but they were separated before he got the chance.

"It's better this way," said Elizabeth. "The fewer the people who have an idea about where you're headed, the better," she said, as she took him outside to an Uplander minivan. "It's used but that just means it'll blend better. I'd ask you to spend the night."

"No, you're right. I'm ready to leave all of this behind and the sooner the better," said Mark.

"You have everything you need?" asked Elizabeth.

"Let me get my kids and get on the road and then I will be set. Do I need to ask about any kind of tracking device on this car?" asked Mark.

"You have my personal word," said Elizabeth. "You are being officially set free. Good or bad, you're on your own."

"Thank God," said Mark.

"Indeed," said Elizabeth. "If you can hang onto that one thought you may just be alright."

CHAPTER

"EXCUSE ME." Wallis was standing in the back of the small Baptist church, not sure what to do next. She could see the back of Pastor Adler's grey head bowed forward in the front pew. "Excuse me," she said, a little louder. The elderly minister jerked around, startled and quickly got to his feet, still standing in the pew. Wallis stayed where she was by the door.

"Who is that?" said the pastor, squinting through the dim light coming in through the narrow windows. "Wallis Jones, is that you?" He waved his arm, motioning to her to come forward.

"I'm not sure why I came here," she said. Her knees felt a little wobbly as she slowly closed the distance between them. "I haven't been here in awhile."

"Well, it's always been my belief that a church is the best place to come to when all you know is confusion. Have a seat, dear," he said, sitting down and patting the seat next to him. "Full disclosure, I have to admit that Esther said you'd probably be stopping by to see me."

"How did Esther know when I had no idea till about five minutes before I walked through that door?"

"Esther's a cagey one and she has the experience of knowing she was in a long battle from the very start. You've been able to deny the whole thing for a much longer time."

Wallis put her face in her hands and tried to take a deep breath but all that came out were deep sobs that she had been holding in for weeks. It was as if a wall had cracked inside of her and the pain and confusion of everything that had happened came pouring out of her heart. She felt the weight of the pastor's hand on her back as her body shook. He let her cry until she could catch her breath on her own.

"The truth can be a very difficult thing," he said, "but just as powerful is the idea that when the truth is set free it does its own work."

"What does that even mean?" asked Wallis, taking the handkerchief the pastor was offering and wiping her face.

"Keep it, my dear. What that means is you have become aware of some ugly truths about human beings and along with that your own limited ability to even know what they're up to, much less stop them in their tracks. That is a very frightening perspective. Now, now, there is hope and it's powerful stuff. The hope comes from an abiding faith that there is a God and He loves us far more than we're able to even conceive. If we can pick up that one true thought then all things become possible because we need never feel like we are doing anything alone, again."

"But does it mean we'll always be safe?" asked Wallis, letting out a small shudder.

"I suppose by your definition the answer is no. But even in the middle of this chaos you can find peace and live with purpose. That's something to cherish," said the Pastor, his voice catching with feeling. "As long as there are human beings this fight will probably go on but those of us who are aware there even is a battle can learn how to be happy and be of service even as it swirls all around us."

"How do I get that?"

"By saying a simple prayer and surrendering your life to the Lord. Believe it or not but faith mixed with service is like the great, get out of jail free card. It's a daily practice after that and life will keep on happening but you won't feel it's happening to you quite so much," he said, gently chuckling.

"How can you be so calm knowing what's out there?" asked Wallis, gesturing toward the door.

"Because I believe and that goes before everything else, clearing the way. Are you ready?" he asked, holding out his hands. Wallis felt a weight lift off of her shoulders as she placed her hands in Pastor Adler's. "Now, let us pray," he began, "and repeat after me."

CHAPTER

WALLIS crawled into bed next to Norman and put her cold feet against his leg.

"What?" He jerked awake.

"Sorry," said Wallis, wrapping her arm around his waist. "I thought you were still awake."

"So my snoring wasn't giving me away," said Norman, putting his head back down against the pillow.

"Norman?"

"Is this going to be a conversation where I'm going to have to pay attention? I thought we agreed no more of those when we're in just our underwear."

"Norman."

He rolled over and sat up. "Okay, I'm listening."

"You think we're safe?" asked Wallis. The question still nagged at her a little.

Norman yawned and scratched his head. "I know I feel much better since you let that bruiser, Alice move in with us. Ow, no pinching. Have you heard how loud she snores? That's got to be a little scary for someone. She even managed to make Harriet come around a little less often."

"Norman, be serious."

"Okay, sorry. I suppose we owe your mother something even if we have to pat her down from now on before she can come in that door."

"I'm going back to sleep," said Wallis.

"I think safety is very, very relative. No, wait, I had a little more. To know the real answer to that I'd have to be able to tell you what's going to happen next month or even tomorrow. I can't control any of that," said Norman.

"Okay, let me rephrase. You think that they'll all leave us alone?"

Norman let out a sigh. "Forever? No, that's probably not going to happen."

"Great," said Wallis, resting her head on his chest.

"But I'll give you this," said Norman, "right in this moment, we're all okay. Our son is asleep upstairs and his nightmares have calmed down to one a night. Progress. The rest I am learning to turn over to God."

Wallis lifted her head for a moment. "Really?" she said, surprised. "Did you tell Pastor Donald about this development?"

"Yes, his response was that it was about time."

"What about your brothers?"

"You know Tom had to go back home when they got him in that walking cast, you know that. Having him so close was raising the danger level to a nice burnt orange. But maybe we can visit him this summer and see what it's like out there. Give Ned a break from all of his memories."

"And Harry?" asked Wallis.

"Oh, Harry," said Norman. He stopped talking for a moment and Wallis listened to the sound of his heart beating in his chest. "Harry is another subject I am turning over to God. I have no other idea what to do."

"Maybe that's enough," said Wallis. "Maybe that's how we survive all of this. Living like this between these two giants trying to battle it out."

"We survive by taking it one day at a time and remembering to be grateful for what we have right in front of us. That's the mistake Harry and all the rest of them made. The rest is all optional."

"Amen, Norman Weiskopf."

"Go to sleep, Wallis Jones. Tomorrow will come soon enough."

CHAPTER 52

FRED counted the steps up the stairs and out of the tunnel. Forty-five, forty-six. Soon enough, he was standing in the private quarters of the White House, once again.

"Mr. President, at your pleasure," he said, as he entered the room. The president was sitting back reading the paper.

Fred walked over to him and placed the small race car in front of him.

"I take it this was the source of all our problems?" asked President Haynes.

"Yes sir, for the most part. We've secured all of the information. It's been very informative."

"Are all of the schmetterlings safe now?"

"The list is now safe and all are accounted for, including our two new ones, Trey and Will. They are proving to be very fast learners," said Fred.

"And his father is still with them."

"For now, sir."

When do we estimate that we will have the first strong wave of graduates in place?" asked the President.

"The estimate is now just a year away. We have put some of them on the fast track given the urgency."

"Fred, I hear you're taking some time off? About time," said the President.

"Yes sir, it was a promise I made to my wife," said Fred, smiling.

"Even a smile, this is a new era. Can I ask where you're headed?"

"To Montana to see an old friend," said Fred. "I'm going to catch up and do a little fishing. I'll only be gone a week."

"Did we ever find anyone to replace that old friend of yours at the Federal Reserve?" asked the President.

"We tried, sir, but Management decided to bring in one of their own. He's also their new director to oversee the Richmond area operatives. His name is George Clemente, a rising star. He's a retread from an earlier, darker time and was banished for a number of years."

"Management must be feeling either particularly nervous or cocky," said the President.

"Our operative inside of Management says that he's got everyone living by a strict new set of rules. They've clamped down for now."

"It never ends. When do you leave?"

"Tomorrow morning, sir. But before that, there's a new alert that we need to cover. We have reports that the rogue cell within Management is getting ready to make their move. Their farms are going well in Africa and their new trading routes are flourishing."

"They're trying to draw us in, aren't they?"

"Yes sir, but we've formulated an answer for now. With your approval, we plan to expose two of their key bank accounts."

"To let the old Management structure know of their existence. Very clever. What is our risk level?"

"They are well-financed and have been using some of their funds to arm themselves," said Fred. "We've also found evidence of hundreds of small grassroots organizations they've begun across North America with fundamentalist ideas in an effort to create a new structure here."

"The weed has grown roots, I take it," said the President.

"Yes sir. They could decide to start a campaign against us within our borders but if we do nothing, then the same risks grows even greater with every day."

"Then take the action, Mr. Bowers and let us hope that the sleeping giant will be able to contain its own mess."

"Yes sir, but if Management is unable to do so, sir."

"What is it, Fred, then what?"

"Then we may find ourselves drawn into a war with our own people, right here."

"A new civil war. God help us all."

"Yes sir."

"Go, Fred. Take a break. Surely this will wait another week. When you get back we'll decide how to deal with them."

About the Author:

Martha Carr (Chicago, IL) is the author of three previous works, a national columnist for the Cagle syndicate, a persistent but slow runner, melanoma cancer survivor, former tap dancer & Girl Scout, national speaker and a Southerner in a big city where she lives near her son, Louie.

Carr is currently at work on the next thriller in The Wallis Simpson Series, The Keeper due out in January 2014.

For more information or to get updates by email go to www.MarthaCarr. com. Tweet the author at MarthaRandolph or at Google+ at +Martha Carr. Become a regular fan and like the author at www.Facebook.com/ MarthaRCarr or sign up for blog posts at www.MarthaCarr.com.

Praise for other Works by Martha Carr:

From page one through the last chapter Carr takes the reader on a quick-paced and easy-flowing tour of murder, suspense and steamy romance. Be prepared to stay up past your bedtime with this one.
Library Journal

Every bit as good as Mary Higgins Clark's highly successful novels of psychological suspense. Suspenseful and entertaining.
The Chattanooga Free Press

Simply enjoy being in the hands of an accomplished writer like Carr, whose lively characters and inviting descriptions of family life and love are the hallmarks of a gifted writer.
Grand Rapids Press on The Sitting Sisters

Carr's book should touch hearts and open minds.
Publishers Weekly

Wired is the best novel I have read in years. I'll never look at malls the same way.
Susan Thompson, Little Professor Book Center, Ashland, Kentucky

WIRED, will join other first novels, like TIME TO KILL and GONE, BUT NOT FORGOTTEN as the creator of a new cult following for Carr. We anxiously await her next endeavor.
Mike Cullis, Little Professor Book Center, Middletown, NJ

Carr excels at looking for the human dimension. When she tackls an issue, she explains the connections to real people and the real ramifications for their lives. She then buttresses her analysis with prose that is at once intellectually playful and vivid. That is a powerful combination."
Geitner Simmons, editorial page editor, Omaha World-Herald

Martha Carr is the new voice for Middle America using insight, humor and a common sense approach to spirituality. She's the one to watch.
Cari Dawson Bartley, Cagle Cartoons, Inc.

Martha Carr invites the reader to a journey through the 'change stories'. You will see parallels in your own life's victories.
Bob Danzig, former CEO, Hearst Newspapers, author and speaker

If only more people wrote as Martha Carr does. When I read her work, I feel like I'm sitting across from her enjoying a cup of coffee and a satisfying conversation.
Tom Purcell, National Columnist

9 781620 304303

NOV 1 2 2013